DON ITIA

Jackie Ashenden writes dark, emotional stories with alpha heroes who've just got the world to their liking only to have it blown wide apart by their kick-ass heroines. She lives in Auckland, New Zealand, with her husband, the inimitable Dr Jax, two kids and two rats. When she's not torturing alpha males and their gutsy heroines she can be found drinking chocolate martinis, reading anything she can lay her hands on, wasting time on social media, or being forced to go mountain biking with her husband.

To keep up to date with Jackie's new releases and other news you can sign up to her newsletter at jackieashenden.com.

Award-winning author of sensual, emotional adventures of the heart, **Rebecca Hunter** writes sexy stories about alpha men and spirited women set in Australia for Mills & Boon's Dare line. She lives with her family in the San Francisco Bay Area.

D0995127

X000 000 053 7819

ABERDEEN CITY LIBRARIES

If you liked *Destroyed* and
Best Laid Plans, why not try

Make Me Crave by Katee Robert
Wild Thing by Nicola Marsh

Discover more at millsandboon.co.uk

DESTROYED

JACKIE ASHENDEN

BEST LAID PLANS

REBECCA HUNTER

MILLS & BOON

All rights reserved including the right of reproduction
in whole or in part in any form. This edition is published
by arrangement with Harlequin Books S.A.

This is a work of fiction. Names, characters, places, locations
and incidents are purely fictional and bear no relationship to
any real life individuals, living or dead, or to any actual places,
business establishments, locations, events or incidents.
Any resemblance is entirely coincidental.

This book is sold subject to the condition that it shall not,
by way of trade or otherwise, be lent, resold, hired out
or otherwise circulated without the prior consent of the publisher
in any form of binding or cover other than that in which it is published
and without a similar condition including this condition
being imposed on the subsequent purchaser.

® and TM are trademarks owned and used by the trademark owner
and/or its licensee. Trademarks marked with ® are registered with the
United Kingdom Patent Office and/or the Office for Harmonisation
in the Internal Market and in other countries.

First Published in Great Britain 2018
by Mills & Boon, an imprint of HarperCollins*Publishers*
1 London Bridge Street, London, SE1 9GF

Destroyed © 2018 Jackie Ashenden

Best Laid Plans © 2018 Rebecca Hunter

ISBN: 978-0-263-26648-1

MIX
Paper from
responsible sources
FSC™ C007454

This book is produced from independently certified FSC™ paper
to ensure responsible forest management.
For more information visit www.harpercollins.co.uk/green.

Printed and bound in Spain
by CPI, Barcelona

DESTROYED

JACKIE ASHENDEN

MILLS & BOON

This one's for all the lovely editors at the
Mills & Boon UK office who've worked with me
over the years.

It took me a while, guys, but I got there in the end!

CHAPTER ONE

Summer

BRAVERY WAS NEVER my strong suit, but I guess it takes a certain amount of courage to talk your way into a biker's bedroom in an outlaw motorcycle club's clubhouse purely so you can hide from your father.

Either that or I was simply stupid, difficult as that was to admit for a person with an IQ score over 170.

Whatever it was, as I sat on Crash's bed in his tiny squalid bedroom, my heart racing, listening to the sounds of a heavy driving beat and male laughter going on outside, I was beginning to question my decision big time.

Two doors separated the bedrooms from the main living area of the clubhouse, but the bikers were so freaking loud I could still hear whatever was going on outside. I didn't know whether it was a party or what—I'd only ever been in the clubhouse a couple of times before—but whatever it was, it didn't make me any less nervous.

Crash had left me in his room, muttering something about why don't I relax while he went and got us some beers.

I didn't really want a beer—I wasn't a party girl and I didn't like alcohol—but sitting on Crash's bed, listening to those sounds outside the door, made the idea of some liquid courage not half-bad.

Especially since he'd been gone awhile and my anxiousness was starting to tip over into outright fear.

His room was little more than a closet, the floor covered with dirty clothes and beer cans and all kinds of other things I didn't want to look at too closely. The bed I was sitting on was unmade and there was a smell to the air that reminded me of my older brother Justin's room when he was younger. Sweaty teenage boy, musty and a bit rank. It was unpleasant and made me feel sick.

I wiped my damp palms nervously on my denim mini.

Okay, maybe it really *had* been stupid to come here. Then again, I hadn't known where else to go. I'd been dumb enough to tell Dad about my Silicon Valley job offer, hoping he'd be happy for me, but of course he hadn't been.

He'd told me I wasn't going and that was final, and that he'd do whatever it took to make me stay here in Brooklyn with him.

I knew what 'whatever it took' meant. Emotional manipulation, emotional blackmail, and if I was really unlucky, he might stoop to physical restraint, too. Dad had always hated being told no.

The quiet and introverted teen I'd once been would have automatically bowed her head and agreed with him. But I'd just come back from three years at college and the time away from him had allowed me some breathing room. I'd had space to grow, to realise that there was a better life out there, one that wasn't constantly overshadowed by his presence.

Sure, I was still quiet and introverted, but when he'd told me I couldn't go, I discovered I had a bit of backbone after all.

I couldn't let him take my dream job away from me. I couldn't let him stop me from trying to live my life. My ticket was booked and I'd be out of here in a couple of days. All I had to do was avoid him so he couldn't do his usual emotional number on me and get me to change my mind.

It would have been fine if I'd been a stronger sort of person, but I wasn't. He always found my vulnerable spots and used them against me, just like the bullies in school used to. I knew I was weak so it was better I take myself out of the equation. Go somewhere he'd never think to find me, never in a million years.

The Knights of Ruin MC's clubhouse.

As police chief, my dad had had a few run-ins with the Knights in the past, though these days he was best buddies with Keep, the Knights' president. Dad would never expect me to have run here, not to the most notorious MC in the state, and especially not when Keep would give me up to him first chance he got if I was ever discovered here.

Which was why I'd come in disguise, dressing up the way I'd seen other girls who wanted a walk on the wild side with a bunch of outlaw bikers do—tiny denim miniskirt and stilettos, a tight blue crop top. I'd had to kill the effect by putting a hoodie on over the top, with the hood pulled up, but I couldn't afford for anyone to see my face. Not that anyone would recognise me these days, but still. Better safe than sorry.

Getting in had been a problem. The only biker whose name I could remember—other than Keep—was Tiger. He'd once been my bodyguard for a month back when I was in high school and I still remembered him. I could hardly forget him, truth be told, so his name had been the first on my lips when I'd been interrogated by the prospect at the door. Unfortunately, though, Tiger was 'busy' and so I'd had to think fast and make up some other lie.

I wasn't experienced with men, had no idea that perhaps flashing my tits would have worked better, but luckily at that moment a semifamiliar face had appeared. I'd met Crash only a couple of times, in conjunction with Tiger, and had no idea if he'd remember me or not. I threw myself at him anyway, begging him to let me inside and that I'd make it worth his while.

He grabbed me around the waist and grinned at

the prospect, and before I knew it I'd been bundled down the corridor and into his bedroom.

Unfortunately, I was starting to think that not only had I been stupid to come here, I'd been naive into the bargain. There were stories about the Knights that I'd heard from various friends, about drunken parties and public sex and threesomes and all kinds of things.

And now I was in the thick of it.

Alone.

So much for my high IQ. Panic had made me stupid. Again.

More sounds came from outside the door. A man shouting and then the sounds of a scuffle followed by laughter. Something thumped hard against the wall and I jumped in shock.

God, I wasn't cut out for this.

I was just starting to wonder if I could slip right back out again without anyone noticing when the door banged open and Crash came in. He was a good-looking guy, which made me nervous since good-looking guys always did. Actually, men in general made me nervous, good-looking or otherwise.

You sure picked the wrong place to hide then, didn't you?

Given that the clubhouse was full of men, violent and loud, yeah, it really had been.

'Still here?' he asked, grinning and swaying on his feet.

I decided not to tell him that he was stating the

obvious since men generally didn't like it when I did that, settling for smoothing my miniskirt instead and trying to smile.

Okay, so I was naive. But I wasn't *that* naive. I knew what girls in MC clubhouses were supposed to do and I knew that Crash hadn't brought me into his bedroom because he wanted to chat about the finer points of game theory—my favourite subject. He'd brought me here because he thought I was ready for some hot sex.

As if on cue, he sauntered over from the door, two beers in his hand, then held one out to me. That grin was still on his face and there was a glazed look in his blue eyes. As he stood there swaying, I finally realised what I should have known the moment he'd grabbed me and hustled me into his bedroom: Crash was drunk. Very, very drunk.

Dammit.

Drunk guys were always super fun. *Not.*

I took the beer, the can cold against my damp palm, and tried to resist the urge to do something about my fear by downing the whole thing in one go.

'So-o-o-o…' Crash said slowly, lifting his own beer and taking a swig. 'How long exactly are you planning on keeping your clothes on?'

My palms got even damper and I could feel myself begin to sweat.

Sex. I knew that was what he expected, but… Well, my great plan had kind of ended with me at the clubrooms. I hadn't thought about what I might have to do to *stay* in the clubrooms.

So, is losing your virginity to some guy you barely know in a dirty biker clubhouse really worth avoiding your father for?

That was a very good question. And one I didn't want to find out the answer to. Maybe if I told him I only wanted to hide out here for a while, he'd let me?

I cleared my throat, trying to get the words out. 'I…um…well…there's kind of a reason.'

'Uh-huh.' Crash sat down heavily next to me on the bed, making me aware of him in a way I didn't like. He was in the usual biker uniform of jeans, a T-shirt and the leather vest they called a 'cut' worn over the top, and I could feel the heat of his body next to mine. He wore a lot of aftershave and that combined with the reek of alcohol coming off him made me want to cringe. 'If that reason is to suck my cock, then, baby, I'm here for that.'

Fear fluttered in my gut.

Yeah, I didn't want to do that. Even the thought of it made me feel ill. I'd never done it before and I certainly didn't want to start with some drunken biker, just because I'd apparently lost my mind and made a decision that was, in retrospect, looking to be the stupidest decision in the history of creation.

'W-what if it's…not that?' I asked hesitantly.

'Oh, come on…' He leaned in, nuzzling against my ear, his beer breath wafting over me, deepening my discomfort with the whole situation. 'Uh…what did you say your name was again?'

I hadn't told him, and what's more, I couldn't. Because although he might not have known who Summer Grant was, I was pretty sure he was familiar with Campbell Grant, the police chief and my dad. Not that he'd necessarily draw a link between the names, at least not in his current state, but I couldn't risk it.

Desperately I tried to think of another name I could give him, but for once my dumb brain was empty. 'Do you really need to know that?'

He left a wet kiss beneath my ear that made my skin crawl. 'Nah. Couldn't give a shit. Just gimme a taste of that pussy.'

I cringed again, both at the crass way he was talking and at how he was leaning over me. 'Hey.' I tried to pull away from him. 'What would you say if I… uh…didn't want to have sex with you?'

He gave a drunken laugh, reaching for my hand. 'Are you kidding me? Then what the hell am I supposed to do with this?' And he pressed my hand right down over his fly, where I could feel him already as hard as a rock.

Wonderful. This situation was getting better and better.

I swallowed, my mouth dry, trying to resist the urge to jerk my hand away since I was pretty sure that would offend him and I didn't want to risk that, not when I wasn't sure what he'd do.

Instead, I left my hand there for a second, then carefully drew it back. 'That's, um…very impressive.' I took a quick sip of my beer, grabbing a bit of that liquid courage and trying not to pull a face at the taste. 'But maybe you could get someone else to do something about it?'

He shook his head and put a hand on my knee, sliding it up to the hem of my skirt. 'Oh, no, baby. It's a party and you're the one in my room. You know what that means.'

I shifted my leg away, attempting to put some distance between us. 'No. I have no idea what that means.' Because, although I knew what it was that he wanted, I didn't know how it being a party made any difference.

Outside, the thumping of the music had increased in volume, and there was lots of loud shouting and laughter. More immediate were the rhythmic noises coming from the room next door and someone moaning, while someone else cursed.

I could feel my face flushing.

'Well,' Crash mumbled, trying to slide his fingers beneath my skirt yet again. 'Girls only go into a brother's room for one reason and here's a hint. It's not to chat.'

I knew that. Of course I knew that.

But you didn't think it through first so now you have to deal.

My heart shuddered in my chest, the fear inside me getting wider, deeper. Would he even let me go if

I didn't want to have sex with him? And if I got out of Crash's room, what would happen then? I'd have to run the gauntlet of those men outside all the way back to the entrance of the club.

Yeah, you're a freaking genius. Mensa would love to have you. Not.

I shivered, feeling like the biggest fool to ever draw breath. What had I been thinking? I hadn't; that was my problem. I'd let my anger at Dad and at my own weakness get the better of me, and now I was here, being pressured into having sex with a drunken biker.

Awesome.

I pushed Crash's hand away yet again, trying frantically to think of a solution to this particular problem. But sadly this was real life and it wasn't quite as simple as a math equation. There were no rules I could apply here and way too many variables, and when you were battling panic, logic didn't always work.

'C-can't we chat?' I wriggled away from him. 'Just while I finish my beer?'

But his hand was now sliding underneath my hoodie, over my bare stomach, and he was pulling me very close, his mouth at my neck. 'Nah. I don't wanna chat. C'mon, baby. Put those lips to work.'

I went rigid, my heart now climbing up into my throat. I could feel the strength in his arm going around me. I knew I couldn't fight it.

Men, they were all the same. Even the ones who

were supposed to be the good guys were assholes, and I knew that better than anyone.

In the corridor outside, a woman giggled, the deep voice of a man saying something in return.

'Well, o-okay.' I hated the way I couldn't keep my voice from shaking. 'But I'm a virgin, you know that, right?' It had been my experience that once you said the 'V' word, men usually ran for the hills.

Sadly Crash didn't run, though to be fair, there were no hills he could logically run to.

'Mmm…' he said. 'Then maybe I can teach you.' And he moved his hand up to cup my breast.

I don't know what happened then. Something in me simply snapped, roaring in negation as his hand cupped me, and I found myself shoving him away hard before I could think better of it, yelling 'No' as loud as I could for good measure.

Then, as I was sitting there, trembling with anger and fear, the door to Crash's room burst open with such force that it bounced back against the wall with a bang.

A man was standing in the doorway. A horribly familiar man.

'What the fuck is going on?' the man demanded, his voice deep and dark, rough and gritty. Then his strange amber eyes met mine and my heart clenched tight with a weird combination of absolute terror and utter relief.

Jake Clarke, aka Tiger.

I'd never forgotten the first day I'd met him. He'd

been waiting for me outside my school one day, sitting astride his massive black Harley and smoking a cigarette. He'd worn battered blue jeans, a black T-shirt with a leather vest thrown over the top, and there were chains attached to his belt, huge motorcycle boots on his feet, brightly coloured tattoos wrapping around both his powerful arms.

He was as beautiful as the animal he was named for and twice as dangerous. Mean as hell and sexy as sin.

The sun had struck copper sparks from his dark hair, and when he'd seen that school was out, he'd thrown his cigarette down right there in the street and ground it under his heel. Then he'd looked straight at me.

And I'd forgotten where I was. I'd even forgotten who I was.

His eyes were amber, the colour of expensive whisky or newly minted gold coins, and they had pinned me to the spot. A golden arrow straight through my heart.

His face was all hard lines and arrogant angles, his brows slightly winged at the corners, and he had the hardest, sharpest jawline I'd ever seen. He didn't smile. His mouth was wide and beautifully carved, and the rounded shape of his bottom lip was the softest part about him, but it didn't curve.

All my friends had stared at him—hell, *everyone* had stared at him. No one in my exclusive girls' school had ever seen a man like him.

'There'll be someone there to meet you after school today,' Dad had told me that morning. 'In fact, he'll be taking you to and from school for a little while so be nice to him, okay?'

Tiger had been that someone. An enforcer for the Knights of Ruin MC, he'd been assigned to be my bodyguard to protect me from the death threats another MC had thrown at my father. And Dad, being canny, had decided that the best protection from one MC was a rival MC.

I'd been terrified of Tiger and excited by him in equal measure, and I'd fallen in love with him the moment I'd seen him. But back then I was only seventeen and a nerdy, tongue-tied little girl, while he was twenty-six and a full-grown man, and so far out of my league he might as well have been the sun to my Pluto.

He was a star while I… I was barely even a planet.

It had taken me years to get him out of my head and I'd thought I'd managed it while I'd been away at college. But one look at him was all it took for those feelings to come flooding back. The fear and the curiosity and the dry-mouthed excitement.

I'd thought my situation couldn't get any worse.

I was wrong.

CHAPTER TWO

Tiger

THE SIGHT OF the girl sitting on Crash's bed, staring at me with the biggest, deepest blue eyes I'd ever seen, hit me like a fucking brick to the head.

Not only because she was as white as a goddamn sheet, but also because I knew her.

Summer Grant. Daughter of that well-known asshole Campbell Grant, the police chief.

What the ever-loving fuck was she doing here?

I'd been enjoying the party, aka the usual Saturday night at the clubhouse, and had gone off to spend a little quality time with Mercy, one of the club girls, and hadn't been in the mood to hear some girl shout 'No' from behind a closed bedroom door, and still less to do anything about it.

But I didn't have much patience with brothers who didn't treat the girls right, so I'd kicked the door open to check out what was going on, to make sure things were okay. Only to find Summer fucking Grant sitting there, shaking, on the bed with that dumbass Crash trying to get his hands all over her.

The brother was drunk as a fucking skunk and didn't appear to notice that his door was currently hanging off its hinges. Or that I was standing there. Or even that I'd asked him a goddamn question.

He reached again for the police chief's pretty little daughter.

Fuck. No.

I took two steps into the room, grabbed Crash by his collar, jerked him off the bed, then shoved him up against the wall. 'You hurt her?' I demanded, gripping him by the throat. 'Say yes and I'll punch your fucking face in.'

Couldn't have brothers hurting the girls here. Made for a bad rep and brought trouble, and if there was one thing the Knights didn't need right now it was trouble.

Crash blinked at me, choking slightly in my hold. 'No,' he managed to get out, but I gave him a cuff over the face all the same, because he was an asshole and needed to learn a lesson.

I took my hand away and left him to drop in a heap on the floor, then I turned around to see how Summer was doing.

She was sitting on the bed, giving me big eyes and fear and not saying a fucking word.

'Want to tell me what you're doing here, baby?' I asked her.

Crash croaked something from the floor, but I

stuck my boot in his gut as a warning. 'Didn't ask you, dumbass.' This time he must have found some brains from somewhere because he closed his mouth again pretty quickly.

Summer still didn't say a word, hunching over and looking down at her hands like they were the most fascinating things she'd ever seen her life.

Fuck. Looked like my evening of beer, a smoke and a couple of relaxing blow jobs was toast.

'Summer,' I said, keeping things mild because it was clear she was shit-scared, 'let's start again from the top. What the fuck are you doing here?'

At that point there came a loud burst of noise from the corridor outside and I glanced towards the door-way, catching a glimpse of some shrieking girls and a couple of the brothers laughing as they all came in from the living area, obviously in search of some bedrooms.

Mercy, hanging around by the broken door, gave me a pointed look.

Christ. I needed to lock this shit down before someone going past got a look at Summer and rec-ognised her, and started wondering what the hell the police chief's daughter was doing hanging around the clubhouse.

'Sorry, Merc.' I gestured to the girl on the bed, who was hunching her shoulders and generally try-ing to make herself invisible. A bit of an impossi-bility when she was wearing a miniskirt that barely covered her pussy and left a pair of long slender legs very, very bare. 'Got a situation I have to handle. Maybe we'll have some fun later.'

And I *did* have to handle it. If Summer decided to make a complaint about Crash to her dad, things could go badly for the Knights. We'd already had some drama with the chief's son and we did not need any more with his daughter.

Mercy made a pouty face, but she was a good girl who knew when to back off. 'Yeah, okay, but I'm holding you to that.'

I didn't look after her as she disappeared back down the corridor. Instead, I took a step over to where Summer was sitting with her head bowed. Crash made another sound, but I didn't want to hear it, especially not from him. 'Shut the fuck up,' I warned him, not even bothering to look at him. 'You try forcing a girl again and I won't just punch you in the face. I'll cut off your cock and make you suck it. Understand?'

He didn't say anything, which was just as well since my evening was starting to look less like blow jobs and beer and more like complicated bullshit.

Annoyed, I kicked aside the clothing lying across the floor and came over to the bed where Summer was sitting. 'Baby,' I said again, 'talk to me.'

But she just shook her head and hunched her shoulders even more.

It made me remember when I used to bodyguard for her. She'd been a little scaredy-cat even then, perpetually treating me like I'd frighten her to death if I even looked at her funny.

What was she doing here? And what had Crash done to her to scare her like this?

I crouched in front of her and reached out to grab one of her hands. Her fingers were icy in mine. 'Hey.' I tried to keep my voice gentle, which was difficult since I wasn't a gentle guy by any stretch of the imagination. 'You okay?'

A brother's voice sounded from close to the doorway. Big Red, the VP, from the sounds of things.

Jesus, I really needed to get her out of here.

I rose to my feet and carefully pulled Summer off the bed so she was standing in front of me, her hand still cold in mine.

Her chin came up, her eyes blinking in shock, her hoodie falling back a little, giving me a better look at her face. Yeah, I remembered her all right. Couldn't forget eyes that blue, or that huge and dark. They seemed black beneath her fair, almost colourless brows, and then there was that determined, pointed chin. I remembered trying to tease her out of her constant terrified silence a couple of times, a tactic that had never worked. But that chin of hers used to jut in a way that made me wonder if she wasn't as scared as she seemed, more like pissed instead. And then there was her luscious mouth, all soft and pink and pouty...

Something punched me hard, right in the gut, and since it was pretty much the last thing I expected to

feel when looking at Summer Grant, it took me a
second to realise that my cock, the impatient motherfucker, was very, *very* interested in that mouth.

Fuck. This was all I needed. Getting inexplica-
bly hard for Campbell Grant's daughter, which was
so not happening. Jesus Christ, I'd be lucky if Keep
didn't kick my ass from here to fucking Florida if
he ever found out.

Not that I'd do anything about it. I hadn't been
into jailbait back when she'd been seventeen and I
wasn't into it now. Though I guessed she wasn't seventeen any more. More like...twenty-two maybe?
Except she didn't look it, not with those big, frightened eyes. She looked like a kid who'd just woken
up from a really bad nightmare.

I didn't mind a bit of fear to get a chick turned
on, as long as she was into it. But if she wasn't, then
neither was I, and as for outright terror... Yeah, that
wasn't hot as far as I was concerned and it pretty
much killed the burgeoning hard-on in my jeans.
Good fucking job.

'Come on,' I told her, impatient now to get this
mess sorted out. 'Party's over.'

I began to move back to the doorway, pulling her
with me, but she'd gone rigid, freezing like a block
of wood, staring at me like I was some kind of se-
rial killer.

Christ. Please don't tell me I was going to have to
haul a terrified girl through the clubhouse in the middle of a party. Knowing my fucking luck, she'd start

screaming and then the shit *would* hit the fan. Especially if Keep spotted me and got the wrong idea.

Yeah, that wasn't happening. Except the problem was that I didn't have time to calm her down now, not with a whole lot of brothers out in the corridor. I needed to get her somewhere private, then maybe get her to quit being so scared and tell me what the hell she was doing here. If it was to take a walk on the wild side with some bikers—which a lot of girls did—then I needed to point out what a stupid fucking idea that was. And then I'd tell her exactly what it meant for the club to have the chief of police's daughter found screaming in a brother's bedroom.

If she didn't want to bang a whole bunch of bikers—and quite frankly, given the look on her face right now, I guessed she probably didn't—then I needed to find out what the hell else had brought her there, then take it to Keep for the same reason.

Protecting the club. That was my job and I took it very, very seriously indeed.

'You gonna come with me?' I asked, giving her a chance to move under her own steam.

But she just stared at me, her face completely white, trembling like a leaf.

Shit. She was panicking now and that was another thing I remembered from my time as her protection. There'd only been one instance of trouble and it hadn't been from the MC who'd delivered the death threats, but from some kids at her school. She'd been late meeting me so I'd gone to see where she was, only to find her being bullied outside some classrooms. All it had taken was a hard stare and a couple of threats, and those bitches had run away, but Summer had stood there stock-still, like a deer caught in the headlights of a car. Too afraid to move.

It had taken a lot of coaxing to get her to snap out of it then, but time was something I didn't have right now. Plus, I was an impatient motherfucker, just like my cock. I wanted this over and done with and I wanted it now.

So I put my hands on her hips, picked her up and threw her over my shoulder.

Summer didn't make a sound or even struggle, though I felt every inch of her go rigid.

'Don't scream,' I told her, wrapping my arm around her slender thighs to hold her steady as I turned towards the door. 'I'm not going to hurt you.'

She was completely silent, stiff as a board as I stepped out of Crash's room and into the corridor.

And into the middle of a goddamn orgy.

Great. Something else I was missing out on. Shit.

I tried to ignore all the hot sex happening right in front of me, heading towards my room since that was the only place I could guarantee we wouldn't be interrupted by douchebags.

But, of course, walking down the corridor with a woman thrown over my shoulder wasn't going to go ignored.

Sure enough, as I went past a brother getting head from two different women, he called out something about my 'friend' and that it was rude not to introduce her.

It was going to look unusual for me *not* to join in since it was well known that I was a big fan of the orgy, but since I was damn sure that the pretty little thing over my shoulder wouldn't be thrilled if I suddenly started insisting on her getting to know the brothers and their cocks, I merely gave him the finger and strode on past.

My room was down the corridor a way, and I stopped outside it, my arm still wrapped around her thighs. She was taller than I'd expected and on the skinny side—I preferred chicks with a little more to hold on to—and I was weirdly conscious of the way she smelled, sweet and flowery and kind of innocent. It got to me, that scent. Not sure why, but it did. The club girls I was used to didn't smell like that and I wasn't sure I liked it.

It made me aware of how scared she'd been and of how I was now hauling her around over my shoulder like a sack of coal. Made me wonder if that really had been the best course of action, since it probably wouldn't have helped her fear.

Then I realised what I was doing and glared at my door. What the fuck? I wasn't used to questioning my decisions and I didn't appreciate the fact that I was questioning them now, and all because of the way some scared little girl smelled.

Holy shit. I was going soft.

Irritated with myself, I opened the door and stepped inside.

I actually had a place of my own, but I liked to keep a room at the club because I liked being where my brothers were, where I could get all the cold beer and hot pussy I could handle without having to do a thing.

I wasn't a loner, unlike my buddy Smoke. I liked people. I liked a party, too, lots of music, alcohol and women… Everything a man needed to feel good, and since feeling good was my preferred state, I indulged myself often.

Pity I was missing out on all of that now, though, which was pissing me off. Especially after the day I'd had taking care of some Demon's Share MC assholes who'd accidentally-on-purpose wandered into our territory and had needed a little reminder to stay out of it.

Anyway, I'd been looking forward to some R & R tonight, a chance to forget about my problems for a little while, but now I had to deal with the tiny issue of a panicking civilian who shouldn't have been anywhere near the clubhouse, and that wasn't exactly enhancing my mood.

I kicked the door shut after me, then carried Summer over to the bed and slid her off my shoulder and down onto it.

I reached for her hood and pulled it off so I could get a good look at her, wanting to check if she was okay. A whole lot of silky platinum-blonde hair came tumbling out and down around her shoulders, reminding me of how she used to wear it back in school, in an untidy ponytail or in a bun wound around a pen or pencil. I always used to want to tie it back properly for her since I hated untidiness as a rule, but of course I never did.

Even with her hair all down, she didn't look up. But I wasn't having that so I put a finger beneath her chin and tipped her head back so I could see her face.

Her skin was dead white, her eyes round as fucking saucers and darker than a night sky.

Jesus.

It was all coming back to me now, that month I'd spent taking her to and from school. How pissed I'd been with the Knights' then president for assigning me what had amounted to babysitting duties as a favour to the police chief. How she'd never said a word to me unless I asked her a question directly, and wouldn't meet my eyes. How much that had irritated me because, sure, I was pretty scary but I hadn't thought I was *that* scary.

She was looking at me now the same way she had back then, those big eyes glazed with fear, and it annoyed me at the same time as it made my chest feel tight. Because I hadn't wanted her to be afraid of me back then and I didn't want her to be afraid of me now. It felt…wrong somehow.

I had no idea what was up with that shit because it wasn't as if I was a nice, caring kind of guy. I was an enforcer, for fuck's sake. I made sure the brothers stuck to the club rules. And I only cared about three things—my club, my bike and making myself feel good as often as I damn well could.

Nothing else mattered.

Certainly not this scaredy-cat who'd got herself into some pretty deep shit.

But knowing all that didn't stop the tightness in my chest. And I found myself rubbing her little chin with my thumb as if I wanted to soothe her or something. 'You gonna tell me what you're doing here, baby girl?' I asked, deliberately using the name I used to call her years ago, when I'd wanted to get a rise out of her. I'd always figured that since being nice to her hadn't got her to be less scared of me, maybe getting her angry would work. 'Did Crash hurt you? Because I'm telling you right now that if he did, his name is going straight to the top of my shitlist.'

She didn't respond to me 'baby girl'-ing her. Instead she swallowed and I found myself staring at the pulse beating in the hollow of her throat. It was fast. Way too fucking fast.

'Tiger?' she said at long last, her voice husky and uncertain.

Hearing her say my name like that shocked me. I didn't know she'd even remembered it, because she'd certainly never used it to my face.

'Yeah, you know it.' Her skin was incredibly soft and smooth under my thumb and I couldn't seem to stop myself from stroking her again. I'd touched plenty of other women so there was no reason why her skin should feel any different. But somehow it did.

She blinked a couple more times, staring at me as if she'd never seen me before in her entire life. Then her gaze slowly dropped to… Holy shit. She was looking at my mouth.

That thing inside me kicked again, harder this time, and I felt my cock stir.

Christ, what the fuck was she doing that for? Didn't she know what a come on it was?

As if I'd said it out loud, those big blue eyes came back to mine again, and she must have realised what she was doing because suddenly colour washed over her pale skin and she jerked herself out of my grip.

'Don't,' she muttered, bending her head again and looking at her hands twisting in her lap, the long blonde hair in a curtain around her face.

'Okay. So you can talk.' I resisted the urge to grab her again, settling for putting my hands in my pockets instead. The warmth of her skin against my fingertips lingered, which pissed me off for no good reason. 'You wanna answer my question about Crash?'

She was silent and I thought she was going to retreat, but then she said finally, 'He didn't hurt me. He was just…insistent.'

'More than insistent. Looked like he scared the shit out of you.'

'I wasn't s-scared.'

'Yeah, and I'm the fucking Queen of England.'

She didn't say anything to that, her hands white-knuckled in her lap.

Christ, this silence bullshit was starting to get really fucking annoying.

'What the hell are you doing here, Summer?' I demanded, coming to the end of my patience. 'And look at me when I'm talking to you.'

Finally, she lifted her head, and maybe I was imagining things, but it seemed like her eyes were less dark. I saw a small blue spark had flickered to life in them.

If it was anger, then good. That was way better than fear.

'Maybe I just wanted to hang out with some b-bikers,' she said, a defensive note in her voice.

I nearly laughed. 'Seriously? You were nearly catatonic back there, baby girl. So, no, I'm not buying you wanting to hang out with some bikers.'

That pretty mouth of hers thinned. 'I'm not a baby and I'm not a girl.'

Yeah, looked like I was annoying her, which was excellent. It also looked like she had a bit of spirit in her after all. Certainly more than she'd had when she was seventeen.

Yeah, and you like that, too.

Which I was *not* going to think about.

'I don't care who you are,' I said mildly. 'You've got five seconds to give me the truth or I'm taking you straight to Keep and you can tell him.'

Fear flashed in her eyes again, but this time that determined chin firmed. Another good sign. 'Don't do that. Please.'

'Okay, well, you'd better start doing some talking then, hadn't you?'

Her gaze flicked away from mine. 'Well…um… I… It's…uh…'

'Use your words, baby girl.'

It flicked back, another of those blue sparks flashing, the colour in her cheeks pinker. Much, *much* better. Annoying her was clearly the way to go. Which was excellent considering I was a master at annoying the shit out of people.

'Give me one good reason I should tell you.' She lifted that chin, looking down her nose at me, all haughty and shit. And fuck knows why, but my cock found that extremely hot.

'Because I asked you,' I said gently, ignoring my impatient dick.

She frowned. 'That's not a good enough reason.'

Holy shit, this woman was a problem.

'Baby girl,' I explained, trying to be patient, 'the way I see it, you have two choices. You either tell me what's going on right now. Or you tell me what's going on right now.'

Her frown deepened. 'But…those two are the same.'

I folded my arms and gave her my enforcer's smile. The one guaranteed to make a brother wish they'd never been born. 'Yeah. I know.'

CHAPTER THREE

Summer

I SAT ON Tiger's bed and stared at him, feeling something deep inside me quiver in a way that had nothing whatsoever to do with the weird panic that had overtaken me in Crash's room.

Or rather, it felt related to fear but not like I was in imminent danger of death or anything. More like when you get on a rollercoaster or a plane taking off, and everything is fast and out of control and it's freaky and scary at the same time.

Tiger had always had that effect on me. He had been exciting and scary and I just hadn't known what to do with myself around him.

I still didn't.

Him suddenly appearing in Crash's room like some kind of tattooed avenging angel, bringing all my confused teenaged feelings about him flooding back, had made me freeze. Like I just…couldn't deal with Crash and him *and* where I was and what was happening all at the same time. And then he'd picked me up and tossed me over his shoulder like I weighed nothing at all and my brain had simply shut down.

Sometimes it happened to me like that. When I got overwhelmed, I froze. As if I was afraid something worse might happen if I moved.

I hated it. Or rather, I hated myself when I got like that. Especially when it happened in front of someone so strong and in control.

Someone like Tiger.

And he was just as strong and in control now as he had been back when I was seventeen. Just as tall and muscular. Just as scary. And just as freaking hot.

He was in jeans and a blue T-shirt, that biker leather vest over the top, and he had his arms folded, giving me a glimpse of the incredible tattoos inked into the bronze skin covering the powerful muscles of his biceps and forearms.

On his right arm, a tiger prowled, long and lean and dangerous, its teeth bared. On his left, an intricate, dizzying design of interlocking circles and spirals and all sorts of other geometries. For a second I got distracted, too busy staring at it and trying to follow all the angles to remember that he'd asked me a question.

'Baby girl,' he said quietly, in that deep voice that I felt right down low in my belly, 'I'm not gonna ask again.'

Baby girl. Hadn't he heard me when I'd told him I didn't like it? How annoying. I'd hated it back when he'd been my protector, had found it incredibly patronising, but I'd been too shy to tell him to stop.

I had a bit more backbone now, though I got distracted again by the warning note in his voice.

Crap. He was going to make me tell him, wasn't he? God, what the hell was I going to do now? I didn't want him to find out what a coward I was. Or how ridiculously stupid I'd been to come down here without a plan.

No, I shouldn't have cared what he thought of me, but the fact was, I did.

He was so strong and bright and...vivid. He didn't give a shit what anyone thought of him. He did whatever the hell he wanted.

He was everything that I wasn't and that intimidated the crap out of me, and the thought of having to spill my guts to him about Dad and my generally being pathetic when it came to emotional manipulation made me feel ill.

But what choice did I have?

Well, you could try distracting him...

That was an option, of course. But how? I wasn't especially good at small talk and found talking to people in general difficult. Particularly people who intimidated me.

I bit my lip and frowned at him. My panic seemed to have receded, which was a mercy, my brain functioning again, formulating several plans, then discarding them.

Maybe I should ask him about his tattoos. Didn't

guys like talking about themselves? And if I managed to get him talking, then I wouldn't have to, an added bonus.

Taking a silent breath, I pushed myself off his bed and took a couple of uncertain steps towards him.

He watched me approach, those golden eyes on mine, unblinking, and I felt fear curl up tight once again inside me. But I made myself take another step or two, getting nearer.

He was even more intimidating close up. I wasn't short, yet he towered over me, a wall of hard muscle and raw masculine power, sending my heartbeat racing into overdrive.

My mouth was dry and I felt shaky, and I had to force myself to speak. 'Your t-tattoos are amazing,' I stuttered weakly. 'Where did you get them?'

This close to him I could feel the heat of his body and smell that delicious scent I remembered from years ago. Leather and engine oil, and some kind of dark spice that made me want to bury my face in his neck and inhale.

Unlike Crash, the thought of being near Tiger didn't make me want to either cringe or pull away. No, it made me want to get even closer.

God, he made my head swim. Like he had when he'd taken my chin in his hand and rubbed it with his thumb. I'd forgotten my fear the moment he'd touched me, the very second those incredible eyes of his had met mine. And instead of feeling like I was going to freeze to death, I'd felt hot instead. Far, far too hot.

He'd been so close, his beautifully sculpted face right in front of me. And I hadn't been able to stop myself from looking at his mouth, with that full bottom lip that had fascinated me so completely at seventeen.

It still fascinated me, and, like I had back then, I'd found myself wondering what it would be like to have that mouth on mine. I'd never been kissed before so I had nothing to compare it to, only that half excited, half fearful wondering…

'Jesus Christ,' Tiger said, his dark voice rolling over me, making me feel like he'd wrapped me up in black velvet. 'I swear to God if you don't start telling me what the fuck is going on, I'm going to call the cops right now and get them to pick you up.'

His golden eyes were full of impatience and anger, and the way he was staring at me made me feel lightheaded and dizzy.

So much for distraction. It had been a lame conversation starter anyway.

I dragged my gaze away, trying to control my sudden breathlessness, not wanting want him to know how badly he affected me. I was even shocked at it myself, especially since it had been a good five years since I'd seen him.

'Okay, okay.' I turned around and went to sit on the double bed pushed up against the opposite wall.

Unlike Crash's room, Tiger's was scrupulously

neat, which surprised me, though I wasn't sure why. The floor was clear of clothes, the quilt straight on the bed. Even the male toiletries and other paraphernalia on the dresser were neatly lined up. Obviously Tiger liked a tidy room, a fact I filed away like I'd filed away other salient facts I'd learned about him in the one month during which he'd guarded me. Not that there were many, since I'd been too tongue-tied to ask him any questions.

But I knew he kept a gun in the small of his back and that he had the most amazing, sexy grin that he turned on any pretty woman who came near him. I knew he rode his bike like it was part of him and that he'd taken his job of protecting me very seriously indeed. Even though he'd hated it, which he'd made very obvious.

You know there's another way to distract him. One that doesn't involve conversation.

My brain came to a screaming halt as the thought crossed my mind and my face heated.

Oh, yes, well. There was *that*. Which was all very well if I'd been some kind of practised seductress. But I wasn't. I was Summer Grant, and I'd spent most of my life trying to be invisible to as many people as possible.

I was the classic nerd. I had been at school, and the same in college. And since mostly it made people leave me alone, I was okay with it. I didn't miss parties or the desperate drama that went along with dating. I was happy with my studies, losing myself in numbers and equations, where everything was logical and followed clear rules. It was easier and way more interesting than all the usual college/teenage stuff that other people got up to.

I'd never met anyone I'd wanted enough to bear the hassle of it anyway.

Well, anyone except Tiger.

He was staring at me, that gaze of his almost flattening me with its intensity. He was leaning back against the closed door now, his arms folded across his muscular chest, the black geometries of his fascinating tattoos dark on his skin.

I felt his stare like a pressure around my throat, closing off all my air, leaving me in no doubt that he wanted an answer and he wanted it now.

Taking a breath, I got up again, a weird kind of restlessness pacing under my skin. I closed the distance between us, coming right up to where he stood. Even nearer than I had before.

His amber gaze followed me so intently it made me almost dry-mouthed with terror. I didn't quite know why. I only knew that the way he looked at me, as if he could really *see* me, made me feel vulnerable in a way I couldn't describe.

It made me want to run away and hide.

But I couldn't, not here. There was nowhere to run to and, besides, I had a feeling Tiger wouldn't let me anyway.

All I could do was keep walking until I was right up close to him, so there were only inches between us. He never took his eyes off me, not once, and again, this near to him, I felt the weird dizziness take over. His scent and his heat and his golden gaze…

'I was in Crash's room because…' I faltered but then made myself go on. 'Well… I wanted to see what being with a b-biker was like.'

Tiger stared down at me for a long moment and I could see something that looked like annoyance glinting in his gaze. Then his mouth curved in a smile that had nothing to do with amusement and he gave a soft laugh that made a shiver chase down my spine. 'Right,' he said. 'So all you want is biker cock.' He gave another laugh. 'Try again, baby girl.'

I don't know what happened then. Maybe it was just being here and running out of options. Maybe it was some leftover stupidity from me shoving Crash away. Whatever it was, his obvious disbelief made a small spark of annoyance ignite me.

It was insanity to argue with a man like Tiger, a man who radiated violence and danger, who had menace inked into his skin. Yet for some reason I opened my big fat mouth and said, 'How do you know that's not why I'm here? Biker c-cock might be exactly what I want.'

There was a stunning silence.

Tiger finally blinked and I was conscious of a weird warm feeling in amongst all that cold fear. Had I finally surprised him?

Of course it didn't last long.

He bent his head and suddenly his face was millimetres from mine, those amber eyes boring into me, that beautiful mouth so close. 'If biker cock is really what you want, then what are you waiting for? I'm a biker and I have a cock. Get down on your knees and suck it.'

The shock of the words and his abrupt nearness froze me in place. But not like before, in Crash's room. I wasn't rigid with fear this time, because I could read in his gaze that he wasn't serious. This was a dare. He used to do that in the month when he'd been my protector, teasing me to get a rise out of me. I'd always been too afraid to respond to him then but now…

I don't know what came over me. A sudden rush of anger filled me, along with a determination to show him that I wasn't the scared 'baby girl' he seemed to think I was.

Forgetting my fear, I gave him one furious look. Then I dropped to my knees in front of him.

CHAPTER FOUR

Tiger

NOTHING SURPRISED ME much any more. But little Summer Grant dropping to her knees right in front of me, ready to prove she was desperate to suck my cock?

Yeah, not gonna lie, that surprised the hell out of me.

Telling her to get on her knees was supposed to have made her back off, not actually do what I said.

I didn't move, looking down at her as she knelt in front of me. Of course I knew that she didn't actually want to do this—I hadn't missed that blue spark that had lit in her eyes just before she did what I told her to do.

She was calling my bluff the way I'd called hers.

And, fuck, she might just have won this round, because, Christ, I couldn't actually let her suck me off. Not given how terrified she'd been not fifteen minutes earlier in Crash's room. And not when she was only doing this because it was clear she didn't want to tell me what she was *actually* doing in the clubhouse.

Unfortunately, though, my goddamn cock didn't seem to understand that.

There was something about the way she knelt in front of me, with her chin lifted, her eyes on mine. And I could see that spark of anger dancing in them. Yeah, she definitely wasn't the scaredy-cat she appeared to be.

In fact, if I wasn't much mistaken, she was giving me a challenge to answer the one I'd just given her.

Not many brothers took me on these days, let alone one little girl. That took guts.

And it made me hard.

Made me want to reach down and bury my fingers in all that silky blonde hair, hold on to her as she took my dick, as she worked her mouth on me, taking me deep.

Made me want to know how far I could push her, how far I could go. Did that little spark of hers mean she was steel all the way through, or would she shatter if I put pressure on her?

I suspected I knew already, though. I suspected she was steel. It was always the quiet ones you had to watch out for, those were the ones with claws.

Christ, that mouth of hers was to die for. Perfectly shaped and a little red from where she'd been gnawing on it. I could imagine those lips wrapped around my cock, could imagine tasting them as well.

Maybe biting on them to see if they were as soft as they looked.

But, shit, I had to get a handle on myself. I couldn't goad her into blowing me. It wasn't what she was here for, no matter that she was insisting otherwise. And apart from anything else, I wasn't in the mood to be giving dick-sucking advice to virgins.

Yeah, sure. You're not in the mood. Like hell.

Ignoring my cock thoughts, I didn't move, only shook my head. 'I'm glad you're keen, baby, but no. We're not doing that.'

Those big blue eyes widened in what I thought was genuine surprise—for some reason it made me glad I could surprise her the way she'd surprised me—and that pouty mouth opened. 'Oh, but I thought you said—'

'I know what I said.' I cut her off. 'I fucking changed my mind. Now, go sit back on that bed like a good girl.'

Again that blue spark jumped, like she was pissed or maybe disappointed, which I didn't mind at all, not one bit, then she got to her feet and went slowly back over to the bed once more. She sat down and looked at her hands again, resolutely avoiding my gaze, her shoulders slumping.

Okay, so it was definitely disappointment. But… why? She hadn't *really* wanted to suck my dick, had she? Not after she'd been so goddamn terrified.

Why are you thinking about this shit? Why the fuck does it matter?

Both very good questions and ones I didn't have the answers to.

Just like I *still* didn't know why the hell she was here.

I was about to give her the hard word yet a-fucking-*gain*, when someone's fist connected loudly on the door at my back. 'Tiger.' It was Keep, sounding pissed. 'I need to talk to you. Open the fucking door.'

At the sound of Keep's voice, Summer's chin came up, her gaze getting wide and dark, frightened again.

Interesting. So given how she hadn't wanted me to talk to Keep earlier and her reaction to the sound of his voice now, it was obvious that she really didn't want him to know she was here. Which kind of made sense. She probably knew he'd bundle her up and ship her out the moment he discovered her.

Keep hammered on the door again, louder this time, and Summer's gaze came to mine, the desperation in it loud and clear. She *really* didn't want me to give her away.

It was crazy. The first thing I should have done was open the door and let my president inside, show him who was hiding out in my room. Because the club came first and always had done, and she represented trouble for it, no doubt about that.

Yet for some reason, that look in her eyes made my chest tighten yet again. Been a long, long time since someone had looked at me like that. Not since my little brother had disappeared along with my mom. Looking at me as if I could help them. As if I could save them.

So when I opened my mouth, it wasn't 'Sure, Keep, come in' that came out. It was 'Gimme a minute, Prez. I'm kind of busy.'

Summer let out a small, sharp breath, like she'd been holding it.

Then Keep said very distinctly, 'Open the fucking door. I don't care who you've got in there.'

Shit.

I couldn't say no to my president and Summer must have known that, because her face went white, and she went very still. And she kept her gaze on mine, silently pleading.

So I made a snap decision.

Pushing myself away from the door, I strode over to the bed and jerked the quilt out from under her. 'Get in,' I ordered.

She blinked rapidly. 'W-what?'

'You want me to hide you? Then get the fuck in my bed.'

She hesitated only a second, kicking off her stilettos before crawling into my bed and drawing the covers up to her chin. While she did that, I shrugged off my cut and slung it over the end of the bed, then pulled my T-shirt off.

'Tiger!' Keep was sounding really pissed now. 'For fuck's sake.'

Summer was watching me with those big eyes getting rounder as I pulled the quilt from her fingers. 'If you want this to work,' I said shortly, quietly, 'then don't argue and follow my lead, okay?'

She didn't speak, only nodded.

So I got into bed with her, positioning myself over the top of her, covering her with my body. Then I pulled the quilt over us.

And not before time.

The door slammed open and there was Keep, standing in the doorway, one of the meanest motherfuckers in the whole MC.

'Sorry, Prez,' I said lazily, looking around at him. 'I should have said. The door's open.'

He gave me that long, hard president's stare, taking in the fact that I was in bed and that there was very obviously a woman with me. My elbows were on the pillows on either side of Summer's head, my upper arms shielding her. Her hair was all over my pillow and she'd turned her face away. There was no way Keep would know who she was, as long as I didn't move.

'Thought you would have been out in the corridor,' he said flatly. 'You're such a fucking exhibitionist.'

Summer was trembling a little, her body warm and soft beneath mine, the flower scent of hers wrapping around me like I'd stumbled into a fucking garden. Her legs were spread and I could feel the intense heat of her pussy pressing against the zipper of my jeans, soaking into the denim.

This wasn't a mistake. At all.

Christ, what the hell else was I supposed to do? There'd been nowhere else for her to hide. Pretending she was some chick I'd brought in to fuck had been the only option.

I forced myself to ignore the feel of her beneath me and said, 'Yeah, well, today I thought I'd be really kinky and try for some privacy.' I shifted my hips, like I was halfway up inside her already and wanted to keep going. 'Speaking of, you got something serious to ask me? 'Cause as you can see, there's something else I'd much rather be doing.'

Keep grunted, his blue eyes cold. 'Got word that Campbell Grant's daughter has gone missing and he wanted me to keep an eye out for her.'

I could feel Summer go rigid under me and I didn't need to see her face to know that the thought of being discovered scared her. Of course it made me want to know why, because although I didn't know much about the police chief, I knew plenty about his asshole son, Summer's brother. Justin Grant was the ex of Cat Livingston, my friend Smoke's old lady. He'd been violent towards her and some shit had gone down that had included Smoke teaching the prick a lesson.

I didn't like the thought of Summer being exposed to that kind of crap, and if the son had been like that, what about the father? Sure, I'd never known what it was like to have a dad since I'd grown up without one, but I knew what had happened with Smoke's old man and Smoke had told me about Cat's.

Seemed like fathers in general were assholes.

'Yeah, I haven't seen her.' I looked down at the

woman lying very still under me. She had her face still turned away, her hair covering her cheek.

Was it her father she was scared of? Was that why she'd come down here? But why here? There were plenty of other less dangerous places to hide than a biker clubhouse. What about friends? Other family?

'Maybe you should start looking,' Keep said. 'Once you've finished, obviously.'

I didn't look at my president, as I was too busy frowning down at Summer. 'Yeah, okay. Might take a while, though.'

'This is more important than your dick, Tiger,' Keep growled. 'The chief's still pissed about that fucker Justin so we've got some ground to make up. Be good if one of the Knights could locate her and bring her in. If she hasn't simply run away, of course.'

Summer did that freezing-in-place thing again. And I wanted to grip her chin and turn her head to face me, look into her eyes to make sure she was okay. But I didn't want to risk Keep seeing her, so all I said was 'Gotcha, Prez. I'll finish up here and then I'm on it.' Quite literally in fact, but he wasn't to know that.

Keep didn't say another word, but I heard the door slam shut and then silence.

Summer remained still and that was actually starting to become something of a problem. Because my brain kept on wanting to concentrate on that heat between her legs and it was starting to get me hard.

No, scratch 'starting to.' I'd been hard even before getting into bed with her.

Which makes getting into bed with her a pretty fucking dumb idea, don't you think? Especially when you shouldn't even be touching her.

Yeah, okay, maybe it was. But I wasn't a goddamn teenage boy. I was the one in control, not my fucking cock. Which meant I should have been throwing back the quilt and getting off her, putting some distance between us.

Yet I didn't move. I stayed right where I was. I was bracing myself on my elbows so I wasn't actually lying on her, but her tits were almost brushing my chest. I couldn't see much of them since she was wearing a loose hoodie, but they seemed high and rounded, a nice handful.

And now you're staring at her tits? What the fuck is wrong with you?

It was an excellent point and yet I still couldn't seem to make myself get off her. And what was more, I was beginning to think that this was actually a great time to make her tell me what the hell she was doing here.

'Summer,' I said quietly. 'He's gone.'

A quiver ran the entire length of her body. I could damn well feel it. Then, slowly, she turned her head, giving me a quick glance from beneath her lashes, like she was afraid to look at me. But there was a flush of pink on her cheekbones, a pretty good indication to me that she wasn't scared. Or at least not as scared as she had been.

Fuck, she was so hot, though. That little pussy of hers felt like a fire burning through my zipper and if I wasn't much mistaken—and I seldom was—I thought I'd caught a hint of musk threading through her sweet, flowery scent.

Whatever you're thinking, it's not a good idea, dumb fuck.

Of course it wasn't a good idea. It was a fucking terrible idea. Yet I still wasn't moving, staying there braced on my elbows with my cock pressed hard between her legs.

She made a restless movement and her hands came up, long, pale fingers pressing against my chest. Then, like my body was a stove she'd accidentally burned herself on, she jerked them away again. 'T-Tiger…' she muttered thickly, still avoiding my gaze. 'I th-think you should…uh…move.'

I don't know what it was about hearing my name in her mouth. Plenty of women called me by it and yet I'd never once felt it go straight to my cock the way it did right now. Maybe it was her voice, all soft and husky and uncertain, and that goddamn stutter on the *T*. Like she was afraid to say it.

The club girls didn't say my name like that. They didn't avoid my gaze, jerk their hands away from my bare skin and blush like a fucking rose. And when they did look at me, it wasn't with fear or excitement or any shit like that. Sure, they wanted me, but they didn't much care who got them off. One cock was as good as another as far as they were concerned.

It had never bothered me before.

It had never bothered me before that one cock was as good as another for them. As long as everyone came, I was fine with it. And as for civilians, well, I didn't mess around with them, because I wasn't up for anything more complicated than fucking.

But Summer, she was lying there all pink and flushed, and avoiding my gaze. And it wasn't because she didn't want me. Because if she hadn't, she'd be shoving me like she'd shoved Crash, and there was definitely no shoving going on.

Yeah, I knew when a woman was into me and this little girl was into me. Not Crash. Not some other brother. *Me*.

And I didn't just like that.

I fucking loved it.

'Uh-huh,' I murmured, staying right where I was, because I was an asshole. 'And how exactly do you want me to move, baby girl?'

CHAPTER FIVE

Summer

I COULDN'T THINK. I could barely even breathe.

I'd always been proud of my brain since it was about the only thing about me that made me special. But right now, with Tiger lying right on top of me, it was like I'd lost several thousand brain cells and the stupid thing was refusing to work.

He was just so...*hot*. And...*big*. And he was everywhere, his bare chest right in front of me, his wide shoulders blocking out the rest of the room, his long, lean, muscular body pressed the whole length of mine.

And his gaze looking down at me, drowning me in gold.

I didn't know what to do with my hands. I didn't know what to do with my entire *self*.

It had happened so fast. One minute I was feeling half disappointed, half relieved that he'd pulled me up off my knees, and maybe a little angry at myself, too, since I hadn't managed to distract him, which meant that now he was going to make me tell him my real reason for being here. Then the next minute there had been a knocking at the door and I'd heard Keep's voice.

I'd thought Tiger would turn me in.

But he hadn't. He'd come across to the bed and told me to get in, and since I hadn't exactly had a lot of choice, I'd kicked off my shoes and done so. The next thing I knew, he'd ripped off his T-shirt and had climbed in, too, lying on top of me, bracing himself on his elbows so he wasn't resting his whole weight on me.

I'd never been in bed with anyone before, let alone the man who'd been lurking in my head ever since I was seventeen. The man who was now half-naked, his hard, sculpted chest and powerful shoulders on show. And somehow it didn't matter that he wasn't resting entirely on me, I felt flattened by him anyway. By the sheer intensity of his physical presence. By his closeness. By the heat of his body and the scent of his bare skin.

My brain shut down then, simply unable to function with Tiger being so near. And then Keep was in the room and finally I realised why Tiger had told me to get into bed and why he was lying on top of me.

He was hiding me from Keep.

The thought was brief and bright and then it disappeared, and I forgot completely that Keep was even in the room. Because somehow my skirt had got rucked up around my waist, my bare thighs brushing against the denim of Tiger's jeans. His hips were resting between my legs, forcing them apart, and there was something big and thick and hard pressing against the front of my panties.

And once I'd become conscious of that, I couldn't concentrate on anything else. There was something about the pressure of him right *there* that made me go hot all over. That made my thighs tremble and my breathing catch. I tried to hold myself rigid, to pull away from where he was touching me, but it was impossible.

He was everywhere. His heat and his dark, spicy scent and all that smooth tanned skin right in front of me. The fascinating tattoo of all the spirals and circles that was on his upper arm went up and over his shoulder, too, spreading halfway across his broad chest. I had to turn my head away to stop from staring at it, my fingers itching to touch it.

But not looking at him didn't do anything to stop the aching awareness of him. The feeling of his long, hot body over mine, pressing down on me, overwhelming me.

He was still overwhelming me.

Keep had gone, yet Tiger was still lying on top of me, braced on his elbows on either side of my head, looking down at me. I could feel myself getting hotter and hotter, and I didn't want to meet his gaze. I didn't want him to see what he was doing to me, how completely overcome I was about this whole situation.

God, my fingertips were tingling from where I'd made the mistake of touching his chest just before—his skin had been so hot I felt like he'd scorched me—so I closed them into fists, not sure where to put them except awkwardly down at my sides.

I knew he'd asked me a question and I was struggling to remember what it was, acutely conscious of the intense heat between my legs where his zipper was pressing against me, making me feel restless and achy and desperate.

He'd said something about moving, right?

'I don't want you to move.' I tried not to look up into his unblinking amber gaze. 'I just want you to get off me.'

'Uh-huh.' His voice sounded lazy, a deep rumble I felt echo down the length of my body. 'Okay, just gimme a second. I'm getting all caught up in the sheet.'

Then he shifted his hips.

It was only a slight movement, but somehow it nudged the hard ridge of his zipper over my clit, sending a lightning strike of sensation firing through me, lighting up every single nerve ending I had.

I tensed, gasping in shock at the unexpectedness of it.

Tiger stilled. 'You okay?' he asked in that same soft, lazy rumble, sounding completely unconcerned.

I couldn't look at him, little pulses of sensation sparking everywhere and my heartbeat—already fast—starting to get frantic.

I might have been a virgin, but I wasn't completely ignorant. I mean, I had a vibrator and I knew how to use it, so this feeling wasn't exactly new. Except that it wasn't anything like the calm, gentle pleasure I gave myself on occasion. This sensation was brighter, sharper, more vivid. Electric.

And one I had no control over whatsoever.

'I…uh…' I tried to catch my breath, tried to hide how much that slight movement of his had affected me. 'Y-yes. I just…need you to get off me.' Now. Please, God, right now.

'Impatient, huh? Where's the fire?' He shifted again, another roll of his hips over that achingly sensitive spot between my thighs, sending another burst of that intense, brilliant sensation exploding through me.

I jerked, instinctively looking up at him, as if his gaze was a magnet and I couldn't resist the pull.

Gold slammed into me. Bright, flaming gold. Burning me, *seeing* me. A forest fire and there was nowhere for me to run, nowhere for me to hide.

I trembled, scared for reasons I couldn't have described. 'T-Tiger…'

'Yeah, I know.' His hands moved, cupping either side of my jaw, the touch of his palms against my skin making me tremble harder. 'I like the way you say my name. Thought you didn't remember it.'

I blinked, trying to breathe. Trying to concentrate on what he was saying and not on the ache that was building between my thighs, right where

he was pressing down. But it was so difficult. 'I…
I…just need…'

'Need what, hmm?' He rolled his hips yet again,
another slow, delicious grind that pressed against my
clit, making me jerk and shiver like he'd given me
an electric shock. 'You need more of this, maybe?'

I could feel myself break out into a sweat. My
thighs were trembling and I wanted to lift my hips
against that tantalising pressure, to chase that incredible friction. But enough of my brain was operating
to know that this was a really bad idea. Because letting *anyone* know how you felt was always a bad
idea, especially when you were as lousy at hiding
your feelings as I was. Especially when you were
somehow in bed with a dangerous biker who'd been
in your head for years. Who lingered there like a
fascinating equation you could never quite work out
the solution to.

'N-no.' I tried to get my voice working, the word
coming out thick and husky and ragged. 'I want to…
get out…'

'Really?' He shifted, another subtle movement
of his hips rubbing against me, that ridge somehow
bigger and harder than it had been before. I groaned,
unable to help myself, pleasure beginning to wrap
itself around me.

'Are you sure you want to get out?' His thumbs
moved over my jaw, stroking my skin, adding more
fuel to the fire burning hotter and hotter. 'Seems
to me like what you want is more of this.' And he

moved again as if to illustrate the point, nearly making my eyes roll back in my head.

I'd begun to pant, my pulse thudding so loud it was a wonder he couldn't hear it, too. I could barely take in what he was saying to me. All I was aware of was the gold in his eyes and the sweet, sharp pleasure he was giving me.

He began to set up a rhythm, making the whole world shudder. Making my skin feel too tight and like I couldn't get enough air. Like I was hot. Too hot.

'What are you doing?' I gasped rather belatedly, raising my fists to push at him, only remembering at the last moment what a bad idea that was. 'I can't... This isn't...'

'It's okay, baby girl,' he said in that dark rumble, his thumbs moving in a gentle back and forth along my jawline. The touch was almost tender in comparison to the way he was moving against me, the pleasure as he rolled over my clit almost vicious, making me moan helplessly. 'Just making you feel good.'

And it *was* good. It was *so* good.

'W-why?' I stammered, trying not to let myself get swept away by what he was doing to me. Trying not to give in to the urges that my body was sending me, to spread my legs wider, lift my hips, rub against him, grab some of that insane, delicious friction that was driving me crazy.

'Why?' Tiger echoed, seeming almost surprised by the question. 'Why the fuck not?' He slowed the rhythm a little, making it hard, more relentless, sending a shower of white-hot sparks cascading through me. 'You're sweet and you're sexy. And your little pussy's as hot as fuck.' His gaze intensified, his thumb brushing along my lower lip. 'Also, I don't like it when little girls who don't know what they're doing try and use blow jobs to distract me. Makes me want to give them a taste of their own medicine.'

I couldn't process that. I couldn't even breathe. The pleasure he was giving me was crushing me completely. 'I can't tell you,' I whispered, barely aware of what I was saying. 'I c-can't… I don't want to…'

'Hey, hey. Stop that.' His voice was dark and rough, and felt like a caress over my bare skin. 'All I want you to think about is what I'm doing right now, hmm?'

Again he moved, another slow grind right against my achingly sensitive clit, and this time I couldn't stop my hips from lifting and my back from arching, pressing myself harder against him.

'Oh, yeah,' he whispered roughly. 'That's it. Rub that little pussy against my dick, baby. Get yourself off.'

I should have hated the dirty words. They should have made me uncomfortable the way they had when Crash had said them. But they didn't. Somehow, spoken in Tiger's rough voice, they only made everything ten thousand times hotter.

His movements got faster, and I was moving with him, entirely by instinct. The pleasure rolling through me was making me pant, my face so hot it was like my skin was on fire.

'You're all wet.' The relentless grind of Tiger's hips was an irresistible rhythm I had no hope of fighting. 'I can feel you soaking my jeans. You like this, don't you? Feels good, right?'

'Y-yes.' I couldn't stop the word from slipping out and as soon as I said it, the brilliant gold of his eyes flared even hotter.

'How good, baby? Tell me how I'm making you feel right now.'

It was an order and I found myself obeying helplessly. 'S-so good,' I gasped. 'I can't… It's too much…'

His beautiful mouth curved in a slow, deeply sexy smile, as if he liked what I'd said. 'Oh, it's not too much. In fact, I'd say it's not nearly enough.'

Then he slowed his movement right down, each shift of his hips lazy and relentless, the pressure on my clit becoming almost unbearable.

I groaned, starting to shake and unable to stop.

'You ever had a guy do this to you before?' Tiger's gaze was inescapable as it searched mine. 'You ever had anyone make you come?'

I didn't want to admit it, didn't want him to know exactly how inexperienced I was. But there was no way I could pretend I did this kind of thing all the time. There was no way I could pretend anything at all right now.

So all I did was stare back at him, letting him read the truth plastered all over my face.

His smile got hotter, as if this was the best thing he'd heard all day. 'You didn't come down here for Crash, did you? You came down here for me.'

There was something in the way he said the last sentence that I knew I should pay attention to. But the sensation between my thighs was getting too much to bear and all I could think was, yes, I *had* come down here for Tiger.

He's the one you run to when you want to be safe.

The thought flashed through my brain, bright as a comet, then disappeared, crushed by the weight of the pleasure that was building inside me.

It was too intense, too fast, and for some reason it scared me.

'Tiger,' I whispered yet again, abruptly frantic. 'I don't know… I can't…'

'Hold on to me.'

It was another order and I obeyed without thought, too, my hands clutching on the heavy muscle of his shoulders. I felt him tense as I touched him, the heat of his skin like a hot coal against my fingertips. I didn't jerk away this time, my nails digging in. He was solid, grounding me, an anchor holding me down as the storm building inside me began to shake me apart.

I said his name again, sweat breaking out all over my body as the dark pleasure he was giving me began to escape my grip.

No, this was *nothing* like my vibrator, where I could control the pleasure I gave myself. Where I could stop if it got to be too much or make it harder if it wasn't enough. This was out of my control completely.

The sensation was terrifying, like I was on the back of a motorcycle I had no idea how to ride, and it was going faster and faster. And I couldn't find the brake to slow it down or the keys to turn the engine off.

I had no choice but to hold on and pray to God I didn't fall off.

My nails dug harder into his shoulders as everything began to spiral out of control. I didn't know what was going to happen when this pressure released and I was afraid I was going to shatter or break apart. That I was going to be in pieces and no one was going to be able to put me back together again.

He must have known what was happening to me, must have read my fear. Because his long, muscular body settled over mine, his weight pressing me down against the mattress, surrounding me. Holding me. And he lowered his head, so his face was only inches away. 'Look at me, baby girl,' he murmured, those gold eyes of his taking up my whole world. 'And hold on tight. I've got you.'

So I did. I held on and I looked at him.

And when the pressure began to release and the orgasm exploded through me, and I opened my mouth to scream, his lips were on mine.

And all I could see was gold.

CHAPTER SIX

Tiger

I KISSED HER. Not because I wanted to keep her quiet—I loved making women scream—but I just couldn't keep myself from tasting her.

Just one kiss, that was all I was going to let myself have, which, considering the fact that her little pussy was creaming all over my jeans, was the epitome of fucking restraint.

She screamed into my mouth as she came, her body tensing and arching up into mine, her nails digging into my skin. I'd meant to simply give myself a taste, but she was so sweet, like a hit of pure sugar, and I was kissing her harder before I even realised what I was doing. Her mouth was so fucking hot, and she was shuddering under me, and I couldn't seem to stop myself, sliding my hands beneath her head and cradling it as I slid my tongue between her lips.

I'd never been particularly interested in kissing. Seemed a pointless waste of time when orgasms could be happening instead, yet I found I couldn't stop kissing Summer all the same.

There was a flavour to her, one I couldn't quite put my finger on, that was erotic as hell, and was making my cock ache even more. I didn't know what the fuck it was, whether it had something to do with the fact that she was coming against me, or whether it was because she'd never had anyone do this to her before.

Yeah, okay. It *was* because she'd never had anyone do this to her before and I was the first—I'd read that particular truth in her face. Which shouldn't have turned me on, because I didn't get possessive or territorial with chicks, but it just fucking did.

No one had made her come before. And now I was kissing her, I was certain no one had done that to her before either, because although she was trying to kiss me back, she was all hesitant, like she didn't know how.

There was no reason it should have got me hard, especially when virgins weren't exactly my style. Yet I was hard. So *fucking* hard.

I wanted to rip her panties off and bury my aching cock deep in the hot pussy that was currently soaking my jeans, and fuck us both into the middle of next week.

But I wasn't going to.

She was trembling underneath me and the small, hesitant movements of her mouth beneath mine were a reminder—as if I needed one—of her complete inexperience. Which made me pretty much the worst guy on the planet for her.

I'd done everything there was to do with a woman and it took a lot to get me off these days. Dirty as fuck tended to do it and there was no way I was going to do dirty as fuck with pretty little Summer Grant, the police chief's virgin daughter.

Apparently, you don't have any objections to messing around with her, though.

I wanted to ignore the thought, to push it completely out of my head and keep on kissing the hell out of her. But it was enough of a kick in the balls to actually stop what I was doing and lift my mouth from hers.

She was staring straight up at me, the dense blue of her eyes nearly hypnotising. As was the look in them. Straight out shocked and confused, yet with an edge of what looked like wonder. Like I was the most incredible thing she'd ever seen.

It made something shift and tighten in my chest. Something uncomfortable.

Shit, no one looked at me like that any more. My little brother once had, and my mom on the nights when her clients had got rough and I'd had to intervene. But no one else. I was just another cock for the club girls, and as for the brothers, well, I was an enforcer who made them toe the line, which some of them didn't appreciate.

Irritated, I shoved the feeling away, trying to ignore it like I was trying to ignore the pain in my dick. Because apart from any of that, she was a god-damn civilian and I didn't involve myself with civilians. Not to mention the fact that she was Campbell Grant's fucking daughter, which was a whole other load of complications that neither the club nor I needed right now.

Oh, yeah, plus I *still* didn't know why she was here.

She came here for you, right?

Christ, why had I said that? I didn't actually *want* her to have come down here for me, not when I hadn't thought about her in years. Clearly a case of my dick doing my thinking for me.

'Now we've got that out of the way,' I said, my voice a lot huskier than I would have liked, 'I think it's time for you to tell me why you didn't want Keep knowing you were here.'

Her lashes came down, veiling her gaze, and her hands pushed ineffectually at my shoulders. 'Could you…give me some room?'

'No.' I made the word hard. 'No one's going any-where until you give me the truth.' Even if my blue balls killed me.

Her cheeks were very flushed and her mouth was very red, and the heat of her pussy against my crotch was driving me fucking nuts. But I didn't move. 'Ten seconds, baby girl. Or else I call Keep right back in here.'

She let out a breath. 'I'm trying to get away from my dad,' she said at last. 'I just…wanted to go some-where he couldn't find me.'

I gave her an incredulous look. 'What? So you thought a biker clubhouse was the perfect place? Seriously?'

This time her lashes rose and I got a hit of that little spark I'd seen in her eyes earlier, a flash of temper. 'It's the only place I could think of. The only place he'd never expect me to go, not with Keep being his friend. Also…he wouldn't think I'd be brave enough so…' She trailed off, looking away again.

Okay, so she *was* here to hide out.

Tension wound through me, and this time it didn't have anything to do with the feel of her body under mine. 'Why are you hiding from him?' I couldn't quite keep the edge out of my voice. 'He knocking you around?'

She gave me another quick, sharp glance, and I could see the fear in it this time. 'No.'

'Summer,' I said warningly.

'It's true. He hasn't.' She gave another shove at my shoulders. 'Tiger, please.'

I relented this time, both to give my fucking cock a rest and to give her some space, rolling off her and onto my side, propping my head on my elbow. My back was to the door—just in case I had any more surprise visitors—while she lay between me and the wall. It wasn't exactly what she wanted, but it was all I was prepared to give her.

This time I wasn't fucking around. I wanted answers. Because if Campbell fucking Grant was as violent as his son, I wasn't going to be very happy.

I hated men who beat on people weaker or smaller than themselves. I'd watched it happen with my mom, when I had been too small to help her, and I'd hated it then, not being able to do a thing except watch her cry.

I'd hated it even when I was bigger, when I could give those assholes a taste of their own medicine, making them cry the way they had my mom.

And I hated it now, looking at Summer. The police chief was a big man, and even though Summer was tall, she was slender. If he wanted to hurt her, he could.

The thought made me furious.

'I know your brother,' I said flatly. 'I know all about his little anger management problem. Is your dad the same? Because if he is…' I didn't finish the sentence. I didn't need to. Too bad if the asshole was a cop. He'd get what was coming to him, I'd make sure of that myself.

'Dad doesn't hit me, no.' She sat up, pulling down the hoodie she had on, then reaching down under the quilt, presumably to pull down her miniskirt.

I stared at her, watching her face and the movements she made. Her hair was a mess of white blonde all over her shoulders, and it looked pretty against the pink of her skin. She was still flushed from the orgasm I'd given her, which was incredibly fucking satisfying, even though it shouldn't have been. I could still feel her heat against my zipper and I wanted to put my hand down to feel the denim, to see if it was as wet as I suspected it was.

But finding out what she was doing here was more important than that so I stayed where I was, looking at her.

'So why are you hiding then?' I asked. 'If he's not going to hit you, then what's he going to do?'

She gave another sigh, then she bent her knees and leaned forward, wrapping her arms around her legs. 'It's a long story.'

'Baby, I've got nothing but time.'

The look in her eyes was serious. 'No, you don't. You're supposed to be out looking for me, remember? Wasn't that what Keep told you?'

'That can wait.' At least it could until she'd told me why she was hiding. Then, depending on her reasons, I'd decide what to do about it.

'Okay,' she said, clearly reluctant. 'I graduated from college a couple of weeks ago, and just before I left, I got a really cool job offer from a tech company in Silicon Valley.'

'Oh, yeah?' After my bodyguard stint with her had ended, I'd lost track of what had happened to her, but I'd always known vaguely that she was smart, so hearing she'd gone to college wasn't a big surprise. 'Congrats.'

She flushed, as if embarrassed, which was weird. Fuck, if I'd been smart enough to go to college, I'd have been so goddamn full of myself, you wouldn't have been able to fit me and my ego in the same fucking room.

'Thanks,' she said. 'I mean, it's exciting, and I really want to go…'

'I can hear the but.'

'Yeah.' Her shoulders hunched. 'I thought Dad would be pleased about the job thing. Actually, no, I knew he *wouldn't* be pleased about the job thing, but I thought I could talk him round. Except when I told him, he wasn't happy.'

I frowned at her, not quite sure what the problem was. 'So your dad wasn't happy about you leaving. So what?'

She shook her head, the blue spark in her eyes back again. 'You don't understand. He doesn't want me to go. He wants me to stay here with him.'

Yeah, and I still didn't see the problem. 'And? Tell him to fuck off. He can't stop you.'

She glanced away, looking down at the quilt covering her knees, and shook her head slowly. 'It's not that simple.'

'Sure it is. Three words. *Fuck. Off. Dad.* Then you go. End of story.'

But she kept on shaking her head. 'It's not. I can't…say that to him. I don't…' She stopped and looked at me again. 'I can't explain it to you. It's not something you'd ever understand.'

I didn't like being dismissed. Didn't like it one fucking bit. And I especially didn't like the part about how I 'wouldn't understand.' I shouldn't have let it get to me, but for some reason, coming from her, it did.

'Ah,' I said. 'Right. So the dumb-fuck biker won't know what you're talking about, is that it?'

Her eyes widened in surprise. 'Uh, no. That's not what I meant at all.'

'Then what did you mean?'

Her colour deepened. 'I only meant that you're…' She gestured at me, as if that would explain everything. 'Well, you're tall and…strong. And you're dangerous. And you don't take crap from anyone. And I'm…not any of those things.'

Nope, still didn't know what the fuck she was talking about. 'Baby, you're gonna have to get clear about what the hell is going on real quick. Because none of this is making any sense.'

Frustration crossed her face. 'Dad manipulates things, okay? He manipulates me. And I don't want to be around him right now, because I'm afraid he'll make me change my mind and I'll end up not going to Silicon Valley after all.'

That sounded weird. But clearly it was an issue for her. She wouldn't have come down to the clubhouse in the middle of a party if it hadn't been.

'Listen,' I said, trying for gentle. 'No one can make you do anything you don't want to do. You know that, right?'

That chin of hers jutted. 'Easy for you to say. Like I told you, you're strong.'

Christ, did she really think she wasn't strong?

What the fuck was that sparky attitude she kept giving me if it wasn't strength? 'And what? You're not? Bullshit to that. Anyway, being strong starts with knowing what you want and fucking taking it, not running away and cowering in a corner pretending no one can see you.'

Something flashed in her gaze again. 'I'm not running away. I just don't want to be anywhere near him for a couple of days. And anyway, I *am* taking what I want. I'm flying to California and taking that damn job.'

'Sure you are. But you're so worried your father will make you change your mind that you had to run to a biker clubhouse to hide.' Perhaps I shouldn't have said it but, shit, it was the truth.

But she didn't like that, anger lighting in her eyes. 'All that's beside the point. Are you going to hide me or not? Because if you don't, I'll find someone else who will.'

'Right, so you're going to go wandering out into the orgy currently happening in the hallway, looking for a brother to hide you?' I stared at her, not bothering to mask my scorn because—seriously?—she actually thought she could do that with no consequences whatsoever? 'Hate to say it, but if they don't take you to Keep straight away, they'll make you join in. And they're all drunk and they're all assholes. All of 'em. They'll eat you alive and I do mean that literally.'

Fear flickered across her face—she was so easy to read it wasn't funny—but that chin of hers was still stubborn. 'You'll have to hide me then.'

I nearly laughed. 'You don't get to tell me what to do, baby girl.'

'Please, Tiger.' Those big blue eyes held mine, determination and temper glowing in her gaze. 'I'll… I'll give you a blow job if you do.'

Fuck, as if I needed a reminder that my dick was still hard. 'Haven't we had this conversation already? I think I remember telling you no.'

'Please. It's only for a few days.'

'You're seriously asking me to risk my rep and my club's, not to mention my relationship with my president, just so you can hide out from your dad?' Christ, now that I'd said it aloud, the whole thing sounded insane. What the fuck was she even still doing here? I should have given her up to Keep the moment he'd come into my room and asked me to find her.

Summer swallowed and I found myself watching the movement of her lovely throat. 'What can I give you then?'

I should have said that there was nothing she could give me. Because hadn't I already decided that getting any more involved in this was a mistake? She spelled nothing but trouble for me and the club, and I'd be a fucking idiot not to get rid of her. Like, right now.

But apparently I *was* a fucking idiot, because I didn't say 'nothing.' Instead, I said, 'I don't know, baby girl. What you got?'

She squared her shoulders and looked me in the eye without a flicker. 'Me,' she said. 'I got me. You hide me, Tiger, and I'll let you do whatever you want to me.'

CHAPTER SEVEN

Summer

TIGER DIDN'T SAY anything immediately. He simply lay there on his side, his long, lean body stretched out down the entire length of the bed, his head propped on his hand, his amber gaze pinning me where I sat.

I could hear my heartbeat thumping loudly in my head and again I could feel that irritating cold current of fear. But I was determined. Sure, he might say all those things about taking what you want and not hiding, but it was fine for him. He was a man. He was strong, he took what he wanted, and most of all, he didn't care what anyone thought of him.

But that was my problem. I *did* care. I cared way too much. Yes, my dad was difficult and living with him was like living in a house made of glass. You had to be really careful because if you walked too heavily, the floor might crack and shatter under your feet, cutting you to pieces.

I'd learned to walk softly over the years, to not

make a fuss. To be invisible when his mood was bad, which since Mom had left was pretty much all the time. But he was all I had. There was my older brother, Justin, but Justin had a violent temper like Dad and often flew into terrible rages. He used to pick on me a lot when I was younger, but then I got the hang of being invisible and so he left me alone.

After a while, they both did. But only because I didn't rock the boat or cause a fuss. Telling Dad I would be leaving for Silicon Valley whether he liked it or not was definitely causing a fuss, and I was afraid of what he might do. Of what he might say. He'd be angry and I hated his anger. I always had. It made me feel small and weak and powerless.

But what was the use explaining that to Tiger? Of hoping he'd understand? He wasn't a guy who let anyone's anger bother him. He just didn't give a shit. And since I couldn't explain it to him in a way he'd get and hope he'd help out of the goodness of his heart, I was left with only offering myself in return.

I knew it wasn't much, but it was all I had.

He said nothing for a long time, simply watching me, and I had to resist the urge to shift around restlessly, because there was something in his eyes that made me hot. That made me aware of the throb between my legs and the tingle of my mouth where he'd kissed me.

But I couldn't think about what he'd just done to me or about that kiss. God, I could barely deal with the fact I was sitting on his bed and he was still half-naked and only inches away, let alone anything more.

Sure, you can't deal. That's why you told him he could do anything he wants to you.

Crap. I was getting myself in deeper and deeper, wasn't I?

The quilt had slipped down to his waist, leaving a whole lot of hard, sculpted muscle and tanned skin bare, along with the ink of his tattoos. And I had to fight not to drop my gaze to stare at his body.

Except looking at his face wasn't any better. His eyes glinted and his beautiful mouth curved in a way that made sweat break out all over my body. 'You'll let me do *whatever* I want?' he asked, his voice low and lazy.

'Yes.' It was difficult to say the word, but I forced it out. If that's what I had to do to get him to hide me, then I would.

The flame in his eyes burned, his smile deepening. As if he knew things I didn't. 'Yeah, I don't think you actually want that.'

'Why not?' I felt suddenly irritated at the arrogant way he seemed to think he knew things about me when he didn't. 'You have no idea what I want.'

He laughed, the sound so soft and sexy it made the breath catch in my throat. 'Baby girl, I'm an extremely dirty guy. Telling me I can do whatever I want to you is *not* something you can handle, believe me.'

I glared at him, my irritation deepening for reasons I couldn't quite explain. He was right, of course.

I probably wouldn't be able to handle him. But, still, his assumption annoyed me. 'How do you know? Just because I haven't had sex before doesn't mean I can't handle it.'

'Sure you can't. That's why you pushed Crash away.'

'Yes, but that's different. I didn't want Crash.'

His eyes glinted and I realised with a start what I'd implied.

Oh, shit.

I could feel that damn blush flooding through me and I opened my mouth to tell him that didn't mean I actually wanted him, but he got in there first.

'Oh, no, don't spoil it,' he said lazily. 'And don't try to deny it either. Not that I'd believe you anyway. Not given how wet the front of my jeans still are.'

I kept my mouth closed, feeling like I was going to burst into flames with embarrassment right where I was sitting.

'It's not a big surprise anyway,' Tiger went on in that same lazy tone. 'I know you want me. You don't have to pretend otherwise. Didn't I tell you that's why you came down here in the first place?'

I wished I could have shrugged and dismissed it, or simply done what I normally do, which was not to say a word either way. Because it felt wrong that he knew what I wanted better than I did myself. Yet I couldn't seem to keep quiet. 'You're really arrogant, you know that?'

'Yes,' he said, like it was no big deal. 'I'm an asshole, too. Anything else you want to add?'

Frustrated, I looked away from him. Perhaps if I was quick, I could slide off the bed and make a break for the door. Then again, that would mean braving the guys in the hallway, and from what Tiger had said about them, perhaps I actually didn't want to do that.

Better the asshole you knew, right?

'That doesn't answer my question,' I said, changing the subject, determined to get an answer out of him one way or the other. 'Are you going to hide me or not?'

'What? In return for letting me do whatever I want to you?'

'Yes.' I made the word as definite as I could.

He was silent, his gaze roaming over me in a way that made me acutely conscious of the remains of the pleasure he'd given me, glowing inside me like hot coals, banked yet still burning. 'I'm risking a lot for you,' he murmured. 'A lot of complications. You're the chief's daughter and a virgin. A lot of shit will hit the fan if anyone found out.'

'No one will find out.' I tried to steady my voice. 'I promise I won't tell a soul.'

'Uh-huh.' His amber eyes came to mine and held them, heat flickering in them. 'Okay, then, maybe you got a deal.'

My heart leapt, relief filling me. 'Oh, that's great—'

'On one condition.'

The relief ebbed, trepidation taking its place. 'What condition?'

'Tell me you want me. And make me believe it.'

I blinked at him, not expecting it. 'Excuse me?'

'I'm thinking you need a couple of lessons in how to be strong. In how to take what you want.' The flames in his eyes leapt higher. 'Consider this your first lesson.'

Being strong starts with knowing what you want and fucking taking it...

I swallowed yet again. 'W-why do you want that?'

'Because I'm not into virgins. And unlike Crash, I'm not into having sex with girls who don't want it either.'

'Well…uh…we don't have to have sex,' I pointed out, feeling strangely disappointed in myself for doing so.

'Gotta get something in return for potentially sac-rificing my club for you, baby.' Another gleam in that stare of his. 'Though I'm not sure why we're arguing about this, since you wouldn't have offered yourself if you hadn't actually wanted me to take you.'

He's right and you know it. He knows you want him, too, so what's the point in hiding it?

That was true. I just hated the vulnerability of having him know, that was the problem. The worry that he might potentially use it against me the way Dad often did. Then again, what else could I do? If I wanted him to hide me, this was the only way. Which meant I had to make it convincing.

Slowly, I shuffled over to him on my knees, and, God, even lying on his side he was intimidating. He looked at me intently, just like the big cat he shared his name with, and because he wasn't wearing a T-shirt there was nothing to hide the naked physical power of him. It was there in the hard-cut lines of his chest and stomach, and the broad width of his shoulders.

Okay, so how to convince him I wanted him? I lifted my hand to his groin.

'No,' he said before I'd even touched him, the hard, flat note in his voice freezing me in place. 'You think I'm just another cock? That a simple blow job is all it takes to convince me? Think again, baby girl.'

I met his glittering eyes, my heart thumping in my chest. He was angry—I could see that—and I wasn't sure why. Did it really matter to him whether I wanted this or not?

Of course it matters to him. He wouldn't have bothered giving you that condition otherwise.

I blinked, the realisation shocking me. I hadn't thought about him, not once. In fact, the only thing I'd thought about since I'd got here was myself. My fear and my need to hide. My desperation to avoid my dad.

But I'd made things difficult for him, hadn't I? I'd caused trouble. And asking him to hide me was going to cause him even more trouble.

Then maybe you shouldn't.

I should. I should woman up and go face my dad. And maybe if I'd been a stronger person, I would have. But I wasn't a stronger person. I was the woman who crept around not wanting to make a noise, not wanting to draw attention. Who stuck to the corners of the room rather than the centre.

The easy to manipulate target.

I couldn't stand up to my dad, not yet. But… Tiger had mentioned lessons in strength, and maybe that was worth taking. Maybe it was even worth making myself a little vulnerable for.

I stared at him, looking straight into his golden eyes, knowing he was right. That I hadn't offered myself to him simply so I could hide from Dad. Because if it had been, then I wouldn't have shoved Crash away. I would have let him do whatever he wanted to me.

But I hadn't. I'd let Tiger take me away instead and I had to admit that there was a very good reason for that. He was different. He'd always been different. He wasn't like any other man I'd met either before or since, and he'd been in my head so damn long I couldn't get him out.

I *did* want him. I'd wanted him the moment I'd met him.

I took a slow, silent breath. 'How do you want me to prove it to you then?'

'You're the genius.' Gold glinted in his gaze, a direct challenge. 'You figure it out.'

That was all very well if I'd been a genius with any experience, but I wasn't. I had no experience whatsoever except the orgasm and the kiss Tiger had given me just before.

My heart began to beat faster.

Oh, he was so close. So very, very close. All I had to do to touch him would be to reach out and I could brush fingers across the hard plane of his chest...

My palms felt sweaty, my breathing ragged, nervousness twisting inside me. And he wasn't giving me any help, simply watching me with that unblinking stare.

I was afraid and I wasn't quite sure why. Yeah, asking for what I wanted was hard for me, especially when it was often used against me. But I knew Tiger wasn't the type of guy who'd do that. He wasn't manipulative and never had been. He was straight-up. Honest. Blunt, yes, and not exactly sensitive. But he wouldn't hurt me. I'd always known that. Not the way Dad would sometimes hurt me.

So maybe feel the fear and do it anyway?

I took yet another breath, then I lifted my hands, not to make a grab for his groin this time but to cup his face between my shaking palms, his jawline hard and hot and a bit prickly against my skin.

The look in his eyes flared in surprise as I touched him, but he didn't pull away or say no this time. Instead he simply looked back, his smile gone, the expression in his gaze fierce and challenging. Daring me to make the next move.

So I did.

I bent my head and did what I'd been wanting to do since I was seventeen.

I kissed him.

His mouth was warm under mine and he didn't

move, giving me no response whatsoever. I let my lips linger on his, hoping he'd take charge and show me what to do, since I had absolutely had no idea, but he didn't. He remained utterly still.

Dammit.

My pulse began to ratchet up, the heat of his skin burning against my palms. I could feel the heat of his bare chest, too, could sense the long length of his body so still and so very close to me.

He smelled *so* good.

I pressed my mouth harder against his, wanting him to do something, at least give me a hint of what to do next, but he didn't. Frustrated, I touched my tongue to his lower lip, licking at him, and finally his mouth opened and he let me in.

The taste of him hit me hard, like the kick of the bourbon I'd tried once in college. The alcohol had burned going down, which had been horrible, but then there had been a nice warm feeling in my gut afterwards, leaving my head swimming. This kiss was like both of those combined and none of it was horrible. Absolutely none of it.

I wanted more. It was like I'd discovered a brand-new addictive flavour that I couldn't get enough of. That I'd been starving for without realising it.

I held him more firmly and slid my tongue deeper into his mouth, exploring him, my whole world narrowing to the incredible heat of him and that raw, alcoholic taste.

My hands slid into his short dark copper-tinted

hair, all thick and silky against my fingers, the way I'd always guessed it would be. And... *God*, he tasted good. I moaned helplessly, deep in my throat, wanting more yet not knowing what more I wanted. All that mattered was that I got more of *him*.

Except he still wasn't moving and it was driving me crazy.

Then suddenly I felt his fingers wrap around my wrists and he was pulling my hands from his hair and drawing back from me, leaving me panting and shaking, my lips feeling hot and tingly and my mouth full of his intoxicating flavour.

The amber colour of his eyes had turned into molten gold, gleaming and hot, and I could feel myself begin to catch fire right where I knelt.

'W-well?' I asked shakily, my voice thick. 'Was I convincing enough?'

That beautiful mouth I'd just tasted curved. 'No.'

'Tiger—'

'You can finish convincing me back at my place. Where we've got a bit more privacy.' Abruptly, he let go my wrists and rolled out of bed, reaching for his T-shirt and leather vest, then pausing to put on his boots.

I sat there watching him, my heart pumping furiously, full of the weirdest combination of emotions. Excited. Thrilled. Afraid. Desperate. Angry. Wanting.

I didn't like it. I'd never been comfortable with extremes of emotion and I didn't know what to do with all those extremes now. What I wanted was to crawl under the quilt and pretend I was back at home, that I hadn't come down to the Knights of Ruin's clubhouse purely on a stupid, cowardly whim.

But it was too late. I was getting myself deeper and deeper into trouble with every passing minute.

Tiger finished with his boots and stood up, glancing down at me, reading me perfectly. 'Second thoughts?'

I couldn't deny it. 'Y-yes.'

He held out his hand to me. 'Come on. I promise it'll be okay.' Then he smiled and just like that, everything fell away.

No one had ever smiled at me like that before, with real warmth, like a ray of sunlight on a midwinter day. It probably meant nothing. Maybe it was simply his normal, average 'Hi, how are ya?' smile. But it felt like a kick to the chest, jolting me all the way through.

Sure, it might simply have been because he was going to get laid and that would make any guy smile—or so I'd heard.

But suddenly I didn't care. He'd given that smile to *me*. That gorgeous, incredible smile was *mine*. And I knew I'd do anything to get him to give it to me again.

So I took his hand and let his warm fingers wrap around mine.

And then I let him take me away.

CHAPTER EIGHT

Tiger

I MADE SURE Summer's hoodie was pulled over her head as I stepped out into the corridor once again. The orgy was still going on, this time with a different combination of people, but once again I ignored what was going on, pulling Summer with me as I strode past.

Again, a couple of the brothers yelled at me to join in, but I ignored them, too. All I wanted was to get Summer out of there as quickly and with as little fuss as possible.

I couldn't stop thinking about that fucking kiss she'd laid on me, though.

I knew she wanted me, it was fucking obvious, but what I'd wanted was for her to admit it. I wasn't going to take her back to my place and do whatever the fuck I wanted with her if she wasn't into it. Then again, I'd been the one who'd wanted something in return for hiding her from her dad.

I shouldn't have insisted. If all I'd wanted was pussy, then I could have let her go and got all the pussy I wanted right here, right now, and with way fewer complications.

But the fucking annoying thing was that I didn't just want any pussy.

I wanted *her* pussy in particular.

So when she'd offered herself to me... Christ, I hadn't been able to get it out of my head. I shouldn't have encouraged her. I should have told her no. Kept on spouting that bullshit about how I wasn't the right guy for a little virgin like her.

Except I hadn't. I'd let her offer herself, let her push it. And now here we were, going down the corridor to the entrance to the club, because apparently my dick was doing my thinking for me.

Of course I didn't stop walking, though, my head full of that goddamn kiss and my heart racing like I'd spent all day in the fucking gym.

When I'd told her I wanted her to convince me, all I'd wanted was some sign that she was into it. But when she'd gone for my cock like every other club girl, for some reason I'd just felt...angry.

I had no idea why it mattered so much that her attention should be about me, but it had. Then she'd looked at me with those big blue eyes, like I was an ice cream she was desperate to taste. And she'd taken my face between her hands, and bent her head, putting that soft, pretty little mouth on mine.

Her kiss had been so shy and unpractised, and it

shouldn't have lit me up inside like a fucking match to a skyrocket. I didn't like that kind of innocent shit.

But there was something about the way Summer looked at me, about the way she kissed me, that stole the air from my lungs.

I wanted to take her home. I wanted to get her naked. I wanted to do every dirty thing to her that I could think of and then I wanted to do it again.

Hiding her, having her, was going to complicate the fuck out of things and for someone who didn't like complicated, that was a problem. But when I wanted something, I didn't like to deny myself.

Shit, apart from anything else, I wanted to get to the bottom of whatever was going on with her fucking father, because hearing her talk about him gave me a bad feeling. And if there was one thing I didn't like it was a bad feeling.

I pulled Summer past the prospect guarding the clubhouse entrance, then went down the steps outside to where all the rides were parked up.

My buddy Smoke was in the process of helping Cat, his old lady, get off his bike as I approached mine, and he lifted his chin in acknowledgement.

Smoke glanced at Summer, then down at our joined hands. 'Who's this?' he asked, raising a brow. 'Anyone special?'

Even though Smoke was my best friend, I knew what he'd think about me hiding Summer. Or screwing Summer. Or doing anything at all with Summer.

So I gave him my usual shit-eating grin. 'Nope. Just some fun.'

Cat came up beside Smoke and gave me a cool look.

Cat and I had had our differences. She'd never liked the club or me, and I'd always thought she'd treated Smoke like shit, not to mention being judgey as hell. But since she and Smoke had got together, she'd mellowed. Though not enough to approve of what I was doing now with Summer, that was for sure.

And that was another thing I should have remembered. Cat had shacked up with Summer's brother for a time, even had a kid with him, so if there was anyone who'd recognise Summer, it was her.

Fuck. I needed to get out of here and fast.

'Going to join the orgy?' I asked her conversationally, when it didn't seem like they were going to leave without a chat. 'Looks like everyone's having a great time.'

Cat sighed. 'An orgy. My favourite.' She looked at Smoke. 'Can we go home now, please?'

Smoke shot me a 'fuck you, asshole' glance before starting the placating process. Poor bastard.

My work done, I quickly grabbed Summer and lifted her onto my bike. There was a helmet in the saddlebags that I took out and put on her head, straight over the top of her hoodie. Then, wasting no time, I got on myself, fired up the engine, then lit on out of there.

Summer didn't make a sound, but her hands abruptly came down on my hips as the bike took off, and her body leaned into mine. I could feel the warmth of her settled against my back as if she'd done this a thousand times before, which was weird. I'd given her a couple of rides while I'd been guarding her and I seemed to remember her almost falling off because she hadn't wanted to hold on to me. Apparently she had no problems with it now and, fuck, neither did I.

She was hot and her bare thighs spread on either side of mine felt insanely good. And the feel of her fit in perfectly with the usual thrill I got out of riding. With the freedom of it.

I didn't like the thought, though, didn't like the way it tightened in my chest, so I ignored it, opening the throttle and going faster instead.

My place wasn't anything fancy, just an old warehouse building that had been converted. I had the bottom floor, which suited me fine, because it gave me a ton of room for a workshop where I could work on my bikes.

I liked dicking around with engines and parts. I liked taking them apart and putting them back together again. I liked making shit go. An engine was simply a giant puzzle and I'd always liked puzzles, even back when I was a kid.

Couldn't read, but give me a Rubik's cube and I could solve that motherfucker in ten seconds flat.

I rode straight up to the automatic roller door at

the back of the building and pressed the button to open it—I'd rigged up an automatic door opener since I hated getting off my bike to open fucking doors—then I rode straight inside.

The whole place was just a wide-open space, with a few walls to separate off the bathroom and a set of iron stairs that led to a mezzanine where I had my bed. Down one end of the giant room was a kitchen—simple, like me—and down the other was the workshop, with a big workbench that ran along the wall and lots of shelves above it. I had a few bikes parked up—the brothers often got me to work on theirs—and there was one up on a stand.

In the middle of the room was a couch and a couple of chairs as a living area, plus a huge-ass TV—I liked movies and plenty of the brothers had enjoyed the odd football game around here, too.

Parking the bike down the workshop end, I kicked down the stand and got off, turning to help Summer. She was fiddling with her helmet, trying to get it undone, but I knocked her hands away and pulled it off for her. She blinked up at me, her hood falling back and revealing her face, all pink and pretty, and her pale hair spread over her shoulders.

My groin ached, my fucking dick reminding me that it was impatient and now she was here, in my territory, I could do whatever the hell I wanted with her.

Starting fucking now.

'Lift your arms,' I ordered and her arms came up just like that, as if she'd been born to obey my orders.

My cock got even harder.

I saw belated realisation cross her face about what she was doing, but by that stage it was too late. I already had my hands on her hoodie and I was pulling it up and over her head, then dropping it to the floor. Finally getting to see what she was wearing under all that cotton.

And, fuck me, I nearly had a heart attack.

All she had on was the tiniest, tightest, stretchiest blue crop top in the entire history of the world. It left a whole lot of the pale skin of her stomach on show and pulled tight across a pair of small, perfectly rounded little tits. It also left her shoulders bare and I found myself fascinated by the delicate shape of her collarbones and by the hollow of her throat where her pulse was beating hard and fast.

She wasn't wearing a bra, her hard nipples obvious through the fabric of her top, a fact she clearly had no idea about since she made no effort to cover them. Instead, she glanced away from me, looking curiously around at the apartment like a kid in a toy shop.

I didn't usually bring chicks back here and the few times I had, it wasn't my place they were interested in, not when they could get their hands on my cock. But not Summer apparently, and it put me off guard. Made me feel…uncomfortable, as if she could see things about me just from my place that I wasn't ready to show anyone.

'Wow,' she murmured, staring at my workbench, her eyes widening. 'You've got a workshop in your apartment. How cool.'

Oh, no, I didn't want her getting interested. Not now.

I reached out and put a finger under her chin, urging her gaze back to mine. 'Nice distraction, but I'm up here.'

Pools of wide, dark blue hit me hard, like a sucker punch, and for a second all I could do was stare back.

I was standing very close to her, those pretty tits almost brushing my chest, and that innocent, flowery scent was doing things to me it shouldn't. Like getting me even harder than I was already.

I'd planned to get her comfortable here first before we moved onto anything else, but after making her come back in the clubhouse, I honestly wasn't sure I could wait. Which was a massive fucking first.

Reaching into my pocket, I grabbed my phone and hit Keep's number. 'Prez, it's me,' I said when he answered. 'I'm out looking for her. Let you know if I see anything.' I didn't wait for him to speak, I simply hit Disconnect before he could say a word, then pocketed the phone again.

Summer swallowed and looked away from me before glancing back. Yeah, she was nervous. I could see her trembling. 'S-so,' she said uncertainly. 'What do we do—'

'Quiet.' I lifted a hand and gently rubbed my thumb along her full lower lip in a slow back and forth.

She took a sharp breath, stiffening as I touched

her. I could see she wanted to pull away, but she was trapped by the bike behind her and me in front of her.

Poor baby girl. Nowhere to run to this time.

I didn't give her any space and I didn't stop touching her lip, the soft give of it under my thumb such a damn turn-on. I'd never bothered to take my time with a woman before, mainly because the club girls all tended to be as impatient as I was when it came to fucking. But it turned out that just running my thumb across Summer's silky skin made me as breathless as being balls-deep in club pussy, so Christ knew what was going to happen to me when I actually did get inside her.

'You're shaking,' I said after a moment. 'That me? You afraid?' I didn't like that idea. She shouldn't be afraid, and definitely not of me.

'N-no.' The stutter in her husky voice revealed the lie that it was.

'Bullshit.' I pressed down on her lip slightly. 'Gimme the truth, baby.'

She took another sharp breath, her blue eyes coming to mine. 'Okay. Yes. A little. But not…not the way you think.'

'Uh-huh. So what then?'

'I just…' Her lashes fluttered. 'It's only that I've wanted you since I was seventeen.'

This time it was my turn to stare at her, my thumb pausing on her mouth, feeling like I'd taken not only that punch to the gut but a kick to the head, as well.

Seventeen? She'd wanted me since she'd been *seventeen*?

Holy fucking shit.

'I know, it's stupid,' she went on, the words coming out of her in a rush. 'But I thought you were… amazing. You weren't like any other guy I'd ever met, dangerous and mean and hot. And I… I'm afraid, Tiger. I'm afraid I won't be able to handle you. But I want to. You've been in my head for so long and I can't… I just…' She trailed off, blushing, clearly embarrassed by what she'd said, looking away from me yet again.

For a second I wasn't sure how I felt about that and then I realised that of course I knew how I felt about it.

I fucking loved it.

I'd been in her head all that time. Five goddamn years and all she'd been thinking about was me.

'Hey,' I growled softly, urging her gaze back to mine. 'Do you trust me?' A dumb fucking question when I'd never done anything to earn her trust, but I had to ask her all the same.

She took a second, but only one before she nodded. And that got to me, too, couldn't deny it. Been a long time since a civilian had trusted me, not since Mom and Tommy. The brothers, sure, that was a given, but everyone else? Nope. Not that I'd given a fuck about a civilian's trust, not when they didn't exactly figure in my life, but this one right here? Yeah, hers mattered.

'Don't worry about whether you can handle me or not,' I went on, starting up that caress on her bottom lip again. 'I know you can. But we're gonna take this nice and slow to start with. Everything I do is supposed to feel good, so if it doesn't, you let me know, okay?'

She gave a little shiver. 'Okay.'

'Good.' I let my finger trail down from her lip, over that stubborn chin and down over the soft skin of her neck and throat to her collarbones, tracing the shapes of them lightly.

She inhaled, goosebumps rising all over her skin wherever I touched her, the pale, creamy colour of it beginning to flush pink.

'Fuck, you're sensitive.' I slid my finger just underneath the neckline of that stretchy blue crop top, stroking the warm silky skin of her chest in another slow back and forth. 'I love it.'

Her cheeks began to glow, the blue of her eyes darkening as I stroked her, and I couldn't take my gaze off her face as the effects of my touch began to take hold. Christ, it was addictive watching her get aroused. Knowing that it was me doing this to her, that no one else had ever made her feel this way.

'So, what's with the virgin thing?' I didn't stop stroking her, back and forth beneath the fabric of her top, grazing the tops of her pretty tits. 'Never met a guy you really liked or what?'

'Well…yeah.' Her voice had got even huskier and

breathless sounding. 'Plus, I'm just not very good with people.'

'Are you sure? Maybe it's that people aren't very good with you.'

Her lashes fell, hiding all that blue from me. 'I don't mind. I don't much like people anyway.'

'But you like me.' I hooked my finger into the neckline of her top and tugged gently, testing to see how much it would stretch. 'I think you like me a lot.'

She took a ragged breath, glancing up at me, then away again, shifting restlessly on her feet. 'M-maybe.'

Didn't take a genius to figure out why she was moving around like that. Or why her nipples were pressing in stiff little points against the material of her top.

It was definitely time to take this up a notch.

CHAPTER NINE

Summer

TIGER WAS STANDING so close I could barely breathe. He was so tall and his shoulders were so wide; he was like a wall right in front of me. A wall made of hard muscle and covered with tanned skin and ink, with a layer of cotton and leather thrown over it.

And he was touching me. He had the tip of his finger inside the neckline of my top and was slowly stroking me back and forth. It felt like he was painting me with flame, leaving scorch marks all over my skin.

Not that I could look down to check, not with the way he was watching me. So carefully and intently, as if he was fascinated by what he saw in my face.

I'd never had someone look at me like that before. It made my heartbeat do that thumping thing again, and made my skin too hot and too tight. I felt like I wanted to rip it right off or climb right out of it.

I shouldn't have told him all that stuff about how long I'd wanted him, not straight out like that, but I hadn't been able to stop myself. He'd asked me if I was afraid and I didn't want him to think that I was, but the truth had slipped out all the same. Along with my pathetic confession.

I'd had no idea how he would take it, but I really hadn't expected the look of satisfaction that had gleamed in his eyes. As if he'd liked the idea of me lusting after him, and liked it a lot.

I hadn't expected him to ask me whether I trusted him either, and I was even more surprised when I found myself nodding almost instantly. But then maybe it wasn't such a surprise. Tiger had never hurt me, never manipulated me. Sure, he'd teased me but it had never been malicious or cruel. And it had only made me feel irritated, not hurt.

So, yeah, I trusted him, and the fact that he'd even asked me had eased my nervousness somewhat, but now, with that finger tracing patterns on me, it was all flooding back again full force.

I hadn't been expecting for him to get straight to the sex part of the evening. I'd thought we might talk for a bit or watch TV or have a drink or something first. And I wouldn't have minded looking around his apartment, because the minute we'd ridden inside, I'd known it wasn't like any other apartment I'd ever seen before and I was curious.

But then he'd caged me against his bike and had taken my hoodie off and right then and there, I knew he wasn't going to wait.

Perhaps I should have been flattered with his impatience. Then again, it wasn't really me he wanted, was it? It was what I'd promised him. The sex.

Something that felt an awful lot like disappointment shifted inside me, but I didn't give it any time to sit there. Of course this wasn't about me; it never had been. So I should just enjoy what was happening and the fact that after so many years, I was finally going to get what I wanted. Him.

If I didn't completely freak the hell out first.

He tugged my top again, his amber gaze gleaming as it dropped to where the fabric stretched over my breasts. 'Hmm. I think I see something that wants to be touched.'

I glanced down, too, wanting to see what he was talking about, and then, with a jolt, understood. My nipples were hard and were pressing very obviously against the thin material.

Full of embarrassment, I raised my hands to cover myself, but he grabbed my wrists and held them down at my sides. 'No, don't do that. Just keep them there, okay?'

I gave a shaky nod, because I'd told him I trusted him and I did.

Releasing my wrists, he hooked the fingers of both hands into the stretchy fabric of my top and began to ease it down my upper arms. Though it had sleeves, the neckline was supposed to leave my shoulders bare, but now Tiger was pulling it down further so it stretched tight across my chest, binding my arms to my sides. And he didn't stop, pulling the fabric down so that it slid over my acutely sensitive nipples and off, baring my breasts completely.

I hadn't put a bra on underneath it, because the girls that usually went to the clubhouse didn't wear them either, but I'd forgotten that fact since I'd had the hoodie on over the top. But I was acutely aware of it now, a sharp, ragged breath escaping me as cool air washed over my heated skin.

The instinct to cover myself was almost overwhelming, but the way he'd pulled my top down made it impossible for me to lift my arms.

'Well, look at you,' Tiger breathed, his eyes deep gold as he stared down at my naked breasts. 'Absolutely fucking perfect tits.' He lifted his hands, cupping me, his big warm palms on my aching flesh making me shudder.

His gaze came to mine again, watching me as his thumbs moved to slowly circle my throbbing nipples. He knew what he was doing to me, no question, not that there was any way for me to hide it. Not when his touch drew a gasp from my throat and sent a hot jolt of electricity straight between my thighs. He circled his thumbs again and again, then brushed them right over the hard tips of my breasts, studying me the whole time like the predator he was.

I shuddered, my brain slowly shutting down as a hot, molten feeling grew between my thighs. 'Tiger,' I said shakily, feeling suddenly unsure about what was happening.

No one had touched me like this before and his

fingers on my skin were like flames. It made me afraid that I'd been right all along. That I wasn't going to be able to handle him. I was so inexperienced and this was so new and I...and I...

'Hey.' His voice somehow caught my flailing attention, calling it back. 'Look at me.'

An arm slid around my waist, easing me close so my body was pressed right up against the hard, hot length of his. I hadn't realised until that moment how weak my knees had got until I found myself leaning against him, as if I needed him to hold me up.

My bare breasts grazed his chest, the cotton of his T-shirt rubbing against my nipples, drawing yet another shudder from me and making my breath catch.

He held me tight, his free hand catching my chin and tilting my face up so I was looking right into his eyes. 'Remember. This is all supposed to feel good, okay?'

He was so hot and hard. Solid and muscular. Reassuring and protective. I felt as if I could lean all my weight on him and he wouldn't let go or drop me. He'd let me lean against him forever, holding me tightly so I wouldn't fall.

'I know,' I managed to get out. 'And it does. But I've never done this before and it's so new. I... I don't know what to do with myself.'

That beautiful, sexy, delicious mouth curved in a smile that took the rest of my breath away. 'You don't have to do anything with yourself. All you have to do is relax and let me do the rest. You can do that, can't you?' There it was again, that look in his eyes, that challenge. The dare that made me want to put back my shoulders and show him that of course I could do it. I could take whatever he threw at me and then some.

'You want me, though?' The words came out before I could think better of them. 'I mean me. Not one of the club girls, right?'

He frowned, searching my face, his eyes full of amber heat. 'I told you I was a dirty guy, and I meant it. Nothing I like better than a full-on fucking orgy. But did you see me stop in the hallway in the clubhouse? Did you see me even look?'

I shook my head slowly, remembering that he hadn't.

'No, because I didn't.' He let go of my chin and grabbed one of my hands, drawing my palm directly over the hard, thick ridge behind his zipper. 'This is for you. This is *all* for you. Understand me?'

I caught my breath, feeling the length and breadth of him beneath my palm. So hard and getting even harder. I was doing this to him, wasn't I? This was me.

As if that reassurance was exactly what I needed to hear, the uncertainty inside me began to recede, leaving behind it a kind of wonder. At myself and my own power. A power I hadn't ever explored before or even realised I had.

If I could do this to him, what else could I do?

But Tiger didn't give me any time to think about it. He picked me up as though I weighed absolutely nothing at all and turned, carrying me over to the battered leather couch in the living area and setting me down on it.

I tried to raise my arms again, but my top was holding them tightly to my sides and I couldn't move. He didn't seem to think this was a problem and took no notice of my wriggles to try to free them. Instead he eased me back into the corner of the couch, between the arm and the back of it, positioning me so my legs were stretched along the cushions and he was kneeling astride them. Then he put his hands on my thighs and pushed the stupid denim mini right up to my waist.

I tensed, shivering, because now he was looking down right between my thighs, and the expression on his face had got even more intense. 'Hmm. What do we have here?' He reached out and brushed his fingers lightly over the front of my panties, making me jerk and gasp as if he'd electrocuted me. 'White cotton. Very pretty. Very innocent.' His fingers moved again, tracing the outline of my sex through the fabric as he lifted his hot gaze to mine. 'And very, very wet.'

My face felt like it was going to burst into flames for the millionth time that night, heat like the back-draft from some massive fire washing over me. I wanted to bend my knees, hide myself somehow, but the way he was kneeling meant I couldn't, and with my arms bound to my sides, I couldn't even push my skirt down.

Except I was supposed to be dealing with the challenge of him, right? Not getting shivery and scared the way I had back in the clubhouse.

So I made myself stare back, ignoring how vulnerable I felt with my top bunched under my bare breasts and my skirt pushed up around my waist.

He grinned and I thought I saw approval in his eyes, which made a hot glow start up in my chest. But then he stroked me again, and the hot glow turned into short sharp spikes of pleasure.

'I know,' he said lazily, sliding the tip of his finger under the cotton of my panties an inch, teasing me. 'You don't like having your top pulled down like that, do you? Well, sorry, baby, but I don't want you touching me just yet. And I don't want you covering yourself either.' He stroked along the edge of the cotton, over the incredibly sensitive skin at the crease of my thigh. 'I want to play with you without your hands in getting in the way.'

I shook as that teasing finger stroked over the front of my panties yet again. 'But I—'

'Quiet,' he ordered, glancing down between my thighs again. 'I want to get a look at this little pussy.' He leaned over me, one hand braced on the couch cushions beside my hip while with the other he pulled aside cotton, baring me.

I squirmed, uncomfortable with the intent way he was studying me and with the way I was exposed, bound and helpless. But he ignored me, smoothing his fingers over the slick flesh of my sex instead. 'Nice.' His voice was warm with approval as I stiffened in response, gasping as another hard spike of pleasure jolted the length of my spine. 'Pretty curls and so pink. So wet.' His fingers slid over me again, tearing a groan from my throat. 'Is that all for me, baby girl? Are you all wet for me?'

I could barely hear him. His fingers had found my clit and he was circling it, his strokes slow and firm, the pleasure making my head tip back against the arm of the couch and my eyes close tightly.

Ohmigod. *So* good.

'I'm looking for an answer. Come on, tell me.'

'Y-yes,' I gasped. 'It's all…for you.'

'Yeah, it's all fucking mine, isn't it?' He gave my clit a flick and I almost sobbed at the intensity of the pleasure that lanced through me. 'Just the way I like it.'

My nails were digging into my palms and I couldn't keep still, my hips shifting restlessly as that finger resumed circling again and again. I was desperate to spread my legs but he had his knees on either side of mine so I couldn't, and that hint of restraint somehow made everything ten thousand times hotter and me ten thousand times more impatient.

'Tiger,' I groaned. 'Please…move. I want to…'

'Not yet.' He brought his knees together, holding my thighs even more tightly closed, and then he put both hands down on either side of my hips, bending down low over me. I could feel the warmth of his breath against my wet flesh and my brain seemed to freeze.

God, was he really going to…?

Then I felt it, his tongue on me as he gave me a long slow lick straight up the centre of my pussy.

I went rigid, pleasure exploding the length of my body, a choked cry escaping me. Tiger only made a low, rumbling satisfied sound. 'Fuck, you taste good.' Then he licked me again. And again.

I shuddered, writhing beneath him, my awareness narrowing down to the lash of his tongue between my legs and the almost unbearable pleasure that came along with it. And it only got worse as he wrapped his arms around my hips, holding on to me and burying his face between my thighs.

I gave a hoarse scream, even more desperate to move, to spread my legs so his tongue could get to the place where I needed more pressure, more friction, more…something. But he was holding them closed and even though the way he was licking me was pushing me nearer and nearer to orgasm, it wasn't quite enough to push me over completely.

I sobbed in frustration, my hips shifting as he toyed with me, as he licked me, as he used his fingers on me. And it was only when I was begging, babbling and incoherent, that he concentrated his tongue on my clit, a relentless pressure that eventually pushed me over the edge, making pleasure explode like a bomb inside me, my screams so loud that the room echoed with them.

Afterwards I lay there, boneless and heavy, not wanting to move or even open my eyes. I could feel his weight on me shift, his hands on my thighs, spreading them finally wide apart.

I groaned, a different, luxurious kind of pleasure rolling through me, as he positioned me, hooking one leg over the arm of the couch while pushing wide the other.

Then his fingers were on my pussy again, spreading my wet flesh apart, and he was back, licking and exploring me relentlessly.

I twisted, panting, trying to avoid his clever tongue, but he held me still, made me take it. 'It's too much,' I protested weakly, writhing. 'I can't...'

'Yes, you can.' His breath was hot against my sensitive skin. 'I want you wet, baby. Really, really wet.'

'I think I'm wet enough already.'

He laughed, a deep, rough, sexy sound. 'No, you're not. Besides, I fucking love eating you out. Deal with it.'

I didn't know if I could deal with it to be honest, especially when I couldn't do anything with my hands.

'Look at me,' he said, as if he knew I was having trouble.

And idiot that I was, I did. And as soon as I opened my eyes I knew it had been a mistake to look because the sight of him lying between my spread thighs hit me like a punch to the gut.

His gaze was molten and feral, gleaming and hungry, and as I met it, his fingers slid through my slick folds, toying lazily with me and watching me as he

did so, taking in every shudder, hearing every desperate moan.

It was unbearably erotic.

'You wanted to handle me? So handle me.' He slid
one finger slowly inside me, the smooth glide of it
making me shudder and sweat. 'Handle me, playing
with your pussy and making you watch.' He slid another finger in beside the first, stretching me gently.

I tried to say something, but I couldn't think of
what words to say. The sight of him with his hand
on me, his fingers disappearing inside me, made everything vanish.

He pumped his fingers, sliding them in and out,
slow and deep. 'You're really tight, baby girl. But you
feel so good. I can't wait to get inside you.'

I couldn't stop shaking, my body already starting
to get desperate again, and I couldn't drag my gaze
from his, lost in all that gold.

He kept playing with me as if he had all the time
in the world and then he added his tongue again,
exploring me once more with a relentlessness that
had me sobbing.

It was only then that he moved away, kneeling
upright on the couch cushions and grabbing his wallet out of his back pocket. He took out a condom
packet, tossed the wallet on the floor, then ripped
open the foil without any hurry. Then he unzipped
his fly and reached down to get out his cock. Gripping it in one hand, he casually rolled down the condom with the other.

I couldn't remember whether I'd seen a naked dick before or not, but right now my brain wasn't working. At all. Then again, it didn't matter whether I'd seen one before or not, since the only dick that mattered was Tiger's.

God, he was big. Really, really big. And long and thick.

My fingers itched. I wanted to touch him, to see what he felt like. To see whether he was as smooth and as hot and as hard as he looked.

Except he wasn't going to give me a chance, that much was obvious as he finished with the condom and moved forward to kneel between my thighs. The smile and the laziness had vanished, a raw, hungry light in his eyes.

He slid one big hand beneath my butt, lifting me up a little, while with the other he gripped his cock, rubbing the head of it through the wet flesh of my pussy. I groaned, electricity sparking, making me arch up into him.

'Fuck, I want you,' he breathed, a strange note in his voice. As if he was shocked by the fact. 'What the hell are you doing to me, baby girl?' He searched my face like he was looking for answers. 'Straight vanilla fucking and I'm almost ready to come. This is not normal for me, understand?'

I didn't know what he wanted me to say, but then I wasn't thinking straight, not while I could feel the head of his dick nudging against my clit, making me jerk and shudder like I was holding on to a bare electrical wire.

'Christ, you're hot.' He slid the head of his cock down the length of my pussy, finding my entrance and pushing lightly. 'I don't want to hurt you, so I'll try and go easy.' He pushed again and I heard his breath catch along with my own as my flesh parted around him. 'Holy *fuck*…' he whispered, staring down at me, his amber eyes darkening. 'You feel insanely good.'

He began to push into me, slow and steady, leaving me no time to be scared, no time to doubt. No time to pull away or change my mind. I was so wet there was no resistance and the only pain I felt was a slight pinch. It was more the unfamiliarity of it that made me tremble, that made me gasp. The stretch and burn of my sex around his as he invaded me. Filled me. 'Tiger…' My voice shook. 'Oh, my God… Tiger.'

He kept on going, kept on pushing, steady, relentless, his golden eyes all I could see. And when he was finally all inside me, as deep as he could go, he paused, his gaze still pinning mine. He had one hand on the arm of the couch, the other on the back, and I could hear the harsh sound of his breathing.

And I knew—I just *knew*—that this was affecting him as much as it was affecting me. I could hear it in his breathing and in the look of shock in his eyes. He was staring at me as if he'd never seen anything like me before in his entire life.

'Summer.' The way he said my name went through me like a knife and I wasn't sure why. There was a note of something in it, like wonder, and it made me feel like crying all of a sudden. Then he said it again, *'Summer,'* harsher this time, and he drew his hips back, thrusting into me.

I wanted my hands free. I wanted to touch him but I couldn't. I could only lie there and watch the flames leap in his gaze, getting hotter and rawer as he moved.

Another deep thrust and the orgasm swept over me so unexpectedly that I didn't even have time to scream, conscious only of the pleasure detonating inside me, leaving me writhing. Then another one began to build, and I think I sobbed, because I wasn't sure I could survive. Because if this was what sex was all about then I was ruined. Destroyed.

But something inside me knew that all sex wasn't like this. That it was only like this because of him. Because of Tiger.

Because he was the one who'd destroyed me and kept on destroying me with every thrust of his hips, every gasp he drew from me, every sob.

He began to move faster, harder, shifting his hold and gripping my hips, showing me how to move with him. Then he angled his thrusts so he hit my clit every time he sank into me and I was gone.

I didn't scream this time, only sobbed.

As I came apart in his hands.

CHAPTER TEN

Tiger

I KNEW THE moment she came, could feel her tight little pussy clamp down hard on my cock, gripping me like a fist. And I don't know what happened, but a hot rush of pleasure flooded through me, and I realised that instead of the hours it normally took me to get off, I was on the verge of coming already, even though I'd only just got inside her.

It didn't make any sense. There shouldn't have been any reason why I suddenly felt at the edge of my control. I wasn't a teenage boy and this wasn't my first fuck. This was a virgin and straight out missionary, and yet if I didn't get myself under control, I was going to lose it on virtually the first couple of thrusts.

I had no idea what was wrong with me.

She was laid out underneath me, her head back against the corner of the couch, her eyes closed, her mouth open. Strands of hair were sticking to her neck and I could see sweat beading on her forehead where more strands of hair were sticking. Her cheeks were deeply flushed and there was a trail of moisture out of the corner of one eye.

She looked so fucking beautiful, so fucking sexy. She looked wrecked and I was the one who'd wrecked her. And I wasn't even sorry. I hadn't even come yet and I wanted to wreck her again and again. And maybe wreck myself along with her.

Fuck, where had all of this come from? I wanted to pull away, because if there was one thing I hated, it was feeling uncomfortable, but the ache in my dick wouldn't let me.

Jesus, she was so tight. And hot. And wet. And she smelled of sex and flowers. And the way she was lying there, all abandoned, was driving me insane.

There was no fighting this. I was going to come and come hard.

I thrust again, harder, pushing deep into her pussy, gripping her hips in my hands. She shuddered and her back arched, and before I knew what I was doing, I was moving faster, even harder. Slamming myself into her. Losing myself in the feel of her tight pussy around my cock.

Then, just before I lost it completely, she opened her eyes and looked up at me, and it was like I'd fallen into the depths of the sea, nothing but dark blue all around me.

She said my name, very softly, in that husky voice and, fuck, it sent me straight over the edge.

I bent and kissed her savagely, roaring into her

mouth as the orgasm hit me like a fucking baseball bat, my hips thrusting wildly, out of control and not giving a shit as pleasure exploded inside me like a goddamn nuclear bomb.

Not thinking straight, I loosened my grip on the couch and leaned forward, gathering her up and pulling her into my lap so her legs were around my waist. Then I turned my head into her damp neck, inhaling that sexy scent of hers, breathing it in and trying to calm myself the fuck down.

I was still inside her, though, and I could feel my cock slowly hardening yet again. Jesus, I'd barely got this round down and already I was up for another.

Even though I didn't want to, I pulled out of her, loving how she gave a delicate little shudder as I did so. 'Be right back,' I murmured, releasing her and letting her slide down onto the cushions. I got off the couch and went into the kitchen area, getting rid of the condom in the trash before coming back to her, pulling off my clothes as I went.

I'd left hers on because I liked the half dressed, half naked look, but now I wanted nothing between us but skin.

Those big blue eyes opened wide as I kicked my boots off, then peeled my T-shirt up and over my head, then shucked my jeans and underwear. Gave me a fucking huge thrill the way she was looking at me, not hiding the fact that she liked what she saw. Most women did and, shit, what man didn't like that?

But there was something about the way this little

girl was staring that made me hard instantly, and when her gaze dropped to my dick, I got even harder.

'Time to get naked, baby girl.' I stalked over to the couch and her eyes were like goddamn saucers as I reached down and pulled her top off. Then I got rid of her miniskirt and her panties, too.

Once she was finally bare, I laid her down flat on the cushions, then I eased myself over her the way I had back in my room in the clubhouse, her warm little body beneath mine, my hips resting between her thighs and that hot little pussy right against my dick.

I braced myself on my elbows on either side of her head, leaning down to nuzzle her neck, licking her throat to get another taste of the salt on her skin. I wanted to spread her thighs and bury my face in her pussy again, but I figured she'd need some recovery time. I hadn't gone easy on her, that was for sure.

She shivered as my tongue touched her throat, and I felt her palms press against my chest.

Yeah, I really hadn't gone easy on her.

I lifted my head. 'You okay? Not sore?'

'Tender maybe, but not sore, no.' Her hands slid from my chest up to my shoulders, her fingers spreading out. 'I want to touch you. Can I?'

'Baby, you don't need to ask permission. But right now, since I'm already pretty fucking hard and you need a break, I don't think that's a good idea.'

She sighed. 'Maybe you're right. So…you said you liked orgies and being dirty. Does that mean that later you want to…um…you know, with me?'

It was obvious what she meant and, prick that I was, I just had to tease her about it. 'What? You want some group sex? Well, sure. If you're into it we could—'

'No!' She gave me a slap on the shoulder, which I found weirdly hot. 'I definitely do *not* want group sex.'

I grinned, putting her out of her misery. 'Good. Because as of now, I've decided I don't like sharing.' The addition *what's mine* echoed inside my head, but I managed not to say it aloud. Because it was fucking strange enough that I found the thought of sharing her vaguely enraging, let alone thinking of her as mine.

Hell, I'd only been with her a few hours and it was way too soon to be thinking about shit like that. If ever.

'That's okay then.' She gave me a stern look, absently stroking my shoulder. 'I don't want to be shared.'

My brothers getting their filthy hands on her... Yeah, I did *not* like that thought. At all. 'Don't worry. There's plenty of other dirty things we can do that don't involve other people.' The way her hand was moving on my shoulder made me want to shiver, which was just flat out fucking weird. No one touched me gently like that and I wasn't sure I liked it. Trying to ignore the feeling, I grinned. 'You leave the dirty part to me, okay?'

She gave me a solemn nod. 'Okay.'

Jesus. She was fucking adorable.

Her gaze dropped to the shoulder she was touching, her fingers beginning to trace my ink. 'By the way, this tattoo is incredible. I love all the angles and stuff. Where did you find the design?'

I shrugged. 'Drew it myself. I liked it so I thought I'd get it inked.'

She gave me a startled glance. 'You did? Because wow.'

That look in her eyes. Christ. Like I was something amazing she'd never seen before, which only made me more uncomfortable.

I tried to brush it off. 'It's just a tattoo.'

'No, it's not.' Her finger traced one of the circles. 'Look at it. The way this spiral interlocks with the others. And the circles here and all the arcs… It's beautiful, Tiger.' She glanced up at me again, blue glowing in her eyes. But it wasn't anger this time. In fact, it looked a hell of a lot like…interest. 'I love the geometries in it.' She gave an odd little smile that made something kick hard in my chest. 'Math is kind of my thing and I love it when everything— I don't know—just fits.'

'Like parts in an engine.' Shit, why I had said that? Chicks didn't like talking about engine parts. At least not the chicks I talked to. Not that I did much talking with them, to be honest.

But the blue glow in Summer's eyes flared as if she knew exactly what I was talking about. 'Oh, yes!

Exactly. And when it all fits together and it works, and it's like…'

'Like solving a puzzle,' I finished, because clearly this was what I was doing now. Finishing her fucking sentences.

She smiled, and honest to God, it felt like the sun coming out. 'Right? I love puzzles.'

That weird feeling in my chest tightened, which, again, I didn't like. I'd had conversations with the club girls before, but it was only small talk. They'd never been interested in what I had to say anyway. They only wanted my cock.

But there was something about Summer's confession that got to me. She'd said it completely without embarrassment, as if she was comfortable talking to me. As if she thought I'd understand.

Strange, when only a couple of hours before she hadn't been able to get a word out.

'So, you're some kind of genius, right?' I shifted on her, adjusting the way my cock was pressing against her and liking the way she shivered in response.

'Y-yes.' Her nails dug into my shoulder, a flush beginning to creep up her throat.

Oh, I liked that. A lot. 'What's your IQ then?'

'Um…last test I did, over 170.'

Super smart then. Yet, just by shifting my cock, I could make her unable to speak.

Not bad for a dumb fuck.

I grinned and moved again, her breath hissing as I did so. 'Okay, so you actually *are* a genius then.'

'I am.' She arched, her lashes drifting closed. 'Um... Tiger?'

'Yeah?'

'Can you...um...'

'What?' I pushed myself up and back so I could look at her perfect tits. Then I lowered my head, licking one of her hard nipples, loving the way she gasped. 'Am I killing some of those super smart brain cells of yours, baby girl?'

'Yes...oh, *yes*.'

I put my mouth over her nipple and sucked hard, feeling her shudder. Yeah, taking her apart like this was fucking amazing. Addictive even.

'Oh...' she breathed, pressing herself up into my mouth. 'I never thought it would be like this.'

She tasted so sweet and the way she gave a jolt every time I teased her with my tongue was insanely good. I'd never been with a woman who was so sensitive before. I could get used it.

I released her nipple, nuzzling her breast. 'Basically, it's because my IQ is pretty fucking high, too. I'm talking about my sex IQ here.'

'No, I'm serious.' Her blue gaze met mine. 'I thought it would be all really scary, but it wasn't. You made it okay. And you made me feel good. Really, *really* good.'

I didn't know what the hell to say to that, because there was nothing but honesty in her eyes, and it felt kind of…painful. Made me want to wrap her up and protect her, tell her not to make herself so vulnerable. Especially not to me.

'I have to tell you something,' I said. 'You might have thought about me for five years, but I didn't think about you. Not once.' If honesty was what we were going for here, then she had to know. I didn't want her making this into something it wasn't. 'So, if you're thinking that we're—'

'I'm *not* thinking that,' she interrupted, a flash of that temper she hid so well crossing her face. 'That wasn't what I was trying to say. I only wanted to tell you that I think you're amazing. And, well… I *do* like you.'

Again, that honesty. It was a problem. 'Baby,' I said gently. 'You don't know me. And good sex doesn't mean a fucking thing.'

She frowned. 'But I do know you. You carry a gun in the back of your jeans and you love riding that bike. And you used to like teasing me—which, FYI, you still do. Oh, and you're very protective. Also, you have an amazing smile and I used to wish—'

'Everyone knows those things.' I cut her off before she could make me any more uncomfortable than she already was. 'They're not secrets.'

I didn't bother to keep the warning note out of my voice, but apparently she either didn't hear it or simply flat out ignored me, because she gave me a very direct look and said, 'So tell me something no one else knows then.'

Shit. How the hell had I got myself into this situation? There were plenty of things no one else knew about me and I wasn't ashamed of them. That wasn't why I didn't talk about them. I didn't talk about them because they weren't anyone else's business and why she thought they were hers, I had no fucking idea.

You should tell her, dumb fuck. If you're not ashamed, it won't make any difference.

I shook the thought away. Later, I'd tell her later. Right now, my dick was hard and I wanted to suck on her tits some more, then maybe eat her out again, teach her how to ride me just the way I liked.

So I shook my head. 'Later, baby girl. Right now, that hot little pussy of yours is driving me crazy. So how about you just lie there and I'll see if I can cool her down a bit?'

Then I bent my head and took her nipple in my mouth again and tried to ignore the voice in my head that was telling me I was a coward.

CHAPTER ELEVEN

Summer

I DON'T KNOW what time it was when I woke up, but light was streaming through the big windows of Tiger's warehouse apartment, illuminating the vaulted ceiling above me and the heavy beams that crisscrossed it.

I lay on my back staring up at it, for a second disorientated about where I was. But then Tiger shifted beside me, his arm tightening around my waist, and I remembered.

After another intense round of sex on the couch, he'd picked me up and carried me into his bathroom and got in the shower with me. Then he'd washed me carefully, like I was a child, before drying me off and carrying me up to the mezzanine floor where his big low bed was.

He'd done things to me in that bed. Things that had made me scream and cry out his name over and over again. Things I was never going to forget.

I wanted him to do those things all over again, but a quick glance revealed he was still asleep and if I wanted to have a look around his apartment without him getting in the way, it was going to have to be now.

Carefully I wriggled out from under his arm and slid out of bed, wincing a little at the way some of my muscles decided to remind me of what we'd been getting up to the night before.

It had been worth it, though, *so* worth it.

My clothes were downstairs, so I went down the iron stairs still naked, coming down into the living area. The dark blue T-shirt he'd been wearing the night before was on the floor and on a whim, I picked it up and put it on myself.

It was massive, falling to midthigh, but it was soft and it smelled like him and for some reason I didn't want to take it off.

You don't know me and good sex doesn't mean a fucking thing.

His words from the night before echoed suddenly in my head, making my chest tighten. Which was stupid. Of course I knew it didn't mean a fucking thing and, sure, maybe I didn't know him.

So why do you want to then?

Good question, and one I didn't have an answer to. Perhaps it had been something to do with the sex after all. Or perhaps it was all about the past and my fascination with him. Or maybe it had simply been after I'd gone on and on embarrassingly about how wonderful his tattoo was, and he'd finished my ravings about how everything had fit together by saying it was like a bike engine.

It had been the most perfect simile, the way he'd understood thrilling me deeply. There weren't many people I could talk to about what excited me, mainly because people's eyes tended to glaze over whenever I mentioned math. But Tiger's hadn't. In one simple sentence, he'd managed to encapsulate my feelings about puzzles and equations, and life in general so perfectly that I knew he'd understood.

Even thinking about it now made a jolt of excitement go through me, making me want to charge right back up the stairs and wake him up, talk to him some more about the similarities between bike engines and mathematics.

Except that wouldn't let me explore and I *really* wanted to do that.

I began to slowly poke around his apartment. It was a massive place, a basic galley kitchen down one end, a motorcycle workshop up the other, with a living area sandwiched in between. Everything was scrupulously clean and tidy, the remotes for the TV and stereo neatly lined up on the coffee table next to a sleek laptop and a stack of bike magazines.

Interesting how he was so tidy, because most guys weren't. Or at least, not the ones I'd had any dealings with.

There were no bookshelves and no books, though. At all. Maybe bikers didn't read? Or were only in terested in magazines? There weren't photos or anything either, which was annoying. I'd been hoping to find a few family pics to give me some insights.

Moving past the living area, I wandered over to the workshop end of the space. There was a workbench running along the length of one wall with cupboards and shelves above it, plus a few larger metal cupboards down one end. A big bike was up on a stand, the chrome gleaming in the morning light.

This area too was neat and tidy, the workbench clean except for a shiny piece of metal that looked like it came from the inside of an engine. I picked it up, the weight of it pleasing in my hand, and turned it over, thinking about him, thinking about the tattoo he'd apparently designed himself, the way all those shapes, the spirals and circles and arcs and squares all fit together.

There was more to him than sex and an easy smile, I was sure of it. And I wanted to know what more there was. He was a puzzle and I wanted to solve him.

I turned around to put the piece of metal back down on the workbench, leaning against it, still thinking. Then I suddenly felt heat along my spine, as two large masculine hands came down onto the bench on either side of me.

I went still, shivering as Tiger's tall, rangy body pressed me up against the workbench, his breath feathering the side of my neck. 'Good morning,' he murmured. 'What are you doing down here? You should be upstairs, naked in my bed and ready to suck my cock.'

The feel of him against me and the scent of him, musky and spicy, made my head swim. I sighed, leaning back into him. 'Nothing much. Just looking around.'

'Uh-huh. Stay out of my stuff, baby girl.' His mouth brushed over the nape of my neck, the kiss taking the sting from the words. 'I like you in my shirt, though. You can keep wearing that.' He shifted his hands, sliding them underneath the hem of the T-shirt I wore, cupping my bare butt, squeezing me. 'No panties either. I approve.'

I wanted to arch my hips and press myself into his hands, but I had a feeling that was another distraction technique, like he'd used the night before when he'd avoided telling me something that no one else knew about him.

I turned my head, trying to ignore the feel of his hands on my bare skin. 'Is it later yet?'

'What do you mean later?'

'You were going to tell me something about you that no one else knows.'

He squeezed me again, his hips flexing, and I felt rough denim and heat as he pushed himself against me. 'Yeah, it's not later yet. Not when my dick is hard.'

Definitely distraction techniques. If I wasn't careful, they were going to work, too. Because his fingers were skimming down over the curve of my butt and pressing gently between my thighs from behind, brushing the folds of my sex. And I could feel the pleasure already starting to take hold, the deep, intense throb of it stealing my breath.

But I wasn't going to let him distract me, not this time.

'I'll tell you something that no one knows about me.' I tried to disguise the breathlessness in my voice. 'I…get afraid a lot. In fact, I'm pretty much always afraid.'

His stroking fingers gentled. 'Hate to break it to you, baby girl, but that's not news. I knew you were afraid the moment I met you.'

I could feel my face get hot. I thought I'd hidden it better than that, but obviously I hadn't. 'How did you know?'

'Because you didn't say a word to me. Could barely even look at me. Plus, you seemed to spend a lot of time trying to blend into the background, trying not to be noticed.' His fingers spread out on my butt, then slid up to my hips, holding on to me. 'Seems to me there's a reason for that.'

I swallowed, falling back on my old excuse. 'I don't like people.'

'Yeah, I don't think that's the issue.'

But I didn't want to talk about my dad and the glass house I lived in. It felt too revealing, even more so when I was wearing hardly any clothes. The only reason I'd said it in the first place was to get him to talk.

'You don't want to hear about my pathetic weakness.' I tried to turn around.

But his fingers firmed on my hips, holding me still. 'Fear doesn't make you pathetic, baby. You're only pathetic if you let it stop you from doing what you want to do. And you definitely don't let it stop you. Fuck, you talked your way into the clubhouse in the middle of a goddamn party, even though you were terrified. That's not pathetic. That's gutsy.'

The way he said it, quiet and yet full of conviction, made my throat get tight and a weird prickle start up behind my eyes. Of course I knew I wasn't really as pathetic as I made out. And I didn't need him to tell me that, right?

I opened my mouth to say something, I don't even know what, but he was still talking in the same quiet tone. 'And if you've got the guts to do that... Okay, you want to know something about me that no one else knows? I can't fucking read.'

Shock pulsed through me and I was turning around before I could think better of it.

He'd loosened his grip on me and had taken a step back, standing there staring down at me with those dark amber eyes. He was only wearing a pair of half-buttoned jeans, leaving a whole lot of gorgeous sculpted muscle and dark ink on show. He casually put his hands in his pockets, his posture loose and easy, but there was a guarded expression on his face.

'You can't read?' I echoed stupidly.

'No. Always had difficulty with it when I was at school and then I had to leave and...' He lifted one of those powerful shoulders. 'I never learned.'

I couldn't believe it. He was so strong, so sure of himself. So confident and yet for some reason he'd never developed one of life's most basic skills. 'Why not?'

Something crossed his face, gone too fast before I could see what it was. 'Like I said, I could never get the hang of it at school. Not that I was at school a lot anyway.'

'But how come? Why weren't you in school? Surely you had someone who could teach you how to—'

'My mom was a whore.' The words were sharp, cutting me off. 'She took johns during the day because she didn't like doing it at night, and she needed me to look after my kid brother. So I did. And when I got older, she needed me to look after her as well, because some of those johns were violent fucks who had no respect.' Something dark and metallic glittered in his gaze, not the bright gold of arousal but what looked like a sullen kind of anger. 'She left when I was sixteen and took Tommy with her, and then it was too late to go back to school, so I didn't. Joined the Knights instead. Don't need to fucking read to be a brother.'

I blinked at him, trying to take all this in. His childhood sounded…awful. Worse than mine by a long shot. 'Your mom was a…p-prostitute?'

'Yeah.' The anger in his gaze burned a little brighter. 'You got a problem with that? She had to feed me and Tommy somehow and that was the only way she could do it.'

'No, no problem,' I said quickly. 'But she left you? At sixteen?' There was something painful in my chest, a terrible sympathy, because I knew what it was like to have a mother leave you. I knew the hole that it left, even though I tried not to think about it too often.

Unexpectedly he looked away, but not before I caught the flash of pain that glinted in his eyes. 'She had to go. I don't blame her for leaving.'

'But you were sixteen. That's so young. Why did she go?'

Another shrug, as if he didn't care. 'I don't know.'

I blinked again. 'You don't know?'

'She didn't fucking tell me, okay?' His rough voice had got sharper, harder, the anger in his eyes bleeding into his words. 'One day I got home and she and Tommy weren't there. She'd just…gone.'

The painful feeling in my chest ached. At least my mom had kissed me goodbye before she'd left. Told me to be a good girl for my dad and that one day she'd come back for me. She never had of course, but that was a whole other story. At least I knew why she'd gone—because living with Dad had become impossible for her.

'I'm so sorry.' It was trite, but I didn't know what else to say. 'That must have been awful.'

'You don't need to be fucking sorry.' Tension had crept into his posture, his shoulders going tight. 'Got nothing to do with you.'

'I know that, but I know what it's like to have a

parent walk out on you. My mom did when I was little. She always told me she'd come back, but…' I stopped. I didn't want to make this about me. This was about him. About the fact that he'd been left alone at sixteen years old. God.

'Parents,' he said, as if that explained everything, his mouth twisting into a mirthless smile. 'What are you gonna do?'

It sounded flippant, but I knew it wasn't. I could see the anger there, glowing beneath the smile he was trying to cover it with. 'What about your dad? Do you have any other relatives?'

'No. Never knew who my dad was and never wanted to find out.' He rolled his shoulders like he was trying to get rid of the tension in them. 'The Knights are all the family I need.'

'Do they know you can't read?'

''Course not. Why do you think I said it was something no one else knew?'

'But why didn't you learn?' I couldn't seem to leave the subject alone. 'I mean, how do you do anything? Do you get people to read to you or what?'

'Technology, baby. It's a wonderful thing.' He took his hands out of his pockets and stalked towards me again, slow and fluid, tiger by name, tiger by nature. 'I got a phone that reads shit out to me and I can dictate texts. Same with my computer. And I don't need to read to be able to put an engine together.'

He closed the distance between us, backing me up against the workbench and pinning me there with his body, his hands coming down on either side of me once again. He was hard, I could feel him pressing against me, could see the glint of arousal in his eyes. But that anger was still there, too, and it was glowing hot.

He might act like he didn't care about his mother leaving, or about not being able to read, but he did.

'Why did you tell me?' I ignored the hard ridge that was nudging between my thighs, looking up into his strong, fierce face.

'You wanted to know. So I told you.'

'But you haven't told anyone else.'

'No, because it's a fucking depressing subject.' He nudged me a little more firmly and a hot burst of sensation flooded through me. 'Don't go thinking this makes you special, baby girl. I don't care who knows.'

Oh, yes, he did. Why else would I be the only one? It hurt that I wasn't special to him, because he was special to me, but still…he'd told me all the same. He'd given this secret to me and no matter what he said, it *did* feel special to me.

I lifted my hands to his face, obeying some instinct that told me that touch was the way to connect with him, the prickle of his morning beard against my palms a delicious roughness. 'I think you do care,' I said calmly. 'So why don't you let me teach you?'

CHAPTER TWELVE

Tiger

SUMMER'S BLUE EYES had that serious look in them again, and she'd taken my face between her palms. And for some reason I could feel that touch settle down through me like I'd popped a Valium or something. It made me feel warm, made the tension in my shoulders and neck release.

Crazy. I wanted to lift her up and fuck her right here on the workbench, not fall in a damn puddle at her feet.

I should never have said anything. I didn't know why I had. Just…her confession about being afraid had hit me hard and I hadn't been able to let it go. For some insane fucking reason, I wanted to give her something back and so the words had come out, like I'd been waiting to say them for goddamn years. Then I'd poured out the shit about Mom and Tommy, too, and the mistake had got worse and worse.

Now she was looking at me like I was a lost puppy

she wanted to take home with her and I didn't like how that made my heart kick hard in my chest. This girl wasn't looking for a cock to ride. She was looking at *me*.

It made me feel naked. Like walking into a rival MC's clubhouse without my cut.

I didn't like that. Because, really, who the fuck liked being vulnerable? I didn't. It reminded me of getting home that day when I was sixteen, and coming inside to find it empty. I'd thought Mom had taken Tommy out to the park, so I hadn't worried. But then it had got dark and she still hadn't turned up. I'd gone out searching for her and couldn't find her, and had started to get worried. It wasn't until I'd come home again and gone up into her bedroom that I saw the empty closet. And the dresser top that used to have all her perfumes and shit on it wiped clean.

I'd never forget that feeling. My stomach had dropped away and I'd thought I was going to be sick. I'd gone into Tommy's room to see what was going on there, but all his clothes were gone, too. And so was the stuffed bear he took with him everywhere.

That was when I knew for certain.

They were gone and they weren't coming back.

So, no. I didn't want to feel like that ever again.

'I don't need you to teach me.' I couldn't keep the edge from my voice. 'I'm happy with things the way they are.'

What about the letters, dumb fuck? Don't you want to know what's in them?

No. Those letters could stay unread until fucking Doomsday as far as I was concerned.

'I don't think you are.' She was so goddamn serious. 'Why won't you let me help?'

''Cause I don't want your help. I didn't bring you here to teach me to read, I brought you here so I could fuck you, end of story.'

She frowned, temper shifting in her eyes. 'Why do you say stuff like that? Why do you make it sound like nothing?'

I opened my mouth to tell her that was because it *was* nothing, no matter what she thought. But then I felt my phone buzz in my pocket.

I held up a hand and pulled away from her, grabbing the phone and looking down to see Smoke's picture on the screen. Fuck. What was he calling about?

I turned away from Summer and hit the answer button. 'What?'

'Keep's getting antsy about the chief's daughter,' Smoke said, getting straight to the point. 'And he thinks you're either hiding something or letting yourself get distracted.'

Jesus, this was all I needed. 'Am I the only fucking brother in the MC?' I didn't bother hiding my temper. 'Why's he fucking on me about it?'

'I dunno, man. You protected her once and have a connection with her?'

'You're with Cat and she was once her sister-in-law. Why don't you find her?'

'Hey, chill the fuck out.' Smoke sounded as pissed as I felt. 'What's your problem?'

I took a breath, trying to get a handle on myself. Because I knew what the problem was. That little girl behind me asking me questions I didn't want to answer and telling me things I didn't want to hear. Not to mention Keep being on my butt about finding her and taking her in.

And I didn't want to do that. I hadn't finished with her.

Apart from all the serious fucking I was planning on doing, I hadn't discovered anything about why she was so afraid all the time or why she'd run from her father in the first place, and I wasn't going to let her go anywhere near Keep until I'd found those things out.

Sure, she was asking me about uncomfortable shit, but I could deal. I wasn't a pussy-ass bitch. It had been years since Mom left and I had a whole new family now. A family that had my back and wouldn't ever leave.

She could help you out with those letters.

Ah, fuck the letters. I didn't want to read them even if I could.

They'd started arriving about a year after Mom left and I knew what my own name looked like; they were addressed to me. The handwriting was familiar, too. I knew they were from Mom.

When the first one had arrived, I'd carried it around with me for weeks, wanting to know what it said and yet so angry I could hardly deal. I could have asked someone to read it for me, but that would have meant giving away the fact that I couldn't, and at the time I hadn't been able to stand the fact that someone would know.

I'd nearly thrown that letter away a thousand times, but something wouldn't let me. In the end, I'd stuffed it in a box and forgotten about it. Same thing happened a year later, I got another letter. Then another. And pretty soon I had a little pile of letters all from Mom, all of which I couldn't read. Which she knew.

I don't know why I kept them, but I still had 'em all in a drawer upstairs. Waiting for the day that I'd rip them open and read them. But that day hadn't come.

'There's no problem,' I growled to Smoke. 'I've got more important things to handle right now.'

'What? That girl you took home last night? Didn't mention her to Keep, by the way. Thought he didn't need to know.'

Well, that was something. 'Thanks, man,' I said grudgingly. 'So am I gonna get him riding my butt this morning about it or what?'

'Leave him to me. I'll deal with it.'

Smoke was Keep's nephew and had a different kind of relationship with him than the rest of us. The prez was a fucking hard-ass, but Smoke seemed to know how to handle him and I appreciated my buddy putting his neck out for me.

But that was the thing about the club. We had each other's backs and in the shitshow that was life, that was the most important thing in it.

'I fucking owe you,' I muttered.

'Yeah, you do.' There was a pause. 'That girl one of the important things to do?'

What I should have said was 'What girl?' But I didn't. Instead I nearly said 'Yeah' without thinking about it. A mistake. Especially when it came to club business, because *nothing* was more important than club business to me.

'No,' I lied, conscious of Summer standing behind me, watching me. I knew she was watching me because I could feel her gaze boring into my back.

'Yeah, sure,' Smoke said, like he knew exactly how big a liar I was. 'I've got one of my own at home, remember?'

I scowled. 'It's not like that.'

'The fuck it isn't.' The prick sounded amused.

Still scowling, I disconnected the call without a response, which would probably give me away as much as more denial would, but I didn't care. I didn't want to keep talking about the subject.

'Well?' Summer asked quietly. 'You didn't answer my question.'

I flung the phone over onto the coffee table, then turned around.

It made no sense why the sight of her with all that pretty white-gold hair down around her shoulders or the fact that she was wearing nothing but my T-shirt should get me harder than steel, but it did and suddenly I didn't give a shit about anything. Not about those letters, not about the fact I'd told her something not even Smoke, my best buddy, knew. And not about the fact that for some inexplicable reason she wanted to help me.

All that stuff was bullshit.

Feeling good, that was the point of everything, wasn't it? Because life was short and shitty, so you grabbed the good times while you could.

'Come here,' I said.

She didn't hesitate, coming to stand right in front of me. There was a crease between her fair brows, her gaze searching mine. 'Are you okay?'

'I will be once my cock is in your mouth.'

Her eyes narrowed and I had the weird feeling that she saw right through me.

Then she said, 'Don't think I don't know distraction techniques when I see them.'

Shit.

I forced a smile. 'You make me come, then maybe we'll talk after.'

'Is that a promise?'

'Depends on how quickly you make me come.'

Her lips pursed and she fixed me with that stern look she did so well. 'You know I'm going to hold you to that.'

Christ, this little girl challenging me all the fucking time. I shook my head. 'Aren't you supposed to be scared of me? Maybe you'd better stop ordering me around.'

Her mouth twitched and I found myself staring at it, already imagining it wrapped around my cock. 'Apparently I'm not *that* scared of you any more.'

'It's my dick. It's magic.'

She laughed. 'So, do I get to see this magic dick of yours then? Or are you going to keep talking?'

This was a side of her I hadn't seen before, a glimpse of the spirit that lurked underneath her fear. Fuck, it was sexy. 'You're very forward for a virgin, you know that?'

'But I'm not a virgin. Not any more.'

'Thank fuck. On your knees, baby girl.'

She didn't even blink, doing exactly what I told her and graceful as hell with it. Then she looked up at me from her position on the floor, all big eyes and white-blonde hair and innocence, and I was suddenly hard enough to hammer nails.

'You'll have to tell me what to do,' she said, all seriousness now. 'This is another first time for me.'

It would be the gentlemanly thing to do. But then, there was nothing gentlemanly about me. And besides, I actually didn't want to tell her. I wanted her to find out what I liked on her own, because she was interested. Because she wanted to explore me, discover me. *Me.* Not some random guy.

It was stupid. 'Take me deep and suck me hard.' That's what I should have said to her. Yet what came out instead was 'Use your imagination.'

A fleeting look of worry crossed her face. 'I know, but you must be used to women who can do it really well, and I'm hardly in that league. You might not enjoy it.'

Jesus, her honesty. It got to me. The fact it mattered to her that I enjoy it. I mean, sure, the club girls were good and wore that skill like a badge of honour. It mattered to them, too, but for different reasons. Reasons that were more about them and their status than they were about pleasing me personally.

I reached down and cupped Summer's cheek. Her skin was so soft it ought to have been illegal. I was sure my hand with all the calluses and scars I'd got from fixing engines would scrape her. Yet if it did, she didn't seem to care, leaning into my palm like a little cat, her gaze on mine.

My chest went tight and I almost forgot what I'd been going to say. 'Whatever you do, I'll enjoy it,' I forced out, wanting her to know this because it felt important. 'Fuck, I already can hardly speak.'

She flushed and her lashes dropped, her gaze on my dick, which was currently pushing so hard against my zipper it was amazing the thing didn't unzip itself.

Her hand lifted and she put out a finger, tracing my cock through the denim, a slow up and down that made my breath catch. Very similar to the way I'd touched her pussy the night before, come to think of it...

Oh, fuck. This was payback, wasn't it?

'Don't be shy,' I muttered. Hell, was that really my voice? All husky and rough? 'Get my dick out.'

'Wait. I'm just figuring it out.' She kept on touching me, slowly and experimentally, finding the head of my cock and rubbing gently over the top, making my breath hiss in my throat.

Yeah, I liked it hard and fast, not this slow kind of bullshit. But the careful way she was touching me and the look of concentration on her face, as if this was really important to her…somehow I couldn't bring myself to tell her to stop.

'You want to play with me?' I asked hoarsely. 'Is that what you're doing?'

She shot me a wide blue glance. 'Is that okay? I mean, you wanted me to figure it out, so I'd like to try.'

'Sure.' I'd kept my hand where it was on her cheek and couldn't resist stroking her with my thumb. 'You just might kill me is all.'

She flushed again with pleasure. 'Well, you killed me last night so maybe it's my turn.'

And she *was* fucking killing me. Slowly and by inches as she fumbled around with my zipper, then tugged it down. I hadn't bothered with underwear when I'd got up, so the moment she got my jeans open, my dick was right in her face.

Her eyes went wide, which was incredibly satisfying, and I found myself sliding my hand to the back of her neck and gripping on tight. Not forcing her forward, just holding on. I couldn't drag my gaze from what she was doing. She put her hand on me, her fingers stroking my cock, exploring it like she'd never seen anything like it before in her life.

It was the hottest fucking thing.

My pulse was racing, my heart rate through the roof. And she was just touching me. That's all she was doing, just stroking me. Christ, I hadn't been kidding when I'd told her she was going to kill me. She would. Literally.

Then she finally gripped me, curving those pale fingers around the base of my dick, squeezing me. And she looked up into my face as she did so, obviously wanting to see my response.

'I'm not fragile, baby girl,' I muttered. 'You can do that harder.'

So she did, squeezing me harder, and I couldn't stop myself. I held on to the back of her neck with one hand while I lifted the other and covered her fingers where they gripped me, then I showed her how to pump me.

God, it felt good. The warmth of her hand and the pressure. The expression of fierce concentration on her face. It was probably the same expression she got when she was figuring out a math problem, which shouldn't have been sexy but was all the same.

She was a fast learner, though, and soon I didn't have to show her what to do, she had it all figured out without any problems. My hand dropped from hers as she began to find a rhythm, varying the strokes and the pressure. Then she stopped a couple of times, circling the head of my aching dick with her thumb and then slicking across the top of it.

Holy shit, she made me feel so good it was insane. She wasn't practised at all, but the way she approached it, like she was going to work at this until she got it right, was hot as fuck.

'Yeah.' I was fucking babbling now. 'So good, baby girl. That's right. You keep doing that, you're gonna make me come so hard.'

She leaned forward and licked me, and I almost lost it. Almost fucking came there and then. Her tongue was like a blowtorch, setting me on fire, and there was only one way this was going to end.

I thrust both hands into her hair and held on, pushing my aching dick between those pretty pink lips before she could pull away, feeling the heat of her mouth surround me. She made a little sound, kind of like a groan, and her hands came out to grip my thighs, holding on tight.

'You okay?' I demanded hoarsely, feeling the shakes beginning already and wanting to thrust deep into her throat, but holding back because I didn't want to lay it on her all at once.

She gave a nod, so I began to ease deeper, my breathing harsh in the silence of the room, every sense I had centred on the heat of that mouth of hers and the incredible pleasure it was giving me.

I nudged the back of her throat and she tensed, so I pulled back, giving her a moment before thrusting in again. Her nails dug hard into my thighs and she gave a groan that sounded hungry, so I began to move faster, harder.

Her hair in my hands was so silky and warm that I gripped it tighter, pulling her head back a little so I could look down into her face, so I could see my dick sliding in between those perfect lips.

So fucking hot.

Her blue eyes met mine and I could see the hunger in them and the glaze of pleasure, and it was like an extra kick to know she was getting off on this as much as I was.

I'd got head from so many women and it had always been good. But this… Holy hell, I don't know what it was, but what she was doing eclipsed every single blow job I'd ever had.

'Gonna go harder,' I warned her. 'You okay?'

She gave a frantic nod so I went ahead and upped the pace, and it was so goddamn good. Her gaze was trained on mine as if I was the only thing she could see and that lit me up, too, made me feel like a fucking god.

'You're gonna make me come.' I looked down into those incredible blue eyes. 'Oh, baby girl, you're gonna make me come so fucking hard.'

I could feel the orgasm building at the base of my spine, the tension winding tighter and tighter. I was going faster now, fucking her mouth without mercy, and she took it all, gripping onto me so tight it was a wonder she didn't draw blood.

Then she did something with her tongue—I don't

know what the fuck it was—and maybe it was the sheer unexpectedness of it that got me but it made lightning shoot straight down my spine to my cock, and that was it, I was gone.

'Take it all,' I groaned. 'Fucking take everything I give you.'

And she did.

And when the orgasm crushed me into fucking dust and I came down the back of her throat, all I could see were her eyes, blue as the sky.

Making me feel as if I were flying.

CHAPTER THIRTEEN

Summer

WATCHING TIGER COME and knowing I was the one who'd done it to him had to rank as one of the hottest things I'd ever seen. And the most powerful.

It was weird how I was on my knees in front of him, supposedly at a disadvantage, and yet he was the one who'd come completely undone.

His cock was pulsing in my mouth and I could taste him, salty and thick. His head was thrown back, the tendons of his throat standing out rigidly as he gasped, the sound of my name echoing around us.

His fingers were wound in my hair and it was a little painful, but I barely felt it. I was too busy looking at him, watching what I'd done to him and feeling the same rush I got when I solved a complex equation.

I'd done this to him. This experienced, jaded biker was shaking and all because I'd taken him in my mouth and sucked him hard.

He'd had to take over in the end, but I didn't count

that as a failure. I'd filed away what he'd shown me, remembered it so that next time I could fully take charge.

If there is a next time.

I shook the thought away. Of course there'd be a next time. Maybe later, after we'd had the talk he'd promised me. I knew more about what he liked now. I could use that knowledge and maybe it wouldn't be him seducing me. Maybe it would be me seducing him.

The idea sent a thrill down my spine, making me shiver, making the ache between my thighs more intense.

His grip in my hair loosened and slowly he pulled out of my mouth, tucking himself away. His hands shook as he did so and that gave me a thrill, too.

Hell, everything about him gave me a thrill.

Once he'd zipped himself back up, I leaned forward and rested my cheek against the warm skin of his stomach, feeling the rock-hard muscles of his abs tense and flex. His hands returned to my hair, combing through it, then massaging my scalp with firm, circular movements of his fingers.

It felt so good that I closed my eyes, enjoying his touch and the heat of his body, the scent of musk and spice that was all Tiger. But pretty soon I wanted those massaging fingers to touch me elsewhere and so I had to move.

Because I wasn't going to let him distract me again. That was exactly what he'd done with his blow job demands and we both knew it. He didn't want to talk about his mother, or about the fact that I'd offered to teach him to read, and, hell, I couldn't blame him. He was such a tough, strong guy and he must hate having his vulnerabilities exposed.

But I wanted to help him. I'd hated the look of pain in his eyes when he'd told me about his mother's disappearance and I wanted to make it better for him. Because I'd bet the entire, meagre contents of my bank account that he didn't have anyone else who wanted to help him the way I wanted to help him.

It was probably a good time to start asking myself why this was so important to me, but I decided I didn't want to answer that question right now. It was enough that I wanted to. Anyway, he'd brought me here and hidden me from Keep and from my dad, so helping him seemed the right thing to do.

After a moment of silence, I felt Tiger move, bending to lift me up into his arms, and I let him, loving his strength and the feeling of lying against his warm, bare chest. Loving how he held me as if I was made of glass and he had to be careful of me, gentle with me.

It made me feel special, which was a dangerous thing to feel, but I couldn't help it. I wanted to feel special to someone, since I'd never really been special to anyone, and this was as close as I was going to get.

I leaned my head against his shoulder and looked up at him. His golden eyes gleamed as they met mine and there was a very satisfied expression on his face. 'Did I do okay?' My voice was hoarse, probably due to him pressing against the back of my throat, and it felt a little raw.

'Do I really need to answer that?' He headed towards the armchair opposite the couch. 'You made me go fucking blind.'

'Oh.' There was a warm glow in the centre of my chest and I smiled, pleased with myself. 'You did have to show me what to do at the end, but next time I promise I'll do better.'

'If you do any better, you'll fucking kill me.' He sat down in the armchair and arranged me across his lap, keeping one arm around me so I could lie back against his shoulder, while with the other he toyed with the hem of the T-shirt I wore. 'I'm planning on some payback already.'

I shivered again at the heat in his voice. 'I'm sure you are. But that's not what we're doing now.'

'Oh?' One dark brow rose. 'And what exactly are we doing now?'

'What you promised. You told me if I made you come, we'd talk.'

He gazed at me from underneath this long, thick black lashes, dark amber gleaming. 'That was a dumb thing to say, wasn't it?'

'You were the one who said it.'

'Hmm.' His fingers stroked my bare knee. 'Fine, let's talk. Tell me why you're afraid all the time.'

I blinked, trying to ignore the light touch of his fingers on my bare skin and only just stopping myself from pulling a face. Talking about myself wasn't exactly what I'd planned. 'I don't know,' I said vaguely. 'It's just… I've always felt afraid of things.'

'Yeah, and that's not a fucking answer. Perhaps it'll become clearer if I do this.' His fingers slid higher, up the inside of my thigh.

I frowned at him. 'What did I say about distraction techniques?'

'Then answer my question.'

I sighed and looked down, raising a hand to trace his beautiful tattoos. I could see the tiger on his right arm, all strength and grace and ferocity. 'Did you design this one, too?' I touched the tiger's gleaming fangs that seemed to close around his shoulder.

'No. Got that when I patched in and the tattoo guy did it for me. Now you're being distracting.' His finger caught me under my chin and tipped my head back so I met his gaze. 'Come on, baby girl. Talk to me.'

'I don't know,' I said quietly. 'Maybe it was growing up in a house that feels like it's going to collapse at any second if you make a wrong move.'

'Why did it feel like that?'

'Oh, Dad. His moods. You never knew where you stood with him and you never knew what could set him off. He used to shout at me for no reason, and I hated it so I tried to keep out of his way as much as possible.' I swallowed, a familiar tense, anxious feeling gripping me. 'And my brother used to do the same thing.'

Tiger's dark brows drew down in a sudden, ferocious frown. Maybe that should have scared me, too, the way it always had whenever Dad had looked at me that way, but it didn't. Because this was Tiger, and sitting here in his arms I'd never felt safer in my entire life. 'Your brother. My buddy's old lady used to go out with him and he used to hurt her. He ever do that to you?'

I hadn't had much to do with Cat when she'd been with Justin so I didn't really know her. 'No, he didn't. I kept out of his way, the same way I kept out of Dad's.'

But Tiger's frown didn't lift. 'He fucking better not have laid a finger on you, get me? Because I'll kill him if he did.'

At first I thought Tiger was joking, but he wasn't smiling. Shit, he really would, wouldn't he?

I wrapped my fingers around his wrist. 'Don't kill my brother, Tiger. Please.'

He grunted, but the feral look in his eyes didn't waver. 'Just a warning.'

'Look, Dad and Justin didn't hurt me, so I'm not sure why I was even so scared.' Now I'd said it out loud, it all seemed so stupid. A lifetime of fear just because I didn't like my daddy shouting at me? How pathetic. 'They never did anything to me.'

'Fear doesn't come from nowhere, baby,' Tiger said fiercely. 'And being an abusive fuck doesn't necessarily mean punching the shit out of someone. Making you feel bad about yourself, making you feel scared, that's all abusive shit right there, and you know what? At least if someone hits you that's honest. At least you know where you stand. But with that kind of emotional bullshit, it's hard. You have no comeback and no way to protect yourself.'

I stared at him, suddenly thinking about all the things that Dad had said to me over the years, the jabs and criticisms, the subtle way he used my fear against me. 'He told me Mom left because of me,' I said hoarsely, not even realising I was going to mention it until the words came out. 'He said that I'd made him angry and that Mom didn't like it when he was angry and so she'd gone.' There was a lump in my throat and it felt tight and sore. I tried to turn my head away, feeling vulnerable and wishing I'd never spoken, but Tiger's grip on my chin tightened, holding me so I couldn't.

'Go on,' he growled.

I didn't want to, but there was something about his hot amber gaze on mine that felt reassuring. Even though it burned with anger, I knew the anger wasn't directed at me. It was for me. And I liked that. No one had ever been angry on my behalf before.

'He said that if I wanted her to come back,' I went on, even though it was painful to say it out loud, 'if I ever wanted to see her again, I'd better be a good girl and not make him mad.' I swallowed. 'I shouldn't have believed him. I don't know why I did. At the time I felt bewildered because I didn't know what I'd done to make him angry. All I knew was that I had to make up for it somehow, so I tried to be as good as I could be. And eventually I thought that if I made myself invisible, he wouldn't see me and if he couldn't see me, I wouldn't make him angry. And then maybe Mom would come home. It's stupid now I think about it, because how could Mom know if he was angry or not when she wasn't there? Anyway, I don't know why he said those things to me. Maybe he was simply angry about Mom leaving and didn't know what to do—'

Tiger's grip tightened, cutting me off. 'Don't excuse him,' he said, his voice hard. 'That was a terrible thing to say to you. No father worth the name blames his little girl for his own fuck-ups, no matter how goddamn angry he is.'

'It's okay,' I croaked, not wanting to make a fuss about it. 'Look, the whole being scared thing was my fault anyway. I'm kind of pathetic and emotional and—'

But Tiger cut me off again, sharp and hard. 'Is that what he told you?'

'No, of course not. But I know that I am and I—'

'It's *not* your fucking fault your mom left. Why do you still believe him? Why are you taking the blame?'

I stared at him, stunned. 'I'm not!'

'Yes, you are.' There was a fierce, angry light in his eyes. 'You're excusing him. You're saying you're pathetic and you're not. You're just fucking not. You're steel, baby. Coming down to the clubhouse, shoving Crash when he put the moves on you. Getting all up in my grille. Fuck, you wanna know how many people challenge me the way you did? Not one. No one would fucking dare.'

The way he said the words and the conviction in his voice did things to me. I hadn't thought I still blamed myself for the way Mom left. I *knew* it had simply been Dad's anger talking, but…

Realisation began to settle down inside me, and with it came pain. Because all my life my father had made me feel small and weak, and I'd *let* him.

Even when I told myself I hadn't believed the things he'd said all those years ago, there was still a small part of me that did.

A tear slid down my cheek and I didn't bother to wipe it away. 'Mom kissed me goodbye when she left. She said she'd see me again. Dad was always so angry afterwards, no matter how good I was. I wondered if I wasn't being good enough and some-how…she knew and…stayed away.'

The fierce light in Tiger's eyes didn't fade, yet somehow it became warmer. He'd kept that big, rough hand on my cheek, and now he brushed the tear away with his thumb, a gentle movement that pierced my heart straight through. 'You didn't drive her away, Summer,' he said, and that warmth was in his rough voice, too, wrapping me up like a velvet blanket. 'And you didn't keep her away either. Your father's an asshole for telling you that. I bet she left because she couldn't stand his shit, but honestly? She should never have left you behind in the first place.

She should have come back. She should have fought like a fucking demon to get you.'

I felt every one of those words hit me like sparks thrown from a fire. And they touched something cold in my heart that I hadn't known existed, igniting a warmth that hadn't been there before, thawing everything icy inside me.

Another tear slipped out, though I tried not to let it. 'We were supposed to be talking about you. Not me.'

'I prefer talking about you.' His thumb moved, brushing away a tear again. 'Don't let your dad affect how you feel about yourself, baby girl. The only power he has over you is the power you give him, so don't give it to him. And you can do that. You're stronger than you think. Jesus, if you can face down an MC enforcer like me, you can face down anyone.'

He was right. I knew it deep in my bones. Maybe the knowledge had always been there and I hadn't wanted to face it, because the thought of confronting my dad was scary. And not because of what he might do to me, but because of the way he could hurt me inside.

But Tiger seemed to see deeper into me than I saw myself. And if he thought I was strong, then maybe I actually was. He wasn't a guy who would lie or blow smoke. He didn't manipulate people. He told the truth.

I gave him a watery smile, leaning into the comfort of his palm against my skin. 'You're not that scary.'

'I'm pretty fucking tough.'

'Not as tough as you make out.' I put my hand over his where it rested on my cheek. 'Your mother didn't come back for you either, did she?'

His gaze flickered as I hit a nerve he didn't want touched. But I didn't look away and I kept my hand over his. I wanted him to know he could talk to me about that, that he could trust me. 'It's not the same,' he muttered eventually.

'Why not?'

'Your mom said goodbye to you.'

'So? Clearly that didn't stop me from blaming myself.'

'I don't blame myself.'

But he did, that was obvious. 'Tiger…'

He looked away. 'Come on, I'll make you breakfast. But don't forget I owe you one.'

'You owe me one what?'

'One orgasm.' His hold shifted and I found myself sliding off his lap and onto my feet.

Yeah, he really did *not* want to talk about his mother and I couldn't help the sharp spike of disappointment that slid under my skin. I'd laid myself open for him yet he wouldn't give me any of himself? It didn't seem fair.

He got to his feet and then, unexpectedly, reached for my hand and threaded his fingers through mine. His amber gaze was suddenly direct. 'I'll talk while I cook, okay?'

CHAPTER FOURTEEN

Tiger

TALKING TO SUMMER about my shitty past was something I definitely didn't want to do. But she'd looked so hurt that I couldn't seem to stop myself. If she wanted to hear it, then where would be the harm in telling her?

It was all in the past now anyway. It didn't have any fucking power over me.

I got Summer to sit on the stool at the counter that divided the rest of my space from the kitchen, while I opened the fridge and got out some eggs and bacon.

If she wanted to hear this shit, then I'd tell her while I cooked, give me something else to focus on. Of course I'd rather have given her the orgasm I owed her, but she clearly wasn't going to drop this until I'd given it to her.

You want to tell her, come on.

Well, okay, maybe I did. She'd been upfront with me about her asshole of a father and how he'd basically undermined her confidence, making her think she was to blame for her mother leaving. Making her scared of him.

It made me want to punch that fucker in the face so hard it was a good thing Summer was here to distract me with my own issues. Because I was definitely itching to get on my bike, take a trip down to the station and confront that asshole. Not a good idea, what with him being the police chief and all.

Trying to ignore the urge towards violence, I put some coffee in the coffee maker, then got a pan prepared for the eggs and bacon. I could feel her staring at my back, waiting for me to speak, and since this wasn't going to get any easier, plus the fact that I wasn't a fucking pussy, I just came out with it. 'No, Mom never came back for me. I never knew why she left. One day she was there, the next she was gone.'

'Did you…try to find her?'

'Yeah, but I was only sixteen. I wanted to go to the cops, see if they could find her, but I'd got a name for myself by that stage and I didn't want to draw attention. Plus…' I grimaced as I cracked the eggs into the pan. 'Mom was a whore. The cops don't want to involve themselves with that if they don't have to.'

'No, I understand,' she said quietly. 'So what did you do?'

'I'd already started prospecting for the Knights so they took me in, helped me out. Looked out for me. They became my family.'

'Do they know about the reading thing?'

I slapped some bacon down beside the eggs. 'No. Smoke's maybe guessed, but we've never talked about it. I can write my own name and sign shit, so that's not a problem. I can dictate texts on my phone and it reads them out to me, plus I can do the same with emails on the laptop. I've got a system worked out so it's fine.'

'But you never wanted to learn? Not once?'

I stared at the cooking food, pushing it around with a fork. I'd always told myself it didn't matter that I couldn't read. Sure, it was fucking annoying sometimes, but I'd managed to get through life without so far. Why bother learning when I was fine?

You know why you haven't learned.

'About a year after Mom left, I got a letter.' The words were out before I could stop them, and now they were out, there was nothing for it but to go on. 'It was addressed to me and I recognised the handwriting. It was from Mom. She'd tried when I was younger to teach me a few basics of the alphabet so I could recognise a few things, like my name and stuff. But I couldn't read a whole letter and she knew that.'

Behind me there was silence.

I pushed around the bacon again, watching it sizzle. Fuck. This was harder than I'd expected. 'I wanted to throw the fucking thing away, tear it up, but I didn't. I carried it around with me for months. I thought about getting someone to read it to me, but that would mean admitting I couldn't read it. Also I just...'

'You were angry at her.' Summer's voice was soft.

She's not wrong.

I gritted my teeth. Yeah, okay. Maybe I was. 'The next year I got another one and then another. I kept getting them. So now I've got this pile of letters upstairs and I still haven't read a fucking word.'

There was another long silence.

I flipped over the eggs and made sure the bacon didn't burn, trying not to think about those goddamn letters and how much I didn't want to know what was in them.

Because you don't want to know why she left in case it was *your fault.*

It wasn't my fault. I hadn't done a goddamn thing. *She* was the one who'd left *me*. Without a fucking word. Not even bothering to tell me where she was going and taking Tommy with her, too.

I used to tell myself I didn't care, that it didn't touch me. But of course it had. I'd never forgiven her, not after everything I'd tried to do for her. Protecting her from the pricks that would have hurt her, getting some part-time work under the table and giving her the cash for when things were tight, looking after Tommy so she could work…

Then she'd left. Thanks for nothing, Tiger.

The food was ready so I slid the eggs and bacon onto some plates and carried one over to her, getting out a knife and fork for her, too.

She gave me a quick glance as I put the silverware

down before glancing down at her plate. 'This looks delicious. I could read them for you, if you like.'

She said the last sentence in exactly the same tone as the first and I almost missed it. Then I heard. And I had to turn away, going for the coffee maker, because I didn't know what the fuck to say.

Okay, that was a lie. I knew.

'No.' I pulled out a couple of mugs from the shelf. 'I don't want to know.'

Another silence.

Then she said, 'I didn't think you were a coward, Tiger.'

I snapped my head around, a surge of anger going through me, and met her blue eyes. They were clear and direct, and didn't flinch away even though I must have been snarling. 'No one calls me a fucking coward,' I growled. 'No one.'

Her chin lifted a little. 'Then why haven't you got someone to read them to you?'

'Because I don't need to know what the fuck is in them.'

'Bullshit,' she said sternly. 'I think you do. I think you're desperate to know. But you're afraid of what you might find.'

'I'm not—'

'You're afraid you're to blame, aren't you?'

I don't know how she saw through me, right the way through to my goddamn shrivelled-up excuse for a soul, but she did. And this time I was the one who had to turn away, using making the coffee as an excuse not to have to deal with the look in her eyes.

'I know what it's like, Tiger,' she went on, clearly not picking up on my 'shut the hell up' vibes. 'I know what it's like to blame yourself. I mean, wasn't that what you told me about my own mother just now?'

I stalked over to the fridge for some cream. 'It's not the same.'

'You said that already. But it is. We both had people leave us and we both don't know why. God, at least your mother reached out to you. I would have given anything for a letter from mine.'

The wistfulness in her voice hit me like a hammer to the back of the head, making me stop dead.

You tool. Sulking over some fucking letters. She's right. You're being a pussy about this, not to mention selfish. At least you can find out what happened to your mom. She can't.

Slowly I resumed walking to the fridge, pulling it open and getting the cream out. Then I carried it over to the counter where I'd left the mugs of coffee and splashed some in. I stood there for a second looking down at the coffee mugs, my chest feeling tight. Wanting to put my fist through a wall or get on my bike or pull apart an engine or just carry Summer up to the bed and fuck her into the middle of next week.

Basically, do anything but think about those letters.

But they wouldn't let me alone and neither would

her accusation. Yeah, fuck. She was right. I *was* being a pussy about this.

'Tiger, is that the reason you never learned to read? So you didn't have to find out what was in those letters?'

I blinked down at the mugs, the question bouncing around inside me like a pinball in a machine, hitting things, lighting things up.

Fuck, was she right?

'No,' I growled, denying the thought and trying to make it sound less like the lie it was. 'What the hell kind of pussy would that make me?'

'It wouldn't make you a pussy at all.' She sounded very patient. 'That stuff is…hard. And you're trying to protect yourself.'

'I'm not a fucking kid,' I ground out, her tone irritating me. 'I'm not trying to protect myself. And I don't care why she left.'

'I think you do care,' she disagreed, unfazed by my shitty temper. 'Why else have you still got them? If you didn't care, you would have thrown that first letter away. But you didn't. You kept it. And then you kept all the rest, too.'

Jesus. Maybe she *was* right. Why *had* I kept them all this time? I didn't even know. I just knew that every time one came in the mail, I stuck it in the box with the others, closed it up and went on not thinking about them.

You kept them for a reason, douchebag.

Something curled up tight in my chest, a cold, uncomfortable feeling. It was familiar. The same one that had dogged me ever since I'd sat on my mother's bed in that empty apartment, listening for keys in the lock and the opening of the front door. Listening and hearing nothing but silence. Waiting all night for someone to come home, the cold feeling in my chest getting colder and colder, heavier and heavier as I realised that no one was coming home.

No one was ever coming home.

They'd left me and I didn't have the first fucking clue as to why.

So find out.

Ah, fuck.

'You told me that I wasn't to blame for my mom leaving,' Summer said after a moment. 'Which means that you can't blame yourself for yours.'

I shut my eyes, tension crawling along my shoulders.

Maybe I really was afraid of what those letters would tell me and not being able to read was just a convenient excuse. Whatever, she was right about one thing: I needed to know once and for all what had happened to Mom and Tommy, not pretend the issue didn't exist the way I'd been doing for the last fifteen years of my life.

Summer had been able to face the stuff to do with her father, so what the hell was my excuse? I was a goddamn enforcer for the Knights of Ruin MC. I was a badass motherfucker. Yet I didn't want to read a bunch of letters from my own mother?

Fucking hell. What a dick I was.

You could find out where they are. You could see them.

Yeah, that was maybe a step too far. I was too angry, no point in denying it now. *Fucking* angry. I'd been telling myself for years that she must have had her reasons for leaving, for not telling me where she was going, and that I was okay with it.

But I wasn't okay with it. I never had been.

And one thing was for sure; I'd never be okay with it until I found out the truth of why she'd left and put the whole goddamn issue behind me once and for all.

I opened my eyes, picked up the mugs and strode over to where Summer sat, putting one down beside her. She watched me, her food untouched, blue eyes full of concern. Full of caring.

She shouldn't look at me like that. I wasn't her business.

'Eat,' I growled. 'And then you can read me those fucking letters.'

She blinked. 'Are you sure?'

'No. But you're right. I've got the chance to at least find out why she left so I should take it.'

Her expression softened, her mouth curving into the most beautiful fucking smile. Christ, she was like sunshine, sitting there in my shitty apartment, about to eat the meal I'd cooked for her. A ray of perfect sunshine, lighting the whole place up, making it brighter than it was before.

Making everything brighter than it was before.

That cold feeling in my chest began to fade away, melting like goddamn snow, leaving behind it heat.

I wanted to pull her across the counter, put my mouth on her, taste her sweetness. Have all that sunshine on me, covering me. Get it inside me somehow, so that cold feeling would never come back.

Dangerous, dumbass. She's not for you.

No, she wasn't.

But maybe for the next few hours she could be.

CHAPTER FIFTEEN

Summer

THE BREAKFAST TIGER cooked me was delicious and as we ate, he asked me about the job offer I had from the tech firm in Silicon Valley. I went on and on about it—probably way too long—but he seemed interested so I kept talking.

It was just so good to have someone interested in hearing what I had to say, someone who wasn't one of my professors, that I couldn't seem to shut myself up. And then he started asking about what I'd been studying at college and that was it, I started running at the mouth like a stuck faucet.

My head was telling me to shut the hell up, that he couldn't possibly be interested in all the math crap since it went over most people's heads, but he didn't tell me to shut the hell up. He didn't tell me it was boring and no one wanted to hear about it the way Dad did. No, it was the opposite. He seemed to get it, the fascination I had with numbers and the way they fit together.

I found myself describing equations and the excitement I got with solving them the way Dad talked about baseball, and Tiger's eyes didn't glaze over. And he didn't walk away. He asked questions, and even though I was pretty sure he didn't understand my answers, his mind seemed to work enough like mine that he grasped the basics of what I was saying.

More than that, he even seemed interested, offering his own perspective in the form of mechanics and the way he fixed engines. They were puzzles to him and I could see by the light in his eyes as he spoke that he loved solving those puzzles as much as I did.

It was so strange meeting someone who thought the way you did. Who was so different from you in every way on the surface, but underneath...

He was talking about how he'd got into fixing things, doing stuff with his hands since he was good at it and enjoyed doing something he was good at, and the spark in his eyes, in his whole face as he talked made my heart tighten.

Made it kick hard.

He was such an interesting man. Despite the biker macho stuff, he was articulate and thoughtful. And he listened to me, really listened.

This is all very bad news.

But I didn't want to think about that. I didn't want to think about what made my heart kick when I looked at him. I didn't want to think about what it might mean. In just a few days I would be flying to the West Coast and away from him, so there was no point letting myself hope for something that was never going to happen.

Better to enjoy this moment while I could.

We finished up breakfast and I helped him stack the plates in the dishwasher—or at least I tried. He chased me away and wouldn't let me, efficiently taking care of the dishes and mugs and wiping everything down.

I wanted to tease him about being a neat freak but suddenly remembered what I'd promised him after breakfast was over.

The letters he'd received from his mom. The ones he'd kept yet never read.

The ones that for some reason he was going to let me read to him.

I'd felt guilty about pushing him, especially when it was so obvious he didn't want to even think about those letters. But the stuff he'd said about me blaming myself for the way my own mother had left had stuck with me, making me wonder if he felt the same. But then, I *knew* he did. Why else would he be short-tempered about it every time I mentioned it? Why else would he be so angry?

And he *was* angry. I could see it in every line of his body.

This was a painful subject for him and me pushing him to deal with it probably hadn't helped.

As he finished up dealing with breakfast, he

pointed at the couch. 'You go sit there. I'll go get the damn letters.'

So I went over to the couch and sat down while he went upstairs. He was up there awhile and I was starting to think that maybe I'd been wrong to push him. That my need to help him solve this puzzle had been a selfish one.

But then there was something inside me that knew he wasn't going to be able to get rid of the anger I'd seen in him, the pain, until he found out what was in those letters. I wanted him to get rid of the stuff that was hurting him. I wanted to help him be okay, the way he was helping me.

And maybe that *was* selfish, but if it helped him, then where was the harm?

He eventually came back down the stairs, holding a small cardboard box in his hands. His strongly carved features were a mask, but fire raged in his amber eyes.

He didn't give the box to me, merely set it on the coffee table in front of the couch, then he stood there with his arms folded across his broad inked chest. Radiating aggressiveness. He probably didn't realise that was what he was doing, but I could feel the tension and the anger pouring off him all the same.

As if this was a threat he was having to face down.

'Go on,' he said roughly. 'Take a look.'

I moved forward and grabbed the box, sitting back on the couch again. 'Do you want me to read it myself first, then read it out to you?'

'No.' The word was flat. 'I'm done running from this shit.'

He was scared, wasn't he? That was why he was so aggressive and so angry. He was scared about what was in those letters and what they would say.

It made my heart hurt for him. Made me angry at the woman who'd walked out and left her own son without even a word.

Well, there was no need to drag this out any longer than it needed to be.

Taking a breath, I opened the box and looked down. Neatly stacked inside were a bunch of yellowing envelopes. The one on the top was obviously the most recent one, judging by the date stamped on it, so I dug through the rest to get to the bottom of the pile and the first letter. Then I drew it out.

It had Tiger's name on it—Jake Clarke—and my hands shook a little as I opened the envelope and got out the letter inside.

I wanted to check there was nothing in there that might hurt him before I read it aloud, but he was standing there watching me, his golden eyes like a laser beam boring into me, and I knew I had to do what he said, to read out loud straight off.

"'Jake…'" I said, slowly reading out the tangled-up handwriting on the page. "'I know I took a long time to write this, and I know you probably won't be able to read it, but I have to tell you this. My conscience won't let me run away from it any more. I'm still a coward, though, writing a letter to you that I know you won't be able to read. But there's a reason for that.'"

I paused and swallowed, not daring to look at Tiger standing on the other side of the coffee table.

"'I had to leave, darling boy. And I couldn't tell you that I was going. It wasn't an easy decision to make, but I knew I had to do it. Protecting me, helping me, wasn't doing what was best for you. You deserved more than having to protect me all the time. You deserved more of a life than that. I should have told you I was going. I know I should have. But I was afraid you'd come after me. I was afraid you'd try to find me and I couldn't let you do that. So I took Tommy and I left. I wished he was old enough to stay with you, so he didn't have to be with me, but I couldn't let you have to be responsible for him, too. That wasn't the life I wanted for either of you. I'm sorry, Jake. I'm sorry I—'"

I broke off as, without a word, Tiger suddenly turned around, strode to the door of the warehouse, flung it open and walked through it.

My throat closed up tight, my eyes prickling with tears. I wanted to go to him to see if he was okay, but I wasn't sure I should. This wasn't my pain. It was his, and I didn't know whether that revelation had helped him or made it worse.

Was this the blame that he'd worried about? But it hadn't been anything he'd done. It was all his mother wanting to protect him. Sure, she'd used the most hurtful method possible, but it made sense in a twisted kind of way. I could see Tiger taking off after her, trying to find her. Not resting until he had.

But she'd wanted him to have a life. And this had clearly been the only way she could give it to him.

My heart clenched hard. I knew I shouldn't go after him, that this should be a private moment. But I wanted him to know that he wasn't alone. He'd been alone since his mother had left him—and, no, I didn't count his club because I couldn't see him sitting around with a bunch of bikers chatting about his pain—and I wanted him to know that I was here. That I knew a little of what it felt like. That I understood.

That he wasn't alone this time. He had me.

So I put the box back on the table and I stood up. And even though it was scary to intrude on something so deeply personal, I went after him. He'd chosen me to read those letters to him and that meant something, didn't it?

I walked over to the front door of the warehouse and peered outside. There was an enclosed concrete courtyard with other buildings on all sides and an entranceway just off the street. Tiger was standing in the middle of the courtyard with his back to me, his head bent, his arms at his sides and his hands in fists.

His body radiated tension and anger, and I couldn't stand leaving him there on his own. I closed the distance between us and I put a hand on his bare back, where some of those geometric tattoos overflowed from his shoulder and down to one shoulder blade.

His whole posture went even more tense, but he didn't move and he didn't say anything. And neither did I. I remained quiet and kept my hand on his back, letting him know I was here.

'I tried to think of what I'd done so many times.' His voice was so rough it hardly sounded like him. 'I went over and over that last day, that last week, thinking over what I'd done. Wondering. But there was nothing unusual. I remember just before I left the house that day, she kissed me on the forehead. She never did shit like that, because I didn't like it. But she did that day.'

I spread my hand out and pressed harder, giving him my presence and my warmth, his muscles still vibrating with tension.

'It was my fault in the end, though,' he went on. 'She *did* leave because of me. And she didn't even give me a choice about it.'

The note of pain in his voice got to me, burrowed inside me and stuck there like a thorn. I couldn't stop myself. I took my hand from his back and wound my arms around his waist, laying my cheek against his spine, inhaling his warmth and giving him back some of mine. 'No,' I said fiercely. 'It wasn't your fault. She left because she wanted what was best for you. I don't agree with her decision to leave without telling you, but it was her decision and there was nothing you could have done about it. She didn't leave because she didn't love you, Tiger. She left because she did.'

He didn't move, his strong back tense as a board. 'She wanted me to have a life.' There was bitterness tinging his words. 'But what did I do? I got into the MC. I fix motorcycles. That's it. What fucking life is that? I can't even goddamn read.'

I gripped him tighter. 'That's a hell of a life. You have a family of guys who look out for you and you do the work you love. Who else gets to do that? Who else gets to live the way they want? With no rules or restrictions? Isn't that what you love about the MC? You do what you like. You live free and fix bikes, solve puzzles. Sounds like a hell of a life to me.'

He said nothing for a long time, his muscles like steel beneath my cheek. Then his hands came down over mine where they were clasped on his taut stomach and he pushed them away. I let him, thinking he wanted distance.

But then he turned around sharply and before I could move, his arms were around me and he was pulling me close, holding me against his hard, hot body. He turned his face into my hair and for a long moment he just stood there, keeping me tight in his arms.

I trembled, breathless. Hurting for him. Wanting to help him. So I raised my arms and put them around his neck and simply held him the way he was holding me.

For long moments we stood there, not saying a word, holding each other. And I closed my eyes, taking the moment to be with him. To inhale his scent and feel the strength of his arms around me, to feel the need in them, too. I didn't think he was a man who would ever accept comfort, but again he surprised me, squeezing me tight.

Then suddenly his head turned and his mouth was against my neck and he bit me. Not hard, but it sent an electric shock of sensation straight down my spine, making me gasp and shudder.

'I want you to fuck me,' he murmured against my skin. 'I want you to fuck me hard, and I want you to fuck me rough. Can you do that, baby girl?'

His words were a straight out aphrodisiac, firing directly between my thighs, making all the feelings that had gripped me as I'd given him that blow job come flooding back.

His hold on me shifted, his hands curving down under the hem of the T-shirt I wore, reminding me acutely that I had nothing on underneath it. His palms were hot against the bare skin of my butt as his finger curled around each cheek, squeezing me hard, pulling me against the front of his body, his hips flexing as he ground his pelvis against mine.

'Well?' he demanded, and there was a raw note that slid into me, gripping on as tightly as his hands on my ass.

'Yes,' I whispered, my voice as raw as his. 'Yes, I'll fuck you.'

He didn't say anything more. Instead he lifted me up as easily as he had the night before and carried me back into the warehouse. He didn't stop at the couch this time, carrying me straight up the stairs to the mezzanine floor where his big wide bed was.

Then set he set me down on it and stood back, undoing the zipper of his jeans with one hand as he stared down at me, his golden eyes burning. Heat and anger and pain and desire, all mixed together. He stood there almost arrogantly, unzipping his fly, his cock hard and ready as he pushed the denim down his narrow hips. My breath caught, watching the play of all that chiselled muscle and smooth skin. He wanted me to fuck him hard and rough…

I didn't know if I could do that. Could I?

Well, it didn't matter if I could or not. If that was what he wanted, what he needed, then that was what I'd give him. God knew, I didn't have much of anything else to give.

He stepped out of his jeans, naked and strong and so beautiful I could hardly breathe. Then he moved over to where I sat and he pulled the T-shirt off me so I was naked, too. He pushed me back on the bed and came down onto it with me, crouching above me on all fours, just like the tiger that prowled up his arm. Hungry and feral and predatory.

I put my hands up, pressing my palms to his hard, hot chest. 'I thought I was going to be the one to fuck you hard,' I said unsteadily.

His mouth curved in a smile that had nothing to do with amusement, all challenge and fire and not a bit of desperation. 'So do it, baby girl.'

That desperation switched something on inside me,

something aggressive I hadn't known was there. He wanted me. He wanted *me*. I'd been worried about whether I could handle him and I had. I damn well had.

Now I wanted to make him wonder whether or not he could handle *me*.

So I shoved at him—hard. 'On your back, big boy.'

His smile deepened and this time there was definitely a hint of amusement in it. 'Big boy?'

I ignored him, shoving at him again. 'If you don't get on your back, you don't get any p-pussy.' Which would have sounded hotter if I hadn't stuttered over the word, or blushed like a teenager, but, hell, I'd said it. My first dirty talk. Yay me.

Still grinning, he pushed himself away from me and turned over on his back, putting his hands behind his head like he was lying on a beach. 'Here I am. Doing what you say. Where's my pussy then?'

I sat up and before I could second-guess myself, I straddled him, easing my sex up against the hard ridge of his cock. It was long and thick and as hot as he was and it made me shiver. 'Here's your pussy.' I put my hands on the pillows on either side of his head, looking down into his fascinating eyes, the tips of my nipples brushing against his chest. Then I shifted my hips. 'Can you feel it?'

Golden flames leapt in his gaze and I heard the breath go out of him, and that was as massive a turn-on as the pressure of his cock against my sex.

'Oh, yeah,' he breathed, all thick and intense. 'I feel it. Give me more.'

There was something amazingly powerful about having this tall strong, muscled and dangerous biker underneath me. Looking at me like there was nothing and no one else in the entire world. Looking at me like he'd die if he didn't have me right there and then.

It made me want to play with him. He might want it hard and rough, but he was going to have to wait first.

I flexed my hips again, rubbing myself against him, feeling the line of pleasure pull taut inside me, a dragging sensation that made me want to pant.

'Yeah,' he whispered, staring up at me like I was the sun and he'd spent a lifetime in the dark. 'Just like that. More, baby girl.'

I held his gaze, lowering my head so my hair curtained us, falling over his shoulders. He tried to lift up to kiss me, but I pulled back, tantalising him. His beautiful mouth curved again, like he knew exactly what I was doing and approved. So I shifted my hips once more, giving him back a taste of what he'd given me the night before in his room. The night that felt like so long ago but really wasn't.

He made a deep noise in his throat as I ground myself against him, moving along that delicious hard ridge, rubbing my clit against it, panting and gasping in response. 'You like that?' I heard myself say. 'You like this pussy against your hard cock?'

'What do you think?' He lifted his head impatiently, trying to kiss me, but I pulled away again, brushing my nipples against his chest, tantalising him even more.

'Not yet.' I let my mouth hover bare inches above his. 'Beg me for a kiss and I might give you one.'

But of course he cheated. He lifted his head and took that kiss anyway, his mouth hard and demanding. His hands were on my hips, pressing me more insistently against him, his pelvis lifting against mine. And for a second I fell into the kiss, into the heat of him, letting him do whatever he wanted.

'Condom,' he murmured against my mouth. 'Now.'

I knew where they were, having watched him put more than a couple on himself the night before. So I reached over the side of the bed to the small nightstand and pulled open the drawer. He stroked me as I did, one hand curving around my butt, the other finding my breast and flicking my nipple with his thumb.

I shuddered as I pulled the packet out, his touch making the breath catch in my throat and sensation spread like wildfire over my skin. I sat back, ripping open the foil and taking out the condom.

He watched me from beneath black lashes, his gaze hotter than that wildfire sweeping over me. It filled me with power, made me feel like I could do anything, so I didn't freak out that I hadn't put a condom on a guy before. I didn't doubt myself. It was a puzzle to be solved and I solved it simply by putting it on him and rolling the latex down with my hands.

He made another of those deep, delicious sounds in his throat, lifting his hips up into my hands, making it obvious how much he liked my touch. It was such a thrill I wanted to do it again and again, wring some more of those sounds from him.

But there was something I wanted more.

Him. Inside me. Hard and deep and rough like he wanted.

I grabbed his cock, meeting his gaze, holding it. 'You want this pussy?' I teased him, rubbing the head of his dick against the throbbing flesh between my thighs, making him sweat.

'Fuck, yes.' His voice was rough, guttural. 'Do it. Give it to me.'

I gave him a slow, sensual smile and squeezed him. 'Say please.'

His breath hissed. 'You fucking tease. I love it.' He lifted his hips, trying to arch up into me, and I squeezed him again, making him groan. 'Please, baby girl. Please fuck me. *Now.*'

God, he was *so* hot. His desperation was such a turn-on that abruptly I lost interest in teasing him, wanting him inside me.

So I lifted myself up and guided him inside, both of us shuddering as I slid down on him, feeling the delicious stretch of him inside me, the burn as he filled me. He was big and I loved it, the intensity of the sensation making me gasp as he impaled me completely.

I put my hands on his chest, balancing myself, his fingers on my hips, digging in. I looked into his eyes, saw the heat, the need there, and knew he saw the same in mine. The connection was intense and made me tremble, but I didn't look away. He wanted this hard and rough, and he was going to get it.

His hands tightened, but I shook my head. 'No. Let me figure it out.'

'Don't know if I can wait that long.' His lips peeled back in a feral grimace. 'I need you fucking me right now.'

Digging my nails into his chest, I moved experimentally, watching the expression of agonised pleasure cross his face as I did so.

'Oh, yeah, Jesus. Keep doing that.'

I kind of wanted not to, to do something different to shock him, but it felt too good and I was rapidly getting to the point where I wanted the pleasure of him as much as he wanted the pleasure of me.

So I did what he liked, again and again, finding a rhythm that made us both groan. A slow rise and fall, the feeling of his cock sliding in and out making me shiver and shake. I spread my hands out on his chest, moving faster, harder, and he gave me a savage grin. 'Fuck, yes. Ride me, baby girl. Show me what you got.'

So I showed him. Riding him even faster, lifting myself up and slamming myself down on him, digging my nails into his chest so I left little circles on his flesh. Marking him. And he did the same to me with his hands on my hips, holding me so tightly he was going to leave bruises.

I wanted those bruises. I wanted those marks. I

wanted to be branded by this time with him. So I'd carry it with me when I flew away from him and into the new life I was going to have.

So I'd never forget.

Not that I needed those marks.

I'd never forget Tiger. Never. Not as long as I lived.

My heart was thundering in my head and I was moving rhythmically. The slick glide of him inside me driving us both out of our minds. In. Out. Up. Down.

Harder. Faster. The sounds of his flesh slamming into mine and the gasping of our breath echoing around us.

So good. So good.

I fucked him as hard and as rough as I could, and I looked into his eyes the whole time. And I saw the moment he came, golden fire exploding, the roar of my name shuddering against the ceiling.

Then he put his hand between my thighs and pressed down hard on my clit, bringing me into the flames with him.

CHAPTER SIXTEEN

Tiger

I LAY ON the bed, panting and fucking destroyed. Because that was what she'd done to me. She'd destroyed me. She'd done exactly what I told her to, fucked me hard and rough, and now I wasn't sure I'd ever be the same again.

She'd collapsed on top of me, her soft hair all over my chest, and I could still feel her hot little pussy squeezing my cock. Christ, she was amazing. Everything about her was amazing. I wanted to hold her tightly to me, never let her go. She was mine, which was a fucking weird thought since I'd never had it before about anyone.

She knew about my past, about my mother. And she'd been the one to read that letter to me, discovering right along with me the real reason Mom had left.

That had been the hardest thing to hear. To know that Mom had gone to protect me. To give me a fucking life, as if I didn't have one already. I'd been full of nothing but anger in that moment, because it *had* been my fault she'd gone. And if she'd given me the choice, I would have told her not to go, that the decisions about my life were mine to make, not hers. But, no, she'd taken the choice from me. She'd decided to leave me without even talking to me first and I'd wanted to smack something so bad I hadn't been able to think straight.

I'd had to walk out, to leave before I did something stupid and frightened Summer.

I hadn't expected Summer to come after me. To follow and put a hand on my back. Her warmth had been astonishing and her voice calm.

Then she'd put her arms around me, her warmth soaking into me, and it was the strangest fucking thing. No one had ever given me a hug before, not since Mom left, and it made me feel... Christ, I don't even know. Like I wanted to melt back into her. She'd felt strong at my back and it was as if she was giving me a piece of her own strength, filling up something that had always felt hollow and empty before.

Jesus, how had she ever thought of herself as weak? I was the one who was weak and now she was making me strong.

I hadn't wanted to talk about it any more right then. I'd just wanted her.

Fucking hell, I'd never wanted anything so badly in my life.

Then she'd given me more than strength. She'd given me the fire that I knew was inside her, that burning blue spark. Riding me like I was her favourite stallion. So fucking hot.

I hadn't realised what I was missing—that I'd been missing anything at all, in fact—until she'd put her hands on my chest and looked down into my eyes. Holding my gaze as she'd fucking taken me to heaven and back.

Hot and fierce and bright. That was Summer. And I wanted more.

I tightened my arms around her.

She's yours now.

Yeah, she was. She just fucking was. And suddenly it didn't feel weird. It felt right, like it was meant to be somehow.

Keep would probably be after me by now and I thought I'd better check in with him. No, it was going to be more than a check in. It was going to be a fucking full-on denial. There was no way I'd let Summer anywhere near her father. Anywhere near *anyone* who could hurt her.

I was going to protect her until it was time for her to fly out west to her new job and her new life, and if anyone tried to stop her they'd have to answer to me.

I rolled onto my side, taking her with me. Then I pushed her onto her back, sifting her beautiful hair through my fingers. Felt like fucking silk. 'I need to go check in with Keep,' I murmured. 'Don't worry, I won't mention you're here. I'll hide you until it's time to get your flight and then I'll take you to the airport myself.'

Her brow creased, an expression I couldn't quite catch flashing over her face. 'Are you sure? You'd really lie to your president for me?'

'Nothing I haven't done already, baby girl.'

'But your club—'

I put a finger over her mouth, silencing her. 'Leave the club to me. It's my thing, I'll handle it, okay?'

'Okay.' Yet that worried look didn't leave her eyes. 'Tiger, I'm sorry. I don't want to make things difficult for you.'

'Yeah, I know. But that's not your decision to make. It's mine. And I'm making it right now.'

Another flicker of expression across her lovely face. 'Okay,' she said again, sounding reluctant. 'But you know, if there's anything—'

I shut her up by kissing her, sliding my tongue into her mouth so she couldn't speak. And then she didn't want to anyway, giving a little groan and tipping her head back, encouraging me to kiss her deeper, harder.

I growled, because I wanted to. But I had to deal with Keep first.

Giving her a nip, I lifted my head and gently disengaged myself from her, rolling away to deal with the condom in the nearby wastebasket. 'I need to call Keep.' I turned and gave her a look from over my shoulder. 'Don't go anywhere, okay? And definitely don't get dressed. I have plans for you.'

She flushed, which was straight out weird considering what she'd done to me not two minutes ago, but

I was fucking delighted all the same. I was already getting hard thinking of all the other dirty ways I was going to make her come today.

Christ, suddenly two days with her didn't seem enough.

I pulled on my jeans and grabbed my phone, taking it downstairs so I wouldn't stress her out. Then I hit Keep's number.

He answered it almost immediately. 'Where the fuck have you been and why aren't you answering my goddamn calls?'

'I've been out looking for the chief's daughter, just like you wanted, Prez,' I lied without even a twinge of guilt. 'And, no, I haven't found her yet. Anyone else?'

'No,' Keep said curtly. 'Chief's getting fucking pissed, put out a few APBs, all kinds of shit. You don't have a number for her or anything?'

'Why? Because I did some protection for her? That was five years ago. Fuck only knows what's up with her now.'

Keep grunted. 'Yeah, okay. Well, keep your eyes open.'

He ended the call without another word, but I didn't lose any sleep over it. I had no problem with protecting Summer. None at all. And it was kind of weird to think that I didn't. Because it meant that she had become more important to me than the club, which was a worry, but I decided I wasn't going to let that get to me. I could deal with that later, once she'd got safely away. Right now, I had other things to do.

Like making her come some more.

We spent the rest of the day in bed, pausing only for a lunch break and then some sleep in the afternoon. I woke her up after that, flipping her over onto her stomach and pulling her up on her hands and knees. Then I ate her out from behind, making her come a couple of times, before pulling those slender hips up against mine and sliding deep inside her quivering little pussy.

It was hard and it was raw and I made her scream. Then I made her scream some more before I let myself go, pushing her down and slamming her into the mattress over and over until I was blind with the fucking ecstasy of it.

I got her up after that and took her into the shower again, soaping her down, loving the feel of her leaning against me as if she couldn't stand upright on her own, knowing it was me who'd made her feel that.

Afterwards I made her dinner and we sat at the counter and talked about nothing in particular. I liked hearing her talk about her new job and about her interest in math. It all went over my head—she was so fucking smart it kind of astounded me—but she explained everything in such an easy way it was almost as if I could grasp it. She talked about her life at college and then, when she got sick of talking about herself, she began to ask me about life at the club and what it was like.

I was honest with her, didn't gloss over the stuff that wasn't great, but she seemed to get how important the club was to me. How like a family it was. How my brothers truly were like brothers.

After I'd given her a rundown on one of our wilder parties, making her blue eyes go round and her cheeks pink, I took her over to the workshop and showed her a few of the bikes I was in the process of fixing. She was right into it, peering at everything and asking me questions, wanting to know how things worked.

I'd never explained any mechanical shit to a woman before, let alone one who was so interested. She even sat down beside me, watching and getting me to explain what I was doing, making comments and asking yet more questions.

I didn't much like it when people talked at me while I was working, but with Summer I found I didn't care. In fact, I liked it. I liked that she was interested in something that interested me, too, and that it was all completely genuine. There wasn't a fake bone in her body, not one.

A couple of hours passed like that and it was... good. Just fucking good.

Later, I got us both beers and sat on the couch with her in my lap, talking about nothing. Talking about everything.

I was so deep in discussion with her about something she called game theory that I didn't even hear the distinctive rumble of a hog in the courtyard outside. All I knew was that one minute we were alone and talking, the next the door of my warehouse had been kicked open and Keep was there, striding inside with Smoke following along behind him.

For a second Summer and I just stared at them in shock, because what the actual fuck? Then she stiffened in my lap, making a soft, distressed sound.

And I acted without thought.

Pushing her off my lap, I shoved her behind me, then stood up, putting myself between my president and my best buddy, and her.

Keep stopped not far from me, his blue eyes glittering and full of rage. 'What the fuck do you think you're doing?' he demanded, coming straight out with it.

I met him stare for fucking stare. 'I could ask you the same thing.'

Stupid question. There was only one reason he was here and she was sitting on the couch behind me, dressed only in my T-shirt.

A sudden rush of possessiveness filled me. I didn't want these assholes looking at her. I didn't want them even glancing in her direction, so I adjusted my stance, blocking her from them as much as I could. 'What the fuck, Prez?' I decided to go on the attack, since there was no point denying Summer's presence here. 'I'm just having a quiet beer with—'

'The chief of police's daughter,' Keep finished, hard and cold. 'The one you told me you were out looking for.'

Summer started to say something, but I held up my hand sharply to let her know that her talking right now was a very bad idea.

Luckily she seemed to get it and stayed quiet.

'I didn't tell him,' Smoke said from his position behind Keep, his dark gaze meeting mine. 'Crash let it slip this afternoon that she'd been at the party yesterday. We came to ask you where she was.'

Rage turned over inside me. Crash. Of course. That fucking asshole. I thought he hadn't known who she was but clearly he had. 'Why?' I demanded. 'He want some brownie points from you, Prez?'

'Doesn't matter why.' There was nothing but ice in Keep's voice. Always a very bad fucking sign. 'You knew who she was. You knew she was nothing but trouble for the fucking club, and not only did you *not* tell me you had her, you've been fucking her, too, from the looks of things.' The glitter in his eyes got even colder. 'You lied to me, Tiger.'

Aggression poured through my veins. Because he was right, I'd done those things. I'd lied to my president. I'd broken his trust. I'd created a potentially volatile situation for my club, one we really didn't need right now.

I'd fucked up.

And I didn't even care.

There was only one thing I did care about right in that moment and she was sitting right behind me.

The truth of it hit me so fucking hard that I couldn't speak but I knew.

It was her. It was Summer. She was mine.

And I wasn't giving her up, not to anyone.

'Yeah, I did.' I didn't bother keeping the edge out of my voice. 'I did lie to you. But I did it to protect her.'

Keep's expression hardened. 'I don't give a fuck why you did it. That doesn't change the fact that you did.' The look on his face got even meaner. 'I got no room in my club for an officer who lies to his president. I got no patience with that shit.'

'Prez—' Smoke began.

But Keep gave a jerk of his head, silencing him. 'You want to make things right, Tiger?' His blue gaze was squarely on mine. 'You take her to Grant right the fuck now.'

I didn't make the mistake of thinking this wasn't the flat-out choice that it was. Basically, it was her or the club. The club that'd looked out for me, been there for me, that'd been my family since my mom left. Or a woman I'd only really known a matter of days, yet who'd somehow lit up my life in a way no one else ever had.

I didn't even have to think. I already knew my choice.

'No,' I said flatly 'She stays with me.'

Keep smiled and it wasn't a nice smile. It was his 'don't fuck with the president' smile. 'You're seriously going to choose her? Over your club?'

Smoke was silent, giving me a strange look that seemed a whole lot like understanding.

But I couldn't deal with that now. There was only Keep and the knowledge that if he took one step towards the woman behind me, I was going to punch his fucking head in. Which would be crossing a line.

I couldn't come back from that and I knew it. But again, I didn't give a shit. Protecting her was more important. *She* was more important.

More important than the club. More important than me.

More important than any damn thing.

So I put my shoulders back and my hands curled into fists, and I stared at Keep, daring him to come at me. To touch what was fucking mine.

And the tension in the warehouse wound so tight with violence it was a wonder the whole fucking thing didn't explode.

Then there came a sound from behind me, and suddenly Summer was coming around me, putting herself between me and Keep.

'Summer,' I began, reaching out for her. 'What the fuck are you—'

'I'll go with you,' she said flatly, not even looking at me, all her attention on Keep. 'If you want me to go, I'll go right now.'

CHAPTER SEVENTEEN

Summer

I STOOD THERE looking into the cold blue eyes of the Knights of Ruin's president and I'd never felt so terrified in all my stupid life. But I'd known from the moment he'd stormed into Tiger's warehouse that this was what I had to do.

I couldn't let Tiger take the fall for me. I couldn't let him choose between the club that was his entire family and me, a woman he hadn't known for very long. After all, this had all been my fault. I was the one who'd run to the clubhouse. I was the one who'd asked him to keep me hidden. Sure, it had been his choice to hide me, but I was the one who'd put him in this position in the first place.

So no. He wasn't going to have to choose.

It was time for me to face the consequences of what I'd done.

It was time for me to face my father.

'Don't you dare,' Tiger said from behind me. 'Don't you fucking dare, Summer.'

I could feel his heat and then suddenly he was gripping my upper arms and turning me to face him. His gaze was full of angry flames, his expression burning with intensity. 'Don't say a fucking word,' he growled. 'In fact, get your ass up the stairs and don't come down until I say.'

I knew he was trying to protect me. I could see it in his eyes. And there was a very large part of me that wanted to do exactly what he said.

But I wasn't going to.

If I didn't do this right now, if I didn't face my fear of my father, it would dog me for the rest of my life. And who knew who else it would involve? Who knew who else would get hurt? It had hurt Tiger already, I knew it had, and I couldn't stand it. I *wouldn't* stand it.

So I simply stared back at him, letting him see that I wasn't going to back down on this. 'Let me go, Tiger.'

'No.' His fingers tightened, the look in his eyes blazing. 'You're fucking mine now. You're not going anywhere.'

My heart threw itself against my ribs, because there was nothing more I wanted in that moment than to be his. No one had ever wanted me the way he did. No one had ever said it out loud, with other people watching, claiming me for themselves.

I wanted to say 'Okay, I'm yours' so badly I could taste it.

But I couldn't. I didn't want him to have to choose. I didn't want him to have to deal with the consequences of my own cowardice.

He deserved better than that.

He deserves better than you.

The thought whispered through my head and I knew it was true. Because even if all this stuff with Keep hadn't happened, nothing changed the fact that I would be leaving him soon anyway, flying thousands of miles away from him permanently.

I couldn't stay. I wasn't part of his world and I never would be, and I was tired of being where I didn't fit. Where I was invisible.

I wanted to take the job, create a life of my own, and even though the thought of him coming with me made me light-headed with happiness, I knew I couldn't ask him to. Again, I didn't want him to have to choose between me and the life and the family he'd built here for himself. And I didn't want to have to leave him like his mother had left him.

'I'm not.' I struggled to keep my voice level. 'I have to go, Tiger. I *have* to.'

'No, you don't.' His fingers tightened even more, pulling me up against him, his grip almost painful. 'Stay here. I'll protect you.'

'I don't want you to protect me.' My throat felt tight and dry, my body beginning to blaze in response to the heat of his so close. 'I have to face Dad. I can't run away from him any more.'

'I'll come with you. I'll make sure—'

'No,' I cut him off sharply, meeting his gold gaze. 'I have to do it on my own. This is my issue to deal with, not yours.'

He growled, full on, like the big cat prowling up his arm, jerking me even closer to him. Then he bared his teeth, trying to intimidate me. 'Fuck you. Your issues are mine now and I'll help you deal with them whether you like it or not.'

'If I don't do this now, on my own, I'll always be scared.' I kept my gaze on his, willing him to understand. 'I'll always be hiding. I have to face him and I have to do it without you.'

He was silent a long moment, staring at me. 'But you'll come back. And we'll have the last few days together, right?'

My throat closed up and there was a weight on my chest, so heavy.

The last few days. All two of them.

It's not enough.

No, it wasn't. There would never be enough time in the whole world to be with Tiger. I didn't want two days. I wanted forever. But would he? Sure, he wanted to protect me, and he wanted another couple of days of hot sex, but in the end, would he see me off at the airport without a backward glance?

My heart twisted inside my chest at the thought, painful and tight. And in that moment I knew I couldn't do it. I couldn't come back to him. Because if I did, I'd never want to leave. I'd want to stay here with him forever. Except he didn't strike me as a forever kind of guy. Sure, we'd had hot sex and some great conversations, but I was positive he didn't feel the same way about me as I did about him. And, really, why should he?

I was a nerdy girl who liked math and who wasn't anything special. Not to a guy like him.

Perhaps it would be better to save us both the trouble and not come back at all.

Coward.

Yeah, well, that's what I was, wasn't I?

I'd deal with my father. I could handle that. But maybe I couldn't handle Tiger after all.

'No,' I said shakily, forcing the word out. 'I don't think that's a good idea.'

Something leapt in his gaze, a blaze of anger. 'What do you mean you don't think that's a good idea? It's what I want. I thought that's what you wanted, too?'

I was beginning to tremble now. 'Well… I—I've changed my mind.' It was harder than I thought to say it. Harder still with his fierce amber eyes on mine. 'I think it's b-better if we call it quits now.'

For a second something blinding flicked in his gaze, a bright flash of something I didn't recognise. It made my chest hurt, made my pulse start to climb, made me want to tell him I was lying, that I never wanted to call it quits. But I couldn't.

It was easier this way.

Easier for you, coward.

'You really want that?' He searched my face as if looking for something. 'You don't even want another day?' A raw note had crept into his voice and it felt like a knife in my heart.

But I'd made my decision. It was better to be the one who walked away than the one left behind, as I knew all too well.

So does he.

He did. But he was stronger than I was. He always had been.

'No.' It came out as a whisper and I don't even know how I managed to say it. 'I don't.'

Tiger shut down then. I could see the moment it happened. Like a door slamming in my face, shutting out all the heat from his amber eyes, leaving me alone in the cold, with nothing but ashes.

He released me, so quickly I nearly stumbled back. 'If that's what you want.' His voice was absolutely expressionless, his face hard and set. 'You'd better go then. Say hi to your daddy for me.' He flicked a glance at Keep and his friend Smoke. 'You pricks can fuck off, too.'

I hated the expression on his face, and it was agony to know that I'd put it there. 'I…just think this is the easiest way,' I began hoarsely, wanting to explain so he understood.

But he didn't let me. 'I don't want to hear it.' The amber of his gaze had dulled. 'Just go.'

'Tiger—'

'Yours isn't the only pussy in the world, Summer. It certainly isn't going to be the last.'

I hated the flat sound in his voice and I reached out to him, but he'd already turned to his workshop area. 'Have a nice trip. Enjoy your new job.'

The knife in my heart turned, a vicious pain.

'Enough of this bullshit.' Keep's deep voice from behind me. 'You coming with us, Summer?'

Tiger had gone to one of the bikes, the one I'd watched him work on only a couple of hours ago, his clever hands moving with a kind of knowledge and skill that had thrilled me.

There were tears in my eyes, my stupid heart wanting him to come after me, to fight for me, to insist I was his and that he wasn't going to let me go.

But he didn't.

'Yes,' I croaked. 'I'll just get dressed.'

I got my clothes together, then I went into the bathroom for some privacy to get changed, trying to blink back the tears that kept wanting to fall. It was awful, the thought of taking his shirt off, of not being close to his familiar scent and warmth, so because I was selfish at heart, I kept it on, pulling on my underwear and denim mini to go with it.

Then I came back outside to find Keep waiting at the front door of the warehouse. Smoke was down the other end with Tiger, who was bent over one of the bikes. He didn't look up. Not once.

I felt cold and the pain in my chest wouldn't stop throbbing, but I tried to ignore it.

This was the right decision. It was.

Keep eyed me as I approached and perhaps I should have been afraid of him, but I couldn't bring myself to care. Instead I simply met his cold blue gaze and said, 'You tell my dad Tiger found me. And he called you the moment he did.'

Keep raised one brow. 'Why the fuck would I do that?'

I didn't even flinch. 'Because I said.'

He gave me another long look and I knew I was treading on thin ice. But all he said was 'Okay.' And the next minute he was leading me outside to where his bike was parked.

I got on it and as we roared out of the courtyard, I didn't look back.

It felt like I'd left a piece of myself with Tiger and I didn't look to know which piece it was.

Stupid thing was I already knew.

My idiot heart.

Keep took me home, right to my front door. He didn't say a word to me the whole time, waiting silently beside me until the door opened and there was Dad standing on the threshold.

'Tiger found your girl,' Keep said shortly to him. 'You might want to take better care of her in future.'

Dad opened his mouth to say something, but Keep

had already turned around and was off down the steps, leaving me there with my father.

He'd always seemed tall to me, and intimidating, his blue eyes full of a fury that never seemed to go away. He turned that fury on me now. 'Where *the hell* have you been?' he demanded angrily. 'Get in the goddamn house.'

Normally when he got angry like this, all I wanted to do was run away and hide, make myself invisible so he wouldn't see me.

But now…now I could feel my own rage start to rise, thick and hot, fuelled by the pain in my heart at leaving Tiger and by the unfairness of it all. How dare he tell me what to do? How *dare* he threaten Tiger and Tiger's club way he had? What gave him the right? Just because I was his daughter, it didn't mean he could treat me like a possession or use me as a weapon against the people I cared about.

The only power he has over you is the power you give him, so don't give it to him…

Tiger's words echoed in my head and, despite the heartbreak I'd just left behind, I straightened my spine, firmed my shoulders.

No, I wasn't going to run away and hide. I wasn't going to be goddamn invisible, not this time, not today.

Today I was going to deal with him once and for all.

'No,' I said flatly. 'I will not get in the goddamn house.'

Dad's head snapped back. 'What did you say?'

'You heard me.' I met his furious blue gaze, held it. 'My days of doing whatever you say are over.'

He had one hand on the doorframe and his knuckles turned white as an expression of pure fury crossed his face. 'You ungrateful little bitch. You run away for days on end and now you think you can—'

'I think I can do whatever the hell I want!' My own fury leapt high and I let it, taking a step forward, getting right in his face. 'In fact, now it's *my* turn to tell *you* what to do. First of all, you're going to leave Tiger alone completely, and if I *ever* hear of you threatening either him or his club, you will never see me again.'

My father took a half step back, then stopped, as if realising what he was doing. He scowled, puffing his chest up. 'Are you threatening me?'

I ignored him. 'Second, I'm taking that job whether you like it or not. And if you try to stop me, I'll lay charges. Because I know there's at least a couple of good guys at the station who aren't in your pocket.'

'You really think you can—'

'Third.' I took another step, getting closer, holding his gaze, letting him see my strength, my rage, the broken heart in my chest fuel to the fire. 'Don't you ever try to manipulate me again. You've been doing that all my life and it ends right here, right now.'

For the first time, uncertainty flickered behind the anger in his eyes, and to my surprise it was he who took another step back, as if I was the one intimidating him. 'Jesus Christ, girl,' he blustered. 'What gives you the right to talk to me like that? I gave you a roof over your head. I gave you food on your plate and the clothes on your back. After your mother left—'

'You blamed me for her leaving,' I finished for him, anger becoming a strength flowing through me, the strength Tiger had always told me I possessed and yet I'd never felt. Not until this moment. 'You made sure to tell me she left because of me every single goddamn day.'

He said nothing, his mouth gone flat and hard in that tight line, every inch of him the disapproving police chief.

'Fourth, you want to know why I'm really here, Dad?' I lifted my chin. 'I'm here to tell you that you're wrong. Mom didn't leave because of me. She left because you're a bully. A controlling, manipulative prick. It was *your* fault she went away, not mine, and I'm not taking the blame for you any more.'

More fury leapt in his gaze, but he kept the distance between us. And I realised with a shock that it was because he was afraid.

He was afraid of *me*.

'You know why she never came back?' he said suddenly, the look on his face turning vicious. 'Because I told her if she did, I'd take you away where she could never find us.'

It felt like he'd kicked me in the stomach.

I stood there for a moment, the breath knocked out of me, staring at his familiar face, at the lines of bitterness around his eyes and mouth, the deep folds of anger and resentment along the once-sharp jawline.

Pain coiled inside me. 'Why? Why the hell would you do that?'

'Why do you think?' That viciousness lingered in his voice. 'Because the bitch left me and she needed to be punished.'

He'd been handsome once, my dad. A proud, intimidating figure. But he wasn't now. Suddenly all I saw in front of me was an old man, twisted and bitter and mean. A man with no power who was trying to get some however he could.

A weak, hollow kind of man.

This was who'd I'd been afraid of for so long? *This?*

Tiger had told me all this time not to give him any power but this was the first time I'd truly felt it in my heart. Truly seen that far from being this powerful, scary figure, my father had had no power to start with.

Dear God. How could I have let this small, weak man dictate my life?

Especially when I knew—I just *knew*—how much stronger than him I was.

All the air rushed suddenly back into my lungs, the realisation making me feel like I'd been suffocating all these years and only now could I breathe.

Dad's confession would have broken the Summer

that I'd been a week ago. But I wasn't that woman any more. I'd spent three days in the arms of one of the toughest, most frightening men I knew and he'd made me feel like a goddess. He'd made me feel wanted in a way I'd never felt before. He made me feel truly strong.

Because he made me feel loved.

It hit me then, like a bolt of white lightning, how unimportant standing on this step was. How unimportant my father was. That the only person who mattered to me was the man I'd left behind.

And I'd left him because I'd still been scared little Summer Grant, who'd had so little faith in herself and her own feelings that she'd rather walk away than fight for what she wanted.

Dad was blustering, making all kinds of threats, but they slipped off me like rain off an umbrella. They didn't even touch me.

I simply turned around and walked away.

Because there was only one thing I wanted and he'd been left behind by everyone who'd loved him.

I was *not* going to be another.

CHAPTER EIGHTEEN

Tiger

'YOU'RE A DUMBASS,' Smoke said.

I ignored him and kept myself bent over the bike, concentrating hard on the engine and not on whatever it was that kept kicking me hard in the chest, over and over again.

I didn't want to fix the fucking bike. I wanted to smash it. I wanted to knock the whole fucking thing off its stand and watch it crash down. Then maybe smash the headlight and kick the chrome of the exhaust. Take a sledgehammer to the petrol tank, just fucking destroy that motherfucker.

I didn't even know why.

Sure you do, asshole.

Yeah, okay, so I did. I wanted to destroy that bike the way Summer had fucking destroyed me.

Christ, I don't know what I'd expected. Not for her to give herself up like that, that was for sure. Not for her to give me some bullshit about not wanting me to choose between her and the club. And then to say she didn't want to come back to me, not have those couple of extra days before she left...

Fucked if I knew what that was all about. I'd thought she'd wanted it just like I did, but to have her change her mind like that didn't make any sense.

You should have asked her.

Yeah, maybe I should have. But, fuck, if she didn't want me, she didn't want me. I wasn't going to insist. Plenty more pussy in the sea and all that shit.

'I said you're a dumbass.'

I bared my teeth at the engine. 'Fuck off.'

Annoyingly, Smoke stayed right where he was. Prick didn't know when to take a hint. 'Why did you let her go?'

'Didn't you hear me?' I picked up a wrench and tried twisting off a nut. 'I said fuck off.'

'You wanted her, right?'

The wrench slipped and I dropped it. 'Fuck.' I kicked the fucking thing across the ground. 'Motherfucking fuck!'

Smoke stuck his hands into his pockets. 'Are you finished being a damn drama queen?'

I raised a fist, ready to do some damage to something or, preferably, someone. 'Don't make me fucking hit you.'

He didn't even look at my fist. 'Like I said, why did you let her go?'

I could feel my heartbeat raging, the effort it took to keep myself under control slipping, my raised fist shaking. And I didn't want to admit to why. 'Because she wanted to fucking go, okay?'

He gave me another of those long, steady looks. 'You said she was yours.'

'I was wrong.'

'No, you weren't.' He didn't move, didn't even blink. 'You're in love with her.'

The words hit me like a tank rolling the fuck over me, crushing me into the dirt.

He's right. That's why you want to destroy things. Because she left you.

I wanted to deny it, wanted to roar that it was a fucking lie, that I didn't love her. That she was just another girl I'd fucked and had a good time with but didn't give a shit about.

But that lie wouldn't come.

Of course he was right. Of course I was in love with her. And it was tearing me apart.

'What the fuck has that got to do with anything?' I demanded.

'You let her go.'

'What the fuck was I supposed to do? Chain her to my bed?'

Smoke said nothing for a moment and I found myself fighting to breathe. Because my chest hurt. Everything fucking hurt.

'Go after her then,' he said, as if it was easy. 'You want her, go get her.'

'No. She made her choice and it wasn't me. So

I'm making my choice now. And that's to let her the fuck go.'

His mouth twisted. 'You know what you sound like? You sound like me when I had to leave Cat. I was trying to protect her, making all these dumb fucking excuses about why I couldn't have her. Telling myself it was to keep her and Annie safe. But it wasn't. I was just afraid. Afraid of what I wanted and what it would mean.'

'It's not fucking the same,' I snarled.

'Yeah, dumb fuck, it is. You're making a whole lot of excuses about why you let her go. Why you can't go after her now. But don't kid yourself they're actually the reasons you're doing this. The real reason you're not is because you're in love and you don't know what to do about it, and you're shitting yourself.'

I didn't want to hear that. I didn't want to hear anything of what he said. 'Just because you've got yourself an old lady it doesn't make you some fucking love guru.' I kicked at the bike stand, the machine wobbling. 'Now, why don't you fuck off before I call the police about some asshole trespassing on my property?'

Smoke just shrugged. 'Fine. Have it your way. But just ask yourself one thing. What's more important? You or her? And if it's her, then you'll know what to do.'

That was another thing I didn't want to hear, but it stayed in my head long after he'd gone and I was alone, echoing and bouncing around in my skull like a pinball in a machine.

Who's more important? Me or her?

What the fuck did that even mean?

Give me a beer, give me pussy, give me my bike and a whole stretch of freeway, those were the things that were simple and uncomplicated. Things that I could count on to make me feel better. Those were the things I could trust. They never kicked me over and over again like this feeling was. They never made me hurt.

I tried to concentrate on the bikes for a couple of hours afterwards, but nothing seemed to work. I couldn't stop thinking about Summer. About how she'd left. How she'd looked me straight in the eye and told me I had to let her go. Even when I'd snarled at her, she hadn't been afraid. She'd been calm and certain and sure.

It was only at the end that I'd seen something like fear light in her eyes. When she'd tried to explain herself. But I hadn't wanted to listen. She was just like Mom, leaving me with some bullshit excuses. And that was fine, I'd deal, just like I dealt with everything.

But you're not dealing. So why the fuck did you let her go?

I had no answer to that, though I suspected it was there inside me, sitting somewhere I didn't want to see it.

I tried to distract myself with TV and then looking through my bike mags, but nothing worked. I couldn't sit still, couldn't relax.

I wanted Summer so badly it was agony.

So stop being a sulky little bitch and go get her.

Fuck, I'd never had a problem before with going out and taking what I wanted. What the hell was my deal now?

What's more important?

Smoke's voice echoed in my head all of a sudden and I froze midpace, the meaning of the question abruptly hitting me hard over the back of my head.

She was more important, no question. She was so fucking smart, so fucking bright and beautiful. She had everything going for her, a new job and a new life. There was no room in that life for a dumbass like me. An illiterate biker with no education, whose only skill was putting together engines. What on earth would she want with that?

There wasn't one single thing about me—apart from sex—that she'd want. That she would need.

Nothing except the fact that I loved her.

And if there was one thing that Summer Grant needed it was love. She hadn't had it from her mom or her dad, or from her violent brother.

She hadn't had it from anyone. And she deserved it. She deserved every fucking bit of love I had.

She was more important. More important than this pissy fear that she wouldn't want me, that she'd walk away from me the way Mom had.

She was more important than I was.

Which meant I had to suck up this stupid fucking fear of mine and go out and tell her how I felt. How I loved her, how I didn't want to leave her. How I'd do anything in the world for her, anything at all.

She might not want that shit, but she might. And if there was even one chance she would…

I was halfway to the door of the warehouse, all ready to go after her, when someone knocked, and I wondered who the fuck it could be. And then I didn't care because whoever it was could get fucked, because I was going to go get Summer and this time I wasn't going to let anyone stand in my way.

I reached for the door and then flung it open.

And found Summer standing on the other side.

She was in jeans this time, but she was still wearing my T-shirt, and her hair was loose and falling all silky and pale down her back. She had a backpack slung over one shoulder and her blue eyes were gazing at me all wide and dark and vulnerable.

My entire body rang like a fucking bell.

'Can I come in?' Her mouth was fragile, that fucking honesty of hers written all over her face. 'There's something I want to say to you.'

I couldn't believe it. I couldn't believe she was here.

I gripped the doorframe, white-knuckled. 'I thought you didn't want to come back.'

'I know.' That gorgeous lower lip of hers trembled. 'I was wrong.'

Something squeezed hard around my heart. 'You cross this threshold, you're mine,' I said, not taking my gaze from hers, making sure she was absolutely clear. 'I let you go once. I'm not doing it again.'

Colour washed over her face and I saw relief in her big blue eyes.

And she didn't say another word. She simply walked through my door as if she couldn't think of anything she'd like better.

The fist around my heart squeezed tighter as she came in, and I shut the door after her, turning to face her.

She let her backpack slip onto the ground and she was staring at me, her pulse frantic at the base of her throat.

I took a step towards her, wanting to touch her so badly I ached, but she held up a hand, stopping me in my tracks. 'W-wait,' she stuttered. 'I just want to say something. So, I went to my dad. And I basically told him he was to leave you alone and that if he didn't, he'd never see me again.' She swallowed. 'Then I told him I was going to the West Coast and my new job, whether he liked it or not, and that he couldn't stop me.'

'Summer, I—'

'No, I haven't finished. He didn't like it. He told me that the reason Mom never came back to me was because he had threatened her. He told her he'd take me away where she could never find me.'

That bastard. That *fucking* bastard.

But Summer went on before I could say anything. 'I think that was the moment I finally realised that he wasn't scary. He was just a bitter old man who was afraid and trying to get power any way he could.' She took a quick breath. 'He was weak, Tiger. And I was stronger than he was. Anyway, long story short. He won't be bothering you. Keep told him you were the one who brought me in anyway, so there's no drama with the club.' She was talking very fast, like she had to get it all out at once. 'But the main thing is… God, this is hard… I lied. I lied when I told you I didn't want to come back to you. Because I did. I wanted to come back and I… I was afraid that if I did, I'd never want to leave. And then you'd get sick of me—'

'Summer—'

'No. Let me finish.' Her voice was thick and there was a glitter in her blue eyes. But she straightened her spine, threw back her shoulders, looked straight at me. 'I left because I was afraid. And I want you to know that I'm not afraid any more. I know what's important now. And it's you, Tiger. It's you.'

The fist around my heart released all of a sudden and I couldn't hold back any longer. I swept her up into my arms and held her close, feeling her long, slender body shake against mine. 'You brave little idiot. Don't you know that I'm never going to get sick of you?' I said, holding her as I carried her over to the couch. 'What's mine stays mine. And you're mine, baby girl. You were mine the moment I took you out of the clubhouse.'

'Oh, Tiger.' She wrapped her arms around my neck and pressed her face to my throat, her voice going all muffled. 'I'm so sorry I lied. I was scared. I couldn't see how you'd want someone like me—'

'Shush.' I sat down on the couch, everything in-side me suddenly loose and easy, like a rusty engine finally being oiled. Then I arranged her in my lap with her head on my shoulder, so I could look down into her slightly reddened eyes. 'You're the smartest person I know. Plus you're the bravest and the strongest. You stood up to your dad. You stood up to me. You don't take any of my shit and I respect the hell out of that. Not to mention the fact that you're the most beautiful thing I've ever seen. Fuck, you light up this place like the sun.'

She blinked, her mouth going all vulnerable again. 'Really? You really think that about me?'

'Yeah, I really do. I don't know what the hell you'd want with a dumbass like me—'

'You're not a dumbass!' She looked fierce. 'No one else gets me when I talk math, but you do. We think the same way, Tiger. And you're smart. You're probably as smart as I am.'

I shook my head, trying to ignore how much I loved hearing her say that to me. 'I dunno if that's true.'

'It *is* true.'

'You're fierce, baby girl. You're going to give me a big head.'

'Good.' She looked very serious all of a sudden. 'Look, I don't need to go to Silicon Valley. I'll stay here, find something else. I don't care what. As long as I'm with you, it doesn't matter—'

I put a finger on her lovely mouth, silencing her. 'Oh, hell, no. You're not giving up that job.' She began to protest, but I pressed my finger harder. 'Quiet, I haven't finished. I'm going to come with you to the West Coast.' Her lips moved beneath my finger, but I kept it right where it was. 'You need that job, Summer. Like I already told you, you're so fucking smart and you deserve every fucking chance, and you're taking it, end of story.'

Her eyes were very wide and full of questions, so I let my finger slide away. 'But what about the club?' she demanded instantly. 'I know how important that is to you. You can't give that up for me.'

'Bullshit I can't. I'll go nomad. Which means I'll be a kind of a scout for the club, send back intel, that kind of shit. Hell, maybe I'll even think about setting up a new chapter. In the meantime, I can set up a workshop if I want. I can work on bikes anywhere. But the important thing is that I want to be with you. And if that's what I have to do, then I'll do it.'

'But, Tiger—'

'That's not your choice, baby girl. It's mine.'

She let out a sigh, then finally gave a tiny nod.

I tightened my arms around her. 'But there's two things you're going to do for me in return.'

That lovely mouth of hers curved. 'No problem. Especially if it's something to do with sex.'

I grinned. 'I love your enthusiasm, baby, but it's not about sex. First, you're going to teach me how to read, and second, you're going to help me find my mom and little brother.'

Her big blue eyes sparkled. 'Are you sure about this? Are you absolutely, completely sure?'

'I've never been surer of anything in my entire life.' The words were nothing but the truth.

She leaned up then, kissing me, her mouth so soft and sweet. 'I love you,' she whispered. 'That's the main reason I came back. Because I love you and you needed someone to come back to you.'

My heart, that fucking piece of crap, swelled up like a balloon in my chest. 'You know, I was on my way out, just as you knocked.'

'Oh? Where were you going?'

I stared into her eyes. 'To find you.'

She went pink. 'Why?'

'Why do you think? I haven't got much to give you, not for everything you've given me. But my heart is yours if you want it.'

Her blue eyes got even bluer, even deeper. 'You idiot. That's all I've wanted since I was seventeen years old.'

I blinked like the dumbass I was, and then she kissed me again, harder. 'I always had a thing for bad boys,' she went on. 'Particularly ones who like engines and puzzles, and who don't find math boring. And have the highest sex IQ of anyone I know.'

Fuck, she always knew just what to say. 'I think I love you, baby girl.'

'I think that might be my magic pussy.'

I laughed, then I picked her up in my arms and carried her upstairs.

And we made a little magic.

Together.

EPILOGUE

Summer

CAT AND SMOKE took us out to the airport, but I was nervous. Not because I thought Tiger might have second thoughts, but because I was afraid he might regret his decision. Because he wasn't just saying goodbye to his club, but to his family, as well.

We were both a little red-eyed from the party at the clubhouse the night before, both a goodbye party and a public claiming where he made me his old lady in front of his brothers. It had been scary and thrilling, though Tiger had insisted on taking me back to his place before anything had got too wild. Which I was slightly disappointed about. But only slightly. Mainly because I loved him being possessive of me and couldn't get enough of it.

This morning was no different and he kept his arm around me the whole way through check-in.

But I had tears in my eyes when he said goodbye to Smoke, a manly hug and that was it. Then Smoke raised a brow, glanced at me and then back at Tiger 'Guess you found the answer, huh?' he asked cryptically.

Tiger smiled. 'Yeah. Don't worry. Your position as love guru is safe.'

Smoke grinned, pulling Cat tighter against him. She glanced at me and rolled her eyes, which made me laugh.

'I'll see you round,' Tiger said. 'Hey, maybe I'll even write.'

Smoke's grin became wider. 'You do that.'

And that was that.

Tiger didn't let me go as we walked through security and he didn't look back. 'Here's to the future, baby girl,' he murmured in my ear. 'It's gonna be great.'

* * * * *

BEST LAID PLANS

REBECCA HUNTER

MILLS & BOON

To my sister Leah, who tolerates early drafts
of everything I write.

Your adventures in Australia inspired this series.

CHAPTER ONE

"LESS LIKE A fraternity and more like a real company? What the hell does that mean?"

Cameron Blackmore leaned back in the plush lounge chair and massaged his temples. He didn't like this any more than the others, but as CEO of Blackmore Inc. in Australia, he had to be the voice of reason. Or at least survival. He crossed his arms and looked each of the other three members of his team in the eye.

"You all know exactly what this means," he said. "After the recent news coverage we've gotten, we need to lie low for a while. We're in high-profile security, for fuck's sake. No public appearances, no partying and no walking out of a pub with clients."

Derek and Simon nodded. Max's scowl grew.

"Can your father and his board tell us where we can go and who we can bring home with us?" Max grumbled. "All the way from New York?"

Cameron surveyed the dark room and caught a couple glances in their direction from other patrons.

Damn. They were attracting attention. He had moved their impromptu meeting to the hotel lounge to be discreet, but discreet wasn't Max's strong suit.

Cameron lowered his voice and leaned in. "It's not like any of us were planning on finding the love of our lives in the next two weeks." He turned to Max. "And to answer your question, yes. When you land on the front page of the *Sydney Morning Herald*, yes."

Derek and Simon looked at Max.

Max threw his hands up. "Hey, I was fact-finding with her."

Derek smirked. "Is that what you call it, mate?"

"We don't need to get into this again," said Cameron. "You did what you needed to do. The client understood that, even if the board doesn't. They're owned by my father, so what do you expect?"

His smile disappeared. Harlan Blackmore still managed to wield some control over his life, even a continent away. Cameron's dislike of his father was no secret. When he joined the family business, Cameron had expected his grandfather to hold on for a few more years. Enough time to take the ruins of the business his father had left in Australia and turn it into the kind of company his grandfather had built. Cameron had fond, if hazy, memories of Sydney from the two years he'd spent here as a child— back when his parents were together. So, he'd jumped on the opportunity to return a couple years ago. But his grandfather's heart attack wasn't in Cameron's plans, nor was his father's scramble for control over Blackmore Inc.

And Harlan Blackmore had no fucking idea how to run an international security company. He just looked the part and acted the part, all while running Blackmore Inc. Australia into the ground with his US strategies. And the board rewarded him for this grand performance by making him president.

But maybe, just maybe, this whole recent turn of events could be Cameron's chance to run the business his way. His grandfather's way. A chance to show the board that focusing on a strong, loyal team and the demands of the current market had a better business payoff than making strategic golf partners or any of the other shit the board wanted him to do. His father could play golf or do whatever the hell he pleased, as long as he left the business strategy to Cameron.

Low grumbles came from around the table.

"No women? Sounds like a waste of two weeks," said Max.

Derek took a swipe at Max's head, but Max ducked. "You're whining more than you did back on the footy field."

"Piss off," said Max lazily. "Not all of us have a hot woman at home to—"

"Watch what you say about my wife," growled Derek, all two-hundred-plus pounds of muscle ready to tackle his former teammate.

"Enough," said Cameron.

The discussion was over. He trusted this group of men with his life. If he asked them to keep a low profile, they'd all do it. And so would he. Starting tomorrow.

Cameron took a gulp of his beer and scanned the lounge to see if anyone was still watching them. He stopped on a woman sitting at the end of the bar, her eyes on him. Red lips and long brown hair in waves down her back. A silky shirt, see-through, thanks to the angle of the lights, and a black skirt riding up her thighs. She was looking, not listening, and there was something dreamy, unfocused, in her gaze. As if she were thinking through the course of her night, too.

The woman pulled her bottom lip between her teeth and looked down into her drink. Damn. How soon could he get this meeting over with?

Simon leaned in and grabbed the paper off the table in front of him, scanning it again. "So they're sending this asshole—" he pointed at the name in the middle of the page "—Jackson McAllister all the way from New York just to follow us around for two weeks?"

"What kind of wanky name is Jackson McAllister?" Max waved his hand around, almost knocking over his beer.

"The kind that will be firing all of our asses if we're not careful," said Derek.

Cameron sighed. "Look, he'll be around the office a bit, but it's really me he's supposed to follow. To see if a little public relations training can 'fix' our image. Fix my image, actually. It's my job that's on the line. The board was pretty specific on that."

Max blew out his breath. "Sorry, mate."

Cameron swallowed the bile creeping up his throat and shrugged. "So the plan is to give this dickhead a grand welcome to Sydney, show him that this is all a big misunderstanding, that we're not all drunken brawlers who like to pick up women every night, and then send him on his way back to New York."

Derek snorted. "Good luck with that."

"It's fine," said Cameron. "I can play nice for a few days. And so can you all."

Derek raised a skeptical eyebrow at Max.

"Piss off, Derek," said Max and punched him in the arm. "You were partying just as much as the rest of us before you met Laurie."

"Here's the thing," said Cameron, cutting off the exchange. "I called you here because I wanted you to know ahead of time. I'm meeting with the guy to-morrow morning, and we'll all go to dinner at Circular Quay, all nice and civil-like. But until then, you don't know anything. So you all have one last night before the ax comes down."

He looked around the table. The expressions on all three faces of his team grew into grins, as if they were each imagining what they were going to do with this night. Cameron didn't need to use his imagina-tion. The woman was sitting right in his line of sight. Her wine was almost gone, so it was time to wrap up this meeting.

Cameron cleared his throat.

"Oh, well, thanks for the heads-up," said Max, all traces of his frown gone. He stood up and set his beer on the table. "So what are we waiting for? Who's in for the pub?"

Derek smiled. "Laurie's out until ten, so I'm up for a couple drinks. But I want to make it home by then."

Max rolled his eyes. "Me and lover boy. What about you, Simon?"

"Of course."

"And you, boss?"

Cameron eyed the bar. The woman was looking in his direction again. This time, she waited an extra beat before she lowered her long dark lashes. A good sign.

"I'm sticking around here for a while," he said. "But I'll call you if I change my mind."

"Whatever, mate." Max shook his head. "You gonna check into a room here and rent some porn for your last night of freedom?"

"Get the fuck out of here," he said, chuckling.

Cameron watched his team head out of the hotel. He took the last drink from his beer and set it down. He turned for one more look at the luscious woman at the bar. If he ended up alone tonight, he'd have plenty of material to get off on. Her skirt rode high enough to get a good look at her shapely bare legs. Was she the type who liked to ride or be ridden? Or both?

Cameron stood up and started over to the bar. He caught her gaze and held it. She squinted a little.

Then her eyes widened, as if this were the last thing she expected to happen. Hmm. One of those curvy bombshells who somehow hadn't realized just how sexy she was? Even better.

As he came closer, the corners of her mouth turned up into a little smile. He slid into the stool next to hers. His legs were too long to fit under the bar, so he faced her instead.

She turned and brushed her silky hair over her shoulder. Her smile grew wider. "Hi, there."

She was American? She had one of those soft, raspy voices that was going to get him hard right here in the bar if he wasn't careful. This was getting better by the minute.

"What's your name?" he asked.

She shook her head and smiled. No names? He could do that.

"Okay," he said. "Should I start with, 'Do you come here often?'"

She gave a throaty laugh. "Is that all you got?"

Shit, this was going to be fun. He leaned closer and whispered, "Depends on what you want."

A flush crept up her slender neck and onto her cheeks. She swallowed. "Just so you know, I'm not into getting picked up at a bar."

He raised an eyebrow. "Maybe you're looking at it wrong."

"Is that right?" She gave a little snort of amusement.

He nodded. "It's all about having fun. About trying new things you might not try anywhere else. And living for the moment."

"How very philosophical," she said, crossing her arms. "Does that usually work for you?"

Cameron hung his head and laughed. "I've got a good record."

She rolled her eyes. "No wonder you're so cocky. *That* kind of guy."

"If you know my kind, then you know I love a challenge. And you've just raised the stakes, sweetheart," he said softly.

The woman took the last sip of her wine and licked her lips. She met his gaze again, and for a moment, an electric spark sizzled through him, held him there. Did she feel it, too? Her long, dark lashes fluttered.

Then the amusement was back in her smile. And maybe a hint of challenge.

"You're going to have to work a lot harder than this," she said.

Cameron rested his foot on her bar stool to get closer. "I'll work as long and hard as you want me to."

She gasped softly, and her mouth dropped for a brief moment. What was she imagining right now? Then she laughed. "Enough with the lines," she said, shaking her head.

"But they're working so well," he deadpanned. He shifted back. "You're not just a little curious?"

She hesitated, so he continued. "You know what I'm most curious about?"

She narrowed her eyes and slowly shook her head.

"I'm wondering what makes you hot," he said, lowering his voice.

As he spoke, her gaze darted down between his legs, where he was fighting a full-on erection. Maybe this wasn't such a long shot after all.

"Are you wondering how big I am?" he whispered. "What it might feel like?"

She met his gaze, and the fire sparked between them. Hell, she liked this game just as much as he did.

"Does it have any correlation with your ego?" she asked sweetly.

He quirked a brow. "You're welcome to find out for yourself." He fought another smile as her gaze landed between his legs again. Definitely interested.

"Size is overrated," she said, wrinkling her nose. "I'd rather have a man who knows how to use it."

She smelled like something delicious. Her lips were red and wet and only inches away. "What if you can have both?"

CHAPTER TWO

JACKSON MCALLISTER SWALLOWED the flutter in her throat as she stared at this man's soft, full lips. Thick black hair, deep blue eyes and a little stubble along his hard jaw. At least she thought she saw all that. So what if she couldn't actually see him clearly? Her imagination took off where her vision ended. And putting those two together, this guy was unreal. Big and built enough for even her to make out the out-lines of his muscles against his black T-shirt. He was so out of her league. But just a moment ago, she could have sworn something had passed between them.

If she wanted to prove Cheater Rob wrong, now was her chance. She *did* know how to have fun in bed. And even without her contacts in, this guy looked like he was all about the best kinds of fun. He had such big…arms. Sure, he had an ego the size of this hotel, but did it matter? If she wanted to get back in the saddle, so to speak, maybe she needed someone who wasn't so concerned about his own performance.

Best of all, no one would ever know. Jackson had never set foot on this continent before today, and she had sidestepped names. What better introduction to Australia? This trip didn't allow for all the sightseeing in her little red book, so why not try her own private cultural primer? Okay, so he sounded American—she detected a slight accent on a few words—but she could make an exception in this case.

Her mother's mantra rang in her ears: *Good things come to those who wait.* Well, she had put off this kind of careless fun for long enough. And he was looking pretty good. Her mother probably hadn't meant for Jackson to apply her favorite saying in this way, which would make it all the more fun.

She reached for her little red book, tucked inside the pocket of her purse, but stopped. No, she wasn't going to add "hot sex in Sydney" to the Australia page, just so she could cross at least one item off the list. Not here, right in front of this particular tourist attraction.

Jackson bit her lip and met his gaze. He looked familiar, though she had given up any hope of recognizing anyone when she left her contacts back in her hotel room. At least her eyes weren't stinging anymore. Her glasses had gotten her down to the bar, but she'd slipped them back in their case when she sat down. And she wasn't about to pull them out to get a better look at this guy.

He gazed at her like he had all the time in the world. But she knew he was ready to get things started. And she was thinking this just might happen. A kiss couldn't hurt.

"What do you think?" he asked. "Want to see if this is as good as I think it will be?"

She glanced at his left hand. "No ring?"

He laughed. "Do I strike you as the relationship type?"

That deep, sexy voice was killing her. She rested one hand on his hard, muscular thigh. "Okay. Let's see what you've got."

She leaned forward and took his bottom lip between hers. She sucked gently and went back for more, pressing her mouth against his and licking his bottom lip this time. A rumble rose from his chest, and he took control. He slipped his tongue inside her mouth for a few lazy strokes, and he slid his large hand behind her head, pulling her closer. He teased and coaxed until she wove her hand into his thick dark hair, responding, asking for more. Easing off his chair to standing, he ran his hands over her hips as he took the kiss deeper. Harder. His erection pressed firmly against her, and she moaned a little louder than she should have.

He pulled back, and she let go of the handful of hair she was grasping. *Whoa.*

"Fuck," he muttered under his breath and sank back into his stool.

She looked up, and his eyes were closed. He shook his head a little and opened them again.

"I guess we've answered the first question," he said with a wry smile. "It'll definitely be good."

She nodded. This was already sexier than anything she'd done in a long time, and they had only kissed.

His gaze was fixed on her, and she took the opportunity to stare back. At least she tried to. He *did* look familiar. Maybe he was an actor, someone from a movie she had seen? His hair had fallen down into his face. If he were her boyfriend, she'd push it back. But he wasn't. Far from it. Which made this all the more tempting.

"Well, sweetheart," he said. "Are we going to walk away, or are we taking this to the next level?"

This was either going to be the best decision she'd ever made or the dumbest.

"I've got a room," she whispered.

He smiled. "I like your choice."

She gathered her purse and they stood up. *Good God*, he was big. What would it be like to have a man this size over her? He'd crush her if he flopped around like Cheater Rob. She frowned. No more Rob thoughts tonight.

"Can I use your mobile for a minute?" he asked.

Jackson raised an eyebrow, but he looked serious. She unlocked it and handed it over. He found the camera and took a picture of himself.

"Oooh, a commemorative photo of our evening," she said, laughing. "Thanks."

He looked down at her and sighed. "For your safety," he said drily.

Oh. Why the hell didn't she think of safety? She must be loopy on all his super-alpha pheromones.

"Can anyone access your email?"

She shrugged. "My sister, I guess."

"Then email the photo to yourself and write, 'This is who I was with tonight.'"

Well, that *was* a good idea, now that he mentioned it. She typed the message and sent it.

"Ready?" he asked.

Yep, she was definitely ready.

They managed to make it through the lobby, but when the elevator doors closed, all bets were off. He backed her against the wall for another searing kiss. He licked the seam of her mouth, and she opened, answering back with her own explorations. He found her thigh with his hand, and he slipped it under the hem of her skirt. His teeth scraped her bottom lip, and he bit down softly. His hand slid higher, and she squirmed against him. He was rock hard.

"I can feel you," she whispered. "All of you."

He smiled. "You worried?"

"Should I be?"

He didn't answer, so she reached between them and palmed him gently. His groan echoed through the elevator chamber as she stroked from base to tip, and he muttered an indecipherable string of curse words. He grabbed her hand, but the elevator dinged before he could do anything more.

Jackson stepped out and took a deep breath. She had flown from New York to Sydney today and had been awake for God knew how long. Now she was taking the world's hottest man to her hotel room for what promised to be the best sex of her life. Hopefully the jet lag wouldn't catch up with her any time soon.

They turned the corner, and she stopped in front of the first room. He swept her hair aside and kissed her neck as she fumbled with the key. But before she could open the door, his hand covered hers.

"You are on fire," he whispered in her ear. "And I want to give you more pleasure tonight than you've had in your life."

Her pulse pounded in her throat. Damn, this was unreal.

"But if you don't like something," he continued, "just say stop and I'll back off. No matter what we're in the middle of. Got it?"

She nodded.

"Good."

He took her key and pushed it in the lock, and the door swung open. He was right behind her, crowding her. As soon as the door closed, he turned her around and pressed her back against the door with the weight of his body. She cupped his jaw in her hands and pulled his mouth toward hers. His lips came down on hers, hungry and insistent. His grip tightened around her waist, but he pulled back.

"What do you want?" he growled.

"An orgasm, please?" she squeaked.

Jackson covered her mouth. Did she really just say that?

He leaned his forehead against the door, and his shoulders shook with silent laughter. "Yeah, I got that," he finally said.

He straightened up and met her gaze. His smile slowly shifted from amusement back to searing lust. He ran his hands up and down her waist in slow, sensual sweeps. "I mean, what do you like?" he said, his voice low and gruff. "This can be as gentle or as rough as you want it."

The word *rough* sang through her body. What did he imagine when he said it?

"How do you want this to be?" she hedged.

His eyes widened, and he smiled. "I wasn't expecting that answer." He rubbed the stubble on his chin. "I want this to be the best night of your life. I want you to wake up missing the feeling of my cock in you."

A rush of heat flooded her. His words turned her on just as much as his ravenous kisses. Jackson had no idea what to say.

He put his hand back on her waist. "How 'bout we start with this," he said before his lips brushed the base of her jaw.

She swallowed and nodded.

His tongue was soft and teasing. She ran her hands over the thick muscles of his arms. He found the edge of her shirt and tugged it up. She pulled it over her head, and his breath caught. "Mmm... That bra is perfect."

She smiled. See-through lace. Her nipples poked out, hard, begging for attention. "Glad you like it."

"Hell, yeah." He cupped her breasts and rubbed his thumbs over the peaks. She moaned, and his erection throbbed hard against her.

"Turn around," he said.

She faced the door, and he unclasped the bra, pushing the straps over her shoulders. She let it fall to the floor. Her breasts were heavy, and they tingled in the cool air. Would he play with them?

He knelt down behind her and unzipped her skirt. Oh. He slid his hands under the material and pushed the skirt over her hips. It fell to the floor, too, and she stood in nothing but her panties.

He didn't touch at first. His breath came in gentle puffs on her back. "Lace again," he said, running his hands over the material.

A little gasp escaped from her lips. He kissed the small of her back and eased the panties down, as well.

She was naked and giddy, but his caresses slowed. His hand trailed down her spine, and when he came to her rear, one finger continued. Then he stopped at the most daring place of all.

She shivered.

"You ever played here?" he asked softly.

Jackson hesitated. She hadn't, but she was definitely curious. Should she say yes, just to see what it was like? She shook her head.

"Okay," he said, and his finger trailed lower. "Then we'll play here."

His finger teased her clit, and then it was gone. He turned her around and tugged off his own shirt. He undid the front of his pants, and her mouth fell open as he reached in to give himself a long, hard stroke.

He looked up at her darkly. "First I want to lick you, and then I want to fuck you hard. How does that sound?"

"Like the most erotic thing I've ever heard," Jackson blurted. Shit. That had slipped out.

He gave her a hungry smile. "Okay, sweetheart. Put your leg over my shoulder."

She lifted her leg and rested it on the hard wall of muscles along his back. She was so exposed and wound up that she wasn't sure how long she could stand like this.

He wrapped his hands around her hips and buried his face in her. He ran his tongue along her inner thigh until he reached her clit. Then he sucked hard. Pleasure shot through her body. She cried out and her head fell back. So he did it again. His tongue traveled over a new spot, exploring, learning her responses. But he went slowly, so slowly. Jackson tangled her hands into his hair, begging him for more. Shudders of heat rushed through her, more and more intense each time. He groaned when she responded, but he didn't stop; he found new places to lick and suck, bringing her closer and closer until she fell back against the wall. Want turned to need. Then a bolt of ecstasy exploded inside, and she came in white-hot spasms.

She panted, trying to hold herself up. It was too much. He caught her in his arms and brought her down to the floor against him. He held her like that until her breaths slowed.

"That was amazing," she whispered.

"We can do it as many times as you want," he said.

His pants had fallen open, and his erection strained through the last layer of clothing between them. She kissed his shoulder and leaned back, taking in the sight of him. "When do you get naked?" she asked.

He put his hands on his knees and stood up in front of her. Oh. Now. She slid his pants down his legs. He toed off his shoes and kicked his pants aside. Jackson rose on her knees and fingered the waistband of his boxers.

She swallowed. Finally she was going to get a look at what promised to be the most impressive display she had ever seen, with or without glasses. Taking a deep breath, she inched down his waistband. His tip glistened in front of her. She tugged his boxers down farther, and he bent down to help her. He stepped out, and she got a nice, long view of him. *Long* being the operative word.

"Oh, my," she whispered.

He laughed, and their eyes met. His smile faded. For one quiet moment, neither of them moved. The scene was outrageously erotic. She was naked on her knees, with his enormous cock bobbing in front of her, but there was something else, too. A different kind of spark between them, something that made this scene even better.

Whoa, girl. Way too deep for casual sex.

She looked away from his hypnotic blue eyes and began to explore. She traced him slowly from tip to base. His breaths quickened as she stroked and squeezed him, and he rocked into her touch.

He leaned forward to help her up, and he nodded to the bed.

"You ready?" All the smoothness in his voice was gone.

"Yes."

He reached for his jeans and pulled out his wallet. The wrapper crackled as he tore it off and rolled on the condom. She was beyond caring that she was staring at him with open lust.

"Turn around," he said softly, and she did.

He pressed up behind her, his erection hard against her back. Leaning over her, he moved her hair to one side and gently bit her earlobe. He reached around and squeezed her breasts. Oh, yes. He liked that, too. He played with her nipples, squeezing harder until she gasped.

"I want you from behind," he said, his harsh breaths in her ear.

She nodded and crawled onto the bed, and he followed, never letting go of her. Spreading her legs farther with his knees, he slid his erection along every sensitive place. He teased her and played, and she moved to find new angles of pleasure. His tip pressed at her entrance, and her body yielded to him. With a low groan, he pushed himself all the way in.

She cried out, and he stilled, his fingers flexing hard on her hips.

"You okay?" he said through gritted teeth.

"Yes." She could barely get out the sound. Everything felt full, and she squirmed to adjust.

"Hold on," he bit out, and he held her in place. He pulled out slowly and sank back in hard.

A wild moan escaped her.

"You like that, sweetheart?" he growled.

"Yes," she whispered.

In response, he did it again. Then again and again, pulling out and driving back in. Each time, she sank back on her knees, searching for more. Her body felt lighter as the pleasure built, threatening to explode inside her. His thrusts grew harder and more frantic.

"I—I'm going to…" she stuttered just as the pleasure flooded her once more, the long spasms racking her body. Her arms collapsed as wave after luscious wave of heat rolled through her.

His hips crashed against her, driving deeper, and he came with a torn roar. His big body fell over hers, and he rested his chest on her back. She collapsed in a boneless, sated heap.

Moments passed. He eased down onto the bed and shifted her to his side. His heart pumped in overdrive against her back, and his breath was heavy over her as he stroked her hair softly. She couldn't see him, but he was everywhere, all around her, holding her close. Like his body belonged there, right against hers.

Wow. Just wow. This was what sex could be like? It was probably better than anything she'd ever have again. If she weren't so tired, maybe she'd ask to do it one more time.

"My God," she whispered. "If I had known that one-night stands were this good, I would have started doing this a long time ago."

He didn't laugh at her joke. He didn't answer. He smoothed her hair once more and kissed her on the top of her head. His lips stayed there for an extra beat, and then they were gone.

He rolled away from her and wandered around the room, probably looking for somewhere to put the condom. He bent down and untangled his clothes from the heap on the floor. Was he leaving now? He stepped into his boxers and pulled on his jeans. He picked up his shirt, but he didn't put it on. Instead, he sat down on the bed right next to her. It dipped under his weight.

Jackson was still wearing nothing, and she climbed under the covers. Her whole body felt heavy and slow. The jet lag was setting in hard. Her eyes fluttered closed, and she fought to open them again.

He pulled the blanket over her shoulders and studied her, but she couldn't make out his expression.

"I think I should go," he said.

"Okay," she said. "Um, thanks, I guess."

His teeth flashed in a smile.

"You're welcome, sweetheart. I'll think of you often when I'm alone in bed."

Jackson smiled. "Likewise."

He stood up and headed for the door. When it clicked behind him, she closed her eyes and fell asleep.

CHAPTER THREE

CAMERON WOKE UP with a hand on his cock. Damn. It was *his* hand, not the hand of the hot-as-hell woman who had featured in his dream. The woman with a smart, sexy mouth, a nice round ass and no name.

He was already hard as a rock and halfway there, so he slipped down his boxers and closed his eyes. Last night in the shower, he had gotten himself off to all the things he wanted to do with her nice round ass. This morning he'd dedicate to that smart, sexy mouth.

His fantasy began just like she had the night before. She'd touched him with her hands, but this time she'd use her lips and her tongue. Yes, those eager lashes of her tongue. In his dream, instead of walking out, he stayed for another round. He grasped her long, luscious hair in both hands and guided himself in and out of her mouth, thrusting deeper, while she stared up at him with those deep green eyes. Fuck.

Cameron gave himself a few last hard strokes and came with a loud groan. He collapsed back on his bed, panting. As the haze of pleasure faded, he shook his head and frowned. When was the last time he'd woken himself up like that? At least he should be able to lie back for a few more minutes of satisfaction. Instead he was restless. And irritable. And still thinking about her comment from the night before.

If I had known that one-night stands were this good, I would have started doing this a long time ago.

What the hell? One-night stands weren't that good. In fact, Cameron couldn't think of one that had come close. But when he opened his mouth to tell her, he'd stopped. If he said that the night went far beyond any one-night stand, then what? Starting today, he was supposed to keep his dick in his pants. There was no hope for a repeat performance. So he'd gotten dressed and walked out of the woman's room instead.

He had told her he wanted her to remember it as the best night of her life. But by the time he left her, he'd reconsidered. If they were that good together on the first try, what would happen when they really started exploring each other?

No. That couldn't happen. And he wasn't about to ruin the memories of that night with sappy shit that didn't matter anyway.

Cameron kicked off his covers, took a few long strides to the bathroom and slammed the door. He turned the shower on punishingly cold, hoping for a distraction. Because the more he thought about this no-women situation, the madder he got.

This PR bullshit the board had arranged was no

longer just a nuisance. Last night it meant that he had had to walk away from the best sex in a long time. Maybe that woman was staying in Sydney for a while. Hell, maybe she even lived close by and they could have gone on fucking like that for days. Instead he was making a mess of himself in his boxers right before going to meet with that fucker Jackson McAllister.

Screw Harlan Blackmore and his board. This was the last straw. He had been waiting for the right moment to take control away from them for years, and this was it. His grandfather had built this business years ago to give veterans from his unit a purpose after the Vietnam War. It was the bond of the teams that made his grandfather's business strong, not the latest PR. Okay, so his team may have gotten a little careless with their public image, but hiring a babysitter to shadow and report on Cameron smacked of his father's dirty tactics. Harlan had latched on to this situation and intervened as a show of force. There wasn't too much bad press at this point. Wouldn't a warning from the board have sufficed? Then Cameron could've dealt with his team on his own terms. He needed to show his father and the board just how far up their asses their heads were. And the best way to do that would be to send Jackson McAllister home looking like an idiot.

He shut off the water and toweled off, then he strode into his walk-in closet and reached for a pair of jeans. One leg into them, he stopped and cursed. Probably should wear a suit for this meeting.

By the time he climbed the dock off his building, he still wasn't thinking clearly. His boat floated peacefully in its berth. Maybe a good fast ride across the harbor would help. Buying that boat was the best decision he'd made since he moved to Sydney. No crowds, no traffic, everything in sight. Those trips across the water every day were the few moments he didn't have to be on guard. Cameron nodded at the captain and took a seat. He enjoyed this type of travel…and he knew from his army days there were worse ways to get around. Hell, after the plane crash he'd been through, no one could fault him for being picky in that regard.

He pushed those thoughts aside.

If he'd learned anything in the military, it was just how much better things went with a clear plan. And judging from the start of his morning, he was in no state to come up with a good one. But in this pissy mood, any plan was better than none. As the boat passed under the Harbour Bridge, he sent an email to his team. Tonight at dinner they'd figure out Jackson McAllister's weak spots. Tomorrow they'd figure out how to use them.

But planning didn't help. When he walked through the glass doors into the Blackmore Inc. office, his mood was just as dark.

"Good morning, Mr. Blackmore."

He bit out a greeting to Chloe, the receptionist, and headed for his office.

"Mr. Blackmore," she called after him. "Jackson McAllister is waiting for you in the small conference room."

He grunted but didn't turn around. What the hell? The guy wasn't supposed to be there for another thirty minutes. Cameron changed direction and headed straight for the conference room. He was going to have to tell that fuckwit to come back later.

He burst through the door and came to a full stop. In one of the chairs he saw a woman, not a man. The rear of a woman, to be specific, turned away, bending over a mess of papers on the floor. What the—

"Sorry. Just a moment," came a voice from under the round table.

A voice that awakened his entire body. He gave himself a little shake. What the fuck was going on?

"I got the time mixed up…" The woman rose with a pile of papers and turned. And froze.

"Oh," she whispered. "Damn."

It was her. The hot-as-hell woman. His body had known the moment she spoke, and now his mind finally registered it. Her lips were pale, not red, and she was wearing glasses, but this only added to her appeal. She had her long, silky hair up in a bun. He already knew the feeling of a fistful of that hair, and he had gotten himself off to what those lips would look like around his—

"What are you doing here?" he barked.

The words came out as more of an accusation than a question. Lust must have short-circuited his brain because he still couldn't figure out how the hell this woman had ended up at his office building.

But as he glared across the room at her, all the wonder disappeared from her expression. She took off her glasses and blinked at him a couple times before putting them back on. She narrowed her eyes and pressed her lips together into a tight smile. She stood up and stuck out her hand for a handshake.

"Jackson McAllister," she said. "The board warned me about your growling."

Cameron screwed his eyes shut and rubbed his forehead. He opened his eyes again, but nothing changed. The same woman was still glaring at him.

"What the hell?" he whispered. "You're not a man."

Jackson dropped her hand and raised her eyebrows. "I think you and I already established that last night, Mr. Blackmore," she said drily. "And you're supposed to have a beard."

So... *She* was Jackson McAllister. The person the board had sent to rein in him and his team. Or try to. And he had already given her an eye-opening welcome. Cameron rubbed his temples.

"But Jackson's a man's name," he muttered to himself.

She shook her head slowly. "Why do I feel like I'm back in elementary school?"

"I'm long past elementary school, Ms. McAllister," he snapped. "I think we established that last night, too."

Her face betrayed no emotion, but a deep flush crept up her neck. Which brought him right back to the place his mind absolutely should not go now. The last time those cheeks reddened like that was—

Shit. What was he supposed to do now? Pull out a chair for her all gentleman-like? Ignore the fact that he had just had mind-bending sex with her less than twelve hours ago? He huffed out a breath and sank into his own chair at the table.

He crossed his arms and leaned back, scrambling to get a handle on the situation. Wait. He'd had no idea who she was last night, but had she known who he was? Was this part of some larger scheme to "tame" him? He nearly snarled at the thought. It sure as hell hadn't felt that way. And when he walked into the conference room, she'd looked just as confused as he had felt. But he couldn't rule it out.

"You had to know it was me last night," he said slowly. "Didn't the board give you photos or something?"

Jackson rolled her eyes. "I didn't spend hours gazing at your profile, if that's what you mean. You had a beard in most of them, and last night I took my contacts out because my eyes were killing me."

Well, those glasses gave her an innocent-but-naughty look that would turn him on right here if he kept thinking about it. Fighting for calm, he said, "Screw it. Let's do this."

Her eyes snapped up to meet his, and another blush washed over her cheeks. Wait—did he just catch her staring at his biceps? She sat down quickly in her chair and smoothed her skirt over her legs. She grabbed the files she had just collected from the floor and cleared her throat.

"I'm here to give you a boost of intensive public relations support," she said. "I'll be looking at every detail of your day and coming up with a plan for improvement."

"Any suggestions so far?" The comment slipped out before he could think better of it. And fuck if she didn't lick her lips before *she* could think better of it.

But the glossy look in her eyes quickly switched back to a glare. "The board wants a detailed report," she said sharply. "And there I'll make suggestions for the future."

All his retorts faded. He hadn't missed the board's veiled threat. If Cameron didn't run his company the Harlan Blackmore way, someone else would. But he hadn't missed Jackson's threat, either. And the glare she still fixed on him said the same thing: *Don't mess with me.*

Cameron ran a hand through his hair and blew out a breath. "How the hell do you propose we make this work, Jackson?"

She let out a little sigh. Her eyes softened, and she pushed her glasses up her nose. For a moment, she looked just as mixed up about the situation as he was. But when she spoke again, her voice was steady and all business.

"We just forget about last night and do our jobs," she said. "I'm over it. You're a big boy. You can get past it, too, can't you?"

She knew just how much of a big boy he was, but now wasn't the time to point this out.

"I think I can manage that," he said drily. "Let's get to work."

She opened a file and pushed it toward him. He picked up the printouts of newspaper articles and photos one by one. He had seen most of them before. They featured various members of his team with different women from different jobs. Most of them weren't remarkable. He could see her point, too—he did have a beard in most of them.

"These are clients," he said.

She picked up one of Max and a high-profile actress. He was whispering something in her ear, and if the sultry smile on her face was any indication, she was ready for him to do a lot more.

"He looks more like a male escort than a bodyguard," she said.

Cameron took the photo back. "What can I say? He's good at his job."

He continued through the pile. He found a photo of himself coming out of a pub with two women, one on each side. He was talking to one, and the other was holding on to his bicep, her mouth next to his ear.

His gaze flicked up to meet hers. "That's not what it looks like."

"Let me guess," she said sweetly. "You're good at your job, too?"

He rested his gaze on her. "I am good at my job." He added softly, "And aside from that, I prefer to enjoy women one at a time."

She didn't answer, but she lost some of the hardness in her expression. What was going on in her mind right now? Did she like more than one man at a time? The idea boiled in him. Hell, no. But that was the last thing he should be getting upset about right now. Nothing was going to happen between them again. Not a bloody thing.

He leafed through the rest of the photos and articles until he came to one that made him stop. It was a single photo with no words. There was no other indication of where it came from except for a long web address at the top of the page.

"Where did you find this?" he snapped.

Jackson took the paper from his hand and studied it. "I'm not sure about this one. We ran a search on the company's name and all your team members' names and printed out everything we came across from this last year. Why are you asking?"

"That's not a client. That's Derek Latu with his wife, Laurie."

"He's married?" she asked, as if this were the last thing she expected to hear.

"Very happily. Surprised?" Cameron gave her a

pointed look. "I told you this shit doesn't tell the whole story." He gestured to the photo. "Yes, he has a wife, but she stays far away from any press. She's had some stalker issues in the past."

"Oh." Jackson looked at the web address again. "It doesn't come from anywhere I recognize."

"That's what worries me." He looked at the photo once more and set it aside on the table. "Can I keep this? I want to show it to Derek."

Jackson nodded and gathered together the rest of the clippings.

"Whether these photos represent jobs or—" she waved her hand around as if she were searching for the right words "—or other encounters is beside the point from a PR perspective. This is going to become the Blackmore Inc. image if you don't make some changes."

"Says my father," finished Cameron with more than a little bitterness.

He thought she'd deny it, but she didn't. Instead, Jackson gave him a look that was almost sympathetic. "Yes. But it's important for the company, too. Especially if you're saying we're not seeing the whole story."

"Even though the Australian division of Blackmore Inc. is doing better now than it was when my father ran the show?"

"Yep. Probably even because of it."

Cameron sighed. Well, at least they were on the same page in that regard.

"All right," he grumbled. "What's next?"

Jackson flipped through her file to the first pages, biting her lip. Cameron couldn't keep his eyes off those plump, soft lips that had promised him so much pleasure the night before. What would it feel like if she—

"I just want to make sure I have all the basics," she said, looking up at him. Her eyes rounded.

Shit. Were his thoughts so transparent?

Jackson's eyes skittered away and she cleared her throat. "You and three other men make up your main team for on-the-ground security. Max Jensen comes from a prominent ranching family in Australia, and you two were roommates at Princeton. He's the one with his photo on the front page of the papers."

Cameron scowled. "He's also the one who brought both clients and credibility into the Australian market when I took over. His family's name goes a long way down here."

She nodded and jotted a few notes before looking back up. "After you both graduated, he returned to Australia and played rugby, where he met Derek Latu. You enlisted in the army."

Cameron gave a dry laugh. "Much to my father's dismay."

"But not your grandfather's, I'm assuming," she said. "Following his path, the way he built this company."

Very good, Jackson McAllister. He crossed his arms and waited.

"You and Simon Rodriguez were in the same unit," she continued, "and when you both returned, you hired him."

Cameron nodded.

Jackson flipped the page and scanned it. "Not long after, your grandfather put you in charge of Australia and moved your father back to New York." She raised her gaze to his. "I'd imagine your father wouldn't have taken that very well."

Cameron didn't answer. This woman was good. She had done her background work and read between the lines. But even as sympathetic as she had sounded, he couldn't forget for a minute she was working for the board. Not for him.

Jackson looked back down at the pages in her file. "You and Simon Rodriguez came to Sydney, brought Max Jensen and Derek Latu on board, and the four of you started to rethink the company's strategy."

"That's about it," he said.

Jackson looked at him for an extra beat, her green eyes searching his. Then she stuffed her files into her bag. "Let's take a quick tour around the office so I can get a feel for what goes on here. Then we'll look at your schedule. I want to spend the first couple of days getting an idea of what you're doing now."

"Fine," he said, grabbing his briefcase.

Cameron stood up and took a deep breath. He'd just had a conversation with her and hadn't once thought about sex. Well, not for the last part of the conversation, anyway. Progress. He could do this.

She gathered her things, and he gestured to let her go first out of the conference room. Big mistake. Because now he was right behind her with a clear view of that nice round rear he had so appreciated last night. Her skirt was longer today, but it had a slit up the back that got him wondering. How high would it slide up her legs? She was wearing silky stockings. Were they the kind that went all the way up, or did they stop somewhere out of sight and leave the tops of her delicious thighs bare?

Shit. He turned his head and looked down the hall at anything he could find—the plants, the sprinkler system, the lights—anything but the spectacular view of Jackson calling his name.

She turned around. "Which way?"

"I'll lead," he growled. He turned down the hall and headed for the elevators. *Say something, you fuckwit.* Cameron mentally shook himself. "It's just the four of us principals, a couple of admins and some meeting rooms on this floor. The other three guys aren't in the office right now. We'll need to go downstairs for the rest of the company."

He pushed the elevator call button.

"The floor below us is where most of the logistics people sit as well as the teams under each of us four," he said. "Clients want all sorts of security these days, and since I took over the Sydney business, we've broadened according to what the companies here need."

The elevator doors opened, and they stepped in. *Just keep talking.*

"Derek and Max both head up on-the-ground security teams, and Simon is developing our surveillance branch. A lot of the work we do can be carried out in the office, but we work as a team when jobs require more specialized security. That's just for the very high-end clients, and the four of us are on-site for those jobs. Those are the ones that you see in the photos."

Cameron cleared his throat and shoved his hands in his pockets. The doors opened.

"We're two floors down now, in our IT department," he said. "With the kind of security we do, we can't outsource anything."

He led her around, introducing her to employees at all levels. He knew everyone in the company. He had to if he was going to entrust so many people's safety to them.

Jackson smiled and shook everyone's hands, remembering names and asking questions. He had to admit she was really good. But as they made their way through accounting, her eyes began to droop. She must be tired.

"You want to take a break?" he asked.

Jackson took off her glasses and rubbed her eyes. "I think I've seen enough to get us started. Let's head back upstairs."

He led the way back to the elevators. On the ride up, she looked more and more tired by the minute.

They finally came to the door of his office, and he opened it for her.

"Oh, my God," she said breathlessly, walking up to the tall glass windows. "That's the Harbour Bridge."

He started toward her, ready to point out the Opera House, but he froze as his mind kicked back into gear. He was not going to stand next to her and breathe in the warm scent of her hair. They needed to get back to business. "Yes," he grunted, trying not to look in her direction.

He hauled an extra chair over to the opposite side of his desk, then sank into his. She sat down, too, and he pulled up his schedule for the day before swiveling his monitor toward her.

"No meetings this morning?" she asked.

He shook his head. "Moved them all. I wasn't sure what you'd have in mind."

She bent over to look closer at his computer screen, giving him a flash down her button-up shirt. Luscious, round breasts strained against a lacy pink bra. Luscious, round breasts that he spent far too little time on last night. That he would never play with again. He forced his gaze back to the computer screen.

"What's this?" she asked, pointing to the lunch hour block.

"I work out at our gym every day. It's a few floors down from here. Below IT."

"Oh."

"You gonna observe me there, too?" he asked, fighting a grin.

She caught her lip between her teeth. "I'd check out everything with any other client."

"You're welcome to watch." Cameron gave her a lazy smile and added, "If the board insists."

A touch of pink stained her cheeks. "Maybe another day."

"Suit yourself," he said smoothly. "I'll probably be on the phone most of the afternoon checking in with clients. And then we'll meet the rest of the team for dinner tonight."

"They don't come into the office every day?"

"Most days I'm here, and they come in when they're not on security jobs." Thankfully, as CEO, Cameron had a good excuse not to travel—neglecting the daily operations was how his father got the Sydney office into trouble in the first place. The prominent clients in Sydney kept business booming, and his teammates could handle operations farther afield, if they came up. His aversion to flying wasn't exactly good for the business, long-term, but he'd figure that out at some point. "Today the guys are looking at one of the local venues where we're providing security for a high-profile client, a politician. You'll hear the details in this week's meeting."

"Okay," she said, stifling a yawn.

He raised an eyebrow. "This job's already boring you? I told you, our business is a lot more ordinary than your photos suggest."

She shook her head. "It's not that. The jet lag is killing me."

Her eyelids sank for a moment and then snapped back open. He saw an opportunity, and he took it.

"Listen, why don't you take a taxi back to your hotel for a few hours and catch up on some sleep," he said. "Like I said, I'll just be around the office answering messages and talking to clients."

She frowned. "Probably not a good idea on my first day."

"You won't miss anything," he said. "I promise I won't get into any trouble while you're gone."

Her eyelids drooped again. "I don't know... I had planned to cover a bit more."

"We're meeting the team for dinner at seven, so I'll come by your room around six and take you there."

"Okay, maybe you're right. I probably won't be productive like this, anyway," she said, suppressing another yawn. "But I can't miss that meeting."

"I won't let you."

Jackson nodded. "See you tonight, then." She grabbed her bag and he couldn't help noticing the sway of her hips as she walked out the door.

Once she disappeared, Cameron breathed a long sigh of relief. Thank God that was over. And he had just bought himself some time to get his head on straight.

It was only after Jackson was long gone that he realized his mistake. If he was going to forget that last night ever happened, he shouldn't be anywhere near her hotel room.

CHAPTER FOUR

JACKSON WOKE UP to the sound of chimes. She sat up and scanned the room. Her phone alarm flashed in the darkness. Oh, right. The Sydney hotel room. The one she had invited Cameron Blackmore back to for sex last night.

Nice move.

She reached for her phone on the nightstand and shut off the alarm. Stretching, she flopped back onto the bed. After six hours of sleep, the fog was finally lifting off her thoughts.

Which was a good thing because Cameron would be knocking on her door soon.

She rolled out of bed, washed her face and squeezed back into business attire, muttering to herself through the whole process. What the hell was she thinking last night? Actually she knew exactly what she'd been thinking: this guy is unbelievable. Scorching. Tempting enough to have a little of that fun Rob thought she was constitutionally incapable of. The kind of fun she had never let herself have.

Just one night indulging in one of those "good

things" she was long overdue for, and where did that get her? She managed to find the one man in Sydney she absolutely should not have sex with, under any circumstance. She was supposed to be fixing his reputation, not succumbing to it. She doubted the board would praise her thorough investigation skills in this area.

Jackson reached for her purse and pulled out her little red book. She flipped through the worn pages until she found the one labeled Sydney. The last item she had written was Manly Beach. She grabbed a pencil and wrote underneath, "Hot sex in Sydney." And then crossed it out. At least something good should come out of this mess.

Damn Cameron Blackmore and his deep voice and his stupid muscles he'd caught her staring at this morning. Who the hell had biceps you could see through a business shirt? And damn her own traitorous body. This morning she'd pictured office fantasies she didn't even know she had. The kinds of fantasies she should absolutely not be thinking about right before a dinner meeting with his team. The kind her career-oriented mind tried hard to avoid.

Shit. And now he was coming to her room? No.

Jackson stuffed the little red book back into her purse and grabbed her files. She leafed through them until she came to Cameron Blackmore's contact information, then sent him a text.

Meet me in the lobby.

Good. Maybe she could get this whole crazy first twenty-four hours in Sydney under control. And hope Cameron Blackmore didn't figure out that she was probably more at risk of losing her job than he was if anyone found out.

Jackson exhaled loudly and looked at the clock. Enough time to check her messages. She opened her laptop and got to work, reading through the updates from her other clients, responding to Kyle's questions. Luckily, Kyle was a brilliant assistant, much more on top of things than any other twenty-three-year-old she had worked with before. Jackson's shoulders sank in relief. No fires to put out.

She hovered her cursor over the last unopened message, debating whether or not to click on it. She couldn't ignore a message from her own mother, could she? Okay, she'd done it once or twice in the past, but she was in a different country. Maybe her mother was actually worried. Or excited to hear about her first trip to another continent. Right.

She sighed and clicked on the message. Just as she suspected. No *Just checking in to see if you're okay.* No *You're in Sydney! I'm so proud of you.* Instead, her mother had sent a link to her sister's latest blog post featuring the twins. The two-year-olds were feeding each other her sister's latest homemade baby food creation. Okay, it was cute. Very cute. She could almost hear Marcello and Marco's laughter as they stuffed each other's mouths full, dripping all over the expensive tile floors of Jami and Fabio's Brooklyn

town house. But Jami wouldn't worry about that—
the maid would clean up later. Her sister would be
enjoying the moment, enjoying her domestic bliss.

Unlike Jackson, Jami had managed the seemingly
impossible task of living up to all their mother's expectations. She had a faithful husband, adorable kids,
a big house and a successful career. For extra-credit
bonus, Jami was so damn nice and good-natured. Her
sister really was happy, and Jackson admired that,
even if it wasn't quite the kind of happiness she was
looking for. Jami had survived a type-A mother, a
philandering father and their inevitably calamitous
divorce relatively unscathed. Jackson? Well, she had
survived. Unscathed? Debatable.

At the end of the message, her mother hadn't forgotten to add her favorite saying: "Good things come
to those who wait." Thanks, Mom. Really subtle. As
if Jackson were just killing time in Sydney while
waiting for the rest of the things on her mother's
success checklist to fall into place. She was on her
own path…or, rather, she was on a ten-year plan to
get onto her own path.

She gritted her teeth and hit Reply.

Thanks for sending. Marcello and Marco are adorable, as always. PS I'm having a great time in Sydney.

For once, she was grateful her mother would
never think to ask about the nature of her "great
time." Jackson closed her laptop and headed for the

bathroom once more, pushing her mother out of her mind. She was finally in another country, a place where people went about life differently, thought about things differently. What would it be like to live another life, just for a while? That question was what had sparked her dreams of traveling long ago, when her parents were at their worst. But now traveling was more about adventure than escape, though an evening with Cameron Blackmore had certainly given her an X-rated perspective on what another life could feel like. She put on her makeup and practiced her cool, business-only smile in the mirror. She had faced sexy, built men before. She could do this.

Jackson browsed her shoe selection. Flats for walking, or heels to combat the height difference between mammoth Cameron and her? She frowned. Cameron wasn't making any wardrobe decisions based on her. No reason for her to do so for him, either.

She grabbed her flats, put them on and headed for the hotel room door. She swung it open and stepped out. And crashed into a large, solid body.

She heard an "oof," and strong arms closed around her before she fell to the ground.

Cameron.

For a moment, neither of them moved. His arms encircled her and she breathed in his warm, musky scent. God, he smelled good. She softened into him...

What the hell was she doing?

Jackson scrambled away. "You were supposed to meet me in the lobby," she snapped.

A look of realization crossed his face. "I wasn't sure who that message was from."

"You often get messages from women who want to meet you in the lobby?"

He opened his mouth to answer, but she cut him off. "Let's just go."

Jackson brushed by him and headed for the elevator. She reached the doors first and pressed the button. He shifted as they waited in silence. Was Cameron dreading the ride in this particular enclosed space, too? He loomed next to her, his bulky frame distractingly *there*.

The doors opened, and she didn't wait for any chivalrous gestures. She walked in and pressed the button for the lobby. The doors closed. She stole a glance at Cameron. He looked oblivious to her presence.

Damn him. How could he ignore what they had done together in this elevator less than twenty-four hours ago? And then there was the sex. Really, really good sex. She had never believed in all that "men are from Mars" crap, but for the first time, she wondered if men really were fundamentally different from women. Because as hard as she tried, she couldn't just turn off her reaction to him. And he could clearly turn off his.

The elevator dinged, and Jackson stomped out. She started for the lobby doors, not bothering to check if Cameron was following.

"Jackson?"

She stopped and turned around. "What?"

He caught up with her and stopped way too close for her current state of mind. Crap. Stepping farther away meant showing him just how poorly she was handling the "casual" part of casual sex. So she stayed put and wiped all traces of lust from her face. She hoped.

Over six feet of suit and muscle hovered only inches away. She tipped up her chin and met his gaze. Cameron was looking down at her with unexpected softness.

"We're not going to get through dinner like this," he said. His voice resonated inside her, quiet and intimate.

Jackson bit her lip. "You mean *I'm* not going to get through dinner. You seem to be well-practiced at this."

Cameron's eyes hardened. "You don't know anything about me."

"You're right," she said. "And you know nothing about me."

Jackson frowned. Maybe she was being a little harsh, but the gist of this conversation was right on. They knew nothing about each other. He didn't know about Cheater Rob and his "sensitive" dick or her ten-year plan or how much work it took to get this job or anything else that had landed her here in Sydney for what was becoming a nightmare assignment. Their night together was supposed to be about letting go, about fun.

And she certainly did let go and have fun with

Cameron. Now why the hell couldn't she just move on and stop drooling every time he was in sight?

Still, it wasn't his fault that she was temperamentally incapable of just having a fling. They were working together. She had to stop snapping at him.

Jackson took a deep breath. "Look, this has all been a bit much for me. We made a mistake, and there's nothing to do about it but move on." She gave him a smile she hoped looked confident. "I'll be fine at dinner."

The corners of his mouth tipped down, but he didn't say anything.

"Are you ready?" she asked.

"Yeah."

They headed out of the lobby and onto the street. As the warm air hit her, some of the tension eased. While New York was cold and gray in November, Sydney's summer was just coming into full swing. They came to the street corner, and a warm, gentle breeze blew from the direction of the water.

"The restaurant's not too far," said Cameron. "You okay walking?"

"Of course," she said and stepped off the curb to cross.

A large, warm arm wrapped around her waist and pulled her back just as a car swerved around the corner. Her breath caught in her throat. The driver honked his horn, and Cameron gave the guy the finger. He held her against the hard muscles of his chest for an extra beat.

"Look right, sweetheart," he whispered in her ear. "We drive on the other side of the road down here, remember?"

Right. She had managed to make it through the previous twenty-four hours without stepping in front of a car, but with a giant distraction named Cameron Blackmore standing next to her, her brain was apparently having trouble multitasking.

"Thanks," she mumbled. "Maybe you should lead."

He chuckled and released her. She straightened up. *Get it together, girl.* She was about to meet Cameron's team. She gave herself a little shake and tried to focus on the scenery.

Like in New York, tall glass facades mingled with older stone and brick buildings, but the Sydney streets felt cleaner. The whole city felt cleaner and brighter. It was rush hour, and a steady flow of people poured out of the offices and stores onto stone-laid sidewalks. Wow. She was actually in Australia.

Thank God she hadn't worn heels. Even flats were pressing on her toes. "Not too far" clearly meant something entirely different in Australian. Or maybe it was the fact that she took two steps for every one of Cameron's.

Jackson slowed when the harbor came into view.

"This is Circular Quay," Cameron said, pointing at the ferry terminal. "We're going to meet the team at a place out along the water."

Jackson looked where he was pointing out into the harbor. Boats moved slowly through the water, and behind them, the Sydney Opera House peeked out among the buildings. She reached into her purse and pulled out her little red book. She flipped through the pages until she felt Cameron's stare. Wait. Her most recent addition to the list was not exactly the message she wanted to send right now. She stuffed it back into her bag and pretended to look at the harbor. It worked. Cameron crossed the street, and she followed.

But did she write "visit Sydney Opera House" or had she wanted to see a performance there? Probably the former, since her teenage self wouldn't have had much interest in operas or plays. Did seeing the building from a distance count? Nah. Someday she'd find the time to stay in Sydney for a month or two and do it properly.

But since she'd moved out of Rob's apartment, her rent had doubled. Which had turned a five-year plan into a ten-year plan. So for now, she'd have to soak up as much of the city as she could from afar. With Cameron Blackmore at her side. Which, all things considered, might be ideal under any other circumstance but this.

They walked along the water's edge. She stole a look at Cameron and found that he was studying her.

"You were good with everyone at the office today," he said. "Impressive."

Jackson smiled. "Thanks. I like my job."

"What do you like about it?"

"I can do a lot in just a couple weeks, and that

feels good," she said. "Most companies just need to get on the right track."

He looked genuinely interested, so she continued.

"Before I came here I was in California," she said. "This company and its union had been in negotiations that turned sour, and that got lots of press. But when they reached an agreement, both the company and the workers wanted some good PR."

"Did your boost work?"

Jackson nodded. "It did. And they're still following the post-intervention plan I made, which is always a good sign."

He was quiet, and she was perfectly happy to just take in her surroundings. The ferries and smaller boats floated in and out of the harbor. Above them, the bridge spanned the bay. *Climb the Harbour Bridge.* That was definitely on the list. Someday.

"What happens when you get an assignment from a company you don't believe in?" he asked.

Jackson sighed. "I try to find something redeeming about them. But someday I'd like to be able to pick and choose my jobs."

"What would you choose?" he asked.

She laughed. "Definitely more international locations. Maybe Paris?"

If this trip went well, maybe she could. Now that she was getting some of the larger clients, there might be more international travel in her future.

"What do you think about Blackmore Inc.?" he

asked. "Have you found something redeeming about us yet?"

She laughed. "Are you fishing for compliments?"

Cameron grinned and rubbed the back of his neck. "You have a whole file on me. I'm just trying to figure out what I'm in for these next two weeks."

She raised an eyebrow at him.

They had somehow found themselves walking closer, and his hand brushed against hers. He didn't move away, and neither did she. He fell into step next to her, and for a moment she let herself forget he was Cameron Blackmore. She let him be the man he was last night: funny, smooth-talking and tempting as hell. And this time he was in a little better focus. He was such a physical presence that she'd have trouble ignoring him, even if she didn't know just how good a night with him could be. And now that she knew?

Cameron pointed ahead to where the pedestrian walk split. One path led up to the Sydney Opera House, and another lower path continued along the water. Nestled below the higher path was an outdoor bar with tables.

"There's the place where we're headed," he said.

But as they came closer, his easy smile disappeared. They had managed to bridge the awkwardness of their eye-opening introduction for a little while, but that bridge had disappeared. He widened his paces, and Jackson took a couple quick steps to keep up.

Cameron approached the hostess and grumbled

a few indecipherable words at her. The woman nodded and led them inside, underneath the upper level of the promenade, to a table in the back corner of the restaurant. As Jackson's eyes adjusted to the dim light, she recognized the three men sitting around the table from their photos. They were all a lot larger in person.

The blond guy, the one who had been caught whispering in the high-profile actress's ear, took one long look at her and turned to Cameron.

"You brought a date to this meeting, you fuckwit?" he said with a laugh.

Cameron's growl rolled through his chest. "Max Jensen, meet Jackson McAllister. And, yes, he's always this charming."

Max sized her up with new appreciation, and his smile grew wider. He stood up and stuck out his hand. "Welcome to Sydney, Ms. McAllister. I trust Cameron's made you feel welcome."

There was no good way to answer that comment. She shook his hand and gave him a neutral smile. "Nice to meet you."

The other two stood up.

A dark-haired man with stunning green eyes extended his hand next. "Simon Rodriguez," he said.

The last man stepped forward, the one who was pictured with his wife. This guy was the biggest of the group, probably a Pacific Islander, and he was by far the most relaxed. "Derek Latu," he said, reaching out his hand. She shook it, and they all sat down.

The table was silent. Right. Best to get straight to the point.

"I'm sure you're all thrilled to have me here," she said.

The three men chuckled.

"I didn't come to tell you all what to do," she continued. "The numbers suggest you're doing a great job running this business. But after some recent press, the board wants an image adjustment. I'm here to help with that."

She looked around the table for reactions. They were all looking between her and Cameron. So she hazarded a glance at him, too. He was sitting straight up in his chair, arms crossed, with a rock-hard expression on his face. A flush crept up his neck, and she wondered how a man this easily provoked could make it in the security business. She almost laughed.

"Mr. Blackmore, did you want to add something?" she asked calmly.

He shook his head. Derek smirked.

The waitress appeared, and Jackson let out her breath. The woman set down a round of beers in front of the men. Cameron took a long drink from the bottle, finishing half before he set it down.

"What would you like to drink, ma'am?"

Should she order wine? Nope, probably not a good idea. Jackson was going to need all her wits about her for this meeting, especially if Cameron was already this worked up.

"Just water please," she said.

The waitress left in silence. This was going to be painful. She reached into her bag and pulled out a pad of paper.

"Let's take care of this," she said and turned back to the other three. "I'm here to test a couple key public relations opportunities to see what works best and plan accordingly. So as per the board's instructions, I'll spend a few days tailing Mr. Blackmore. I'll shadow one of your jobs—"

"What?" Cameron snapped.

Jackson raised an eyebrow. "I thought that was clear."

"This isn't a sporting event, Ms. McAllister." His voice held contempt. "It's private security that has the potential to be dangerous for everyone involved. It's not for spectators, no matter what the board says." He rubbed his forehead and muttered, "What the hell are they thinking?"

Cameron had a point. What the hell *was* the board thinking? The Blackmore Inc. team was supposed to do their job and make sure Jackson got a good view? From what she'd heard of this board from her colleagues at the PR firm, this sounded like another one of their armchair decisions that had little to do with reality. It wouldn't be the first. Or maybe this was Harlan Blackmore's more personal directive, aimed to take Cameron down a notch. Perhaps Cameron deserved some sympathy… She might have felt bad for him if he wasn't still sneering in her direction. She met his glare and tipped up her chin at him. "The board is thinking that I can take care of myself just fine, Mr. Blackmore," she said slowly, as if she were explaining this to a child.

Cameron clamped his jaw shut and Jackson fought not to roll her eyes. Enough of Cameron Blackmore's caveman tantrums. She had to get out of here and regain her composure.

"If you'll excuse me," she said and headed for the ladies' room.

CHAPTER FIVE

CAMERON WATCHED JACKSON disappear in silence. Only after the door closed did he breathe a sigh of relief.

He turned back to his team. Each was watching him with varying degrees of amusement on their faces.

"Well, that was interesting," said Simon with a grin. "And informative."

Derek raised his eyebrows. "I'm not convinced you're going to make it through this dinner without exploding, let alone two weeks. But it's a fun show to watch."

They all snickered. Cameron pressed his lips together.

"I don't know why you're so wound up, Cam," said Max. "So she's hot. That should make the next few days much more entertaining. Though I don't get the feeling she's the type to—"

"Shut the hell up, all of you," said Cameron.

All three of them laughed at him. He grumbled a few curses under his breath.

"Come on, Cameron. You gotta admit this is a little

funny," said Simon. "We've been in a shitload of intense situations, and you have never once shown signs of cracking. But one day with an attractive woman telling you what to do and you're getting ready to detonate."

"Hilarious," growled Cameron. "It's only my company that's on the line."

That sobered them all up a bit.

He heaved out a long breath. Any time he had gotten involved with someone he'd worked with, he had always waited until the job was over. And it only took one night to scratch that itch before it was gone. So why the hell wasn't this under control?

All afternoon, he had told himself that once the shock of seeing her in the office wore off, everything would return to normal. But she'd ended up in his arms more than once since then. This day was almost over and he was still far from under control.

The last straw was the walk along the harbor. Talking as if they were on some sort of date. As if she and her firm weren't hired by Harlan Blackmore to get Cameron back in line. But as soon as the restaurant came into sight, reality had hit him. She was here because Cameron's successes at Blackmore Inc. were reminders of his father's failures.

He had to get his shit together.

Derek sighed. "I get that you can't stand what the board is doing, but like you said, it's just a couple weeks. You've been in far worse situations. And maybe she can help show the board how important the monitoring side of the business is becoming."

"Maybe you could try to just be decent to her," said Simon. "That might work. Just a thought."

What was he supposed to say? That he had already put their company on the line by screwing the woman that could torpedo their jobs? And now he couldn't stop thinking about what else he wanted to do with her, to her. At least they hadn't gotten into anything dirtier...

"Here she comes," Simon murmured.

Jackson sat down and flipped through her notepad to a bullet-pointed page. She read her first point and began with questions about the team's daily routines. Her voice was clipped and professional, and she didn't once glance in Cameron's direction. He didn't hear a word she said.

Just try to be decent to her? What the hell did *decent* look like when just waiting next to her for the elevator was enough to get him hard? He was supposed to spend the next week alone with her, on full alert, never once slipping up. That alone was bad enough, but struggling through this in front of his team was pushing him over the edge fast.

Even the way Max was looking at her now made his blood boil. And Max wasn't even trying to pick her up. What the hell was wrong with him?

"It's all at your place, isn't it, Cameron?" said Derek.

Cameron blinked. "Sorry. What's at my place?"

"The master list of all clients," said Derek, raising an eyebrow.

Jackson looked at him, all business. "I need it for the conference with the board tomorrow morning."

Cameron shook his head. "It doesn't leave my apartment. That stipulation is written into some of our clients' contracts."

"I need to verify the photos against the client list," she said.

"Not going to happen," said Cameron. "You'll have to trust us when we tell you they're clients."

"That's not going to happen, Mr. Blackmore," Jackson said, matching his tone perfectly. "I'm here because trusting you isn't working for the board."

He bit back an angry retort. The other three were watching this exchange, back and forth, waiting for someone to falter. But Jackson didn't. Her cool gaze was fixed on him, waiting for his next move.

Simon cleared his throat. "As entertaining as this is to watch, I'm going to jump in here with an easy solution. Why doesn't Ms. McAllister go to your place tonight and look at the client list? It never leaves your place, and Ms. McAllister gets to verify the names in person."

Jackson's eyes widened and Cameron froze. Jackson in his apartment? No way.

"Fine. That sounds like a good solution," said Jackson, her voice a little higher.

The whole table turned to him.

"Fine," mumbled Cameron. "Fine." He looked up and met Derek's gaze. His friend glanced at Jackson and back at him, a deep line forming between his eyebrows. Cameron turned away. The last thing he wanted was for Derek to think through this situation further.

Jackson didn't miss a beat. She consulted her bullet-pointed list and asked her next question. But Cameron couldn't move on. Him and Jackson alone in his apartment tonight? Not fine at all.

By the time they left the restaurant, Cameron still hadn't come up with a good reason why Jackson shouldn't go back to his place that night. But the master list never left the privacy of his home. Any other solution had the potential to betray the confidentiality of his most vulnerable—or most secretive—clients. And he wasn't ready to stoop as low as claiming sudden food poisoning to get out of this visit. Almost, but not quite. Besides, excuses would only delay the problem, not solve it.

So, he found himself standing at Circular Quay with Jackson as his private launch arrived to take them home. The captain, Ralph, helped Jackson climb in, and Cameron followed after her. She hadn't looked at him once since they'd left the restaurant. It was going to be a long, hard night in every way possible.

She didn't say a word as they left the dock. Her eyes widened as they passed the Opera House and then she turned for a view of the Harbour Bridge. He leaned back against his seat and watched her. Strands of her lustrous brown hair escaped from the bun and whipped across her face as the boat picked up speed. The corners of her mouth turned up. In the restaurant she was all business, but now, as she looked out into the harbor, she looked softer, the way she'd looked the night before.

The thought dampened his already pessimistic outlook for the evening. He was going to spend the next hour or two trying not to think about all the things he'd rather be doing with her in his apartment.

The launch glided through the waters into his little harbor. Ralph tied up the boat at a private jetty, and he and Jackson wordlessly made their way across the dock to his building. The silence grew heavier as they rode the elevator up to his apartment.

She took the fastener out of her hair to retighten the knot, and he crossed his arms, willing himself not to look at the front of her silky blouse, where one too many buttons had come undone in the process. He was not going to look at the tops of two of the most delicious breasts he had ever seen. Why the hell hadn't he focused more on them the night before? Finally, the elevator doors opened, and Cameron stepped out first. He wasn't going to watch her from behind again. He entered his penthouse, hung his jacket in the hall closet and headed for his bedroom.

"You can wait in there," he said to Jackson, gesturing toward the dining room. "I'll be right back with the list."

When he returned, he found her waiting by the window, looking over the harbor. He sat down at the table and opened his laptop. She spoke to him without turning around.

"Your office isn't your only view of the Harbour Bridge," she murmured. "I like this one even better."

"Thanks." He looked out at the water. He had chosen this penthouse apartment for its view, but how long had it been since he'd actually enjoyed it? All the money spent on furniture and rugs and whatever else the company's decorator had chosen to fill this place was a waste. But the board had insisted. A CEO didn't live in a 300-square-foot apartment without a sofa.

"Head of a successful company in Australia, apartment with a view, commute in your own private boat." She sighed. "Quite a life you have for yourself, Mr. Blackmore."

"Please don't call me Mr. Blackmore. Not here, not after—" He stopped. He shouldn't even mention it. "It's Cameron. And yes, I've made a good life here. Probably should start learning to appreciate it more."

"You should," she said softly. "More than one bedroom in New York is a dream, never mind the view."

She slipped into a chair next to his and pulled out the folder of press clippings. "I'm sorry to do this to you, but I need to confirm that each person in the photos is on your list. If it all checks out, I'll report back to the board tomorrow morning and let them know these are clients, not…anything else."

Cameron's jaw clenched. What the hell? "So the board sent you over to make a list of who my team might have taken home?" growled Cameron. His day was getting worse by the minute.

"Don't flatter yourself," Jackson said coolly. "No one

cares how much mediocre sex you have. The board just cares about your company's image. So let's move on."

Cameron's jaw dropped open. *Mediocre sex?* Was she implying that their night together was mediocre? No. Impossible. The night before was fantastic. She'd thought so, too…hadn't she?

Jackson picked up one of the photos from her file.

"Mr. Blackmore?" she asked in a sugary tone. "Can we get on with this?"

He grunted some approximation of yes.

"Good," she said. "How do you want to work this?"

"I can't show you the whole client list. We're very careful with our clients' privacy, even if the board isn't." He narrowed his eyes, ready for a challenge.

She gave him a look of exaggerated patience. "How about you tell me the name of the person in this photo and show me the name in your database."

"Fine."

She shuffled through the photos, one by one, and he clicked on each corresponding name.

His shoulders tightened with every minute he sat next to her. *Mediocre?* Could it be that he had so completely misjudged her reaction to him last night? Because though he'd been with more than his fair share of women, last night stood out. No. There had been a moment that passed between them yesterday, as she'd looked up at him, and he was under the impression her orgasms were more than satisfying. Both of them.

Maybe she was just taunting him. She must be. He

had to believe that, if only because he really didn't want to think about the other men who had tasted her and made her come in some way he hadn't.

Cameron had to find out for sure.

Jackson came to the photo of him and the two women coming out of the bar. She hesitated.

"Names?" she asked, her face blank.

He mirrored her expression. "Alya Petrova is a client. Her sister, Natasha, isn't."

She stared at him, as if she were waiting for more information. He didn't say anything. Let her think the worst. It was Max who couldn't stay away from Natasha, not him. But that was Max's problem. And none of Jackson's business.

She bit her lip.

"Did you want more details?" he asked, crossing his arms.

She shook her head and wrote the names on the photo.

Jackson continued through the rest of the papers, but she didn't look nearly as composed as she had when they started. Good. When they got to the end, she closed her folder and stuffed it in her bag. She stood up and ran a hand down her skirt. He rose to face her. She was close enough that she had to tilt her head up to meet his eyes.

"Is that all you need from me tonight, Jackson?" he asked.

He had meant to provoke her, but when her first name slipped out of his mouth, the question sounded much more seductive. A few more strands of hair had fallen from the knot on top of her head, and she tucked them behind her ear. He shouldn't be pushing her like this. He should just let it go. But he couldn't bring himself to back down, not when she looked so uncertain. And so sexy.

She swallowed. "Yes."

"Good," he said. "I wouldn't want to subject you to another mediocre night."

She met his gaze and shrugged. "It's okay. Not everything can live up to expectations."

A low rumble escaped from his mouth. Live up to her expectations? What the hell kind of expectations did she have?

She smiled at his reaction and continued with a sigh. "Guys like you always think you're better than you really are."

He narrowed his eyes. "Guys like me?"

She counted off his descriptors on her long, slender fingers. "Tall and fit, used to getting your way all the time, want every woman to think you—"

Cameron was done with her list. He closed his hand around hers and said, "Right now, I'm not interested in what any other woman thinks. I want to hear what you think. When you got down on all fours, ready for my cock, was that just mediocre? Or do we need to do something more to satisfy you?"

CHAPTER SIX

JACKSON'S HEART POUNDED in her chest, and she bit her lip to keep from smiling. Shit. How the hell had this moved so quickly into dangerous territory? Actually, she knew the answer. She had been aching for a chance to push his buttons the way he'd pushed hers all evening. He wouldn't back down from a challenge. So she'd gone straight for it.

And now he had taken the bait.

She could lie to him and end this stupid game right now. She could tell him that their night wasn't exceptional and she wasn't interested in another. He wouldn't push her. That would be her smartest move right now. Just shut this whole conversation down and leave his annoyingly luxurious apartment. But she couldn't bring herself to do it.

Still, Cameron didn't need yet another ego boost. She couldn't tell him that "satisfied" didn't even begin to capture the glow of their night. He had probably heard gushing praise from the long list of women in his one-night-stand history, and Jackson wasn't interested in getting in that line. Or even thinking about it.

So what the hell did she do now?

She stared at the way his hand fit around hers. Damn, he was big. And he waited her out with an arrogant, impossible-to-ignore stance. The wide muscled wall of his chest was directly in her line of sight. Close enough to touch. She balled her fist, resisting.

Then, slowly, he rubbed a calloused thumb up and down the inside of her palm. He leaned forward until his lips were next to her ear, but he didn't touch her. "You weren't satisfied when I got down on my knees and licked you until you couldn't stand?"

Jackson let out a little moan. Shit. She was in so much trouble right now. Her fingers trembled. How much longer could she keep herself together?

"What's your answer?" he whispered. "You can't blame it on bad eyesight this time."

He was going to keep taunting her until she called his bluff.

She couldn't help herself.

She took off her glasses and dropped them in her bag. Then she wove her fingers into his hair. She found his lips with hers and pressed a slow, hungry kiss on them. He groaned and opened his mouth to hers. When her tongue touched his, it was as if his whole body lit up. He let go of her other hand and one big arm came around her back while the other slipped under her rear and pulled her against him. His enormous erection grew against her thigh, and she smiled. Right now, he wanted her just as badly as she wanted him. And that was probably as close to a win as she was going to get tonight.

She sucked his bottom lip between hers and gently bit down. His big body tensed and thrust against her. He pulled away, panting, and met her eyes.

"Done refreshing your memory?" he breathed, the corners of his mouth turning up.

Damn. She should have known he wasn't going to let go of this topic so easily. Still, she wasn't going to tell him what he wanted to hear: that he was amazing in bed. Even if he was. Jackson searched for another diversion.

"This isn't a good idea."

He chuckled. "What the hell is the difference between doing this once or twice?"

Well, he had a point.

Cameron pressed his hips against hers, and her breath caught. One hand found her breast. "It's just a question of whether or not you think you'll be... satisfied."

As the last word came out of his mouth, he pinched her hard nipple through her shirt. She cried out. How could he get her body going so easily? All she wanted was for him to do it again and again.

He closed his eyes, seeming to savor her reaction, and his erection pressed harder against her. She squirmed against his big body, seeking more contact. For a moment, he looked like he was struggling to hold himself together just as much as she was. But when he spoke again, his voice betrayed no weakness.

"Did you wake up thinking about me this morning? Wanting me inside you?"

He was *not* going to push her into lying. But, damn, he was already so full of himself.

"Maybe," she tried. It came out more as a whimper than a challenge.

Cameron's face lit up into a wide smile, and he started to laugh, a deep, low laugh of amusement. "Now we're getting somewhere."

Jackson couldn't hold back much longer. Her own laughter grew inside until she leaned her head forward on his chest and let it out. He let go of her breast and wrapped his arm around her shoulders, pulling her closer. Breathing him in, she relaxed a little. It felt way too good to be there.

She tilted her head, and when she met his deep blue eyes again, the cool distance in his expression was gone.

"What do you think, Ms. Jackson McAllister?" he rumbled. "This has been one hell of a ride today. How do you want it to end?"

She blinked. After their long day of sparring, he was giving in. His guard was down, and behind it there was a hint of tenderness. This was the man she'd caught a glimpse of at the end of last night; the man who had covered her with a blanket and looked at her so seriously, so quietly before he left.

His defenses would come back up soon. Considering his reputation, there was a chance that this side of him wasn't even real. But right now, it felt real.

Sex with someone like him wouldn't—couldn't—be tender, but that wasn't what she wanted.

"I've wanted you all day long," she admitted.

His body tightened against hers, and he drew in a sharp breath. Damn, he was tempting. She wanted to see him react to her again. All her dirty thoughts from the day came at once, and she started with the first.

"When I caught you looking down my shirt this morning, I had this fantasy. I wanted to kneel down between your legs," she whispered, her voice husky. "I wanted to suck you off right there in your office. And make you desperate the way you made me desperate last night. I wanted to hear you beg to come in my mouth. And I'd let you."

"Fuuuck." He shuddered.

His hips flexed against hers. He was thick and hard and hit on all the right places. She had never talked like this before to a man, but if they were going for it tonight, she might as well let it all loose. They had already stepped over the line. And she had a thousand ideas about where to take it.

"You wanna make that fantasy come true right now?"

"Yes," she whispered.

He let her go, and for a moment, she thought he was going to call it all off. That this had been just another game to jockey for power.

But he grabbed her hand and led her to the living

room. A man this sexy didn't deserve to have a sitting room this nice, too. Sparse but warm. Black leather couch, white shag rug and art Cameron Blackmore couldn't have picked for himself. Or maybe he did. She really knew almost nothing personal about this man. Aside from what it was like to have his mouth between her legs.

Cameron leaned against the back of his sofa, and gave her a dark smile.

She toyed with the buttons on her blouse. "If you want something, you need to ask for it," she whispered.

He reached down and stroked himself. "I want you to take me out and suck me. Deep."

Jackson closed her eyes at the erotic rush radiating through her. If last night was sexy as hell, this was even more intense. He was giving a bit of control over to her. Where would that take them?

He pulled his shirt over his head to reveal the insanely carved muscles of his chest. A jagged scar cut across his ribs—she hadn't noticed it the night before. She knelt down in front of him and unbuttoned his pants. His erection pressed against them as she eased down his zipper. It opened up to his boxers, where a wet circle covered his tip.

"Take it out," he rasped.

She eased his boxers over his hips, revealing his thick, hard length. Oh, God. She had seen him last night, but up close his size was still overwhelming.

Cameron leaned against the back of the sofa and spread his legs.

She stepped back and continued to unbutton her shirt, slowly, drawing out each movement. He brought his hand down to his erection for a few final hard tugs, his gaze fixed on her chest. "Just thinking about your breasts all day made me hard."

She let her blouse fall to the floor.

"You're beautiful," he whispered. He rested his hand on the sofa and smiled. "You can taste and play all you want. But I like it rough when I finish. Is that okay with you?"

His eyes were dark and half-closed...with lust?

"I want you to show me just how rough you like it," she said.

He squeezed his eyes shut, as she moved closer, and his erection bobbed enthusiastically.

Jackson reached for his rock-hard length and her body tingled with all sorts of ideas for how this could go. Would he grab her hair? Would he show her how to take more? What did he like best? She tried a few experimental swipes of her tongue. God, he tasted like dirty sex, so she licked him again. She ran her tongue down his long length and up again. He took a sharp breath, so she ran her tongue down it again, stopping at his base.

"Suck on my balls," he groaned.

She took one in her mouth and played with it, then the other. He muttered a low string of incomprehensible words.

She replaced her mouth with her hand and caressed a little more.

Her gaze darted up to his. He was staring at her, watching everything she did with a dark intensity in his eyes. He was unbelievably gorgeous.

"What else do you want?" A tremor ran through his body as she spoke.

"Suck me hard, Jackson," he said through clenched teeth. "I want to give you a mouthful."

She smiled. This was what she wanted. To make him unravel before her, from the power of her touch. God, this was hot. Her own body was on fire as she leaned forward and put her lips around him. He moaned, and she took him deeper. Playing with different techniques, she drew out and in.

His hands wove into her hair, tugging at her fastener, and her waves tumbled down her back. He grabbed on and guided her in and out, setting the pace. His breaths were short and harsh. His hips lifted off the edge of the sofa as he began to thrust into the back of her mouth. Deeper. She gagged, and he froze.

"Shit," he snarled. "Sorry, sweetheart."

She pulled back and looked at him. "I don't want you to be gentle," she whispered. "I want exactly what you're giving me. I want you to lose control."

Her own voice was breathy and full of need. His grip on her hair tightened, and she took him back into her mouth. She reached between her own legs and teased herself. Whoa. She was getting close, too. She sucked hard, and with a groan he took over. Having him in her mouth was perversely erotic. She angled his erection down her throat until he lost his rhythm. He flexed hard and came with a loud growl. Jackson's body was alive with raw, crude pleasure as he panted and shuddered above her.

He unclenched her hair and bent over her, muttering curses. She released him, and he smoothed her hair down her back in soft, almost reverent strokes. He kissed the top of her head, then tucked himself in and held out a hand to help her up.

Jackson's knees ached, and she was a little dizzy from the whole experience.

"I think I should sit down," she said.

He rubbed his eyes and nodded. He still hadn't said anything, and she wasn't sure what she wanted to say, either.

Jackson picked up her blouse and walked to the other side of the dark sofa. She sank into the soft pillows and took a couple long breaths. What now? Did she just grab her bag and leave?

Cameron rustled behind her. His arms wrapped around her from the back of the sofa, and he bent down so his breath was in her ear.

"That was so good," he said, his voice rough.

She nodded.

"Unbelievably good."

Jackson smiled. "For me, too." She turned to look at him, and the corners of his mouth kicked up.

He let go of her, and cool air brushed over her skin. He came around the sofa and knelt down in front of her, resting his hands on her thighs.

"We're not done here," he said.

Why wasn't this a good idea? She could barely remember at this point. Besides, this might be her last chance with Cameron. She swallowed and whispered, "Okay."

"Okay?" Cameron laughed. "You're going to have to do better than that, sweetheart."

He angled a pillow on the arm of the sofa and nodded for her to turn and lean back on it. He guided one of her legs up to rest on the back of the couch and scooted her skirt up over her hips.

"Now, let's try that again," he said, climbing onto the couch between her open legs. He rested back on his heels and smiled. "Do you want me to get you off?" There was dark heat in his eyes, and he put a hand down his boxers and adjusted himself.

She could ask for anything she wanted right now, and he would do it. Should she ask for something that guaranteed pleasure, or was this the once-in-a-lifetime chance to try something that she never thought she would. His question from the night before came back to her. *Have you ever played here?* If anyone could do that right, it was certainly Cameron Blackmore. Her pulse thumped in her throat.

No. Some things were probably better left to the imagination.

Jackson licked her lips as she made her decision. "I want you to get me off with your mouth," she said.

Cameron smiled with a look of smug satisfaction. "You can watch me."

He lowered himself between her legs and started slowly, teasing her thighs and kissing her through her panties. When she moved to slip off the piece of silk, Cameron laughed, tickling her.

"Be patient. I want to take my time with this."

And he did. He explored the inside of her legs, around each sensitive spot. He was leisurely and thorough, and the deep groans mingling with her breathy sighs told her that he was enjoying it as much as she was. As she lifted her hips and arched with pleasure toward his mouth, he held her tighter, attending to each different place, testing her responsiveness. He was relentless, building her up and then easing her down, over and over until she grabbed his hair.

"Please, Cameron," she panted. "Now."

He swirled his tongue, focusing on her clit, pushing her over the edge as she bucked her hips against him. Everything exploded in white-hot shards of pleasure through her. He didn't stop. He drew out her orgasm until it subsided in gentle waves. She let go of his hair, and he sat back. He was a beautiful sight, all tense muscles and a look of triumph on his face. She was open and exposed, but she didn't move. She just watched him. He wiped his mouth with the back of his hand and smiled.

Then he met her eyes, and slowly he lowered his body over hers. His erection throbbed urgently against her, but the rest of him was under tight control. He kissed her on the lips and gave her a soft bite on the neck.

"I want to be inside you so bad, Jackson," he whispered in her ear. "And I don't know if I'll ever get a chance to do it again."

"So do it now," she said.

He rolled his hips into hers with a deep groan. One of his hands cupped her face, and he kissed her.

"It's going to be fast and hard," he said, his lips brushing against hers.

"I like fast and hard," she said.

"Good." He eased back and pulled the wallet out of his back pocket to grab a condom. He lowered his boxers. Did his girlfriends ever get used to his sex drive? But he'd said himself he wasn't the type that had girlfriends.

Cameron tore off the wrapper and rolled the condom down his impressive length. He lifted one of her legs to rest on his shoulder, and he teased her, gliding over her firmly.

"You want this?" he growled.

"Yes," she breathed.

He positioned himself and then slammed into her. Oh, God. She cried out at the overwhelming fullness, and Cameron's face twisted in agonizing pleasure. He pulled out and started to move. He swore and thrust harder. All of his tight control dissolved. It was as if he had given in and let something deeper, something more basic, take over. His eyes were dark and alive, and her body sang under his. Her hips matched his rhythmic movements, seeking a second release that finally came. Explosive pleasure washed over her. He drove into her a few more times and threw his head back in an enormous roar. His big body jerked as he came.

He fell down onto his arms, his head hanging over her. He closed his eyes, and his chest heaved. She wanted to pull him down and feel the weight of him on her. She wanted to draw out the deep satisfaction of this encounter.

But that wasn't what this night was about. That wasn't what Cameron Blackmore was about.

She shifted under him, and he blinked his eyes open. He looked down at her. His gaze was soft, full of wonder. He opened his mouth as if to speak, but he seemed to change his mind. Instead he pulled out and took off his condom.

"You are really fucking hot," he said as he got off the couch and headed for the kitchen.

That was what he wanted to say to her? That she was hot? That look on his face had moved her. Damn him. He had to go and spoil this night by opening his stupid mouth. Because for a moment, she'd almost gotten carried away. For a moment, she'd thought they had hit on something more.

But all things considered, this was probably the best way to end the night. Call it a reality check.

Quickly she squirmed off the couch and shimmied her crushed skirt back over her hips. She shuffled the pillows and dug up her shirt, now crumpled into an ugly mess. She shoved her arms into the sleeves and buttoned it up.

Cameron wandered back into the room with two glasses of water in his hands, but he stopped when he caught sight of her.

"Jackson?" he said. "Are you leaving?"

She had to get out of his apartment before she did anything stupid. He hadn't deceived her. She knew this encounter wasn't about anything more than pleasure, and he had just taken her orgasm to a new level. So why the hell did she feel like snapping at him?

Jackson put on her best business face and smiled. "Early calls, meeting tomorrow with the board. As you know."

She found her way to his ridiculously stylish dining room table and picked up her bag, but by the time she reached the elevator door, Cameron was standing in front of it.

"What's going on, Jackson?" he asked.

"Absolutely nothing is going on, Cameron," she said smoothly, forcing another smile. "Isn't that the point of this?"

She stared at him, challenging him to disagree. He didn't. His deep blue eyes were guarded, wary as he looked down at her. The elevator door opened.

"Excuse me," she said, motioning to the door.

He stepped aside and she walked in. The doors closed, and she shoved her hand into her bag, searching for her glasses. It was only when she reached the street that Jackson realized she had no idea how to get back to her hotel room.

CHAPTER SEVEN

CAMERON BLACKMORE YANKED open the door to his office building. More accurately, his father's office building. It was one of many assets that Cameron had added to the Blackmore Inc. empire, all ultimately controlled by his father.

Cameron was a thorn in his father's side that would never go away. If he had been a little older, a little more experienced when his grandfather died, Harlan Senior would have bypassed Cameron's father altogether and named him chairman of the board. Cameron knew it. His father knew it. The board knew it.

But what Harlan Junior couldn't understand was that Cameron had no desire to take over his job. He'd much rather be in the Sydney office with his team than in a boardroom in New York. Which meant he never had to see another airplane in his life. Let one of his half brothers take on that role and leave Cameron as the master of his own domain.

Harlan Blackmore was good at bullshit like country clubs and photo ops—much better at schmoozing than he was at the actual business of running a company. But no matter what his father threw his way, Cameron wouldn't walk away from his grandfather's legacy. His father had used Cameron's strong sense of loyalty to keep him in line in the aftermath of his parents' awful divorce. And now he was counting on this same sense of loyalty to Harlan Senior to keep Cameron from rebelling against the board outright.

Which was the reason Cameron was in this current mess in the first place.

Though there was no way to blame last night's mess on his father. That fell squarely on his own shoulders. He had replayed the scene at least a hundred times since the elevator doors closed behind her, and he still couldn't shake the hurt on Jackson's face.

Telling her she was hot was about the stupidest thing he had done in a while, and considering the last two days of stupid moves, that was saying something. He had thrown it out to cover up what almost came out of his mouth as he looked down at Jackson, still buried deep inside of her. He'd almost told her that he wanted to do this every day for the rest of his life. That this was what he had been missing. And that would have taken this messed-up situation to a new level of messed-up-ness.

Cameron walked into the elevator and punched the button for the top floor. He gritted his teeth. His entire business depended on his ability to plan, to foresee all potential problems, to make everything run smoothly, but nothing about the last two days had gone right. And he had only a couple hours to come up with a new plan to dig himself out of the latest hole he'd made.

Then Jackson McAllister would show up at the office again.

"Good morning, Mr. Blackmore," Chloe chirped as he walked through the glass doors. "Mr. Latu, Mr. Jensen and Mr. Rodriguez are waiting for you in the large conference room."

Right. First he had to get through this meeting. These guys knew him better than anyone else in the world. One of them was going to figure out how badly he had screwed up soon. Judging from the night before at dinner, Cameron had his money on Derek. But that wasn't going to happen today. Soon this meeting would be over and he'd have time to do a little thinking in the weight room before he had to face Jackson again.

And figure out how not to botch this situation further.

He grabbed the handle to the conference room door and took a deep breath. Game time. He swung it open.

Derek, Max and Simon sat around one end of the long table. Max was in the middle of a story, and the other two sat back in the black leather chairs, watching.

"After we're done I say—" Max turned toward him and smiled. "Cam, just in time."

Derek punched Max on the shoulder. "No way that story ends with 'Cam, just in time.'"

Simon and Max chuckled.

"I'll finish it later," said Max. "Where's your bab-ysitter, mate?"

Cameron sat down in one of the chairs and let out a long breath. "She's got a video conference with the board. She'll be here in a couple of hours."

They all watched him silently, no doubt waiting for more details. Cameron didn't say a word.

Finally Derek broke the silence. "I'm just going to lay it all out for us. We need a new plan. I'm not feeling the idea of undermining Jackson McAllis-ter's reputation. Plus, I'm pretty sure we'd come off as sexist."

Max leaned back in his chair and smiled. "How's this for a new plan? One of us takes her out and gets caught with her in some sort of compromising situ-ation. I doubt the board sends anyone here after that. And she's gorgeous, so I'll volunteer myself for the job. A woman like that's all business on the outside, but when you get her—"

"No!" barked Cameron. He heaved in a calming breath, but the damage was done. Already he was picturing Max and Jackson together. Jackson moan-ing and calling out Max's name instead of his. Cam-eron ground his teeth together hard.

No. Just no.

Cameron unclenched his fists. "No one messes with her," he bit out. "Don't bring it up again. Our plan isn't going to work."

Max rolled his eyes. "Okay, boss."

Derek crossed his arms and sighed. "Hate to mention this, Cam, but how about just finding a way through that flying problem of yours and taking it up with your father and the board in person?"

Cameron shook his head. "Not an option."

They had been over this before. The doctors had called it PTSD, but who the hell would be crazy enough to get on a plane after a crash like his unit had been through?

Derek threw up his hands. "Help me out here, Simon. You talk to him."

Simon shook his head. "Not helping on this one, Derek. Staying away from airplanes is Cameron's thing. Other guys in our unit came home with much more fucked up ways of dealing with it. If he says no, I'm letting it be."

Cameron shot Simon a nod of thanks. They'd been through hell together, and Cam knew his friend had his own reasons for not returning to the States—airplanes had nothing to do with it. "We're just going to get through this. We let her babysit for two weeks, and then it's done."

Max raised an eyebrow, but Cameron ignored him.

"We're moving on," he said. "Ms. McAllister had a bunch of photos that looked like all of us cozying up with clients. Most were on the job, but a few weren't. The press doesn't always get it right. Sometimes they catch us during off hours, but we need to watch that. Not just while she's here. In the future, too."

He looked at Simon and Max. They nodded.

"But there was one photo you all need to see." Cameron pulled the sheet from his briefcase and set it on the table.

Derek grabbed it. "What the fuck?" he said.

"I know," said Cameron. "Take it easy."

Max leaned over to get a look at the paper crushed in Derek's hand. "Is that Laurie?"

"It is," said Cameron. "I checked out the address on the top of the papers. It comes from a social media account, last name Toleafoa. Samoan, right, Derek?"

Derek's jaw clenched tightly, and his lips formed a tight snarl. He gave a curt nod.

"It's Derek's name on the caption, not Laurie's. Scrolling through this guy's other posts, I'm pretty sure his only interest in Laurie is that she's with Derek, not the other way around."

Derek closed his eyes and leaned back in his chair. "I won't let her go through that again," he said softly.

"None of us will, Derek," said Simon, clapping his friend on the shoulder.

Cameron nodded. "Right. And you know I wouldn't play down the risk if I thought there was one."

Derek opened his eyes and met Cameron's. The hard look softened a little. "Okay. But I still think this is messed up. Even if this guy didn't recognize Laurie, someone else could."

"Exactly," said Cameron. "This is why I brought the photo this morning. My father and his board sent Ms. McAllister here to adjust our image, but here is the real reason we need to take this PR thing seriously." He gestured to the photo. "More media interest in what we do, including on our off hours, means more photos like this. Or worse. And we can't have that. Our clients require absolute discretion for their safety."

For once, Max looked serious. He glanced at Derek and then turned back to Cameron. "You're right," he said quietly.

Simon nodded. "And not just this week."

"Right," said Cameron.

He leaned back in his chair and let the others digest the information. Derek picked up the photo again and studied it. He looked at Cameron.

"Do I want to take this home and look it up?"

Cameron frowned. "I'm pretty sure you don't."

Derek nodded. "I thought so."

"One of us will watch it for you," said Simon.

Derek took one last look at the photo and passed it back to Cameron. "Okay. Let's move on."

Jackson spent the morning in her hotel room, on a video conference call with the board. Then she set to rereading Blackmore Inc.'s annual report. She had read it on the plane ride over, but now that she had met Cameron Blackmore, her original plans weren't going to work.

She had assumed he was just another self-centered asshole with an overinflated sense of entitlement. She hadn't necessarily revised the self-centered asshole part, but he was a lot more serious about his business than she had expected. Ignoring the board's push for a more prestigious image felt like a *screw you* to Harlan Blackmore rather than a lack of self-control among the men. In fact, the more she studied the company's information, the more she was convinced of just how careful and calculating Cameron was.

Which made her all the angrier about his comment the night before. He must have sensed her momentary lapse in judgment when he rested over her, still inside of her. The whole encounter had been beyond amazing, but when he looked down at her with what had looked like awe, she had almost taken his face in both her hands and told him exactly what she was thinking. That he wasn't at all what she'd expected. That he made her feel better than anyone ever had.

Thank God she hadn't. She had completely misread him. Of course. A careful and calculating man known for his appearances with some high-profile women knew how to cultivate that feeling of intimacy they'd shared. She didn't assume the media had all the facts straight about his affairs, but she also didn't doubt for a second that Cameron Blackmore had his fair share of lovers. He clearly knew what women wanted. But that didn't make any of it real. His comment last night was a message: game over. And she got that message loud and clear. The fact that it hurt told her that she should never repeat a night like that with him, even if they weren't in danger of getting caught.

Cameron hadn't misled her. He had been perfectly clear the first night in the hotel. He was giving her exactly what he promised: orgasms with his big, hard cock. And yes, he definitely knew how to use it.

She was the one who couldn't just let it be.

She needed to refocus. She was supposed to be revising the PR plan. Most of the tactics she had proposed still worked, but the media coverage ideas were off.

Her phone rang, and her assistant's name popped up on the screen.

"Kyle," she said. "How's the northern half of the world today?"

"Cold. And busy." His voice was as chipper as ever.

Jackson glanced at her laptop clock, still set to New York time. It was 6:30 p.m.—yesterday?—and the man sounded like he was just starting his day. Probably the type that only needed six hours of sleep at night. Which was good for her, since he had taken on a chunk of her clients while she was in Sydney.

"What do you have for me?" she asked.

"I'm sending over the finals that art just passed on for three December campaigns. I just wanted to run them by you before I okayed them."

She clicked on the images in Kyle's email, and scanned them. "Nice. The second one should probably be a shade or two lighter so that everything still shows up on a smaller scale, but otherwise they're good to go."

"Right, lighter," said Kyle. "I should have seen that."

Jackson laughed. "Don't sweat it. You're the best assistant I've ever had. Give it a little more time and you'll be taking over my job."

"And be assigned to hot Australian clients?" Kyle was definitely smirking now. "That alone is reason enough to work for it. Is he as good-looking in person as he is on paper?"

Thank God this wasn't a video conference because Jackson's face had to be beet red by now.

"He's technically American," she managed to mutter.

"Is that a yes?" Kyle laughed. "I'd take him anyway, though I suspect I'm not his type. But you never know."

Jackson knew exactly what type Cameron was. She flashed to the night before, his naked, muscular torso over her as he came. Shit. She cleared her throat. "I've got to go. Send me the revision of the second file when you get it."

She hung up the phone. *Focus on the job, girl.*

Jackson scanned the company's financial statements. Some of the clients were clear, but others were masked by blandly named corporations. Nothing she could use.

She sighed and looked through the document again. The easiest media coverage to get would be to make a public appearance with a charitable organization, but Blackmore Inc. in Australia didn't seem to give exceptional sums to any one place. Maybe she could convince Cameron to. He could give enough to be newsworthy, she'd send out a press release and they could all deliver the check in person in the next day or two. Perfect.

Jackson closed her laptop and headed for the Blackmore Inc. building.

Twenty minutes later, she stepped out of the elevator into the bright penthouse office.

"Good afternoon, Ms. McAllister," said the receptionist. Chloe, Jackson remembered. She was young and blonde with long, manicured nails and… Jackson frowned. Did Cameron sleep with his receptionist?

"I'm meeting Mr. Blackmore," said Jackson.

The younger woman nodded. "He and Mr. Latu just headed down to the fifth-floor gym. He said you could set up in the conference room while you wait."

"While I wait?" Jackson echoed.

"They're usually gone for an hour or so."

Jackson huffed out a breath. Wait for Cameron to lift weights and hang out with his friends? Nope.

"Did he take his phone?" she asked.

Chloe shook her head. "He doesn't usually, but you're welcome to try him."

Jackson grimaced and looked at the clock. Okay, so maybe she should have checked in with Cameron this morning if she wanted him to be available. But the thought of calling him? She pinched the bridge of her nose. *Concentrate.*

She needed to get her plan under way: get Cameron to agree to the idea, choose an appropriate charity, arrange for an opportunity to meet the head of the organization and then spread the press release. And she was already getting a late start.

"You said he just went down?" she asked.

"Yes," Chloe said. "I suppose you could catch him coming out of the changing room, but he might be… Never mind."

"I'll find him," said Jackson as she turned back toward the elevators.

The doors opened onto the fifth floor, and Jackson stepped out into a spa-like atrium, with white walls and pictures of water and sand. The hallway in both directions was wide and empty, and the reception desk was unmanned. How did she find her way to the workout room? Listen for sounds of male grunting? She started down the bright hallway, passing doors with unhelpful labels like Room 1 and Room 2. Maybe this wasn't such a good idea.

A door clicked farther down, and low male voices sounded through the hallway. Jackson looked up in time to see a glimpse of ripped ab muscles and a jagged scar before they were covered in a T-shirt. She didn't even have to look up to see who they belonged to. Heat flooded through her, cutting off all rational thought.

"…Afraid I've fucked it all up—" Cameron stopped midsentence as his head came through the neck of his shirt.

"You still have time to fix it—" Derek Latu followed Cameron through the door and came to a stop. He looked at Jackson, at Cameron and back at Jackson again. "Ms. McAllister. This is…unexpected." Derek's face betrayed only mild surprise, but Jackson could tell he was taking her in with new eyes.

"I'll catch you later, bro," he said and headed down the hall.

Jackson waited for the sound of the door closing behind Derek before she let out her breath. "Were you ladies gossiping about your exploits?" she hissed.

Cameron blinked. "No," he said flatly.

"You didn't tell him about…" She waved her hand between them, searching for a good ending to this sentence. Nothing came.

Cameron gave a bark of laughter. "Hell, no."

"Then why was he looking at me like that?"

The corners of Cameron's mouth turned up. "Um. Well, you were staring at me, and you looked…" His eyes danced with amusement. "Let's just say you might have tipped him off."

Jackson leaned back against the wall. She closed her eyes as heat crept up her neck and into her cheeks. Shit. "Really?" she whispered.

"Mmm, really."

His voice was closer, and when she opened her eyes he was standing right in front of her. Not business distance. He was approaching lean-down-and-kiss-the-hell-out-of-her distance.

"No glasses today," he murmured. "Gonna pretend you didn't recognize me again?"

She put up her hand. "Stop right there."

Cameron furrowed his brow.

"I've been known to do really stupid things when you get that close," she said. "I can feel my IQ dropping as we speak."

Cameron stayed put, smiling down at her. "Can I say something?"

She rolled her eyes at him. "Like I could stop you."

"Look, I messed up last night," he said softly. "I was a little thrown off by how things went, and—"

"No." She shook her head to stop this exchange before it got worse. "It's over."

Cameron frowned.

"I know I said the same thing yesterday, but this time I really mean it," she added quickly. "We'll just get through the next two weeks, and when I leave this goes, too."

Cameron shook his head. "It won't be gone."

Jackson put a hand on her hip and raised her eyebrows. "How do you know? How many times have you done this before?"

"Enough to know that it doesn't usually feel like this." He paused. When she didn't say anything, he continued. "Look, it's good between us, really good, and whether or not we act on it doesn't reverse that. I'm already an ass for not keeping my pants on when I told my team to. If you want me to stay away, I will. Probably better that way, but I wouldn't say no if you change your mind. There's a lot we haven't even explored."

His words echoed in erotic waves through her body. Jackson gritted her teeth. How had they got to this point so quickly? "Can we please move on?"

Cameron inhaled slowly and nodded. Jackson straightened up.

"I came down here because I wanted to run something by you," she said, "something I'd like to work on for the rest of the afternoon."

Cameron folded his arms. "I'm listening."

Jackson set down her briefcase and pulled out a folder. "Your charitable donations aren't standout," she said, pointing to the summary she had put together.

The corners of Cameron's mouth turned down. "Is that so?"

Jackson nodded. "I'm thinking you can pick one of the smaller charities the company already gives to, one where you could make a serious difference in their budget, and make a large public donation."

Cameron scowled. "Not that it's any of your business, Ms. McAllister, but I do give. Maybe I should give more, and we can discuss that, but you don't know what the hell you're talking about." He glanced down the hallway and continued. "Second of all, I'm not picking my charities by how much of a PR boost I'll get. I'm not my father. If I'm giving more it's going to UNHCR."

"What's that?" she asked.

"It's the United Nations' fund for refugees."

The acronym hadn't stood out when she looked over the company's financial records earlier. Jackson scanned the papers she was clutching until she found it. "UNHCR…five thousand dollars. For a company of this size, that's not a lot."

He shook his head. "I give a lot more than that."

"Where?" She leafed through the pages. "I don't see anything else."

She looked up at him. He worked his jaw, and his scowl deepened. "Personally. But I'm not using that to boost the company's image."

Cameron stood over her with his arms crossed. She had somehow hit on a nerve, and his defenses were up. She needed to find a way past them. "So, you donate larger sums from your personal finances?" she asked.

He nodded. "Anonymously. But the director knows me. I checked out the organization pretty thoroughly to make sure the money was really being used to help people."

"Why?" she asked. "Why anonymously? Why not as you or under the Blackmore Inc. name?"

The hallway was still and silent, but he glanced up and down again. Then Cameron fixed his gaze on her. "It's my father's name and my father's company now, and he'd twist it for his own advantage. But he doesn't know the first thing about war or refugees or any of the other fallout."

She met his eyes. "And you do."

"Yes," he said quietly. "And I do." He scrubbed a hand over his face. "I don't want to donate money to get the Blackmore name on some flashy building. I've seen some awful things, and there are smart, good people at the UNHCR who know how to help."

"You've been to their office before?"

Cameron nodded. "And I've met some of the people from the refugee camps who relocated to Sydney."

"I see," she murmured. She let the image of Cameron sitting down with refugees sink in. "That must have been intense."

"I guess," he said slowly. "But it's the reality for a lot of people."

Wow. This wasn't where she'd expected this conversation to go. What could she say to that? Jackson had no experience with anything close to war or refugee camps.

"Look, I believed that I was fighting for a good cause when I was on the ground. I still do. But war means terrible things for everyone it touches. I can't ignore that. I have to do something about that part, too."

Oh. She had gotten one thing right the other night. She really didn't know this man.

"I'm impressed, Cameron," she whispered.

He shook his head. "Don't be. I'm going for decent."

She smiled at that, and he studied her for a moment. She wanted to wrap her arms around him and take away the lost look in his eyes. But she couldn't touch him like that. Never again.

Jackson took a deep breath. "I'm not going to push you into this. I can come up with something else. But I just want to add one more thing to consider."

He nodded. "Okay."

"Making a high-profile donation helps the organization, too. They're in the spotlight, and they can leverage the position to raise more money."

Cameron didn't react, but he didn't stop her, so she continued. "Blackmore Inc. will get press for it. Your father might even take the credit. But if that brings in a few thousand dollars to people who really need it, the whole thing might be worth it."

Cameron's face betrayed nothing, but his arms were still crossed tight against his chest.

"Just think about it," she said.

His expression softened. "I will."

CHAPTER EIGHT

"REMIND ME OF why the hell we're on our way to the UNHCR office?" said Derek, smiling across the taxi at Cameron. "I thought you didn't want Blackmore Inc. anywhere near this subject."

Cameron folded his arms. "I changed my mind."

Derek raised an eyebrow. "You changed your mind, or someone changed it for you?"

Cameron groaned. He and Derek had been friends long enough for Cameron to know Derek would keep pushing the subject until he got his answer. And Cameron really didn't want to get into this. At all.

"The board wants some sort of PR boost, and this is a good option," tried Cameron.

"You sure that's it?" asked Derek, his smile growing. "Because when that Ms. Jackson McAllister caught you with your shirt off, she liked what she saw. And I suspect the feeling is mutual."

"Shut the hell up, Derek," he mumbled. "She's the board's PR woman, and she's flying back to New York next week to report on us. It doesn't matter what she liked because nothing's going on. End of story."

Technically, this was true. Nothing was going on because Jackson had put an end to it. Again. But it wasn't anywhere near over in his mind.

Derek chuckled. "You're getting your knickers in a knot over this woman, mate."

Cameron huffed out a breath and looked out the window. "Knickers in a knot" didn't even begin to describe the mess of feelings that were clogging up his thoughts. It wasn't just the flashes of her tousled on his sofa, skirt around her hips, that were tripping him up now. He had mentioned the army. He never talked about that. And when she'd looked at him like she really heard what he was saying, he'd wanted to tell her more. The decision to follow in his grandfather's footsteps, not his father's. The way his father had turned against him. The kind of shit she needed to know if she was going to understand why he never wanted to be in the same room with his father again. That, long before Harlan started meddling with Cameron's job in Sydney, he'd betrayed his son by leaving Cameron and his mother to start a new family.

"Look, something's up." Derek's voice turned more serious. "I don't even want to know what it is. And I'm the last person to tell you to lay off, after what happened with me and Laurie. But be careful. There's a lot riding on this 'PR boost' or whatever the hell they're calling it. For you more than anyone else."

"Don't I know it," said Cameron. He closed his eyes and rubbed his forehead. "What I want is for my father to leave me the hell alone."

Derek was quiet.

"All three of us would understand if you wanted to leave Blackmore Inc.," he finally said.

Cameron frowned. "It's my grandfather's company, not my father's. Harlan Senior was more a father to me, and I owe it to him to stick it out." He clapped Derek's shoulder. "Besides, you three aren't the only salaries the company pays. If I stepped down, my father would fuck up everything I've done."

"You can't keep your father from screwing up other people's lives, Cam." Derek shook his head. "Just take a shot and hope you get it right. I'm sure you will."

"I don't know about that," he muttered.

And Cameron wouldn't rest until he got out from under his father's control. But wasn't that exactly the way Harlan Blackmore thought? Wasn't that why he'd left all those years ago and moved on to his next family—because his father wasn't willing to bend to anyone, not even his own father?

The taxi pulled up in front of the UNHCR offices, and Cameron and Derek climbed out. They stood next to each other on the sidewalk, the traffic at their backs. A PR visit was the last thing in the world Cameron wanted to do right now. Well, almost the last.

Derek cleared his throat. "I wasn't just giving you shit about the thing between Jackson and you. Neither of you are doing a good job of hiding whatever *nothing* is. I don't know what the hell you're doing."

Cameron shook his head. "I don't know what the hell I'm doing, either."

"That's what I thought," Derek said, swinging the door open. "Come on, everyone's up there waiting for us."

By the time they wrapped up at UNHCR, two hours had passed. Cameron led the way out. He pushed open the front door of the building and stepped out onto the sidewalk. The rush of warm city air hit him, and he took a deep breath.

"That was a good move today, Ms. McAllister," said Max from behind him. "Cam, the board will love those pictures with you and the UNHCR directors."

Cameron grunted but didn't turn around.

"It went well." Jackson's voice rang softly in his ears. What the hell was wrong with him? It was like he grew some sort of super-senses when she was around. He couldn't tune anything about her out. They had come into some sort of rhythm the last few days, and her tone shifted when no one else was around. He wanted the time to just watch her, enjoy her. And he didn't have it.

The group stopped next to the street, and Derek looked down at his watch. "I'm headed to the gym," he said. "Anyone else in?"

"I'm in," said Simon.

Max turned to Jackson and flashed her a smile. "That invitation includes you, Ms. McAllister." Cameron glared, but Max ignored him. "We wouldn't want you to get the impression that Blackmore Inc.

is just a man's club. We welcome women into all areas of our business."

Jackson rolled her eyes, smiling. "Noted. But no thanks."

Cameron was going to strangle Max if he had to listen to his friend harass Jackson for another minute.

"Suit yourself," Max said easily. "Cam?"

Derek gave Cameron a wary look and clapped Max on the back. "He'll catch up with us if he wants to." The three men nodded to Cameron and disappeared into a taxi. Leaving him standing with Jackson.

"Is Max ever serious?" she asked.

Cameron shrugged. "Occasionally. A couple things get under his skin." Like the subject of his family. And Natasha. In the time that Cameron had known Max, those were the only two subjects he had ever seen his friend get heated about.

Jackson tilted her head and looked at him. "Do you mind if I walk with you a bit?"

Of course he minded. It meant every ounce of his energy was going toward not touching her. Not watching her soft, full lips as she spoke in that husky voice.

But if he said no, he was an asshole. Correction: he was already an asshole. But he didn't need to make the situation worse.

Cameron sighed. "I was going to walk over to Haymarket for some dumplings. You're welcome to join me."

She hesitated. "Um, okay."

He nodded his head down the street. "This way. It's a bit of a walk."

Jackson smiled and pointed to her feet. "I bought a new pair of walking shoes."

Cameron made the mistake of looking down at them. He didn't know shit about women's shoes, and these looked roughly the same as any other pair. But of course he didn't stop his observations at the shoes. His gaze lingered at her ankles before tracing the curve of her legs up to the hem of her skirt. Today's was just short enough to get him thinking about her thighs. Shit.

Cameron shoved his hands in his pockets and started walking. Jackson caught up a moment later.

"Listen," she said breathlessly, "I just wanted to thank you for putting in the effort today with UNHCR. I talked with the director for a while before you got there, and he was beyond thrilled about the exposure."

Cameron nodded.

"He said that donations come in at times of crisis, but the money tends to dry up when the crisis is no longer on the front pages," she continued. "Something like this brings people's attention back."

Cameron glanced at her as she spoke. Her cheeks were flushed, and she was gesturing with her hands like she actually cared about what she was saying. Her eyes were alive. And she looked beautiful.

He raised an eyebrow at her. "You already got me in front of the camera. You don't need to sell me the idea anymore."

Jackson stopped in the middle of the busy sidewalk and put her hands on her hips. Cameron turned and met her gaze, and he found more than a hint of irritation in it. The lunch crowd bumped around her, but she didn't seem to care.

"I'm not selling anything, Cameron. Raising money for a good cause is important."

Cameron crossed his arms. "If that's what you feel strongly about, then why are you working in corporate PR, for companies like my father's?"

There. He'd said it. This was the question that had irked him since she'd shown up in his office for the first time. Why had she taken a job with Harlan?

Jackson's arms fell from her hips, and she looked away, frowning.

"That's complicated," she said.

Cameron took a step closer. "We're long past complicated, Jackson. I'd like to know."

"It's personal," she said, still not looking at him. "You know, you're just as much a threat to my job as I am to yours."

He blinked. All this time he had worried about her leveraging her power over his job, and she had been anxious about the same thing? That he'd use sex to manipulate her somehow? Cameron's shoulders fell. It was just the kind of thing Harlan Blackmore would do.

He uncrossed his arms and she turned to meet his gaze.

"I'd never use our personal time together against

you. Or anything else personal, for that matter," he said softly. "Do you really think I would?"

His heart thumped in his chest as he waited for her judgment. Groups of people jostled by, but neither of them moved. Jackson held his gaze, her eyes searching his. She brushed a few strands of hair off her face.

"No, I don't think you would," she finally said. "Maybe I thought so at first, but not anymore."

He was dying to kiss her right now, no matter who was watching. But he didn't want to stop at a kiss. One encounter with her had left him reeling, and the second had left him desperate. Cameron wasn't sure he'd survive another with his sanity intact.

He lifted his hand to touch her but stopped and let it fall. Her eyes flashed with something—disappointment?—but she averted them and started walking.

"I took a job at a PR firm because I needed the money," she said flatly. "The nonprofit I started out with could barely afford my salary, and I needed double what they were paying me to move out of my sister's spare bedroom."

"And the firm you're at now doesn't take on nonprofits?"

"They do, but those accounts don't pay as well. So I started to go for other accounts, bigger ones like Blackmore Inc." She wrinkled her nose. "See, I'm on this ten-year plan…"

He raised his eyebrows.

"Long story," she said. "Anyway, I needed the extra money quickly, and they were looking for someone who would travel internationally. So I took it."

She needed the extra money quickly? The hair rose on the back of his neck, and his hands tensed into fists. How the hell did he ask his next question?

"Were you in some kind of trouble?" He frowned. He'd asked the question much more forcefully than he had meant to.

Jackson shook her head. "Not really. Just the plain old cheating boyfriend kind of trouble," she said. "So I needed my own apartment."

"Oh." Cameron unclenched his hands, and he rubbed his knuckles. "I'm sorry. That's crap."

She gave him a wry smile. "Yeah. I'm sorry, too. Good apartments are hard to find in New York."

Cameron smiled a little.

"You want to know something else?" She looked at him, and he slowed his pace. Her voice sounded less sure. "He's the reason I took you up to my room that first night. He had some…performance problems."

"And you suspected I wouldn't?"

"Well, yeah." Jackson laughed for real this time. "But he also told me that I didn't know how to have fun." Her smile faded a little.

"And he said you were causing his performance problems?" he asked slowly.

Jackson swallowed. "He didn't come out and say it. But he let me know that he didn't have any problems with the woman he'd cheated on me with."

What an asshole. He hissed out a breath. The dickhead was probably lying, too, but Cameron didn't want to push the subject. Jackson looked hurt, and he had to shove his hands into his pockets to keep from taking her into his arms.

They stopped on a corner at a red light. The crowd closed in on them, and he took a step closer to her.

"You know that's not true, clearly not true," he said softly.

Jackson shrugged. "I guess I do now." She looked lost in thought for a moment. "Yep," she added. "Those nights were definitely fun."

She started across the street with the rest of the crowd, leaving Cameron behind. Fun? This wasn't a deliberate insult, the way she had played *mediocre* the other night. *Fun* was ordinary, forgettable. Not something that kept Jackson up late at night or woke her up needy and aching for his mouth and his arms and his cock. And Jackson McAllister was not going home thinking they'd had *fun* together. In fact, he was starting to hope she wasn't going home at all.

She reached the other side of the street and turned around, looking for him, her brow creased. But when she found him in the crowd, her mouth tipped up into a slow smile, as if she'd found exactly what she was looking for. As if he were exactly what she wanted.

Cameron's heart pounded in his chest, and he quickened his pace. Maybe he still had a chance to sort this out. But how much progress could he make in a week?

CHAPTER NINE

Jackson stopped in front of Cameron's office door and took a calming breath. She had managed to get through the last few days without succumbing to the temptation of his godlike body. With effort, she'd stayed cool in yesterday's meeting as Cameron gave her the basics of the security job she'd shadow at an upscale gala. She'd get through this meeting, too.

The problem was the longer she went, the more time she spent thinking up reasons why she should stop resisting and get one more taste of Cameron before she left. And if she was going to have another no-strings night, there were a few more ideas she was interested in exploring. Judging from the way she caught him looking at her these past few days when no one else was around, he wouldn't turn her down.

It wasn't the sex itself she was wary of. But every time they were close, she started reading into all the little things he did. Like remembering what she liked on her sandwich or how she liked her coffee. As if it all meant something more.

But if she could just accept this for what it was—a fling—she could invite him back to her hotel room again. Tonight. Because three nights together weren't worse than two. Nor were four nights. Or five.

And just like that, she flashed back to that first night, her heart pounding as she stepped into her room. With Cameron behind her, his harsh breaths in her ear, she thought she'd explode before she even got her clothes off. And then there was his apartment, when he'd buried his face between her legs and made her pant and scream.

The heat rushed up the back of her neck. Maybe the problem was that she was remembering these two nights as better than they really were. After a dry year, she must have been hard up. Cameron had stepped in at the right time. Times. And now she'd spent every night since thinking about it. Inflating each time in her mind. If she invited him up to her room for one more night, maybe reality would break this spell, and she could go back to New York satisfied in every way.

More rationalization.

Jackson brushed out the wrinkles in the front of her skirt and stared at the plaque on the door in front of her. *Cameron Blackmore, CEO.* As if she needed a reminder of who she would find on the other side when she opened it.

She knocked. "Mr. Blackmore?" Jackson peeked her head in. Cameron was facing his computer. His hair had fallen down on his forehead again, begging

for someone to come fix it. Lots of ex-military men
still wore their hair close-cut, but Cameron's thick
black hair curled around his ears, and she had gotten a good handful of it that night when he... Nope.
Shouldn't be thinking about that at all.

Jackson cleared her throat. "Mr. Blackmore, I just
wanted to show you that the interview ran today."

He turned to her, and his gaze wandered down,
stopping at the open neckline of her shirt. Yep, she
had his full attention now. His gaze snapped back
up, and his lips formed a tight line.

"Please don't call me Mr. Blackmore."

"Right. Cameron," she said, pulling out her laptop. Hopefully she could keep herself from blushing
every time she said his first name.

Jackson opened her laptop on his desk and pulled
up a chair beside him. She clicked on the article and a
photo appeared of Cameron, Derek, Simon and Max
outside the office building, all dressed in black suits
and white shirts. They all looked good. And Cameron looked really good.

"The suits were a nice touch, Jackson," he said.
"Thanks."

She smiled. "You're welcome. The reporter seemed
to like you all. You're lucky. Some of those answers
you gave could've been spun in other directions."

Cameron narrowed his eyes. "Spun? It's none of
anyone's business why refugee organizations are my
giving choice. And you know what I said was true. I
finally made it public because someone convinced

me that it might bring more money to UNHCR." He gave her a pointed look and added, "That's you, in case you don't remember."

Jackson rolled her eyes. "Got it. But I meant the other questions. About the women and the less-than-flattering media attention you've gotten lately."

Cameron pushed his chair back and leaned forward, resting his forearms on his knees. "That was true, too," he said. "We serve our clients well."

Jackson snorted—case in point. But the heat rushed to her face again. Hearing that comment from him shouldn't sting. She knew what he meant, but she couldn't help but think about all the women he'd been with. The press clippings suggested there'd been many, and though Cameron had said they didn't show the whole story, his reputation wasn't a complete lie, either. It was the reason she'd been sent here in the first place. "That sounds like an admission of guilt. You're lucky that guy didn't run with it."

Cameron turned his head, and his gaze was heated. "Are you trying to ask me a personal question?"

The right answer was "no." She was here in his office to talk about the interview she had set up for him. Which he had handled just fine. The rest shouldn't matter…but reading about his implied sexual exploits on the front page of a top business site didn't feel good.

Jackson closed her eyes. "I guess it's personal. I want to know…how much does the media have right about you?"

Cameron expelled a breath slowly. "I never sleep with active clients. I'm not my father."

She blinked her eyes open in surprise. "No, you're not at all. At least not from what I know of him."

Cameron was a clear copy of his father physically, but that was where the similarities ended. While Harlan Blackmore projected a glossy polished exterior, Cameron seemed to want to wear his roughest edges on the outside, for everyone to see.

"Look, my father paraded my mother around like he was a good, married man. My mother thought they were in love. But really he was fucking anyone he wanted, and he moved on when it was good for business. It was all for show. But I didn't find that out until a lot later." Cameron looked at her again. "I'd rather people think the worst of me than lead them on."

"Lower the expectations?"

He gave a humorless laugh. "I guess so." He ran a hand through his hair. "It's not like I never see any action, but it's rarely anything more than one…encounter. And always separate from business. Unless some sexy New Yorker catches me unaware."

"Catches *you* unaware?" Jackson snorted. "You found me at the bar, not the other way around."

Cameron shook his head slowly. "I know. That's not what I meant."

"I get it," she said. He raised his eyebrows at her, and she added, "But you prefer flings. You're not the relationship type."

"I said that, didn't I?" he muttered. "I haven't been for a long time."

"Just keeping the situation clear," she said quickly. "Got it."

Cameron turned to face her. He rested his arm on the back of her chair and leaned closer. "Maybe I need to revise that statement."

Jackson put her hand up. "Not on my account."

"It's my statement," he murmured. "I can do whatever the hell I want with it."

Jackson hadn't breathed in way too long. Her breath came out as a little gasp, and she glanced over at Cameron to see if he had heard it. He definitely had.

"Ready?" he said, leaning closer. "If I got together with someone for more than just a night or two, it would be fun and intense and hot as hell in bed. And it wouldn't be anyone else's business except for mine and hers. And there definitely wouldn't be anyone else for either of us." He paused, playing with a strand of her hair. "You let me know if you want more details."

Jackson's heart was thumping way too hard. He didn't have to spell that part out for her. She didn't need to be told that getting together with Cameron Blackmore would be fun and intense and hot as hell. And after trying to stop obsessing over him for the last few days, she knew better than to rule anything out.

"What kind of details?" she whispered.

His eyes widened, and his mouth curved into a slow smile. "The kind we need to lock my door for."

Jackson's phone rang, and they both startled. Cameron straightened up, and Jackson reached into her bag and looked at the screen.

"Kyle?" Cameron's eyebrows shot up, and he frowned. She stood and took a couple steps away.

"Jackson, I forwarded you a couple emails to look at," her assistant said when she answered.

Shooting a glance behind her, she whispered, "Can I call you back in a bit?"

"Did I interrupt something? Sorry."

Jackson's face burned. "No, you didn't interrupt."

Her back was turned to Cameron, but she could practically feel the tension radiating from him.

"Nothing urgent," said Kyle. "It's late here, so just check your messages and I'll look at it in the morning."

"Okay."

Jackson hung up the phone and touched her heated cheeks. Damn. Kyle had cut them off before she'd done anything stupid. She should be regretting the first steps down the slippery slope of increasingly forbidden territory, but the regret wasn't coming. Just disappointment. She still wanted him, long after her rational brain should have kicked in.

Slowly, Jackson turned around. Cameron's mouth twisted into a scowl. "Who's Kyle?"

She blinked. Kyle? It took a moment to register

his tone. Was it…jealousy? She smiled a little, and Cameron's expression darkened.

"Kyle's my assistant," she said. When the scowl didn't ease, she added, "He'd be more interested in you than me, Cameron."

He let out a breath and his shoulders came down an inch or two. A strange look crossed his face, as if his own reaction had taken him by surprise. Then the tension in his gaze turned hot, setting off a new kick of heat through her body.

She turned away.

"Where are you going?" he growled.

"To lock the door."

Jackson crossed the room on wobbly legs. Hopefully she'd make it to the door without tripping. They could do this just one more time. But who was she kidding? Hell, if he was going to strip her down right here, she'd probably come back for more. Again and again until her time in Sydney was up. And she could save all the issues with hooking up with him for the plane ride back.

Jackson faced him. He leaned back in his chair, legs splayed, not bothering to hide his growing erection. His dark gaze was doing crazy things to her insides.

"Does anyone have a key?"

Cameron smiled darkly. "Derek, Max and Simon. Why? You have some discovery fantasies you want to tell me about?"

A pulse of heat ran from her core. Did she have

discovery fantasies, or was it just the sound of his voice right now? Everything he said sounded dirty.

Jackson had spent the last few days looking anywhere but at Cameron. Now, finally, she could look. Drink in his deliciously large body. His blue dress shirt was rolled up at the sleeves, revealing corded muscles and a spray of dark hair down his arms and on his big hands. It was the same color as the hair on his chest and the hair that trailed down his stomach. His washboard stomach. His shirt only hinted at it, but her memory was more than adequate.

If things were different, if they were together or even lived on the same continent, would she ever get used to being with such a physical man? Would she take him for granted? Or would she forever be fascinated by the power he held in himself? Damn, this man was too much. He brought his hand to the bulge in his pants and adjusted himself. Wait, how long had she been staring at his erection?

Her gaze snapped back up to his face, and he chuckled. "You can look all you want, sweetheart. I don't mind. And the way you lick your lips every time you look down at my pants makes me hard as hell."

She'd just licked her lips? Jackson closed her eyes. There was nothing to do but laugh. "I didn't realize I was that obvious."

"Believe me, I'm not complaining. But you might not want to do that in public."

"Right. Got it."

But as Jackson watched him from across the office, his smile faded. All the teasing was gone. His gaze raked down to the neckline of her shirt, over her hips, down her legs. Now it was his turn to stare at her. But that didn't last long. He stood up and came to her in fast strides. She took a step back and found the door behind her.

Cameron's gaze was raw and hungry, but he didn't touch her. He rested his hands on both sides of her, caging her in, his heavy body hanging over hers. Heat radiated everywhere from him, and it was impossible to tell where her breaths ended and his began.

His voice was a low rumble in her ear. "You still haven't answered my question. Do you have any fantasies you want to tell me about?"

She shook her head slowly. Not exactly fantasies. Curiosities.

"If it's not discovery, what makes you hot, Ms. Jackson McAllister?" He shifted closer. "What about office fantasies? Fantasies about everything we shouldn't be doing right now?"

She nodded slowly. Yes, she certainly had those. She hadn't thought about this kind of thing before she came to Sydney, but since she'd stepped into Cameron's office that first day, her imagination had become more and more...vivid.

He slid one hand behind her neck and she trembled as he wove it into her hair. She was starving for him, and now that he was so close, touching her, she couldn't wait any longer.

"You promised me details." She sighed. "About what it would be like…"

He smothered a grin when she couldn't finish her sentence. "Don't worry, Jackson. I haven't forgotten. I'm just making sure we're both on the same page."

Then finally, finally, he lowered his lips to hers. He was hungry, so hungry, and she was, too. She nipped at him and opened her mouth for luscious, lingering strokes of his tongue. She grabbed on to his hips and pulled him against her, and his hand tightened in her hair. She finally came up for air, and he eased back until their lips were barely touching.

"We're getting way ahead of ourselves," he panted. "Let's start back when you came into my office."

Were they going to play out this scenario, right here during work hours? This was a dangerous mix of real and pretend. What would happen if she played out the dirty office fantasies she had about Cameron? What if they were no longer just fantasies but things they really did together? Maybe it didn't matter. She was leaving soon, no matter what they did here. She tipped up her head, and her cheek brushed against the stubble of his chin.

"You wanna hear how I imagine this little meeting between us today, sweetheart?" he whispered. "I'm thinking you're not just here for two weeks. I'm thinking you work for me. You'd come in just like you did today. You'd lean over to show me whatever the fuck you wanted me to see, and you'd give me a nice view down your shirt, just like you did the first day you were here in my office."

Her eyes flared and he laughed. "And you'd give me that innocent, wide-eyed look, just like right now. I'd get hard, just like this." He took her hand and pressed it against his rock-hard erection, straining against his pants. "You ready to keep playing this out?"

"Yes." Hell, yes.

"So why don't we go back over to my desk and take it from there."

His fingers slid from her neck to her cheek before he let his hand drop. Jackson slipped away from his body. He was right behind her, close enough to hear his breathing. Her heart pounded harder.

I'm thinking you're not just here for two weeks. I'm thinking you work for me.

How much was fantasy, and how much was about making sense of what they really wanted to be true? No, she wasn't going there. Act now. Analyze later.

She reached the desk, and he rested a hand on her hip. She drew in a sharp breath. Heat lingered everywhere he touched her. Where would they take this?

"You look fantastic today, Ms. McAllister," he whispered in her ear from behind her. "I'm so glad you came by my office." His hand made a slow trail over her shoulder and down her back. Lower. "You have a glorious ass," he muttered. "Last night when I came home, I got myself off in the shower imagining you against this desk, bare for me."

She could see him in his shower, his huge body shaking as he stroked himself. A rush of pleasure ran through her, and she moaned.

He traced the curve of her rear and continued down until he found the slit of her skirt. His hand touched the inside of her thigh, and she gasped. His laugh was soft and low.

"You've been wearing skirts like this all week," he said, reaching higher. "You know what I've been wondering? If I can just lift a skirt like this up whenever I want you, or if you'd have to take it off."

He inched her skirt up until his hand was between her legs. *Please, just a little more.* No. She wasn't going to beg.

"Looks like I got my answer," he said, moving her panties aside. "And you're already so wet."

He played with her. Her head sank and she braced herself on his desk, legs shaking as his fingers teased and tempted.

"You've spent the last week telling me what you think I should do and how I should do it," he said. "And you seem to like that. I wonder how far you're willing to go to convince me."

Jackson closed her eyes, letting his hand and his voice fill her. She'd never fully understood the appeal of role-playing before. But whatever this was that they were doing right now was really getting her going. Her breasts tingled, aching to be touched.

"Are you willing to suck my cock?" he asked.

"Because I'd agree to just about anything to have your soft, wet mouth around it again."

Oh, God. Her heart was pumping hard, and her words were stuck in her throat. What was wrong with her? She'd never truly want her job to depend on sucking off her boss. So why did playing like this with Cameron turn her on? Because she knew he'd never really force her? Something about this set her free to explore this scene, and she wasn't going to try to make sense of it.

"Is that what you want from me, Mr. Blackmore?" she asked. "You want me ready and willing when you ask for something?"

His fingers left her, and he pulled her hips back against his erection and gave a slow, teasing thrust. He pressed his lips on the back of her neck.

"You know what I like, Jackson," he whispered. "And there's no one else I want it from."

Jackson. When he spoke her name, the game shifted into something else. She turned around and met his eyes. For a moment, neither of them moved. Raw heat blazed from him, something real and vulnerable. This was more than just getting each other off on dirty fantasies. A part of this was real for him, too. And she had no idea what to do with that.

"I'd like to give you whatever you want, Mr. Blackmore," she said, soft and husky.

Whatever was in his look just moments before disappeared. Lust sharpened his expression.

"Then get on your knees and give it to me."

He let go of her and eased back against his desk, spreading his legs a little, watching her the whole time. She knelt down on the floor in front of him. Thank goodness his office was carpeted. Jackson unbuckled his belt and unzipped his pants. His erection surged forward, straining against his boxer briefs.

"Take it out," he whispered.

She slipped her hands under his waistband and pulled it down, revealing his cock, huge and ready. She trembled, fighting to take this slowly, to tease out all the pleasure they could get from their little game. She closed her hand around him, and he let out a low groan.

"Is this how you like it, Mr. Blackmore?"

"Hell, yes," he bit out.

She smiled and put her mouth on his tip. She teased him with her tongue and her lips and then took in a little more.

He seemed to love this kind of play, having her push the limits of his control and then doing the same to her. It had been that way back at his apartment, and she'd loved being the one who got him off. Today they were playing that she was the only one he wanted to do these things with. Which was even better.

She experimented with her teeth as his knuckles grew whiter on the edge of the desk. His hisses of pleasure grew louder until he thrust once in her mouth.

"That's enough," he choked, urging her head back.

He helped her to her feet. Were they still playing? She didn't care anymore. All she could think about was him sinking inside of her, again and again. She was still fully dressed, and so was he, aside from his erection jutting out at her, calling for attention.

"You like this part of your job, Ms. McAllister?" he whispered. "You like driving a man like me to the point where all I can think about is coming inside of you?"

His eyes were wild, but he didn't move to touch her.

"Yes," she breathed, playing along. "I want to get you so hot you don't want it from anyone else but me."

Cameron stilled. He cupped her chin with his large hand and brushed his lips over hers.

"I'm already there, sweetheart," he whispered, drawing his fingers over her skin. He rested his hand at the base of her neck. "Now we're going to fuck until you're there, too."

He held her gaze, his eyes intense and demanding. She shifted, trying to control the burning need inside. She wanted everything Cameron would give her. She wanted to feel this fire between them explode.

Jackson tried to steady her voice. "Do you want me on the desk, Mr. Blackmore?"

She moved next to him and faced his desk. She looked over her shoulder through her lashes. His eyes narrowed, and he clenched his jaw. He pushed off his desk and came behind her.

The current sparked so strong between them. It

would be fast and rough. She wanted it like that. But he held back. He inched her skirt up until it was around her waist and caressed her hips slowly.

"You like it this way, too, don't you?" he whispered in her ear.

"Yes, Mr. Blackmore."

"You want to please me."

"Yes, Mr. Blackmore," she breathed again.

"How far would you go to please me?" he said, even softer.

Jackson swallowed. "Anything you want." She knew that was true, whether this was a game or not. She also knew Cameron was the only man she'd say that to. He ran his finger under her panties. Then he reached between her legs, slowly exploring, before he pulled his wet fingers farther back and they skimmed between her two cheeks.

She shivered. She'd been curious about this since the first time he offered. But should they try it right now, in his office, in the middle of the workday?

"I want to try," she whispered.

A pause. "You've never done anything here before," he said, his voice barely there.

She shook her head slowly. "No, but I want to, Mr. Blackmore." Before he could react, she pressed her hips back into his finger and gasped. *Whoa.* The sensation was strange…different.

Cameron's laugh was dark, and he pulled back. "I think that's as far as we'll go today. We'll try more next time."

Her body was molten liquid inside. Was it the power game or his finger or something else? Before she could decide, his hands were skimming down her legs, easing her panties off. He stuffed them in the pocket of his pants.

He opened the drawer of his desk and pulled out a condom, then he tore off the wrapper. Wait, he kept condoms in his office drawer? The thought reeled through her mind and took hold as she waited for him to put it on. Jackson couldn't shake it. She turned to face him, and he stopped, midprocess.

"Have you done this before, Cameron? Here?"

He blinked, as if he were taking her in anew. Slowly, he shook his head. "No." He paused. "You want to be the only one to do this with me, Jackson?"

Yes, she did. Cameron was waiting for her, but she didn't answer. Instead she turned around and tipped her hips up.

"I'm ready, Mr. Blackmore."

CHAPTER TEN

CAMERON SQUEEZED HIS eyes shut, trying to screw his head back on after the last mind-blowing turn of events in his office. He was going to come in about five seconds if he didn't calm the hell down.

Was he really letting go of every last shred of sense just for one more glorious time with Jackson? This thought had run through his mind more than once, but he couldn't stop himself. All the hot tension of being close to her every day was short-circuiting his brain. And the insane jealousy that flashed through him as he listened to her call.

Then she had asked about the condoms. Which he had bought just for her, in case she changed her mind. She wanted it that way—just for her.

They were in dangerous territory. This was all supposed to be play, but it wasn't anymore. Not for him. And he was almost sure it wasn't for her, either.

...*So hot you don't want it from anyone else but me.*

Her words rang through him as he guided himself into heaven.

"Fuuuuuuck," he groaned, and she tilted her hips into his.

He was going to make way too much noise if he wasn't careful. His heart was already pounding at heart-attack speed. He moved as slowly as he could.

"Harder," she demanded, her voice needy and desperate.

She moved against him, and he gave her what she asked for. Again and again.

"Cameron," she cried.

He really might not make it through this. He'd die with his pants down, newly emptied, and he didn't even care. He should care, and he probably would later. But right now, that didn't matter.

He gritted his teeth and reached in front of her, finding her clit and that rhythm that would set her off. The only thing that mattered was the two of them. It was all too much. She squirmed and with a muffled shout she came around him. With a growl he came hard, stars filling his vision until he found himself leaning over his desk, holding her.

Cameron gulped in breaths, too stunned to move. He stayed there, even after his heart began to slow. Goddamn, he had almost passed out when he came.

"Wow," she finally said.

"Yeah. Wow."

He didn't want to let go of her. This whole encounter had been about playing with dirty fantasies, but he couldn't stop thinking about how many times he had slipped closer to real. And she had slipped, too.

He was sure the moment she had called his name. *Cameron.*

But they couldn't stay there forever. He propped himself onto his elbows and kissed her along the jaw-line, then ran his hand over her soft curves.

"Let's sit down for a few minutes. Catch our breath," he murmured.

She nodded.

He disposed of the condom and cleaned up at the corner sink. Then he tucked his half-hard dick back into his pants and walked over to the couch to watch Jackson. She was lovely. All that velvety dark hair and her smart mouth and that little game they'd just played that got him off like nothing ever had. He leaned into the couch cushions and rested his arm along the back. He was so gone on this woman, who lived on the other side of the world. And was hired by the board. All he could think about was getting her to lay back in his arms so he could shut his eyes and pretend she was his for a few more minutes.

Jackson shimmied her skirt back down her delicious round thighs and rebuttoned her shirt. She walked over to the couch and sat on the edge, leaving way too much room between them. She turned to him and let her gaze fall over his chest, his arms, everywhere.

"You know, you're really built," she said. "I've never been with someone so…" She waved away the end of the sentence.

What had she thought to say? Cameron studied her smile, but he couldn't read it. "That a good thing?"

Her smile widened. "Yes, definitely."

"Then help yourself, sweetheart." He shifted, leaving room for her to rest on his shoulder. She blinked and furrowed her brow a little, but she moved closer. She rested her head on his chest, and he wrapped his arms around her.

She made a little humming noise as her chest rose and fell in a long, deep breath. Damn. This was just about perfect.

Jackson looked up at him. "I didn't take you for much of a cuddler."

Cameron snorted. "I'm not. And if this gets out, I'll never live it down."

Jackson laughed. "I didn't see any of this coming. When you first walked up to me in that bar, I had all sorts of ideas about what someone like you spent his time doing."

"Oh, yeah? Give me one of your ideas."

She squeezed his arm gently, letting her fingers linger on his biceps. "Personal trainer?"

He laughed and shook his head. "Sounds boring as shit."

"You're right. You'd definitely do something more exciting." She tilted her head and smiled. "I also came up with a couple macho sports like wrestling crocodiles."

He rolled his eyes. "Come on. That's not a real

sport. That's the worst Australian stereotype out there."

She waved him off. "No way. I could see tourists paying to watch you wrestle crocodiles. Though you'd have to fake an Australian accent."

"Would you pay to watch me wrestle crocodiles?"

Jackson tapped her chin. "Hmm…maybe. Would you have a shirt on?"

He laughed. "Would you want me to?"

She rested her head on his chest and he caressed her cheek. He closed his eyes and held her closer.

"Hey, crocodile man," she whispered.

"Am I supposed to respond to that?"

"Shouldn't we be working?" she asked.

He sighed and kissed her on the top of her head. "Yep."

She sat up, shifting out of his embrace, to face him. He rested his arm on the back of the couch again to stop himself from pulling her back against him.

"I'm not here for much longer." She frowned. "We need to be careful."

"Careful of what?"

Careful not to get caught or careful not to get too involved? The former he could handle, but the latter? Jackson didn't answer. Maybe that was a good sign. Cameron let his fingers travel over her shoulder, down her arm. "So tell the board you need more time."

"To fit in more sex with you?"

Cameron gave a little snort. "You're supposed to

be in PR, sweetheart. If you want them to agree, you'll have to come up with something better than that."

She smiled a little. "I can't lie to the board," she said.

Cameron sat up. "Lie? It's not a lie that it would help to have you here."

She shook her head. Shit. He had just stupidly laid down all his cards and suggested she stay. And she wasn't even considering the idea.

"Never mind," he grumbled. "Let's get back to work."

CHAPTER ELEVEN

"You can't stare at her like that, mate," said Derek.

"I know," Cameron muttered.

Apparently he had been staring, as evidenced by the fact that he hadn't heard Derek come up from behind. Which was a bad sign. Cameron rubbed his forehead. He had walked out of his office for some reason, but he couldn't remember what it was. Because seeing Jackson in that same skirt today was driving him crazy.

Another bad sign.

He was dying for a repeat of the other day in his office, and just thinking about how he could lift this skirt over her hips was turning him on.

"You're getting in way too deep, Cam," muttered Derek. "Let's get back into your office before the sexual harassment police come by."

Cameron tore his eyes from Jackson's curves and ducked into his office. Derek shut the door and parked himself on the sofa. This guy wasn't leaving until whatever he had on his mind was said.

"All right, you wanker, what the hell do you think you're doing?"

Cameron sank into the sofa next to him and ran his hand through his hair. He blew out a breath. "I don't know. Something really stupid."

"Yep." Derek nodded. "Because you're staring at her like you're imagining her doing something dirty."

He couldn't stop himself. The moment Derek said those words, he flashed to the scene in his office just a couple days ago. When she'd bent over his desk for him and he'd taken her from behind. He let out a strangled sound of frustration.

"You fuckwit," whispered Derek. He shook his head. "You've already done it for real. Shit."

Cameron closed his eyes. "Remember that night in the hotel, when I told the three of you that it was our last night to have some fun? Of all the women in Sydney, I picked her up, okay? I had no idea. And it was good. I mean, really good. So much more than anything like that has a right to be." Cameron shook his head. "And I might have been able to let it be if she hadn't shown up in our office the next day, all buttoned up and wide-eyed."

Derek clapped him on the back a couple times. He actually looked sympathetic. "And now?"

"Fuck if I know," he said. "Every time I see her, it's like I can't tear myself away from her. Even when we're just sitting in the conference room, I find reasons to keep her talking, just so she doesn't leave. I can't help myself, okay?"

Cameron rubbed his hands over his eyes and let his shoulders sag. "She's going to leave for real. Soon. And I don't know what the hell I can do about it."

"You sure she's not just playing with you?" asked Derek.

Cameron shook his head. "I don't think so. But I guess I can't be sure."

Derek leaned back into the sofa pillows, and he was silent for way too long. Not good. Derek was from one of the biggest families in the Samoan community in Sydney, and both his father and his grandfather were church leaders. Even though Derek had chosen a different path, people came to him with their problems all the time. And he was never silent.

He glanced over at his friend. "Well?"

Derek raised his eyebrows. "I don't know what you want me to say. You won't see a shrink to get over your flying thing. And she lives in New York. There are ten thousand miles of issues. Something's got to give."

"A shrink won't help," spat Cameron. "I can't do it. I can't get myself on a plane. I'm afraid I'll lose it in a way I'll never come back from."

He couldn't even think of airplanes without flashing back to that crash in the desert and the two men who'd never come back. It was still so real. The utter panic of knowing the engine had failed and they were falling... The impossible, jarring impact as one side of the plane hit the ground and went up in flames. The heat from the burning wreckage, the slashing pain in his midsection and the inhuman screams coming from the men. He closed his eyes against it all.

"You made it across the Pacific once. You can do it again," Derek said.

"Simon was with me," said Cameron. "Just ask him about that plane ride."

"Okay, okay," said Derek, his hands up in surrender. "So find another way to spend some more time with her."

"I suggested she ask the board for more time, but she didn't even consider it." Cameron grimaced. "She mentioned a ten-year plan. And she's got this little red book she writes in. If I could see it, I bet I could figure this out. But I'm not lifting it from her. I'm not stooping that low."

Or would he?

His friend patted his arm and stood up. "Sorry, mate. It doesn't sound good."

"No shit," he said.

Cameron walked Derek to the door and rested his hand on the knob. "There's got to be a way."

Derek smiled. "Cameron, Jackson's smart and beautiful, and she stands up to you. I probably shouldn't say this, but I've seen her looking at you when she thinks no one sees. If you want this badly enough, you're going to find a way to make it work."

"Thanks for nothing," he grumbled and opened the door.

And came face-to-face with Jackson McAllister. "Oh." She gasped.

Shit. How much of their conversation had she heard? But she wasn't paying attention to him. She was peering into her little red book again. What the hell did she write in it?

Derek slipped by her with a nod, and then it was just the two of them. Alone.

"Ms. McAllister?"

Jackson stuffed the little book into her bag. "Right. Sorry."

Cameron covered her hand. She looked up at him, her lips parted as if she were ready to kiss him. Except that wasn't going to happen. Not here, in the Blackmore Inc. hallway.

"I've seen you pull that little book out a few times," he said softly. "Can I see it?"

"It's nothing," she said, but her face was bright red. "It's just a bunch of lists. Nothing interesting."

"I'm interested."

She glanced down the hallway. Derek had disappeared.

"Let's go into your office," she whispered. That shouldn't sound so seductive, but he must have reacted because she added, "Not for *that*."

Right. Take it easy.

Cameron stepped back, and Jackson walked into his office. She pulled up a chair to his desk and sat down. Leaning back against his desk, his legs were inches from hers.

Keep focused. The book. She had taken it out a few times, so it meant something. It had to be the key to figuring out her ten-year plan.

"What's in that book, Jackson?"

"Boring stuff," she said quickly. "Just places I want to go, things I want to visit."

"Can I see it? Please?"

Jackson looked up at him. "Okay. But promise not to laugh." She pulled it from her bag and handed it to him.

The cover was soft and worn, and some of the pages had come loose from the binding. He opened the book to the first page. *My Dream Trips* was underlined three times and surrounded by little hearts. He glanced up at Jackson, and she smiled.

"I got it when I was about twelve, in case you're wondering."

Cameron chuckled. "You never know."

"No laughing." She took a swat at his leg as he turned the page.

"'Paris,'" he read. "Of course. 'The Eiffel Tower, the Mona Lisa…' All the things you want to see there?"

"Yep. Some places have more details than others. I had to add another Paris page."

She took the book from him and flipped to a page in the middle. She handed it back to him.

"Rue Cardinale Lemoine? What's there?"

"Hemingway's apartment." She rolled her eyes. "College."

"Have you been to Paris?"

Jackson sighed. "Nope. Not yet." She flipped to the beginning, to the page titled New York. "Look here. I cross out everything I've done."

Cameron raised his eyebrows. "You still haven't seen everything you want to see in New York?"

Jackson smiled. "It's a big city. And I add to the list all the time. Restaurants I want to try, that kind of thing."

He nodded. "Does Sydney have a page?"

Jackson hesitated. She took the little book again and leafed through the pages. "No laughing, remember?"

The Opera House. Climb the Harbour Bridge. Bondi Beach. The list was long, and only two entries were crossed out. *Boat trip in the Sydney Harbour* and... *Hot sex in Sydney?* Cameron's mouth fell open. Should he be offended or flattered?

"Is that me?" he snorted.

He caught the smile on her face just before she buried her head in her hands. Finally, she looked up again. "That's you."

He pumped his fist in the air. "I made your list. Glad to see it's crossed off."

She pursed her lips.

He tried for a straight face but failed. "It's a little funny, isn't it?"

She smiled. "Okay. A little."

He looked down at her list again. The things that were crossed out she'd done with him. One was the night on his boat. While he spent the whole ride thinking about how to deal with her in his apartment, she was thinking about her dream list. Shit.

"You've only accomplished two things on your Sydney list?" He could have spent the last week and a half showing her all the things written there. They could have done them together.

He looked up at her. "That day we ate right on the harbor, you should have said something. We could have walked up to the Opera House."

Jackson shrugged. "I was working, remember? Besides, we're going to the Sydney Opera House in a couple days for the security job."

Cameron nodded. The private security detail at the gala. That was her last night in town. All he could think about was the time they had wasted. He'd spent so much of it thinking about getting her naked that he'd missed this whole piece of what she wanted. Not that she had complained about the getting naked part.

She took the book out of his hands and flipped through the pages. "It's not an itinerary. More like a fantasy life I want to live someday. When I have more money, and I'm not so busy with work."

She skimmed through pages on the French Riviera, Mont Saint-Michel and Marseille. She really had a thing for France.

"The ten-year plan?"

She sighed. "Yep."

"What about vacations?"

Jackson shrugged. "Sometimes. When I have the

money." She flipped to a page titled St. Thomas, Virgin Islands. *Beach cabana* and *waterside restaurant* were crossed off, but *sailing trip* and *snorkeling* weren't. She looked up at him and gave a wry smile. "My ex-boyfriend wasn't into water sports, so we skipped some of the items."

What the hell was wrong with this guy? He had Jackson all to himself on a Caribbean island, and he wouldn't get in the water with her? If Cameron had Jackson to himself, he'd do whatever the hell would make her happy.

Except get on an airplane, you fuckwit. Which means you can't give her any of the things she wants.

Cameron frowned. "Did your ex know about this book?"

"I guess. He saw me writing, but he never really asked about it." She closed it and stuffed it back in her bag. "It doesn't matter. Like I said, I'll probably never make it to most of these places. The lists are just for fun."

He studied her expression. No, this mattered to her. She had kept that little red book for years, adding new places all the time, waiting for a chance to start living her dream. This was what she wanted. But Cameron wasn't any better than her ex-boyfriend. At least the dickhead had actually gone somewhere with her. Cameron scowled and turned away.

"I know it's a little childish," she said quickly.

Was that what she thought was going through

his mind? He was on the verge of screwing this up worse.

"It's not," he said, a little too forcefully. "That's not what I was thinking at all."

She tilted her head. "Then what were you thinking?"

"A lot of things. I wish I would have taken you to some places on your Sydney list."

Jackson's eyes were soft, and she smiled a little. She paused, as if she were really considering it. "Maybe someday."

Someday. As in, probably never. Unless he figured something out.

CHAPTER TWELVE

WHEN THE ELEVATOR doors closed, Jackson hitched up the top of her dress and swiped a hand down the skirt. The black satin bodice still dipped dangerously low. The saleswoman in the department store had assured her that the dress wasn't too small. It was supposed to show a hint of cleavage. But Jackson was showing more than a hint. And it was too late to change her mind.

She folded the wide, silky scarf around her chest as the elevator raced up. Thank goodness she was leaving tomorrow. If she was around Cameron much longer, she might spontaneously combust. When the rest of his team was around, Cameron barely even looked in her direction. He was short with everyone, and when Max patted her on the shoulder, she could swear Cameron growled.

But when they were alone, it was worse. As soon as he came close, the electricity between them sizzled. Like he was silently waiting for her signal. And she couldn't stop herself from giving in to it.

The elevator dinged, and the doors opened to the top floor. She clutched the scarf around her shoulders tighter and stepped out. The reception desk was empty, but she could hear low voices coming from down the hall. Jackson took a deep breath.

How many fantasies had she flashed through these last days? Fantasies of giving in to the magnetic pull between their bodies for another euphoric encounter before she left. The tension between them built all day. When he read a memo over her shoulder or helped her with her coat, all she had to do was meet his liquid blue eyes. She found what she wanted.

Then, as soon as she got far enough away from the tractor-beam pull of his body, she could see this wasn't leading anywhere good. It was one thing to play out an office fantasy, but real life didn't work the same.

Still, as she'd stood in the boutique's changing room, shopping for an outfit for tonight, she knew the dress was more sexy than professional. And she bought it anyway.

Jackson looked down at the crumpled silk in her fists and sighed. Before she walked into the conference room full of testosterone, she needed to pull herself together.

She slipped the scarf off her shoulders and shook it out, but the wrinkles remained. She frowned. Maybe she could—

Footsteps, close by. Jackson lifted her gaze and

found Cameron, only a couple paces away. He wore
black dress pants and a white dress shirt with gun
holsters strapped across his chest. Refined but dangerous. His eyes, dark and hungry, dipped down over
every curve of her body. He rested his gaze on her
cleavage with unrestrained lust.

Cameron took a step, closing in on her. Another
step. She fought the urge to turn the tables on him,
to back him against the wall and make the spark in
his eyes explode. But this was work. He took one
more step. His body was only inches away from hers,
and when she took a breath, her breasts skimmed his
shirt. Her heart did flips in her chest.

Cameron rested his hand on the wall and leaned
over her. The scent of his aftershave took her right
back to his living room couch as he drove deep inside
her. God, she wanted him right now. A low rumble
rose from his chest.

"What the *hell* are you wearing?" he whispered
roughly.

She swallowed and straightened up.

"This is a formal event," she said, her voice far
too breathless. "I'm trying to fit in."

"And you look sexy as fuck," he groaned. "You
said you'd be out of the way, that I wouldn't even
notice you. But you're putting far too much faith in
my self-control if you think I can turn away when
you look so fucking good in that dress."

His breath warmed her neck, and the heat from
his body pulsed into hers. Or maybe it was her own

body. She squeezed her hands into fists to keep herself from touching him. Just one more time. Once more, she wanted to run her hands over the muscles that strained against the fabric of his shirt. She shifted a little, and her hip brushed against him. His erection grew.

"We're working," he grumbled.

She waited for him to judge his next move. He stayed still.

His breaths rasped in her ear. "I'm going to walk back to my office and calm myself the hell down." He pressed his hard length against her hip, in case she wasn't sure what he was talking about.

His lips brushed against her neck. "Or you can follow me back there."

She closed her eyes, trying to steady her heavy breaths.

Then he was gone. Her eyes drifted open in time to see him turn around, his hands shoved in his pockets. He started down the short hallway. Shit. Just thinking of him in his office got her going. Was he going for the cold shower method of calming down, or was he getting himself off? He wouldn't, would he? She wanted to know.

If she followed him for the kind of quick, hard satisfaction she knew he could give her, it might make the night a lot easier. But she knew better than to follow him back before a key job for a little pleasure. Okay, a lot of pleasure. More than she'd probably ever get for the rest of her life. Double shit.

Jackson smoothed out the scarf she was clutching and wrapped it around her shoulders. Then she started down the hall. She got to the end and looked left, toward Cameron's office. His door was closed. Was he sitting at his desk with his pants unzipped, his big cock in his hand? Was he waiting for her? Damn. She was dying to walk down that hall and find out.

She looked to the right. The door to the conference room at the end of the hall was open. Derek Latu sat at the long table, his broad shoulders and his back just in sight. All he had to do was turn his head in time to see her slip into Cameron's office.

Jackson gave herself a little shake. Good God, what the hell was wrong with her? All Cameron had to do was lean over her, and she was panting after him like a puppy. She was a professional adult, not some hormonal teenager.

No more thinking about Cameron's big, hulking body or his intoxicating scent. She was not even going to turn around for another look at his office door. She was going to put one foot in front of the other and walk to the conference room. And not think about what she was missing back in Cameron's office.

Derek turned around just before she reached the conference room doorway.

"Cameron went out to find you," he said, raising an eyebrow. "You didn't see him?"

Jackson fought the heat rising to her face. "He

had to take care of something. He'll be back in a few minutes."

Derek's gaze rested on her for an extra beat. He knew something was up. Thank goodness she'd come to her senses before she followed Cameron back and did something really stupid. Correction: something *else* really stupid.

She tugged her scarf across her chest and walked into the room. Derek and Max were dressed like Cameron: white shirts, black pants and holsters strapped around their shoulders. No wonder Blackmore Inc. was in such high demand. Both of them looked like they were ready for anything.

"Don't let me interrupt," she said.

Max glanced at her dress and laughed. "Good luck with that."

Jackson felt her face heat.

"Enough, Max," said Derek. "Let's review what Ms. McAllister needs to know."

She sat in the empty chair next to Derek, and Max passed her a paper across the table.

"Here's the schedule for the evening," he said. "In all likelihood, you'll see very little action on this job. But you never know. Because of some recent problems, this client suspects he's being targeted, and he's a little jumpy. He has his own full-time security back at the hotel, but he wants us along because we know the area."

She looked at the minute-by-minute plan, starting at an unnamed hotel.

"Who is the client?" she asked.

Derek shook his head. "Sorry. Can't give that information out."

"Fine," she said. "Where's Simon?"

Derek pointed to the top of her sheet. "He's already at the venue. Cameron will drive you there and get you into the place, and Max and I will pick up the client and his wife."

Which meant more time alone with Cameron. Her heart thumped.

Derek pointed farther down the timeline. "The client will stay for a couple hours, and then Max, Simon and I will take him back."

"And Cameron?" she asked.

"He'll take you back. He didn't want you near the client. In the unlikely event that anything would happen."

"Oh." Jackson frowned.

What was the board thinking when they insisted she tag along on their assignment? The more she thought about it, the more she suspected that Cameron was right. She was in the way. Hanging around on a job was risky, both for her and for the team, and Harlan Blackmore and his board had no idea what they were asking her to do. But Cameron did, and he had taken on the job of babysitting her.

Derek was still looking at her.

"He volunteered, Jackson," he said quietly. "He wanted to make sure you were safe." Derek punctuated his statement with a nod and turned back to Max for more planning talk.

Was Derek trying to tell her what a pain in the ass she was for Cameron, or was he saying something else? If it was the former, she didn't need any reminders. If it was the latter? It didn't matter. She was leaving tomorrow, so even if there was something more between them, there wasn't anything to do about it.

Derek and Max stopped talking, and Jackson looked up. Cameron stood in the doorway. His thick black hair was off his face, and his blue eyes were steely and cold. He wore a suit coat, unbuttoned. His hands were shoved into his pants pockets, showing hints of the now-loaded holsters around his shoulders. His eyes met hers, and for a moment, heat flared in them. Jackson drew in a breath, much louder than she meant to. Both Derek and Max looked at her, then back at Cameron. Shit. She had just all but announced her inappropriate interest in Cameron.

Max smiled at Cameron. "I think I better get out of here before I say something stupid."

Derek snorted. "That would be a first."

Max and Derek stood up and headed out the door. Max patted Cameron on the shoulder as he passed, shaking his head. The men's voices faded, leaving her alone with Cameron.

His gaze was steady on her. She wrapped her scarf tighter around her shoulders and stood up.

"You ready?" he asked, his voice rumbling from his chest.

"Yes."

Jackson tried hard not to stare as she passed him. She really did. But his muscular body in a well-tailored suit and armed...well, it was impossible to ignore. He was sex and danger, and he was watching her right now like nothing else in the world existed. Did he do this to every woman he slept with? If so, he must have a long line of stalkers still hung over from all the intense attention he poured on them. Good thing she was leaving tomorrow night. If she lived any closer, she might become one of those stalkers.

He stayed a half pace behind her, his large body looming just out of sight. He was on the job now, ready for anything. And yet the connection between them wasn't broken. Every rasp of his heavy breaths sent a current through her. Every brush of his arm against her flooded her with heat.

Jackson stopped in front of the elevator and pushed the call button. She stared at the doors, steeling herself for a painfully silent ride inside a small, private space. With Cameron.

The doors opened, and they stepped in. Jackson searched for something to say, something to ease the crackling tension between them.

"You don't have to chaperone me tonight, Cameron," she said, keeping her gaze on the elevator doors. "I'll be fine on my own."

"I won't hover over you, if that's what you're worried about."

"That's not what I mean." She turned and looked

up at him. Some of the iciness in his eyes faded. "I'm sorry you had to plan me into your job, too," she said. "I'm sorry about this whole situation."

The heat flared in his eyes again. "I'm not."

Jackson blinked.

"I'm not sorry about anything that's happened between us, Jackson," he said.

His voice was low and heavy. Jackson bit her lip and turned to watch the floor numbers tick down. The truth was she wasn't sorry that they'd gotten together, either. Who would be sorry about scorching-hot sex? Nope, not sorry at all. It was the first time she had done anything this bold and quite possibly the last.

But why did it have to happen this way, when she was supposed to be working with him? Not even working. She was supposed to be training him. And reporting on him. And planning for future actions. Yes, she was doing her job, too, with good results so far, if the press they had gotten was any indication. But the mix of business and *so* not business was a dangerous game.

The elevator doors opened, and Cameron stepped out first, scanning the lobby. He was fully on guard, focused. He walked out first and then waited for her to pass. Her own private security.

A car waited for them at the building's entrance, and the driver helped her in. They rode in silence through the Sydney streets, past tall buildings, past restaurants and cafés, past Circular Quay, past couples enjoying the evening breeze. Cameron leaned back against the seat and looked out the window, his face blank and unreadable.

The car slowed as they approached the circular drive where the road officially ended and pulled onto the narrow path that led to the Opera House. The driver stopped a bit in front of it and opened her door, and she stepped out into the evening air.

The Sydney Opera House was a majestic building during the day, but at night, it was magical. Each rounded white peak glowed, and the interior lights shone through the tall windows of the front entrance, creating patterns of lines and shadows. The building was perched high up above the harbor, and a long red rug cascaded down the enormous mountain of steps to the entrance.

"Wow," she breathed.

Cameron's low voice came from close behind. "An amazing creation, isn't it?"

Jackson nodded. Her gaze dropped lower, and she eyed the stairs. Good thing she wore flats tonight, considering what they were here for. The store saleswoman had almost talked her into red heels.

As they started up the steps, she snuck a glance at Cameron. His face was blank, but his whole body was alert. Not tense, just aware. If the board ever saw him on the job, in this mode, they'd never think for a moment that he didn't take the business seriously.

Everything about him was impressive. And though she had resisted so many times that week, her resolve not to spend another night with him was crumbling. Yes, she read too much into sex with him. But tomorrow night she'd be on a plane back to New York, no matter what she read into it. And it wasn't like anyone would find out. The man was in security, for goodness' sake. He knew how to be discreet if he wanted to. Though the pile of photos in her file suggested otherwise.

Would these stairs never end?

"We can stop and rest a bit," said Cameron.

Jackson gave a little huff and nodded. They took another step and turned toward downtown. The sun was setting somewhere beyond the buildings, and the sky glowed with reds and oranges. The lights on the Harbour Bridge sparkled on the water, and the ferries glided in and out of Circular Quay.

She smiled and turned to Cameron, perched on the step below. For the moment, they were almost the same height.

"Is this in your little red book, Jackson?"

He could have been talking about the Sydney cityscape, which was, in fact, impressive. But he wasn't. She knew he wasn't. He was asking her, *Is this what you want?*

"It's not in there," she said, "but it probably should be."

She meant to give him her best business face, unfazed and assessing, but she couldn't. Maybe it was how close they were standing, his wide shoulders brushing against hers. Maybe it was the sunset, glowing behind the city. Maybe it was his soft, full lips that tasted like heaven. But as she met his eyes, his smile faded. Her heart stuttered.

No. She couldn't be falling for this man. Not Cameron Blackmore.

Jackson gulped in a breath. Cameron, raking his hand through his hair, turned away and checked his watch.

"The rest of the team will be here in about thirty minutes," he said. "I need to get inside and meet Simon."

His gaze was fixed on the entrance. Right. He had a job to do, and so did she. But for one delicious moment, she had let herself want him. Not just in bed. She wanted him for real. She had all her clothes on, so she couldn't blame it on a post-orgasmic haze. Damn.

She looked up at Cameron's face. Did she dare wonder if he wanted her, too?

But the moment was gone. The blank, focused expression he had worn since they'd walked out of the office was back. They finished mounting the stairs and, after being admitted into the event, stopped just inside the door.

"Where's Simon?" she asked. "Or are we using some kind of secret route?" She smiled up at him. He didn't smile back.

"We? *We're* not going anywhere." He frowned. "*I'm* going to meet Simon. *You're* going into the event."

Jackson put her hands on her hips. "You're not

ditching me for the whole night while you go off and do your job. I'm here to watch how you work."

Cameron clenched his jaw. "You're PR, not quality control," he bit out. "You'll see enough from the event room."

What? After the last two weeks, did he still think he could bark at her like she was some disobedient child? This man knew how to piss her off like no one else did.

"Number one," she said, raising a finger in front of his face, "you're not calling the shots alone here, and you can't just cut me off. Number two, Derek said this wouldn't be dangerous. Number th—"

Cameron's enormous hand closed over hers before she could lift a third finger. "You remember what happened the last time you started counting things off for me."

Jackson's heart stuttered. His living room. Oh, yes, she remembered. And with his large chest just inches away, the scent of him all around… No. She pulled her hand away and glanced around. No one was looking. Thank God.

Cameron gave himself a little shake. He closed his eyes, and his chest rose and fell heavily. Finally, he looked at her.

"Okay, Jackson. I hear you." He sighed. "But I don't like this. You can come and get a sense of what's going on while I meet with Simon, but the moment the client gets close or anything else happens, you need to be far away. No questions."

Jackson blinked. Was Cameron Blackmore actually offering a compromise?

"All right." She put her hand on her hip. "That was easier than I thought."

Cameron gave an incomprehensible snort and pulled out an earpiece from the collar of his shirt. He murmured something into it, and after a beat, he took her hand. "Let's go."

They walked up a flight of stairs and down another. She snuck glances into doorways, trying to get a glimpse of the rooms in this iconic building, but after a while she gave up. Someday she'd come back here and take her time.

Cameron pushed through a door into an empty hallway, muttering short phrases, presumably to Simon. He didn't look in her direction, but he kept her hand tucked tightly into his. He stopped at every corner, ushering her behind him. Jackson tried to keep up with Cameron's long strides. She was starting to pant, but she wasn't about to ask him to slow down.

But as they turned down yet another hallway, Cameron stopped and mumbled something.

"Shit," he hissed, turning to her. "We have a problem. I need to get you out of here."

"Okay," she whispered.

Cameron glanced around and pointed at a door. "In there."

He put his hand on his gun and looked into the dark room. Jackson waited in the hall, listening to the noises in the distance. No one was in sight. He grabbed her hand again, and they slipped inside. The space was windowless, lit only from an open doorway along another wall.

"We'll be out of the way in here," he said, his voice low. "But we need to close that door. Stay close."

He led her across the room. But when they reached the doorway, Cameron froze. Jackson bumped into his side, but he didn't move a muscle. She opened her mouth to ask what was going on, but she heard why he must have stopped. Footsteps. Cameron whispered something. Simon must have said something back because his grip on her hand tightened. What was happening?

The footsteps grew louder. Cameron's grip on her hand grew to bone-crushing tight.

A shadow appeared outside the door. And the footsteps stopped. Shit.

"I'm so glad to finally get you alone," said Cameron loudly.

What?

"Go with it," he breathed when she didn't respond.

Oh. Now she got it.

"I've wanted you all night," she said.

"Come here, sweetheart." He backed her away from the hall and into the wall of the dark room, his big body shielding hers. Over Cameron's heavy breaths, the footsteps resumed. Closer. Cameron's fingers dug into her waist. "Don't worry. No one will find us here."

The footsteps stopped again. Then there was a crash. Cameron froze, but he didn't pull away.

Grunts came from the hallway. Cameron shifted, and his arms wrapped around her, holding her against him. His heart pounded in his chest, just as hard as hers.

More grunts. Then came a voice. "All clear."

Simon.

Cameron's lips brushed the top of her head before he let her go. "Stay here," he murmured to her.

He walked to the doorway and stopped. "You look like shit."

"He looks worse," said Simon. "Looks like we earned our keep before the event even started."

Cameron shook his head. "Nice job. Let Max and Derek know."

Jackson took a step forward, but Cameron put out his hand.

"Derek and Max are just around the corner," said Simon. "Go. Take her back."

Cameron gave a curt nod and came back to her. Curiosity was getting the better of her. Just how bad did Simon look? But one glance at Cameron told her that she'd have to leave it to her imagination. He took her hand and headed for the far entrance, where they had come in.

When they walked out, she stopped. "That was the guy you were supposed to look out for?"

Cameron nodded. "One of them."

"That was…close," she whispered.

He nodded, and the corners of his mouth turned down. He reached for her face and brushed his thumb over her cheek.

"You didn't want me to see that guy?" she asked.

"Not that. I didn't want him to see your face."

Oh. She really had no idea what she was getting into.

"I'm sorry," she said softly. "I really shouldn't be here."

Cameron didn't answer. He wrapped his arms around her once again and pulled her in tight. Heat radiated from his body, and desire spiraled in the wake of all the excitement.

"We need to get you back to the event," he said gruffly.

CHAPTER THIRTEEN

CAMERON RUBBED HIS palms over his eyes and gave himself one more little shake. Thank God this night was almost over. He watched two big black cars drive away from the side exit of the Opera House. He had gotten through the event, but just barely.

What the hell was wrong with him? He had stupidly let Jackson come along to give her what she wanted. To please her. Instead of following his instincts and keeping her away from all potential danger.

Thank God the rest of the job had gone smooth and easy. Security was already tight at this event. The politician who had hired them wasn't the only high-profile guest, and even getting Jackson a ticket had been a stretch. They needed to figure out how the hell that guy had slipped in.

He couldn't shake the mistake, even long after he left Jackson perched on a stool at one of the cocktail tables. This was why he kept his dick in his pants when it came to business. His grandfather never would have let a woman cloud his judgment. So why he still couldn't get Jackson out of his mind, even after he'd screwed up, was too much to process as he walked back into the Bennelong Room.

The lights were dim in the grand, cathedral-like space, and the wooden walls glowed in a warm yellow hue. The bar was a raised area in the middle, and he stopped there to survey the scene. The place usually served as a restaurant, but the dining tables were gone, replaced with a few cocktail tables and a wooden dance floor in the middle. A handful of couples danced, and the rest clumped together in groups, deep in conversation.

He found Jackson immediately. She was standing right where he'd seen her last, at a round cocktail table, and from this angle he got an eyeful down the front of her dress. Unfortunately, Cameron wasn't the only one who was enjoying the view. A man set a drink in front of her, and that guy's gaze dipped down more than once.

He started down the stairs and headed straight for her. Her eyes met his as he approached, and she held his gaze for one long, drawn-out moment before she looked back at the wanker who was talking away, his back to Cameron.

"Sounds to me like your date forgot about you," the guy continued. "I'd be happy to take you out on the dance floor if he has something better to do. But to tell you the truth, I can't think of a single excuse for a man not to show a beautiful woman like you a good time tonight."

Cameron stopped within range of a good jab. "Is that so?"

The guy turned around, and his eyes flared open. Cameron didn't love to use his size to intimidate, but this asshole was asking for it.

"Sorry, mate," the guy mumbled and backed away, leaving Cameron alone with Jackson.

"Was I interrupting something?" he growled. Real charming. He had to pull himself together. Had he really sunk as low as petty jealousy?

But Jackson just rolled her eyes. "He's harmless. He just wanted to dance."

"What he wanted was to get a look down your dress," he said drily.

Jackson sighed, and Cameron bit back a curse. He wasn't going to mess this night up. Not with Jackson standing in front of him in the sexiest dress he had ever seen. She could have worn some uptight business suit tonight. Instead, she'd worn that dress knowing they'd go to this event together. Knowing he'd see her in it.

"Are you off the clock?" she asked.

Cameron nodded and looked out at the dance floor. A man a little older than him was holding a beautiful woman in a long red dress. His hands rested on her hips as they moved slowly to the music. He leaned down and whispered something in her ear, and the woman turned to him and smiled like he was the only thing that mattered in the world.

It had been a shitty night, and all Cameron wanted

was to hold Jackson like that right now. He wanted to breathe in her scent and feel her breasts against his chest. Hell, he wanted a lot more than that, but at this point, he was desperate enough to settle for a dance. And he hated dancing. This was only more evidence of how screwed up in the head he was over this woman.

"I'm so sorry I was in the way tonight," she said.

He frowned. "It's my job to deal with any circumstances that arise."

She was quiet. Cameron took a steadying breath and turned to Jackson. She was watching the other couples, too.

"You wanna dance?" he said roughly.

Jackson studied him for a moment. "Are you asking me?"

"Yes, I'm asking you."

Smooth, asshole.

"Sorry," he mumbled.

She glanced around the room, and he followed her gaze. It was a discreet crowd, used to attention, used to blocking out everyone else around them. Perfect. He took a step closer and ran his hand down the smooth, bare skin of her arm.

"We're surrounded by people with royal titles and Academy Awards. No one here gives a shit about you and me." He shoved his hands in his pockets. "If you want to dance, let's do it."

The corners of Jackson's mouth turned up. "You really are a charmer, Cameron Blackmore."

"So I've been told."

He could feel his own smile growing. Hell, he could stand here and talk to her all night just to hear the next sassy remark out of her mouth. But when she looked up at him, she hesitated. As Jackson's deep green eyes blazed further into him, her smiled faded, as if, in that moment, she could see just how twisted up he was about her.

He didn't turn away. Instead, he took one hand out of his pocket and held it out to her. His voice came out low and uncertain.

"Will you dance with me, Jackson?"

Her eyes flicked to his hand, and his heart pounded harder. If she said no, it would hurt like hell. He was dying to touch her, to have her sweet body pressed against his.

Cameron moved a little closer. "Whatever you want tonight, I'll do it better than anyone else."

Jackson closed her eyes. Maybe she was imagining the same things he was. Then her gaze met his and she nodded. "I already know that."

She lifted her soft hand, and his closed around it. If he had any say in this, he wasn't going to stop touching her for the rest of the night. They walked onto the dance floor, side by side, and Cameron stopped in the middle. The slow, sensual music filled the room. He turned to face her, their bodies so close to touching. He placed one of her hands on his shoulder, then the other, before slipping his arms around her and pulling her against him. In case there was still any question about what kind of dancing this would be.

Cameron looked down at her and raised an eyebrow. "You're…shorter tonight than you were yesterday."

"Why, Cameron, how sweet of you to say so," she said drily.

The corners of his mouth turned up. "There's more where that came from, Ms. McAllister."

She let out a little laugh, and he studied her for a moment. "Why wear high heels at all?" he asked. "They can't be comfortable."

"A small woman makes a man feel powerful," she said. "But a tall woman?"

Cameron chuckled. "I'm not touching that one."

"Fine," said Jackson. "You don't have to respond. But if I wear heels, I get more respect. Nothing makes a CEO listen like a woman who's taller than him."

Cameron nodded slowly, weighing her words. "Okay," he said. "I can see the logic. But it doesn't always work that way."

Jackson raised an eyebrow at him. "Really? You, the guy who hulks around growling at anyone who isn't doing what you want, you don't think size matters."

He smirked and leaned slowly toward her. "I never said size doesn't matter. But there are other things that can bring a man to his knees."

She gave him a bemused look, then rested her

forehead on his arm. He moved his hands to the swell of her beautiful, round hips. And he pulled her even closer. Their bodies were flush, and her breasts pressed against his chest, spilling out like two delightful presents just for him.

This was heaven. Her body moved against his, and he responded. His hands traveled lower over her hips, every move playing out under his fingers. He buried his face in her hair and took a long, deep breath. And another. She sighed, and her body melted even closer. The word *more* echoed through him. Her hands moved up his shoulders and behind his neck, slowly weaving through his hair. He was more attracted to this woman than was wise. Maybe he didn't even care anymore. His heart pounded in his chest, begging him for more. Guests chatted, cameras flashed and glasses clinked around them, but everything was muted by this slow, sensual dance, with Jackson's body pressed against his.

The song ended, and they stopped. Jackson's eyelashes fluttered open, and her hands slipped from his neck. It was over. He let go of her, but neither of them moved apart. Her breasts rose and fell against him in short, erratic pants.

"One more night, Jackson."

She shuddered against him. He breathed in her scent again. His heart pounded harder, ready to explode, and thank God his suit coat hid the growing bulge in his pants. Was she going to turn him down, right here in the middle of the charity event dance floor?

"I'm not playing anymore, Jackson," he said in her ear. "This is real."

He straightened back up, and slowly she lifted her gaze to meet his. Her deep green eyes shone with heat and wonder.

"Yes, Cameron," she said. "One more night."

On the ride back to his building, he couldn't keep his hands off her. He was so far gone, and they hadn't even started. She laid her head against his chest, and her hand rested high on his thigh. Whatever she'd had around her shoulders had fallen away, revealing the low cut of her dress. He moved his hand in slow circles up and down her side, and she arched into his touch.

Tonight would never be enough. If she were his, if she stayed, he could wake up to her every morning, hold her every night and lose himself in everything she had to offer. Or whatever the hell she wanted. He could introduce her to all the dirty things she was curious about. And then some.

But Jackson wasn't his. She was flying back to New York tomorrow with no plans to return. And he couldn't get himself on a fucking airplane to save his life. Cameron gritted his teeth. He'd think about that problem later.

They pulled up in front of his building, and he helped her out into the warm night air. The car drove off and left them standing together under the starry sky. Jackson looked up at him, her eyes wide.

"What are we doing, Cameron?"

He chuckled. "Whatever you want to do."

Jackson smiled a little, but she glanced away. Damn. If she was talking about what they'd do once they got up to his bedroom, he could whisper a list of dirty ideas, just to see if she wanted to try one. The electricity that had sizzled between them for the last two weeks was threatening to spark out of control. Each time they gave in, it grew even more explosive between them. And neither of them was backing away. Yet he got the sense that wasn't what she was asking about.

His smile faded. "I don't know what the hell I'm doing."

Maybe that wasn't completely true. Back on the Opera House dance floor an idea had flickered to life inside him, and now he couldn't let go of it. *More*. He wanted more. So what if they lived on different continents. So what if they had only known each other for two weeks. Being with Jackson trumped every single obstacle he could see.

"I guess it doesn't matter," she said. "I'm leaving tomorrow." She blinked a couple times and gave him a tight smile that hit him straight in the gut.

He rested his hand on the smooth skin of her cheek. "All of this matters, Jackson."

No, he didn't feel like doing anything dirty at all. He just wanted her, plain and simple. He wanted to spend the night with his body over hers, her bright green eyes staring into his as they lost themselves in each other.

He looked at her for a long time, thinking everything he wanted to say. That this was so far past just getting each other off. That he was trying his hardest not to beg her to stay. That he wanted her to sleep in his bed every night so he could wake her up in creative ways every morning. How did he want all these things when they had never even spent a full night together? Maybe they would tonight.

She was watching him so intently, as if she were trying as hard as he was to figure out what mattered and why. He had to make tonight matter.

Cameron kissed her softly. "Let's go upstairs, sweetheart."

He took her hand and led her inside. He turned the key to the penthouse suite, and the elevator doors closed behind them. Jackson leaned against the back wall of the elevator, and he came up to her, covering her body with his. She tilted her hips against his hard length and he buried his face in her neck and inhaled. She smelled like heaven, some spicy, flowery shit that was driving him crazy. And then there was just Jackson, whose scent was now so imprinted on him that he'd probably still get hard twenty years from now if he found himself close enough to her.

"You know what I want?" he breathed.

She laughed. "I can guess."

"You're wrong."

She turned to him and raised her eyebrows. "What is it, then?"

He swallowed. "I want to make love to you so long and hard that you miss your plane tomorrow. And the next day. And the next."

There. He'd said it. Cameron watched her expression. Her gaze was soft and her mouth was parted, but she didn't say anything. Maybe that was a good thing.

"Stay the night, Jackson," he whispered. "Just to see what it's like."

Cameron's heart pounded, but he didn't move. She closed her eyes, and when they opened again, the dreamy look was gone. She wrinkled her brow. "I don't know. I—I didn't bring clothes. Or a toothbrush."

"I don't mind."

Was that a yes? If she stayed the night, he could show her what he had known that very first time in her hotel room. That this was different.

The elevator came to a stop, and the doors opened. He found her hand and squeezed it. She dropped her purse on the hall table and stopped. He came up behind her and rested his hands on the soft curve of her waist.

"Does this mean I'm going to see your bedroom tonight?" She smiled a slow, seductive smile that pushed away all thoughts of the future.

"Is that what you want?" he asked, pressing a kiss on her shoulder.

"Yes." She gave a sexy sigh.

"Good."

And Cameron needed to get there right about now. He dipped down and hooked his arm under her knees, lifting her up. Jackson sucked in a breath and laughed.

He carried her through the hall and set her down in the doorway. Jackson walked across the bedroom to the French doors that opened onto his balcony. The white walls twinkled with the harbor lights. Thank God his cleaning service had come the day before.

"It's beautiful here, Cameron," she said. "You're a really lucky man."

Cameron shoved his hands in his pockets. "I'm feeling pretty lucky right now, but it has nothing to do with my apartment."

She turned around and smiled a little. That dress was killing him. It was classy and sexy and showed off all the good parts. Which was basically everything. Jackson's smile grew wider.

"You know what I thought of when I put on this dress tonight?" she asked.

Cameron shook his head.

"I thought it might be a fun dress for a striptease."

She spoke these last words in her low, husky voice that gave a jolt to his already hardening cock. He nodded, not trusting his voice yet.

"You want to see me do that?" she asked softly.

"You have to ask?" He chuckled. "Hell, yes, I want you to strip for me."

Jackson bit her bottom lip. "I've never done anything like this. It might just look silly instead of sexy."

Cameron shook his head. "I'm going to find anything you do sexy, Jackson. You should know that by now." He let his gaze drift down her body. She had to know just how much he wanted her, no matter what she was doing. He met her eyes again and smiled. "If you can make me laugh when I'm this hard for you, all the better."

She licked her luscious lips and gestured to his bed. "There. Please."

Cameron took a few leisurely steps to the bed, slowing this game. He sat down on the edge and rested his forearms on his thighs. She slipped off her shoes and padded over to stand in front of him. He looked up at her.

"No touching," she whispered.

He smiled at her. "What about touching myself?"

Her eyes flared with a mix of surprise and heat. "Oh," she murmured. Her eyes darted down between his legs. "Yes. In fact, I want to see you make yourself come while you're watching me."

"Oh, fuck," he muttered, squeezing his eyes shut as his erection surged against the zipper of his pants. His heart pumped hard against his chest. He was going to come way too soon if he wasn't careful. "Just give me a moment."

Cameron took a deep breath and stood up. He brushed a kiss over her lips and moved past her, heading for his closet. He slipped off his jacket and unbuttoned his shirt, trying to calm himself down. This was getting hotter by the minute, and they weren't even touching yet. He walked back over to her and unfastened his pants.

After spending the last two weeks hiding his interest in the office, he could drink her in slowly. This was his own private fantasy world, tailored perfectly to the two of them. He eased back onto the bed.

Her gaze dropped to the bulge in his pants, and she smiled.

"Okay, here goes," she said.

She turned around and moved aside her hair. The dress fastened behind her neck, and she fumbled with the clasp for a moment before the two silky straps fell over her shoulders. Cameron stared at the soft, bare skin of her back. She looked over her shoulder, and her smile was more seductive this time.

She turned around. Her hands still held the two straps of her dress that had fallen over her shoulders and down her arms, revealing the tops of her breasts. She let the fabric fall a little farther until he could see the hint of her nipples.

All night she hadn't been wearing a bra.

Cameron reached into his pants and took himself in his hand. Jackson's gaze followed his hand, and her eyes widened. He eased down his pants and let his erection free. His tip was already wet, and he rubbed his palm over it.

"Keep going, sweetheart," he said.

Her eyes darted back up to his, and he drank in all her want, the need that he hoped went beyond physical satisfaction.

Jackson slipped her thumbs under the satiny black fabric and rubbed her nipples in slow circles. Her breath caught, and she teased harder. Cameron gave himself a couple rough strokes and moaned. She let the straps fall so the dress hung at her waist, revealing the most beautiful breasts. His mouth watered as he imagined taking one in his mouth and playing with the other. There were so many things he wanted to do with her nipples, much dirtier. His hand moved faster as pleasure rushed through him. She took her breasts in her hands and squeezed, and his cock throbbed hard in his grip.

"I'm close," he ground out.

"Good."

She teased her nipples and watched him get himself off for another few beats. Then she turned in profile and found a zipper hidden on the side of her dress. Slowly, she pulled it down, revealing more and more of that creamy skin. He was going to come any second now. She shifted her hips and guided the silky material down her thighs to the floor. All that was left was a pair of lacy red panties. He swallowed hard, fighting against the building surge.

Jackson stepped out of the dress and within his reach. She watched over her shoulder as she slipped her fingers into those lacy panties. Just as she bent over to lower them, her gaze opened into something raw and vulnerable.

Everything exploded in a frenzy of euphoric bursts. He kept his gaze fixed on Jackson, her eyes wide, as he let out a torn cry and emptied himself into his hand and onto his stomach. His whole body contracted, and he growled out her name.

Seconds passed. Or maybe minutes. Cameron tried to kick his mind back into gear.

Jackson stepped forward and caressed the back of his neck. "That was really…" she faltered. "Thanks for playing out this little scene of mine."

He hung his head. It was incredible. He had seen other women strip before, and none of them had gotten him going like this. Not even close. But this was probably the wrong time to bring up other naked women.

How could he make her understand? Just carrying out their fantasies wasn't what made this little strip show good. She was the one who brought this beyond teenage jack-off dreams into something much more for him.

He had this one last night to show her. And he wasn't going to screw it up.

Cameron looked up at her. Jackson was naked, and he was a mess.

He kissed the swell of her hips. "Shower?"

She smiled a little. "Sure."

She followed him into the bathroom and leaned against the counter. She was biting her lower lip again.

"You okay?" he asked.

She nodded. "More than okay. I just didn't realize sex could be like this." She chuckled. "I'm not sure I can go back to a regular relationship."

What the hell?

Cameron crossed his arms over his chest. "You think good sex and exploring what turns you on don't go together with a regular relationship?"

Jackson shrugged. "I don't know. I've had a few relationships, and I certainly never had sex like this. Not even close."

"And you've developed a theory based on those assholes?"

She pursed her lips.

"In my experience, guys either want sexy or they want a relationship. I've never been the sexy type." She glanced away. "After my last boyfriend cheated on me, it made me wonder. So here we are. I get to see what it's like to be the sexy type instead."

He raised an eyebrow. "You like it?"

Jackson smirked. "Definitely has its advantages."

Steam came from the shower, and Cameron felt the water with his hand. He stepped in and motioned for her to join him. Jackson entered the shower, her body skimming against his.

"Keep going," he said, running his hands over her bare shoulders. "I'm curious to hear your theories on what men want."

"You don't agree? Men want to have lots of sex with a certain kind of woman. Then they settle down with another kind of woman." She tilted her head. "The reason I'm here is because of your reputation with that first kind of woman, right?"

"What my reputation is and what I want are two different things."

"You don't want to pick up women in hotel bars for sex?"

Cameron sighed. "You want to hear what I think men want?"

Jackson swallowed. "I'm not sure, but go ahead."

"I think men want a lot of hot sex, and if it's in a relationship, all the better. But that's hard to find. So some men go for the relationship and compromise on the sex." He tucked her long damp hair behind her ear and caressed her cheek. "And other men go for the sex, knowing something is missing. Hoping that at some point he meets a woman who can show him what that *something* is."

He found her mouth, wet and warm, and he kissed her. He ran his hands down the curve of her waist and up again, and he nuzzled her cheek with his chin.

"Maybe that second kind of man doesn't even know that's what he's looking for until he finds it," he whispered. "But once he finds it, he doesn't want to go back."

She stilled, and her expression was unreadable. But there was one little tell that gave him hope that she was just as twisted up about this as he was. His hand stopped over the furious pulse at the base of her neck.

The familiar desire for her was returning, but he wasn't giving in to it yet. Losing himself inside her wasn't enough. He wanted something beyond that tonight.

He didn't move. "What do you think about my theory?"

"I'll have to think about it," she said. "Now I'd like to wash you. Slowly."

Her mouth curved into a lazy, seductive grin. She reached for the soap and rubbed it between her hands under the water. She set it back on the shelf and began with his shoulders. In slow circles, she washed his arms, her soft fingers gliding over his skin. Her eyes had a look of wonder in them as she traced the lines of muscle and trails of hair. How these things held her attention was a mystery when she had her own gloriously curvy body, but he wasn't going to point that out right now.

She turned for more soap and worked her way down, across his chest and over the tense muscles of his stomach. And lower.

Heaven. He was in heaven.

He grabbed on to the shower wall to steady himself. She circled closer as he grew harder. She gave his cock a few sudsy strokes, and he tipped his head back and groaned.

All his frustrations and self-recriminations from the night were gone. The water ran down her arms and over her magnificent breasts.

Cameron swallowed hard. "My turn."

He soaped up his hands and smiled. He started at her feet and worked his way up the swell of her thighs and hips, around her beautiful rear and narrow midriff. And her breasts. Goddamn, he was obsessed. He tore his eyes away. But after a few sweeps of her smooth arms, he was done with the washing. He closed his eyes and rested his forehead on hers. He let his fingers glide over her back, her waist, memorizing each curve, as they stood under the faucet. She rested her head on his chest, and he closed his arms around her. "Let me take you to bed, Jackson."

He turned off the shower, grabbed a towel and wrapped her in it. After drying himself off a bit, he took her hand. "Ready?"

She didn't move. She looked up at him hesitantly. "There's a lot of things we haven't tried yet."

She wanted to play again, and his dick didn't miss the message. But he wanted more than just playing around.

He shook his head. "Not tonight."

"Tonight is all we have." Her eyes seemed to glaze over, like she was already halfway through her fantasy. Which he was not giving in to.

Cameron put his hand on her cheek. "You miss your plane tomorrow and stay with me, and we'll try whatever you want. We'll try things you've never even thought of." He brushed his lips over hers. "But not tonight. If this is our last night, we're done with fantasies. I told you before. This is real."

Her eyes widened. The creases still lined her forehead, but he waited her out.

Finally she nodded. "Okay." She walked over to the bed and sat down primly on the edge. Her wet hair dripped down her body, and she shook it behind her shoulders. "So, what do we do?"

Cameron laughed. "You've never had vanilla sex?"

Jackson rolled her eyes. "Until two weeks ago, that's all I'd ever had. After I leave this apartment, it's probably all I'll do for the rest of my life."

Cameron sat down next to her on the bed. Their bodies brushed against each other's, but he didn't touch her. He inhaled deeply and exhaled slowly. Here lay the biggest problem. She still thought what she felt was about sex. Because she was trying things she had never tried. But he had played more than his share of dirty games before. He had played enough to know that no game was enough to make him feel like he did on the Opera House dance floor with Jackson in his arms. And he had felt that with all of his clothes on.

But he couldn't explain that. He had to show her instead.

Cameron leaned over and traced Jackson's wet hair down her back. "I think vanilla could be just as good as any game if we do it right."

"Is that so?" Her voice was soft and dreamy.

"Let's find out." He nodded to the pillows. "Come lie down with me."

He lay on his side, and she settled against him. She looked at him expectantly, as if she had no idea what to do next. Maybe she didn't. And maybe he didn't know what he was getting into, either.

Cameron found her hand. Was it trembling? He brought it to his mouth for a soft kiss and placed it on his waist. He cupped her cheek with his hand and kissed the corner of her mouth, then her bottom lip. He slid his hand down her shoulder and back up behind her neck as he opened his mouth and found her tongue. Her fingers tightened around his waist, so he did it again. She pulled him against her and rocked her hips. He twitched and ached, and she rocked again. Her round breasts pressed against his chest, and he cupped one with his hand, squeezing as he deepened the kiss. She moaned and sighed, moving against him, setting his body on fire.

He rolled her over onto her back, spreading her legs with his knees. He settled onto his elbows and caught her gaze. And held it. His mind reeled through all the things he couldn't say. That this had somehow become more than just a complicated mistake. That he was starting to think his own ten-year plan included her. That he couldn't imagine a life where he never did this again.

And then she moved. All thoughts disappeared except one. Jackson. Cameron couldn't hold it together any longer. He ran his length over every wet, delicious fold. Her eyes grew hazy with pleasure, but she didn't look away. It was incredible. This time he wasn't going to bury his head between her legs or tease her ass or do any of the other nasty, hot shit to make her come. This time, it was just the two of them, face-to-face. And if she could just see what he was feeling right now, everything might turn out right.

He glided along her slippery core and restrained the urge to move faster. He wasn't going to come on her stomach, no matter how good it would be. She widened her legs, opening herself to him, and she tilted her hips, meeting each of his movements. Her breaths got shorter and louder, and she chanted his name, how good he felt, how big he was.

Something inside him was about to explode.

"Now, Cameron." She gasped, her eyelids fluttering. "I want you now."

He stilled. "You can have me anytime you want, Jackson," he breathed. "Anytime."

He pushed back and grabbed a condom from inside his nightstand. He rolled it on as she watched, her mouth parted. She was so beautiful. He had to make her see just how right they were together. If he could get this one last night together right, maybe she would stay a little longer.

He pressed his tip at her entrance and slipped his arms under her shoulders.

"Yes, Cameron," she whispered, moving her hips.

He buried his head in the warm, lush scent of her neck and, slowly, he pushed in. At her sounds of pleasure, he pushed deeper and deeper. Finally, he was buried inside her. And he could have stayed there forever, on the edge of infinite bliss. But Jackson wanted more.

So he gave her one hard thrust, and she cried out.

"Vanilla feels good to me right now." He caught her earlobe between his teeth. "What do you think?"

"Yes." She sighed. He gave her another unyielding thrust. "Yes. Yes."

He moved inside her, setting a slow, relentless pace. She matched his rhythm, urging him on faster, harder. *Yes, yes.* Her voice echoed inside him, over and over. Cameron bit his tongue, distracting himself from the urge to come. He held her face in his hands and looked down at her, giving her everything.

"I'm so close, Cameron," she whispered.

He reached between them and found her clit. Her mouth fell open and he swirled his fingers firmer. She clawed at his back as he drove into her steadily. Her body shook and clenched under him as she fell apart in his arms, calling his name.

"Oh, God, Cameron. Yes."

At the sound of his name, his whole body exploded. He came in long spasms, emptying inside her. He held her tightly as his hips moved against hers, over and over in the most primitive urge to drive himself deeper, deeper inside her forever.

Jackson melted under him, her gaze dreamy and unfocused. It was them, together, that made her look that way. Did she understand that now?

She stroked his arm, pressing her fingers against his muscles.

"You're amazing," Jackson whispered. "I still can't get over it, and I don't think I ever will."

She used the word *will*. Did she imagine a scenario where they were together?

Cameron smiled. "You really know how to make a man feel good." He wove his hand into her damp hair. "Just the way you're looking at me right now. I feel like my heart's going to burst."

The corners of her mouth turned up, slowly spreading into a smile. She looked genuinely surprised. "You know, you're good at keeping these kinds of things to yourself. I can never read you."

He blinked down at her, registering her comment. Did she not understand that he was affected, too? He tried for the best answer he could come up with.

"Actions speak louder than words, right?"

Jackson laughed. "Are we talking about actions in bed?"

"Yes, we are." He bent down and brushed his lips against her. "You need me to spell it out for you?"

She nodded. "Humor me."

He pulled out and rolled out of bed to throw away the condom. She didn't move, but she followed him with her eyes. He slid back over her, resting on his elbows.

He brushed his thumb along her bottom lip. "This is good between us. Really good. And not just in bed. So don't go. Stay here in Sydney with me."

She puffed out a breath and looked away. "Even if I wanted to stay, I have to go back. I have a job and an apartment. And a ten-year plan."

Cameron's heart gave a surge. Not the answer he was looking for, but maybe there was hope. She had thought this through. Which meant maybe she had considered staying.

"A plan to quit your job and travel?" he asked.

"I just want to explore a little," she said. "Travel and work in new places, that kind of thing. But first I need to get myself on better financial footing, pay off my student loans. Someday."

He raised an eyebrow. She gave him a wry smile.

"Good things come to those who wait, right?" she added. "My mother's philosophy."

"Did it work for her?"

Jackson snorted. "Not really. Which is why she wants me to firm up my plans."

"How much money do these plans involve?"

"I'm still working that part out." Jackson frowned.

"Maybe you've waited long enough, Jackson," he said slowly. "Maybe it's time to stop waiting and start doing the things you really want to do."

She wrinkled her nose. "Give up my hard-won apartment and my job to travel until the money ran out?"

"I'd give you a job," he said.

Jackson laughed. "Was that an interview the other day in your office?"

"If you want it to be." He leaned down to kiss

her neck. "But I'd hire you even without the extra services."

"Good to know."

He cupped her face in his hands so she was looking at him. "I'm serious, Jackson."

She blinked at him, and for a moment her eyes welled up.

"I can't just abandon my life in New York. Not right now, when my only Plan B involves moving back in with my mother." She shuddered. "Maybe I'll come back sometime and visit. When I can afford to take some time off."

He shook his head slowly. "Not good enough."

"Just pick up and go? That is what my mother would call completely unrealistic thinking." She brushed her fingers over his jaw. "I have monthly payments and no real savings. I'd be completely dependent on you."

Cameron shook his head. "It doesn't have to be that way."

She was silent for a while, her fingers lingering on his jaw. "Maybe you could come to New York instead."

He froze. He should have prepared for this question, but he hadn't. The board must have mentioned that he never traveled. Cameron closed his eyes.

"I can't," he said flatly. He tamped down the panic that came from even thinking about that last time. Cameron took a deep breath. "Look, even if I wanted to, I wouldn't make it there. When I flew here to

Sydney, I went a little crazy. If Simon hadn't been there to talk me down, I would have been led off in handcuffs."

"Oh. I'm sorry," she whispered. But there wasn't a hint of pity in her voice. A crease formed between her eyebrows. "Is that why you don't go to board meetings?"

Cameron sighed. "Partly. But the other reason is true, too. I'd rather not be in the same room as my father."

"But the no-flying thing isn't public, right?" she said quietly.

He gave her a tight smile. "Bad for business."

So there it was. He had laid it all out for her and gotten his answer. She wasn't staying in Sydney, and he was too messed up to be able to follow her back.

Her fingers moved to his neck, and she played with his hair.

"What happened? I mean, what made you lose it?" she asked. Then she shook her head. "Never mind. You don't have to talk about it."

But she deserved to know. Cameron rolled on his back and looked up at the ceiling. "On our last mission, the plane was hit. Some of us got out, but others?" He shook his head. "Every time I think about flying, I flash to those seconds when the plane crashed into the ground. The other side went down first and killed the two guys closest to the rear. I was sitting on the other side, watching… Why the hell did I make it and not those guys? One of them was married with a kid and another on the way. His family needed him. I was a young, cocky shit, and I didn't need to live. But I did."

Jackson slowed her movements. "I'm glad you did. Really glad."

Those words felt good. He glanced down at her and frowned. "Just about everyone who goes to war has a story like that. It's nothing special."

"That doesn't make it easier," she whispered. She propped herself up on her arm. Her soft breaths tickled his chest, and he couldn't stop thinking about how warm and perfect her body was against his. It made everything just a little better. And her soft, husky voice was already getting him hard again.

Cameron reached out to find her hand, and he laced his fingers in hers.

She leaned forward for another soft kiss. "If this really is our last night, let's make it good."

CHAPTER FOURTEEN

JACKSON SANK INTO an airport security seat and slipped her shoes back on. She hadn't gotten much sleep the night before, and her mind didn't seem to be functioning properly. Questions like *Why the hell did you walk out of Cameron's apartment this morning?* and *When did you get to be such a mess over a man?* had been running through her mind for hours.

She wasn't really considering quitting her job in New York for more time with Cameron, was she? Cameron, the man who wouldn't fly. Goodbye, ten-year plan. Goodbye, dreams of travel and adventure. No, she couldn't do that.

The ache of leaving him would fade at some point, wouldn't it? Because this was unbearable. She had turned him down when he'd offered to take her to the airport. Out of sight, out of mind. Now, only a few hours after she had last buried her face in his chest and breathed in his warm, musky scent, she already regretted it. A few more minutes with his arms around her in the back of the car wouldn't have made this moment better, but it would be one more memory. And in their two-week history, that was something.

But maybe it was better like this. Most of their morning had been without clothes, and it was hard to think about much of anything when Cameron wasn't dressed. But if he had come back to her hotel room when she'd packed, she would have probably forgotten half her belongings. If she had spent the ride to the airport against his warm, hard body, she might have begged him...

But begged for what? For Cameron to come with her? He had already made it clear that he didn't do airplanes.

So what if staying here in Sydney with him would mean crossing off pages of entries in her little red book. So what if he introduced her to games that were made for porn movies. Really good porn movies. She had wanted to travel for her whole life. She wasn't giving up her little red book or her ten-year plan for a guy she had met two weeks ago. And that was that.

Jackson blew out a breath and looked at her watch. She still had another hour before her plane took off. She stood up and grabbed her carry-on bag. Coffee usually made everything a little better. Maybe it would even work for heartbreak. Not that this was heartbreak. It was just...readjustment.

The nearest café had a line to the door, but Jackson didn't have anything better to do. She rolled her bag over to the little shop and parked herself behind the last person. And tried not to look at her phone. She had already looked at Cameron's message about a hundred times. He wasn't going to send another one unless she responded. Which she wasn't going to. At least not until she was far away.

Jackson rubbed her eyes and looked for a distraction. She grabbed a paper off the newsstand and scanned the front page, slowing to a stop when she reached the bottom. There, in full color, was a photo of two A-list actors posing on the dance floor of the Bennelong Room at the Sydney Opera House. But it wasn't the actors who caught her eye. It was the little black dress in the background.

Her little black dress. And Cameron's large, sensual hands in the middle of her rear. His face was lowered to hers. The photo hadn't caught either of them directly, but it was enough.

She remembered that moment. He was already half-hard and had whispered words in her ear that had made her forget they were in a public place. And she had brushed a lock of hair off his face, as if he were hers for real.

She stared down at the photo as she raced to spin this most public breach of conduct. Technically, they were off the clock at that point, but the board probably wouldn't care. Could they just make some claim about helping her blend in? Besides, her face was turned, so maybe she wasn't so identifiable. Damn.

She was in PR, for God's sake. She could do better than that, couldn't she?

Except she couldn't. All she could think about right now was the look on Cameron's face. It was a combination of want and longing and something else she didn't even know how to process. And it was printed on the front of the *Sydney Morning Herald* for everyone to see.

Maybe the Blackmore Inc. board didn't read the *Sydney Morning Herald*.

Jackson refolded the paper and slid it back into the newsstand, photo side down.

Shit.

She couldn't even pretend this was a mistake. She had known the risks, and that hadn't stopped her. Because in the end she didn't want to stop. This time, she'd wanted to give in. And she couldn't make herself regret it.

What the hell was she going to do? Maybe her brain would kick back into gear somewhere over the Pacific. Because she had forty-eight hours before she'd be standing in front of the board. And Harlan Blackmore. If she didn't come up with something, Harlan Blackmore and his board would come up with their own explanations. And none of them would be good.

Even the magical powers of coffee couldn't help make this disaster better.

Just as she squeezed her eyes shut in a futile attempt to make it all go away, her phone rang. She pulled it out of her bag, the word *Mom* in large letters across the screen.

"This isn't such a great time, Mom," she said.

"Oh, honey, you're always too busy," her mother said. "How do you expect to keep a good man if you don't even have time for your mother?"

What was Jackson expecting? Anything in the range of *What's wrong, honey?* was a stretch, of course, but maybe just *I'll try you later?*

"My plane is boarding soon," Jackson said. Soon, as in within the next forty-five minutes. "Was there something quick you wanted to say?"

That got her attention. "Oh, no. Am I calling internationally? Heavens." Her mother let out a long breath. "Well, I just wanted to remind you that Marcello and Marco are turning three in a few weeks. I didn't want you to forget. You know, some single dads are coming, some who might consider—"

"Thanks, Mom. I'll be there," she said. "Look, I have to go."

Jackson stuffed her phone back into her bag. Her career was teetering on the edge of disaster, her whole body ached for Cameron and her mother was trying to fix her up with single dads. Welcome home.

Jackson smoothed her dark blue skirt and checked to make sure the top button of her blouse was still buttoned. She had dressed in her most conservative suit, but it wasn't helping. She was the woman who they had sent over to tame Harlan Blackmore's rebellious son, only to fall headfirst for his charms. And land on the front page of the *Sydney Morning Herald*. Which maybe, by some miracle, the board hadn't seen.

She wasn't the woman they thought they'd hired. She wasn't the woman *she* thought they'd hired, either.

"I'm Jackson McAllister, to see the board," she announced to the receptionist.

The woman gave her a once-over and raised her eyebrows. "Right this way, Ms. McAllister."

Jackson followed the receptionist down the hall, ignoring the top-floor view of New York City. It was hard to believe that she had walked down this same hall less than three weeks ago. The person she was the last time she met the board felt far, far away. Her fling with Cameron was stupid and unprofessional. She had known it at the time, and she had still gone back to him, again and again. It was exactly the kind of mistake Jackson thought she wasn't capable of making. The board must have thought the same, since they'd sent her over there, despite Cameron's reputation.

Now she had to hope that none of them happened to scan the front page of the Sydney newspaper two days ago. If she could just get through this meeting and close the file with Blackmore Inc., she could catch her breath. And try to figure out what the hell she was doing.

The receptionist opened the door to a large con-

ference room at the end of the hall. The first slide of
her presentation was already displayed on the wide
screen across the room. Harlan Blackmore sat at the
head of a long table, and the board members took up
the seats along the two sides. The only empty seat
was at the other end, nearest the door. She walked
to her place, pulled out the chair and froze. On the
table in front of her was the *Sydney Morning Herald*
from two days before. Her own little black dress was
no less recognizable, nor were Cameron's strategi-
cally placed hands.

Cameron. Just this little glimpse of him brought
on a wash of want and longing she had tried so hard
to put behind her these last forty-eight hours.

Don't go. Stay here in Sydney with me. He had
held her face and kissed her until all doubts were
gone. But the next morning she had left. And now
she was here in New York, across the conference
table from his father, about to discuss the specifics
of her last two weeks. Shit.

Jackson swallowed hard and straightened up. At
least her first question was answered. They knew.
She had played out this scenario in her head, but how
did she decide to spin it? Her mind had gone blank.

So she sat down, folded the paper back up and
set it aside.

"You have my report, but—" she gestured to the
newspaper next to her "—it seems you want to discuss something else."

A smile formed on Harlan Blackmore's hard

countenance, but it held no warmth. "I already knew my son would go to all lengths to tell me to fuck off. I just assumed you were too smart for that. Apparently, I was wrong. But who knows how a woman's mind works."

Jackson pressed her lips together, shutting down various hotheaded responses that came to mind. She didn't even know where to start being offended. At the insult to her intelligence? At the insult to women in general? Or should she be offended that not one of the board members spoke up?

"What can I say?" Blackmore's voice held a hint of admiration. "He's my son. He's good at what he does."

He took a single sheet of paper from in front of him and passed it down the table. Each man glanced down at it before passing it on. Harlan Blackmore was putting on a show, reminding her of who ran this meeting.

The paper landed in front of her. Jackson clenched her jaw and forced herself to look down. It was a printout of an email from Cameron to the other three members on his team, written on the first day she had been at the Blackmore Inc. office. It was short, and one of the sentences was highlighted in yellow, doubtlessly by Blackmore himself, just to make sure no one missed the message: *Figure out Jackson McAllister's weak spots at dinner tonight. Tomorrow we'll discuss how to exploit them.*

Jackson could feel the heat creeping up her neck

as she reread the sentence. No. This couldn't have come from the man who'd asked her to stay yesterday. It just couldn't.

Except that everything else about it looked real. Surely it was below even Harlan Blackmore to fake something like this. And what would he gain by doing it? But if it wasn't faked, then Cameron took her back to his apartment just to discredit her.

He wouldn't do that, would he?

"Ms. McAllister?" Harlan Blackmore's voice boomed from the other end of the table.

Shit. She was still at the beginning of this meeting from hell, with no escape in sight. Yes, she could get through this. She had been through worse. But what this meant about her last two weeks with Cameron stung more than she wanted it to.

Jackson took a deep breath and met Harlan Blackmore's cool gaze. "You have an email that says your son will discredit me, and you have a news photo of him fondling me. It's my job to worry about what these items say about your son, not about me. We can start that discussion by looking over my report."

The board members were watching this discussion play out, tennis-match style. Their heads turned together for Blackmore's response. Except nothing came. His expression didn't falter, but the hesitation itself was all the answer she needed.

The corners of his mouth turned up in what could have been amusement. "I can see why he went for you."

"I'll take that as a compliment," said Jackson with a tight smile. "Shall we begin?"

Jackson settled into her seat and leaned over to pull her files out of her bag. But as she reached in, the conference room door handle clicked, and the receptionist's clipped tones came through the doorway.

"...in the middle of a meeting, but—"

"Thank you for escorting me. I'm here for the board meeting, too."

His voice. No. Impossible.

She sat up straight and slowly turned toward the door. Cameron was taking up most of the doorway, dressed in jeans and a black T-shirt, carrying a leather jacket. He had grown a beard again or forgotten to shave. More likely the latter, considering the messy hair and dark circles under his eyes. Those deep blue eyes were a little glazed over, but they were alive with emotion. And he was staring right at her.

"What?" she whispered. "What are you doing here?"

Cameron had the nerve to chuckle. "I came to help you through this. Though by the look on my father's face, I'm guessing you're doing just fine on your own."

Jackson's heart raced faster, and her fingers tingled. Somehow, he had made it here. The man who had sworn off planes forever had flown here, to New York. She ached to touch him, to make sure he was real. She ached to do a lot more than that. So she grabbed the file in front of her and held on tight.

Because...that email. He had planned to discredit

her. He had written it out and sent it to his team. Had he come to New York to play her, start off nice before he finished her off? She didn't want to believe that the Cameron she knew would do that, but he was the son of Harlan Blackmore. Good at what he did. And he had shown her just how much he loved playing games. And winning them.

But Jackson wasn't going to think about that. She sat on the edge of her chair, searching for something to say. Harlan Blackmore beat her to it.

"Well, son, this is a surprise," he rumbled. "If I had known that pussy would bring you to a board meeting, I would have arranged for it long ago."

Jackson sucked in a harsh breath, and Cameron froze. His hands balled into fists, and his jaw worked angrily. This was bad in so many ways. Harlan Blackmore was just as awful as Cameron had insinuated. Even worse. And Cameron looked about two seconds away from punching his father in the face.

"Don't, Cameron," she said. "What's the point?"

Her voice shook a little, but she was beyond caring.

Cameron closed his eyes and let out a long breath. He unclenched his hands, and his heavy shoulders came down a fraction of an inch.

"I would have thought a comment like that was beneath even you, Father," he said slowly. "But you're full of surprises, as well."

He headed for the corner of the room and grabbed an extra chair. He set it down next to Jackson. What the hell was he doing? She couldn't sit next to him. She couldn't listen to his smooth, deep voice and smell his musky scent and not react.

She took a steadying breath. It didn't work.

Cameron was watching her. Waiting. She couldn't do this. She glanced over at him, but he was looking down at the printout of his email. And frowning.

Slowly, he met her gaze again. He didn't reject the paper or call it out as a fake.

"Later," he said softly. But his eyes said more. *You know me.*

Jackson swallowed hard. Did she?

But they were in a meeting. Her voice was going to shake if she spoke again. Which would only feed Harlan Blackmore's attacks. Cameron was still waiting for her to begin. He thought she could do this. And she still couldn't get her mind back into gear.

Finally, Cameron leaned back in his chair and looked out at the board. "Ms. McAllister spent the last two weeks boosting the Blackmore Inc. image, and the write-ups we've gotten are evidence of her success. So I'm ready to listen to her plan for our next steps."

Right. Just talk about the plans. Don't think about anything else.

So she pulled out her file, cleared her throat and started to speak.

CHAPTER FIFTEEN

CAMERON HADN'T MOVED a muscle for the last thirty minutes. Jackson's presentation was full of angles he hadn't even considered. She had dropped hints about her ideas during her stay in Sydney, but she hadn't asked for his approval. She had managed a perfect balance between respecting his freedom when it came to running his business but answering first and foremost to the board. The woman was amazing.

But he already knew that. What he hadn't counted on was her ability to take control of the meeting and steer it right back on her course. She had completely and unapologetically shut down the discussion of the front-page appearance of their less-than-professional dance. Even his father looked impressed. And that was saying something.

"That's my proposal for future actions," concluded Jackson. She turned off the projector and returned to her seat. "Any questions?"

Harlan Blackmore leaned back in his chair and

laced his fingers together. "So you're proposing that
we hire a Sydney-based firm for ongoing strategy?"

Jackson shook her head. "No, Mr. Blackmore. I'm
suggesting *your son* hires a Sydney-based firm. This
is an ongoing project that Cameron needs to be a part
of if we're looking for success." She turned to the
rest of the board. "The virtual conferencing system
I'm recommending is standard in most companies
now, and it will allow for regular updates from the
Sydney office."

The room was silent. Jackson had just proposed
a giant step toward getting him out from under his
father's thumb. And not just in the PR department.
He'd rejected the idea of a virtual conferencing system before, thinking his father would abuse it. All
this time he'd thought distancing the Sydney branch
was the best way to keep the board from meddling.
But from the way Jackson had presented it just now,
this tool would give him his independence; it would
ensure that decisions regarding the Sydney office
weren't made in his absence. And Jackson had carefully presented her recommendations in a way that
sidestepped Harlan Blackmore.

"So, Ms. McAllister, you're writing yourself out
of this plan?" his father asked. "What will your firm
say about that?"

Cameron clenched his fists. His father hadn't
missed any of the subtleties of Jackson's plan. The
board had assigned her the task of boosting the company's image and getting his errant son under con-

trol, and she had come back with a plan that gave that same son more power. Which meant Harlan Blackmore had less. He was too savvy to outwardly dismiss Jackson's plan, but he wasn't above looking for ways to put her at a disadvantage.

But Harlan Blackmore wasn't the first CEO Jackson had met. She raised an eyebrow at him. "My job is to recommend the best plan of action for your company, not ours. My success record speaks for itself. That's why I was assigned this account in the first place."

The room grew quiet again. Finally, one of the board members leaned forward and picked up the sheet of recommendations Jackson had passed out.

"This is a really solid plan." He looked down at Cameron. "But some of this depends on whether you want this role, Mr. Blackmore."

Cameron nodded. "After I've taken a little time off, I'll be ready."

"I'm in favor, as well," said another member.

"Should we take it to a vote?"

Cameron blinked. Maybe the board wasn't completely under his father's command. Maybe showing up at this meeting was enough to get them to listen. And Jackson had just created a way for him to do it. One that didn't require flying or being in the same room as his father.

Yep. He was definitely in love with her.

The vote passed, and they adjourned. He hung back as one of the board members shook Jackson's hand. He couldn't stop himself from staring. But the hard clap on his shoulder jolted him back to reality.

"You flew all the way here for this meeting, son."

Cameron flinched at the word *son*. There was no escaping it. He was Harlan Blackmore's son, not just Harlan Senior's grandson. But he had a choice in how he lived that out.

He cleared his face of emotion and turned to his father. "It was important, so I came."

His father scowled. "You're making a mistake if you let a woman like that make decisions for you."

Cameron smiled. "You're in a room full of people who disagree."

His father was quiet.

"How long will you be in New York?" he finally asked.

Cameron took a deep breath. "Not sure yet."

"Come by the office again," said his father.

"I'll think about it."

Cameron shook his father's hand, and his father left. Slowly, the board members trickled out until it was just Jackson and him left. She looked at him carefully.

"You heading out?" he asked softly.

She nodded. She gathered her belongings with the delicate hands he had dreamed about last night, and they headed for the elevator.

The tension between them crackled. Every move she made echoed in his body, as he waited for that first touch. She was all buttoned up in that suit, and her hair was twisted into a tight bun like she was waiting for someone to take it down.

Please let it be me.

The elevator doors opened, and she stepped in and pushed the button. She didn't look at him until the doors closed.

"I thought you didn't fly."

He crossed his arms. "Until yesterday I didn't."

"And then you suddenly got over your fear?" She raised an eyebrow.

"Not quite," he said. "The real story involves a shitty day on my part when you left, enough tranquilizers to subdue a horse and a really big favor by Simon."

Her eyes softened. "He came with you? You told me he was never coming back to the US again."

"He wasn't. As I said, it was a really big favor."

"Oh." She looked down at the floor.

He frowned. It was the second flight Simon had coached him through, and Cameron hoped to God that it was the last time he ever had to ask for a favor like that again. He hoped that the next time he had to force himself onto a plane, Jackson would be sitting next to him instead. He shuddered. Just thinking about climbing into that metal coffin was going to flip the switch back into that awful abyss. And he wasn't going back there. Not now. Not if he didn't have to.

After descending a few more floors, she turned to him again. "Why are you here?"

He blinked. Did she really not understand?

"I'm here for you," he said slowly. "Because your career is at stake while the board just thinks Harlan Blackmore's stubborn son is acting up again. And if you got fired and I just got a new PR plan, then…"

She looked up at him, eyes wide. He couldn't stop himself this time. They were still in the elevator of his father's building, where they were probably being watched by someone, but he couldn't wait any longer. He turned to her and ran the backs of his fingers down her cheek.

"Then none of this could work out right," he whispered.

The elevator dinged, and the doors opened into the lobby. Their shoes echoed as they crossed the stone floor, but she didn't say a word. They walked out into the November wind. Damn, it was cold. Why the hell did anyone live in this climate? Cameron put on his jacket and zipped it up, then he looked down at Jackson. She had some sexy little pair of shoes on, and she was already shivering.

"Can we find somewhere to talk?" he asked. "Somewhere a little warmer?"

She studied him. "I don't know. I really appreciate that you came all this way to help me out today, especially considering you never fly. But spending time together is only going to make the goodbye harder." She blinked up at him, and for a moment, she looked young and vulnerable. This was the same woman who could handle Harlan Blackmore and his board.

But the way she was staring up at him, so lost and worried, he wanted to hold her and make her smile again. He was so gone on this woman.

He gently interlaced her cold fingers in his. "Jackson, let's get a taxi and go somewhere far from here. Somewhere warm. Then you can spend all the time you want telling me why we shouldn't do this."

She smiled, and some of the lost look faded. Finally, she whispered, "Okay."

The taxi ride was quiet, and the car dropped them off in front of an old-fashioned Italian café. He held the door open for her, and the warm air flooded out. The place was nearly empty. Jackson sat down at one of the tiny tables by the window. She crossed her legs and rubbed her hands together. God, she looked cold. She belonged in Sydney with him. But they were a long way from that.

The waitress came up to take their orders, but Cameron had no idea what the hell he was supposed to order in a place like this. There were all sorts of girly-looking breads and desserts, but he wasn't hungry. Jackson was the only thing on his mind right now.

Thankfully, she just ordered a coffee. He did, too, and the waitress disappeared, leaving them in silence.

"Where's Simon?" she asked after a while.

"Miami."

Her eyebrows rose. She waited for more, but he wasn't going to get into that.

Simon hadn't said a word about his plans, but

Cameron knew what he was doing. If Simon had flown to Miami, he was going to the house of the woman he'd never got over. Who he thought he never deserved in the first place. Who was now married. Even moving halfway around the world hadn't helped that wound heal. But that was Simon's shit to tell, not his.

Besides, he hadn't come here to talk about Simon. It was time to clear the air. "First, about that email my father showed you. I wrote it the morning before we met." Cameron added, "Before we met in the office. As soon as I saw who you were, I called that off."

She looked at him for a while, and a little of the hurt in her eyes disappeared. But not all of it.

"You were amazing today, Jackson," he whispered.

She gave him a wry smile. "I didn't get fired today." Her smile faded. "But the board found out about us. I felt unprofessional. And cheap."

"My father's such an asshole," Cameron muttered, hanging his head and closing his eyes. "You're not cheap, Jackson. So, so far from that." He rubbed the back of his neck.

"Besides," he added, "the reason I picked you up that night at the hotel was because I found out the board was sending someone over to get me in line. So I did the opposite. How's that for unprofessional?" He looked up at her again. A strand of hair had escaped her bun, and she tucked it behind her ear. Damn, she was beautiful. "Well, maybe that wasn't the only reason. You also looked sexy as hell."

She laughed a little. "Still, it was a stupid thing to do, Cameron. It didn't sound like Blackmore Inc. was going to pass on all the details to my firm, but either way, I never want to face that board again."

Cameron froze. "Will your firm ask questions?"

"Probably. And I'm not going to lie."

The waitress returned with their coffees, and Cameron took a scalding drink. When he looked up, Jackson was staring at him, her eyes filled with disbelief.

"Sorry," she mumbled, finding her cup. "It's just…well, I really didn't expect you to be here."

Cameron sighed. "Me neither, to tell you the truth. After I saw the paper, I spent the day all worked up. I was trying to find a way to manage the situation from Sydney."

"What did you come up with?"

"Nothing good. I had an assistant gather all the press you arranged, and I sent a letter to your firm praising you in detail."

Jackson's eyes widened. "Oh?"

"Not that kind of detail." He chuckled.

She blushed.

Should he tell her about the other things he'd done? Cameron shifted in his chair. Was she going to appreciate the gesture, or would she think it was excessive and invasive? Heat stole up his neck and onto his cheeks. He was blushing now, too, for God's sake.

He cleared his throat. "I…um…well, I also paid your rent for a year."

Jackson froze. "What?"

This wasn't going well. He had to just get it all out.

Cameron drew in a breath. "I know it's a little strange, but I was worried you'd lose your job. Because of me. And I knew I wasn't going to lose my job even though I had an affair at work, the same as you." He glanced over at the deep lines in her forehead. "Look, it just didn't seem right. And you mentioned how expensive your apartment was now that you'd moved out from your ex's place. And your ten-year plan…" Cameron scrubbed a hand over his face. "This isn't sounding good, is it?"

Jackson rubbed her temples. And then she started to laugh. Just a little at first, but her smile grew. She shook her head slowly. "What the hell am I supposed to say to that?"

"Thank you?"

Jackson rolled her eyes. "You are an arrogant man, Cameron Blackmore."

He chuckled. "I've got a lot worse faults than that."

Cameron leaned forward and slipped his hand under the table, resting it on her leg. She didn't move away.

"Anyway, I did a couple of other things that we can talk about later, but nothing I was doing felt right." He slowly rubbed her thigh with his thumb. "Jackson, I didn't just come to the board meeting because I wanted to help you out. I came because I wanted to be there for you. Do you see the difference?"

She tilted her head a bit, regarding him warily.

No. He was going to mess this up if he didn't hurry. He just had to say it.

Cameron leaned closer. "I'm falling in love, Jackson. With you. That's what got me on that plane. So I could be with you."

She drew in a quick breath. Then, she reached over and rested her hand on his cheek. Leaning forward, she pressed her mouth to his. Dear God, that felt good. Her lips were so soft and warm, and she tasted like coffee and mint and something so right. He tilted his head for a better angle, but she was already a step ahead of him. Jackson opened her lips and tasted. And just like that, the kiss spiraled out of control. A hot, aching release of all the tension from the last few days. Her hands were in his hair and he was searching higher on her thighs.

The waitress loudly cleared her throat.

Right. They were in a public place. He released Jackson, letting his fingers linger on the soft skin of her neck, and she sighed.

"I've wanted to do that since you walked into the conference room today," she said with a small smile. She shook herself a little, and the smile disappeared. "But I still don't understand how this could ever work between us."

He had gotten through the last twenty-four hours without a heart attack, and that included a plane ride from hell. If he could make it through that, he could tell her this last bit.

"Well, I also took some time off," he said carefully.

"Right." She feigned shock. "So, Cameron Blackmore took a vacation from work?"

"Yep. And I left Derek in charge."

Jackson paused. "For how long?"

"A couple months," he said softly. "I was hoping I could spend it with you."

"In that apartment you just paid for?" Her eyes danced with laughter.

"If you want. Or we could go somewhere you've always wanted to go." He pointed to her purse. "You have that little red book with you?"

She nodded and pulled it out. He took it out of her hand and opened to the first page, filled with school-age script. "Why not Paris?"

She frowned. "But on a plane?"

"I have a whole bottle of pills for that," he said. "You're also welcome to try more traditional relaxation techniques with me. First class has a little private space." He raised his eyebrows at her, and she smiled a little.

Cameron took a deep breath. "Seriously, it'll be tough, and I may need a break before I board a plane again. But if we're going to have a shot at being together, I have to deal with my shit. It might take a while, but I'll find a way."

Jackson found his hand and laced her fingers with his. "So you're moving in?"

"If you want me," he whispered.

The corners of her mouth turned up. "You already know I do." She closed her eyes, and when she opened them, she smiled. "You're still here, right in front of me. I can't get over it."

"Does this mean you're open to revising your ten-year plan?"

Her eyes met his directly. "Yes, but I'm starting to suspect the old adage is true—the best laid plans often go awry."

"Maybe," he said, squeezing her hand. "But this is the best version of *awry* that I can think of."

* * * * *

COMING
SOON!

We really hope you enjoyed reading this book. If you're looking for more romance, be sure to head to the shops when new books are available on

Thursday
26th July

To see which titles are coming soon, please visit
millsandboon.co.uk

MILLS & BOON

LET'S TALK
Romance

For exclusive extracts, competitions
and special offers, find us online:

f facebook.com/millsandboon

○ @millsandboonuk

🐦 @millsandboon

Or get in touch on 0844 844 1351*

For all the latest titles coming soon, visit
millsandboon.co.uk/nextmonth

*Calls cost 7p per minute plus your phone company's price per minute access charge

Want even more
ROMANCE?

Join our bookclub today!

'Mills & Boon books, the perfect way to escape for an hour or so.'

Miss W. Dyer

'Excellent service, promptly delivered and very good subscription choices.'

Miss A. Pearson

'You get fantastic special offers and the chance to get books before they hit the shops'

Mrs V. Hall

Visit millsandbook.co.uk/Bookclub and save on brand new books.

MILLS & BOON